# With Guilt and Promises

I D Hamilton

This paperback edition was first published in 2023

First Edition 2023

Copyright © I D Hamilton 2023

This is a work of fiction. Names, characters, businesses, places, events, locales, and incidents are either the products of the author's imagination or used in a fictitious manner. Any resemblance to actual persons, living or dead, or actual events is purely coincidental.

I D Hamilton has asserted his right under the Copyright, Designs and Patents Act, 1988, to be identified as the author of this work.

All rights reserved. No part of this publication may be reproduced, stored in a retrieval system, or transmitted in any form or by any means, electronic, mechanical, photocopying, recording or otherwise, without the prior permission of the author.

Cover photograph by Emma Hamilton @wallsandweaves

Cover and spine font Theaterv04_Bold by Adrian Jordanov Design

Also by I D Hamilton

*Different People*
*Five Times Twelve*
*Old Threads*

*We made our mistakes*
*The price we paid*
*With guilt and promises*
*Our journeys made*

*We looked for truth*
*Our path was laid*
*With guilt and promises*
*The balance weighed*

*We found our home*
*Love was our aid*
*With guilt and promises*
*The price was paid*

*Anon*

# *Mistakes*

# Chapter 1         1979

## Fiona

IT'S JO'S SUMMER wedding. The guests have just driven from the church to the reception. Fiona Donney notices them watching her park the car. It was the same at the church – the glances, the turned-away words to the person next to them. She still hasn't spoken to the bride, her stepsister. The worst part was the photos – standing in the family group, pretending they *were* a family group. That hurdle is over, but there's more to come. She gets out and locks the car. One of the groom's friends watches her, interested, appraising. In the church, he'd looked across the aisle at her – several times. The woman next to him says something to him but doesn't get his full attention. Fiona can't lip-read, but she guesses one of the words is 'sister' and the other is 'prison'. Behind them, Jo and David appear in the hotel entrance. The ornate pillars and stone steps will be the backdrop for yet more photos. Jo looks away when she sees Fiona.

The Austin Maxi looks out of place amongst the

newer, shinier cars. Its dented side faces the onlookers, just one of its many blemishes. It's next to the vintage Rolls Royce with its white ribbons. She wonders if they intended the place for someone else. But there are no other spaces. She leaves it and walks towards the entrance.

Oliver Donney, Fiona's father, Jo's stepfather, descends the hotel steps. Fiona thinks how grey his hair looks. He's being cajoled by his wife, Margaret, as she rounds up the guests for the next shot – one of many on her list. The photographer looks at his watch. Oliver forces a smile at Fiona, goes to move towards her, but is stopped by Margaret's impatient hand, steering him into place. It annoys Fiona. They'd only managed a couple of words at the church; there are things to be said. Margaret glances at Fiona with the acid look she's never been able to control, then changes it to a smile for the camera. Fiona wonders if that phony smile could have attracted Dad to her. She remembers Margaret and Dad's wedding. Margaret wanted a lot of photos then too. It was as if the more she had, the more legitimate it would be – when Dad had been at the same church for Mum's funeral less than a year before. Later that day, she'd asked Dad why there weren't any photos of his and Mum's wedding. He'd got annoyed and said they were lost.

All around Fiona, Jo's friends point cameras, gather into groups and chat. The sly looks in her direction increase her feeling of exclusion. It's strange, she thinks, how few of the guests she knows, how few from her past are here, even her dad's past. But then, after Mum died, after Margaret came along, most of that past was erased. Like now, the connections were broken; like the wedding photos, they'd been lost.

She had been invited though. After the shiny card arrived in the post, Dad had telephoned to check she'd got it. He'd said he really wanted her there. Considering how things had been when she'd left, she knew he must have battled to get that invitation past Margaret – maybe Jo too. She couldn't refuse him. Then again, Fiona had missed the expensive engagement party. Maybe Jo wants her at the wedding to make sure she sees her achievements – all the things Fiona doesn't have: a man with a good job who wanted to marry her, a big wedding, lots of friends to celebrate with.

A lot of the people here must be Jo's university friends, Fiona decides. She was in Holloway when Jo graduated. Dad had brought the photos in when he'd visited, mentioning that Margaret had arranged another big party to celebrate Jo getting a first. He hadn't said much about the big twenty-first party she'd had earlier that year – a month after Fiona had hers, when the girls on her wing had scraped together every penny they had to come up with a cake, and made streamers and decorations. She remembers Dad asking if there was anything he could do for hers, and her petulant reply, saying she didn't want anything – asking had he forgotten where she was. She'd wanted to ask if he'd forgotten he'd been away at sea when she'd had her eighteenth at school, and if he remembered his card and present arrived almost a month later. Yes, Jo had quite a few parties around that time, Fiona thinks. Doubtless, Margaret thought they were important, that they built contacts, helped cement friendships. And Jo needed friendships. In one of his letters, Dad had mentioned Jo's place on the graduate training scheme at the bank, where she'd met David, and how they'd both applied for the corporate Masters' programme – more evidence at the time that Jo's life was taking off, while hers had hit a brick wall, a prison wall.

Now Jo is about to start another new life, with a new name. She's no longer a Donney, the name she'd only borrowed for a dozen years. Fiona thinks how Jo must have wished her birth name hadn't been changed when her mother married Dad, that she'd have been glad of a different name when it had been in the tabloids: *DONNEY AND CLIVE! Hold-up duo still on the run.*

Jo looks over at her. Fiona notices the familiar smugness around her eyes that says Jo knows something she doesn't – still playing that game. She thinks how they'd looked so alike as children. Now, both twenty-two, only their fair hair and brown eyes lend the slightest similarity. Now, Jo's hair is in elaborate curls under her veil and hers is short and spikey. She's nothing to do with me, Fiona thinks. Why did I come?

David says something to Jo and she looks up at him. He's a tall and very groomed groom in his morning suit and fashionable aviator specs. Fiona had first met him when she'd lived at home for a few months after Holloway. Dad had said David was a 'nice chap', very grounded. Not like Clive, thought Fiona. Clive might have been out by now – if he was still alive, if he hadn't slashed his wrists after he'd got her letter, the one telling him not to write again, not to keep writing to her about what they'd do when they were both out, because that wasn't how it was going to be. Then he'd gone and done that, and left her feeling she was to blame, still feeling it.

The friends of the bride are being arranged for the next shot. Fiona knows she won't be needed in that one. She spots another way into the hotel and slips inside. As she checks in, she asks herself again, why is she doing this, why doesn't she just go? She'd thought maybe it would be different, that's why. As she takes the room key, she hears her dad's voice behind her.

'There you are.' And he hugs her like he means it.

As she hugs him back, she wonders why there is such a gap between her and her dad. The answer comes from the hall beyond, from where Margaret calls his name – because of that woman, that's why. Over his shoulder, she comes into view, stopping when she sees them embracing, avoiding looking at her, telling him he's needed outside for the next photo.

'We'll catch up later,' he says.

Fiona just nods and looks for the stairs.

Dad has booked her a lovely room. She can see out over Greenwich through the large windows. The marble en-suite, with its large shower and massive free-standing bath, seems palatial. In the last year, she's only known the dated bathroom in Hettie's café and boarding house in Lincolnshire, her mother's sister's home, where the bath and its ugly pipework were put in for guests before the war. She knows every stain on that tub. She's grown used to its erratic hot water supply and slow plug hole. Hettie said it was like herself – it had seen better days.

She should ring Hettie. She'll be worrying that the car

had made it down there, worrying about her driving across London. She picks up the phone, telling herself she should pay for the call when she checks out. This day must be costing Dad enough already. Hettie answers straightaway. Fiona knows she was waiting.

'Are you alright?' Fiona asks her.

'Are *you* alright?' Hettie replies.

Fiona tells Hettie everything is fine, knowing her tone isn't convincing. She says she'll be back tomorrow; she'll get going early, like she did this morning. Hettie tells her not to hurry, to enjoy herself. Fiona stops herself saying that's not very likely, repeating that she'll leave early. She says goodbye and hangs up.

She should go downstairs. The reception is starting. Everyone will be filing in past Jo and David, saying nice things to them, saying how lovely St Alfege Church looked, how lovely they looked, a lovely couple, a lovely wedding; how much planning it must have all taken, and what a wonderful touch that they had a choir too. What can she say to them? Isn't it nice that Dad gave you the deposit for the house?

Walking down the stairs, Fiona thinks how worried Hettie sounded on the phone and how she was always there for her. She remembers how Hettie had dropped everything and rushed down to be with her after Mum had died, how she'd scooped her up, how she'd hugged her like Mum used to. But Hettie couldn't stay and be her mum. She had the boarding house and café to run. There was something else in that memory though, something about the reproachful look she'd given Dad, and the tight murmured words they kept having behind the closed dining-room door, something Fiona had never understood. Then Hettie was gone, and Fiona had thought it would just be her and Dad. He wasn't going back to sea on his supertanker. They'd given him a job in head office as a concession, until the end of the year, to 'sort things out.' Even as a ten-year-old, Fiona wondered how you sorted out the death of a wife and mother.

There's a line of guests filing into the function room. Fiona steps back to let them go through first. Oliver sees her. He hurries over, ignoring Margaret, who was by his side in mid flow, asking him something about the wedding gifts' table.

'How is everything?'

'Alright,' she replies.

He manoeuvres to get out of Margaret's line of vision. 'Hettie?'

'She manages.'

They watch the queue of guests, the smiles, the hugs and the handshakes.

'You're helping though.'

She notices his face is tightly drawn, eyes frightened of her replies. It still puzzles her, that thing he has about Hettie.

'Yes,' Fiona says. 'I'm helping.'

'What's the place like these days?'

'Just as it was.'

'She can't be getting guests. I mean, it was basic back then.'

'There haven't been any guests – but there's still the café. I know you never liked the place.'

'It's just a bit... But you going up there was a good thing. It'll give you a chance to...' He tails off, shrugging, unsure.

'Keep out of the way,' says Fiona.

'No.'

She can see he's finding this hard. She doesn't want to punish him, but she can't stop herself. 'No more embarrassment for you all,' she says, not giving him the chance to reply, carrying on, 'Was Jo's house expensive?'

He breathes in deeply. 'I'd do the same for you,' he says. Then, correcting himself, 'I'll do the same when, if you...'

'If Margaret hasn't spent all the money from the old house first,' she says.

'Fiona—'

'Don't worry, I never wanted to go back there anyway – not with her there. But it was my home, and it was Mum's too.' She looks over at Margaret, who hasn't taken her eyes off her.

'You can't expect—' he starts to say.

'I don't expect anything, Dad. Thanks for paying for the room though.'

He looks at the shuffling queue and back at her. Fiona sees the worry in his eyes. He'll know she and Jo haven't spoken yet.

'You won't... I mean, this is Jo's day. Please don't upset things.'

'I'm going to congratulate her,' says Fiona. 'That's all.'

'I know this must be hard for you, but I thought maybe it was a chance...'

Margaret has edged closer. Fiona isn't going to give her the satisfaction of hearing what they're saying. She leaves him, joins the queue and waits for her turn.

The smile goes from Jo's face when Fiona is next in line. David does his best to look like he's relaxed about seeing her, not quite carrying it off, nor the clumsy embrace he gives her. Jo watches, immobile, face blank. Fiona doesn't close the gap between them.

'Congratulations. I hope you'll both be very happy, she says.'

Someone behind her loudly congratulates David, and Jo puts the smile back on her face for them. Fiona passes into the room, aware that Margaret's eyes are still on her, then of another pair of eyes – him again, the one from the church. He can't keep the interest from his face.

She finds the seating plan and looks for her name. She's been put on an outer table by the door – Margaret's doing, no doubt. She knows only one name on her table – the Davidsons, neighbours from Beckenham, years ago. She heads for her place, aware he's still watching.

The couples already seated at the table are strangers. They smile and say very little as she takes her seat next to a large perspiring man and introduces herself, thinking they must all know who she is, what she did, and where she ended up. She's relieved to see Mr and Mrs Davidson approaching. They're soon sharing memories of her childhood. They talk of her mum and how much they liked her. For the first time that day, being here feels good. Mr Davidson remarks on her dad finally leaving the sea for an office job.

'I don't think he wanted to,' says Fiona, thinking he'd done it for Margaret, but he wouldn't do it for his own daughter years before.

'It can't have been easy for either of you – back then,' says Mrs Davidson.

It's no off-the-cuff platitude. She's saying something else with her eyes. Fiona just nods in response. No, it wasn't easy, she thinks, Mum being dead only seven months when Dad married Margaret, sending us away to school, keeping him all to herself. Fiona looks over to where her stepmother presides over the main table. Margaret looks back with what, triumph? Fiona can't decide. She meets her eyes calmly and holds them. Margaret has to look away. Amazing what prison can do for you, Fiona thinks, teach you how to watch people, read people, give off the right signals. This will be the last time she tolerates Margaret's presence, she decides. No more games of happy families.

The speeches are very polished – too polished and a bit too long. Someone has been studying the format and protocol, she thinks. Oliver's is the shortest, referring to Jo as his daughter – when she never was or never will be, thinks Fiona. As soon as she can, she's going to slip away. But there's still the evening do, and a lot of time to kill before then. She asks herself if anyone will notice if she doesn't come back.

Leaving the table, she sees most of the other guests have formed groups, moving out to the garden. It's lovely out there in the sun. But who is she going to sit with? She can't hang on to the Davidsons. They're already talking to someone else. It's feeling like a mistake again. She has a book upstairs in her bag. She tells herself she should make the most of the nice room, fill that big bath right up, soak and read, have one of those fancy teas from the complementary tray. It will be better than trying to look like she's not feeling alone in that crowd.

She almost makes it through the main lobby to the stairs without being seen. But her watcher is there too, a few steps behind her.

'Not going already, are you?'

She turns. Dark brown hair and brown eyes, nice skin, he's certainly good looking. The jacket is off now. It looks like he does some kind of training or sport or something. She wonders what his connection to David is. Before she can reply, he tells her.

'I'm Paul – David's cousin.'

'Fiona,' she says, declining to explain further. Besides, he already knows who she is.

He's looking right into her eyes. Yes, he's very interested. She returns the gaze; his falters. He's not had her kind of training, she thinks. She turns back to the stairs.

'I'll see you at the evening do,' he calls after her.

'Maybe,' she replies, thinking it might be nice. It's been a long time.

In her room, she dismisses the idea. She doesn't need the complication. She catches sight of herself in the mirror, in the floaty cream skirt and short jacket bought specially for today, the sort of things she never wears. She wonders if she'll ever wear them again. She takes her lacy black evening-do dress from its hanger and holds it against herself. They'd gone to Lincoln to shop, a rare day out. Hettie had insisted on paying for both outfits. She'd said she didn't pay her much for working in the café, but Fiona still feels bad about the clothes.

She should at least wear the evening dress, put in an appearance, she decides. She undresses and runs the bath, marvelling at the speed it fills with all that hot water.

As she soaks, she wonders how long she'll have to stay downstairs later. Someone at her table told her the bar will be free all evening – another bill for Dad. It's tempting to get tanked up, wipe it all out, get that Paul bloke into her enormous bed. She thinks about it as she lets the hot water soak in. It's a nice thought, she decides, that's all. How many stories had she heard about using booze or drugs to deaden the pain? How many crap relationships from random pickups? Loads of girls she'd met inside had done that. She can manage without. She's not going down that road. She'd been thinking she was entitled to something. She wasn't. So what if Dad had given Jo money for her house? It was his to give to anyone he wanted to. Jo had got her degree, she was doing a job, she had a proper career. It wasn't one Fiona wanted, nor a life she wanted – but that wasn't the point. Let her have it, Fiona thinks. I'll make my own way – Hettie has. Although there'd once been a husband, Ted, someone Hettie never speaks of. Hettie's managed without him. She might not have much, but what she's got is her own. She answers to no one. Fiona has learnt that's worth a lot. And it's better than working in a fucking bank, like Jo, isn't it? She gets out of the bath, gets dressed and goes downstairs.

'A lime and soda, please,' she says when the barmaid looks over.

She sits on a bar stool. The last time she did this was with Clive, she thinks. It was vodka and tonic back then. They'd have been out on the town, having a good time, before all that stupidity.

'That doesn't look like a wedding-do kind of drink,' says a voice from behind her.

She half turns, knowing who it is.

'It's all free, you know,' Paul goes on.

'So what?' she says.

He shrugs. There's uncertainty in his eyes. He's not as brave as he's trying to look, she decides. He hangs in there though. He's still intrigued. He orders a pint of lager. He takes the stool next to her. The DJ starts the background music. They talk about the wedding and how nice the weather has been. He's easy to talk to. The room is filling up. They talk about the hotel, his job in the City – everything but her. When the best man takes the microphone from the DJ, they turn and face the dance floor.

'Requested by David for Jo, his lady,' he says.

As The Commodores 'Three Times a Lady' starts up, they watch Jo and David take to the centre of the floor. Jo used to be useless at dancing. She's taken lessons for this, thinks Fiona. Towards the end of the track, a few more couples join them. Paul poses an invitation with his eyes and gets off the stool. Why not? She follows him as the tempo changes and 'Ain't No Stopping Us Now' takes over. More couples get up. She can't help noticing how many are looking at her and Paul. She gives them something to look at, loosens up, and lets herself go. He smiles. They dance on through Donna Summer's 'Hot Stuff'. By the time Sister Sledge finishes 'He's The Greatest Dancer', Fiona is nicely warmed up and keeps him on the floor for the next few tracks before letting him get another drink.

They repeat the cycle. She stays with the lime and soda. He keeps going on the lager. They dance on. He takes almost two hours to ask the question. They're sitting at a table now, taking a break. He's just got another lager, given up trying to get her to have something stronger. She doesn't need it. She hasn't done this for so long and it feels so good. She's running off the music.

'When did you..?' He looks down and back up at her.

'When did I what? Get out?'

He shakes his head. 'I've never met anyone who... I mean, you were kind of coerced, weren't you though? I'm sorry, I shouldn't be saying this, should I?'

'Say what you like,' she replies. 'Everyone else is thinking it.' She looks at him. 'Over a year now, if you really want to know.'

He smiles sheepishly and looks down. He still can't hold the eye contact. She's already planning her exit. She's decided it's best to leave when he's next at the bar. Then, when she looks around and sees Dad still with Margaret, both chatting with David's parents, she knows that big bedroom is going to feel very empty. Besides, she still wants to dance. The DJ puts on Chic's 'I want your Love'.

'Come on,' she says and pulls Paul back to the dance floor.

They stay there. The DJ keeps the disco stuff coming. It's working. Everyone's dancing. Even Jo's uni friends, who'd all looked a bit stiff and reluctant, are on the floor. They're pulling Jo back into the mix of bodies. It looks like she's having fun. Fiona is too. She's not thinking much about this Paul guy now. She's lost count of many lagers he's had. He's just someone to dance with. So long as he doesn't fall over just yet, she thinks. She's no longer out of place; she's moving with everyone else. She tips her head back and lets the strobe light wash over her. They dance on.

When Paul makes another trip to the bar, she sees Oliver crossing the room. She intercepts him. He looks glad to see her, a guilty kind of love in his eyes. He's still her dad, he's not Jo's dad, she tells herself again. He asks her if she's alright. But there's something she needs to ask him, something she'd wanted to ask for a long time. Maybe it's not the place to say it, but she has to.

'Do you ever miss Mum?'

He can't stop the contraction of his face from the shock of the question. He looks away. 'Why are you asking me that now?'

What difference does when make? she thinks. You either do or you don't. She nearly says it but stops herself. 'I wish you'd been on those holidays with Mum and me,' she says instead.

This time there's just confusion in his eyes. He waits for an explanation.

'We had some lovely times at Hettie's.'

'I'm glad you did.'

'But you weren't there.'

He looks down. 'I know,' he says. He looks over to where Margaret is sitting. 'Are you really alright up there with her?'

'I don't know about long term. But for now, yes.'

'I'm glad.'

'She wrote to me every week, you know, just like she

did when I was at school.' She wants to remind him how Hettie has always been there for her.

'I should have done more,' he says. 'I'm sorry how it turned out.'

But it's not guilt in his eyes, she decides, it's fear. She puts the thought aside; there's something else she wants to ask him.

'What happened with her?'

'What do you mean?' There's fear in his voice now.

'Her and Ted.'

His features relax a little, like he was expecting worse. 'Ted died in a car crash,' he says.

'Is that all? She never talks about him.'

'It wasn't a good idea, her going up there to run that place – it wasn't as if it was where your mum and her were from. She knew no one up there.' He pauses. 'Her and Ted weren't a good match.'

Margaret has caught his eye. They seem to have an invisible messaging system, Fiona thinks. She's nearly said all what she wanted to say though.

'You could come up. She'd be glad to see you.'

There's that look again. She knows he won't. She turns and leaves him. When she sits back down, she sees he's back with Margaret, staring into space.

The DJ is on a roll now. He's not drawn a blank yet. 'Boogie Wonderland', 'Dancing Queen', and 'Staying Alive' have come and gone. The floor is packed when 'I Will Survive' starts up. She pulls Paul to his feet and absorbs Gloria Gaynor's voice in the alternate light and dark. She's back to where she was earlier, forgetting where she really is, letting the music take her, thinking *she* can survive.

The DJ moves into his smooching tracks with 'It Sure Brings Out The Love In Your Eyes'. The transition signals the end of the evening is near. They stay on the dance floor. Paul puts his arms around her. He feels heavy, like she's taking too much of his weight. He slurs into her ear. He's saying something about going upstairs. She's not sure if she's hearing him right. She pulls back. He grins stupidly.

'Come on, you know you want to.'

'Hopelessly Devoted To You' pushes the couples closer to each other. Fiona wants the opposite. She tries to disengage his heavy arms. But Paul's not giving up. He hangs on tighter. The floor is jammed with hot bodies. Everything's too close now. He's suffocating her. She pushes back at him.

'You know you do,' he says in her ear. His breath seems very wet. Even if she wanted to before, she certainly doesn't now. She pushes back harder. His hands slide down her back and grasp her buttocks, his nails dig into the thin dress. When she brings her knee up into his crotch, it's sharp and decisive. His features can't react quickly enough to the disbelief or the pain in his testicles. She hadn't held back. He lets go and staggers back, groaning.

'You fucking bitch! What did you do that for?' He folds forward, clutching himself.

The couples around them move aside and stare in disbelief. The effect ripples out to the edge of the dance floor. Some have stopped dancing; others turn to look. A few can't resist smiling. Later, she'll wonder if they knew something about him. Just then, she's too aware of what she's done.

He lurches towards her. 'Fucking cow!'

It feels like everyone is looking now. Their attention goes from him to Fiona, standing alone, before she dashes for their table, grabs her bag and heads for the door. Before she reaches it, she catches Jo's eyes – alight with anger.

# Roy

IT'S LONG PAST midnight. The rattling diesel engine echoes down Poplar High Street. Roy Brady waits until it fades away so the driver won't see him cross the road to take a circuitous route to Sally's place. He turns the corner at the long row of flats, feeling the cool evening air waking him up. He'd dozed on the journey from Victoria Station. He's almost forgotten the £70,000 in cash in the bag he's holding – or his slice, the £20,000 that Luiz promised him. The weight of the holdall reminds him. He quickens his pace. The sooner he gets the money to Luiz, the sooner it will all be over; this whole bloody thing, this obligation that hangs around his neck. And it has a companion: survivor's guilt, an even heavier weight, one that won't be cast off so easily. Or maybe it finally will. With that money, he can get away, put it all behind him and make a fresh start. Why not? Maybe that's all he needs. He concentrates on that, trying to believe it.

The street is quiet. He walks on. He'd got the driver to drop him well beyond his destination. They had to be careful, Luiz had kept saying. His repeated warnings had irked Roy. He was the one taking the risks, taking the fucking diamonds to Antwerp and bringing back the money. He's through with all this. Luiz will get his money, and that will be it, Roy tells himself for the hundredth time. In a very short while, he'll drive back along this street and it will be done. Except for Geri – he's still got to tell her he's leaving her and he doesn't know how. And there's her dad, Kirk, who gave him a job when he needed one. Kirk's treated him like a son. That thought adds to his guilt. Not that long ago, a Friday lunchtime in the pub near the garage, he'd promised Kirk he'd look after Geri. Now he's going to let them both down.

He owes it them to tell them face to face; tell them he's grateful, but he can't do this any longer. He can't live with Geri, and that means he can't work for Kirk – not when she works there too. Besides, he needs to be somewhere else, far away. Living here, living in this vacuum, living with his memories, is killing him. And Geri knows as well as he does it isn't working between them, that it's not what either of them wants – not that he knows what she wants, or what he wants, come to that. But he doesn't want this.

As he rounds the next corner, Sally's flat almost in sight, the bitter desolation threatens to overwhelm him. Thirty-five years old and he doesn't know what the hell he's doing with his life; in a relationship with a woman who knows hardly anything about him – no basis for a relationship at all. As that thought hits him, someone steps out of a doorway right in front of him. He swings the bag up instinctively and draws back his other arm to strike. His assailant raises his own arm in defence and steps back.

'It's me, you fucking idiot!'

Roy lowers his fist. 'For Christ's sake, Luiz, what are you playing at?'

'Get in here.' Luiz Freitas pulls him into the doorway.

Luiz's features are rigid, fear oozing out of him. What's he doing here? In his gut, Roy knows something's badly wrong.

'You got the money?' Luiz's question is quick and nervy.

'Yes,' says Roy, handing him the bag. 'What's going on?'

When those piles of notes were packed into the boxes of fancy Belgium chocolates, and sealed with fresh cellophane, and he'd put them in the bag, he'd known it couldn't be as simple as Luiz had made out. Luiz had said these people were buying diamonds from him instead of some big company, that they were the same diamonds at a lower price, that's all there was to it. Then he'd said he couldn't risk the trip himself and asked Roy to go in his place – one last favour. Roy knew there'd been more to it than that.

'We can't go to the flat,' Luiz is saying.

His accent has slipped, his native Portuguese coming through, like it does when he's uptight. This is serious. He means Sally's flat – Sally and little Tina's home – a few hundred yards away, where they'd agreed to meet.

'Why not?' Roy asks, scared of the answer, knowing he'd brought this on Sally and Tina. It's not cold, but his insides are chilling.

'They're at her sister's in Plaistow – just for tonight.'

Roy knows Sally doesn't get on with her sister. She

must have been desperate to go to her.

'Some men came to the flat,' says Luiz.

'What?'

'There's been a few problems. I've been—'

'If anything happens to them...' Roy grabs Luiz's jacket.

Luiz pushes his arm away. 'Nothing will happen to them. It's me they're looking for.'

That was supposed to make him feel better? Anger balloons in Roy's head, anger and more guilt. It's just as much his fault as Luiz's, but he's not going to ask who these men are. Who else is involved with those diamonds isn't Roy's concern. Yes, he knew they'd been smuggled from Angola, he'd even suspected Luiz had pulled a fast one on someone, but he's done with that now, they're quits now. Except there's Sally and Tina. He'd promised Shane he'd look out for them, especially Tina, Shane's little girl. Shane, whose body he'd seen scattered in pieces over that faraway soil, that hostile African bush, the place that Luiz had got him out of. And no matter how much he wants to walk away from Luiz's mess, he knows he can't. Debts, always fucking debts, owing someone for something. This was supposed to change all that; this was going to be the answer to all that.

When Luiz had turned up, over six months ago, there'd been no talk of any of this. Roy had introduced him to Sally then. They'd got on so well. He'd thought he'd done them both a favour. Luiz had been good to Sally, he'd doted on Tina. Everything looked okay. Yes, Luiz had been cagey about why he'd come to London, and Roy knew he had connections with diamond smuggling. But he'd thought all that was in the past. He'd been glad to see Luiz. He'd had no friends then. Sally wasn't really a friend – their relationship rested on something else, someone else. It was pathetic to admit to feeling like that, to admit Luiz had fitted that role and he'd been glad of it.

It had been over three years since they'd seen each other, since Luiz had helped him and he'd helped Luiz get his family's money, converted into diamonds, out of Angola. The Freitas family was amongst the thousands of *retornados* who'd fled when the civil war broke out, after independence. They were back in Portugal and Roy had thought Luiz had joined them, that he'd never see him again.

He'd had no idea what Luiz had been doing since the hot, humid day they'd parted in Pointe-Noire. The details came out gradually, as Luiz got to know Sally and started talking about making big money. And Roy had gone along with it. It had been good to have a sidekick again, someone who knew about that part of his past, the part he couldn't speak of. Then, when he realised where things were going, and there'd be some money, a chunk of money he could do something with, it had seemed a way out of the rut he'd found himself in. That's when he'd decided to tell Geri it was all over and start afresh somewhere else. That's what was supposed to happen – not this.

'I need you to take them somewhere safe,' Luiz is saying. 'Just until I sort this out.'

Roy wants to believe him, but he doesn't. He knows Luiz better now. He looks around them. Despite being surrounded by buildings, he feels like he's out in the

Angolan bush again, danger seconds away. 'That wasn't the deal,' he says. 'I've got my own plans.'

'I know, I know. But just a few days – that's all I need.'

Roy can't hold back his anger. 'If they're in danger…'

Luiz shakes his head. 'I can sort this out.'

Roy notices his own breathing, pressure in his forehead. What can he do? He can't leave them like this.

'We need to get going,' Luiz says. 'Get your car. I'll wait here.'

Roy's glad to be walking again. He avoids the street where Sally's flat is and skirts around to where he'd parked his car early that morning. It had been alright then, when Luiz had driven him to Victoria to get the train to Dover. Now nothing is right. He grips the steering wheel for a few seconds, wondering, as he sometimes did if his dad had assembled this Cortina, taking comfort from knowing he might have, that connection. He drives back to where he left Luiz. Again, he avoids passing Sally's flat, looping round a couple of side streets, scanning the pavements and the parked cars for anyone suspicious.

Luiz is still there. He hasn't done a runner. Whatever else he is, that isn't Luiz. He has to give him that. All the same, this has to be it. No more.

'Where's your car?' Roy asks as Luiz gets into the passenger seat.

'At your flat,' says Luiz. 'But I can't risk going back there.'

'So where are we going?'

'Dalston.'

Luiz has some mates up that way. Roy's not going to

ask how much they're involved in this. As he pulls away, Luiz undoes the chocolate boxes and separates the cash from the cardboard and cellophane, ranting about how 'those bastards' want to rip him off, how they'd demanded half of the cash when that wasn't the deal. Roy doesn't respond. He doesn't ask who 'those bastards' are. He wants to drop Luiz off and never see him again. But Luiz is spewing the whole mess and Roy knows he's getting sucked back into it.

'I can't look after Sally and Tina,' he says, over Luiz's rant.

Luiz stops talking. He finds a couple of carrier bags in the door pocket and starts stuffing bundles of notes into one and the packaging into the other.

'I mean it, Luiz.'

'I just need a few days. I'll have somewhere for them then.'

'You can't do this to them,' says Roy. 'You fucking well can't.'

'I can fix it,' says Luiz.

Roy's thinking, fix it, yeah. What does that mean? 'She won't stay at her sister's,' he says.

Luiz finishes separating the cash. 'Do you know of anywhere?'

'No,' says Roy.

They're crossing the Mile End Road. He's got less than twenty minutes to get out of this.

'You've got to help me,' says Luiz.

He's really saying Roy wouldn't be there if it wasn't for him. It's a reminder to Roy that if they'd caught him, the best he could have hoped for was thirty years in an Angolan jail. The alternative was the firing squad.

Others had escaped, only to be interviewed by Special Branch and chased by the press. But not him. No one knew he'd even been there – no one but Sally and Luiz. Maybe that was the problem; maybe he should have talked to someone else about it. He stares at the oncoming headlights. Even if he wasn't doing this to help Luiz, there was the promise he'd made to Shane. What if he *could* take Sally and Tina somewhere? Maybe that way none of them would see Luiz again. Maybe then it might all finally be over.

'Would Geri..?'

'No,' says Roy. 'I'm not getting her involved. I told you, I'm leaving her.'

As they pass Victoria Park, Luiz shoves bundles of twenty-pound notes into Roy's holdall. 'You can buy your own place with this.'

Roy doesn't reply. He thinks how he's never had his own place, never expected to. The flat he'd once shared with Shane, the flat Luiz is borrowing now, is rented. Before that, before the army, home was a council house in Dagenham. Before that, all he can remember is the room in the children's home, stained wallpaper, his bed and three other beds. After the army, it was back to Dagenham until he'd shared the flat with Shane – then back to the flat without Shane. Now home is Geri's place, the terraced house she'd bought with her husband, Vic, a few streets from where she was brought up. The bed Roy shared with her was the one she'd shared with Vic before she'd divorced him. None of those places were really his. The idea of choosing somewhere of his own seems like a mirage.

It wasn't that he'd never had a proper home. When

Jean and Alan, Mum and Dad, fostered him, they'd done everything to make him safe and happy, and he was still grateful for that. Earlier that year, when Mum died, just a year after Dad, he'd cleared that home out, put aside the charity stuff, and taken car loads to the dump. He'd finished up with a small box of things he couldn't throw away – personal things: photos, Mum's jewelry box, Dad's watch, bits of their lives, the lives they'd shared with him. That's all he had left. And he'd let them down.

After the army, he hadn't known what he wanted. Dad getting him the job at Fords hadn't helped, although Roy could never say it. He'd become a regular working man: leaving the house at the same time, getting home at the same time, same programmes on the box, same routine. There'd be a big session on Friday night and he'd be just about capable of football on Saturday. Sunday was a wilderness of nothing much to do. Then it was Monday and it started all over again. It made him feel hollow inside to think of that time, how he couldn't deal with that life and what that made him do.

When Shane had fallen out with Sally, no more able than he was to cope out of the army, it was almost like old times. Shane had got the flat in Enfield and had found casual work in the building trade. Roy upped and left Dagenham to share the flat and just do something different. They'd roamed around doing odd jobs, somewhere different each day, no routine, no one breathing down their necks. Roy had hardly ever visited Mum and Dad then. When he did, he'd kept it short and avoided talking about what he was doing, ignoring their worried looks. And when Shane saw that advert and they'd gone off to Angola, he didn't even tell them he was going. He was glad he hadn't. When he'd got back, there was no way he could tell them, tell them what happened.

Back in February, at Mum's funeral, Geri had said 'Pity they hadn't bought their own house.'

He'd just looked at her, about to explode.

'I just mean, you know, it would have been something to leave to you.'

'Fucking hell, Geri!'

'Keep your hair on, I only meant it would have been nice.'

'Nice?'

'Oh, forget it.' She'd turned away and looked around the social club hall, knowing no one there, having no connection to the place, his home town.

He'd known she'd felt out of it. She'd only met Mum a few times and they hadn't really hit it off. He'd told her she didn't have to come, but she'd said she should. He'd put aside what she'd just said. There were people he'd had to talk to, say thank you to, just acknowledge. He'd already talked to quite a few of them, but he wanted to make sure he hadn't missed anyone. He didn't even know who some of them were. He'd looked for Hettie. He'd seen her at the crematorium. She'd been talking to one of Mum's old workmates, 'One of the girls from the old days,' Mum would have said. There were quite a few from that era at the funeral, women who, back then, had looked after houses and families and still did their long hours of war work at the Ford factory. They'd all known each other, known each other's boyfriends and husbands, all the men that had been called up – the ones who'd come back and the ones that wouldn't. Dad had come back, married Mum and they'd adopted him. After that, their lives had followed the prescribed pattern – the last thread of which had just snapped.

When Roy was going through his mum's things, he'd found her address book. He'd written to several people in there with the news of her death. Amongst the names, he'd found Hettie's. It wasn't in the faded ink of the relations who'd emigrated years ago and who she'd send Christmas cards to; Hettie's name had been added more recently. Mum had mentioned she'd got back in touch with Hettie, that she was still up in Ebwich. He'd had an idea his dad's death had triggered that renewed contact. When she'd told him, he'd thought she might explain why, but she'd just breezed on, saying something about Hettie still running the café. He'd sent her the details of the funeral. It was a long way for her to come and he hadn't expected her to be there. But she had. And now she stood by the door. He left Geri getting sandwiches. Hettie watched his approach, smiling as he got closer.

'Hello Sunshine,' she'd said, exactly like she used to.

As they embraced, it felt like he was holding the last connection to Mum and Dad.

They talked for ages. They started with the things everyone else had said – how Jean was only sixty, how she'd had heart problems for a while, but no one had expected this, and how Alan had been cheated of his retirement plans when he'd died the year before – then they went on to those visits to Hettie's in the summers of the 1950s. He'd been aware of Geri standing alone, but he'd wanted to hear Hettie talk. He'd wanted to remember how much he'd loved those holidays. Then he'd waited to see if she'd say anything about how the last one had ended. She didn't. Just like with Mum and Dad, it never got mentioned. And he noticed she hadn't mentioned Ted, dead now but still alive the last time they'd seen each other.

By then, Geri had stopped hiding how uncomfortable she'd felt. He'd gestured for her to join them. She'd put on a fixed smile as he'd made the introductions.

'I expect you've got lots of other people to talk to,' Hettie had said.

He'd looked around. She was right, he should. But he'd hesitated, wanting to keep talking about the past. 'I often think about the last time we were up there,' he'd said, watching her face to see if there was any reaction.

But she'd just smiled. 'I've stopped taking guests,' she'd replied. 'But you're always welcome.' She'd taken a notebook from her bag and was writing down a number.

'I'd like that,' he'd said, thinking Geri certainly wouldn't.

She'd torn out the page and handed it to him. 'Give me a call if you do.'

As she'd said it, Albert, one of Dad's old workmates, had bowled up. He'd recognised Hettie and was soon reminding her of their shared past at the factory.

'—ambulances, Bren carriers. The girls worked on all of them. Do you remember when you and Jean—'

Roy had left them to it and talked to some of his old neighbours, laughing about broken windows and having his football confiscated. He'd known Geri was eager to go. He'd seen how frustrated she was when he'd insisted they were the last to leave.

In the car on the way home, he'd told her about Hettie and the holidays in Ebwich and how they'd suddenly stopped going, how there'd been a falling out that no one spoke of. She wasn't interested. That annoyed him and he hadn't known why.

'You weren't serious about visiting her, were you?' she'd said. 'I thought we were going abroad for our holiday.'

'If you want to,' he'd replied. And he'd never mentioned Hettie again.

Luiz gives him the last of the directions and they pull up outside a terraced house. He's back on the subject of Sally and Tina.

'You must know someone.'

Roy thinks of Hettie's offer. No one would look for them in Ebwich. No one would know they were there. He still has the phone number on that bit of paper in his wallet, but how could he explain this to Hettie? She'd probably take it in her stride, he decides.

'There is somewhere I could take them,' he says.

Luiz smiles at him and opens the car door. 'I knew you'd think of something. Tell Sally everything will be okay,' he says. 'You can contact me at Tomás's place. You've got his number, haven't you?'

'For crying out loud, Luiz—'

'Roy, please, I just need a few days.'

'You expect me to believe all that?' says Roy, still thinking about Geri, that he had his own problems to deal with.

'I'll sort everything out – I promise. Pick them up tomorrow. Leave a message with Tomás.'

'Today, you mean.'

'Yes, today. Trust me, Roy. I'm going to fix everything. You'll see.'

# Chapter 2      1967

## Roy

I WAS ON LEAVE in April 1967 when I asked Dad why we'd stopped going to Hettie's. I don't know why it took me so long. I'd thought about it over the years, wondered if what I believed had happened was what had really happened. But I doubted my own memory. The early parts of your life, remembered in separate incidents, seem to get compressed. All the space in between seems to vanish, all the other things that must have happened seem to dissolve somewhere. I've often thought about what it would be like if we could remember absolutely everything. It's probably just as well we can't.

After Mum and Dad had adopted me in 1949, we used to go to Hettie's for our summer holidays. It felt like we spent ages there, going year after year. But it was really just a week or two each summer. It must have been odd: a Dagenham girl running a boarding house and café in a seaside village in Lincolnshire. From what Mum said, the place was used in the war as accommodation for girls from the land army. But there had been a spare room, and Hettie had managed to get it for her younger sister, Roni, when she was evacuated. That's when Hettie met Ted.

Hettie and Ted married at the end of the war and she moved up there. Ted's parents weren't in good health. His father had been gassed in the Great War and his mother was a frail woman. After the war, they were trying to get the place back on its feet and Hettie ended up running it for them, getting it ready for the post-war holidaymakers. By the time I first went there, Hettie's father-in-law had died and his wife was bedbound. It was a going concern again then, albeit basic and paying just enough for them to live on.

Its lino floors, brown paint and worn furnishings didn't matter to me. The café food made up for any lack of comforts. A lot of food was 'coming off the ration' as they said then, and Hettie's generous meals have blended into my memory with the salty coastline, the sunny early mornings with the birds outside my open bedroom window, and the sense of freedom of those summer holidays. Those days have since merged into one long day on the beach, building sandcastles, playing in the sea, eating picnic lunches, and taking the long walk to the cabin that sold ice creams. It had everything I needed. It was perfect.

We drove there. First in an early Ford Anglia, then in a Prefect, cars that Dad cherished, cars he'd probably assembled on the Dagenham production line. He treated his cars with care and respect. Helping him with jobs on the car at the weekends was what made me go for vehicle maintenance in the army.

I was in the working men's club with Dad. It was Sunday lunchtime. Usually when I was on leave, I went round to Wendy's mum and dad's house for lunch. But not this Sunday. Since my last leave, I hadn't heard from Wendy. I'd known her since school. I'd seen her whenever I'd been home on leave. I don't know if I was keener on her than she was on me because she was sometimes very cool with me. Then she'd get all serious and say she missed me and it would be nice if we saw each other more often. She'd ask why I'd gone into the army when there were local jobs I could do. But I'd seen my old classmates who were working at Fords, stuck at home, saving up to get married, looking forward to one night out at the weekend, two weeks' holiday in the summer. That wasn't what I wanted. On the previous leave, I'd said something along those lines to Wendy.

'If that's how you see things, you needn't come round here anymore,' she'd snapped back at me. 'Not everyone's like you. Some people want to settle down and have a family.'

I'd left her at her parent's front door, taking those words with me down the path. Sunday lunch with the Groves was no longer part of my leave routine. Mum had quipped that her roast was better than anyone else's anyway. But she wasn't happy. Like Wendy, she'd been pinning her hopes on me settling down. I told her she was right about her Sunday roast and said no more about Wendy.

In the club, we'd been talking about the attacks in Aden. I'd already told Dad there were rumours my unit would be sent there. Dad read his Daily Mirror from back to front every day, so he knew a bit about what was being called 'The Aden Emergency'. He told me not to say anything to Mum about it. He said she'd been watching the stuff on the telly about the American boys in Vietnam and had got upset. He told me to keep my head down, 'Look after your mates and they'll look after you'. Dad had got off the beach in Dunkirk and went back on the D-day landings. So when he gave a rare bit of advice based on his service, I paid attention. It was then I told him I was thinking of signing on for another stint. He'd just shrugged and said, 'It's your decision, boy.' We were both quiet for a few minutes after that. That's when I asked him what I'd often wondered.

'Why did we stop going to Hettie's for our holidays?'

He picked up his pint and drained it before answering. 'It were my fault.' Then he got up. 'Your mum will have that dinner on the table.'

I followed him out. We never talked about it again.

I was five when Mum and Dad adopted me. I remember them picking me up. I had a tiny cardboard suitcase and a bear whose stuffing was coming out – and who Mum set to work fixing that same day – and a bundle of picture books tied up with string. When we got home, Dad said they had chosen me and they were going to look after me the best they could. No man had ever picked me up and hugged me like he did when he said that. From that day on, we were the best of mates, and later on I wished I'd been better to him. I wished when I was growing up I hadn't ever, for one second, thought he could have done better than his job at Fords and our council house. And I'd wished I'd had more respect for Mum too. Too often I'd just seen her as a housewife, someone who was always at home. It wasn't until her funeral I realised how it must have been for her when she did her war work in the factory, a tough, dangerous job that she never spoke of. She'd done her bit too. I wondered if she'd missed it, like I'd missed the army.

A lot of people thought it was bloody stupid joining up like Shane and I did in 1960, when national service was ending. Unlike the thousands before me, I didn't have to go. Dad had said stopping national service was MacMillan's ticket to winning the election a couple of years before, a mistake when the Soviets were flexing their muscles. He said it was good there were still lads who were willing to join up. The national servicemen who were there when we started our basic training didn't see it that way and took the piss out of Shane and me.

I met Shane at Arborfield. We were training to be mechanics in the Royal Electrical and Mechanical Engineers, or REME. We hit it off from the word go. We wound up back at Arborfield together a few times and we were on the same deployments more than once. Neither of us had great ambitions. We enjoyed doing the hands-on stuff, and we both remained corporals. But we were good at what we did. At the time, at that age, it seemed enough. The stuff Dad and his mates used to talk about – the pay deals, the unions, the state that the car industry was getting in, and the battle against the wage freezes – all passed us by.

It wasn't until much later I understood what it was like to be a working man like Dad, when I'd had a taste of it myself. It had been the time of some of the biggest changes the country had ever seen, and I'd hardly noticed any of it. That's what being in the army does for you; you live in a different world. While Dad lamented the Tories gaining control of the GLC and other councils in the local elections, and how British industry was on its knees and exports were still falling, and that Labour was on the way out, I'd been oblivious. He used to read out bits from the paper about the EEC and how North Sea oil would bring in new money. He'd go on about the continuing battles for pay rises and the criticisms of poor productivity. I remember thinking none of that applied to me – I was staying in the army.

The rumours had been right. In June that year, I was in Aden, along with Shane. We were based at 52 Command Workshop. But with a shortage of bodies, we had to do other duties, including patrols. The situation in Aden was complicated. That part of what is now Yemen was then a British colony. The surrounding area was the Federation of South Arabia, which was fragmented and, for the last few years, in a civil war. Britain had been supporting the Yemeni monarchy, while a National Liberation Front (NLF), backed by Egypt, was intent on taking over the country. A second group, the Front for the Liberation of Occupied South Yemen (FLOSY), split off, and the conflict grew.

Then you had the Southern Arabian Army (SAA), based in Aden. Until 1967 it had been commanded by British Officers. It was a sizeable outfit, 15,000 or so, and had plenty of hardware. Britain was due to pull out of Aden later that year, so Arab officers had been appointed to the SAA. We'd heard that amongst them were supporters of both the NLF and FLOSY. When it became known that the British troops would soon leave, things hotted up. Egypt's President Nasser stirred this up, supporting FLOSY, and with the stuff going between Egypt and Israel, the British government procrastinated, fearing another Suez cock-up. The NLF and FLOSY groups saw their chance and stepped things up. These rebels were based in the so-called Crater district, the packed-in little streets in the old Arab area. The place was a death trap with just a couple of ways in and out. It was no picnic being in Aden in 1967.

Britain was thought to be helping Israel at the time, so things were already tense between Britain and the SAA. Then, after some of the Arab officers were suspended, the armed police rebelled and let out hundreds of prisoners. Fighting broke out between factions of the SAA and they were soon firing on British soldiers. They killed eight of our transport lads in one day, shot in a lorry returning from weapons training.

Worse was to come. Two of our Land Rovers were passing the Arab Police Barracks when the police opened fire on them. These were supposed to be our allies, for Christ's sake. The lads in the Land Rovers didn't stand a chance. The ones who were still alive fired back. But with no real cover, they were easy targets. Twelve were killed. We couldn't even get their bodies out of the place. If they'd let us use some serious weaponry, we could have sorted things out. But we'd been refused permission – more bloody softly-softly stuff when they'd murdered their own allies and even fired on an ambulance.

Shane and I were on Marine Drive when all this was going off. We'd been pulled back and heard the mortars, and later the anti-tank rockets. The whole place erupted, bringing out all these fanatics with hardware we didn't even know they had. The worst thing of all was that three more blokes from the Royal Northumberland Fusiliers who'd gone back into the Crater hadn't come out. Everyone hoped they were dead before they were mutilated and dragged through the streets – a technique the fanatics were fond of. I knew long before then I was never a hardcore, up-for-it combat soldier, but when I heard what happened to those lads, I knew what it meant to feel your blood boil and I'd have been happy to hit back as hard as we could. We felt we'd been blindsided and humiliated. Worse still, it had been kicked off by people we were supposed to be helping. When we finally got in to recover the remains of the ambushed Land Rovers, it really came home what a fucking mess the whole thing was and we were asking each other what the hell was Britain doing there anyway.

After the ambush, over twenty British soldiers were dead and the Crater area was held by hundreds of terrorists, along with the Arab police – against us, and it seemed each other too. The Crater area was sealed off, and it was almost two weeks before Operation Stirling Castle was launched to retake it. That's when they found the mutilated bodies of our lads.

In September, the service families were evacuated, and we were soon on our way home too. As we were preparing to leave, the SAA had joined with the NFL and together were giving FLOSY a pasting. But I don't think anyone cared anymore. By that November, Britain was out of its former colony and the likes of Shane and me were still asking what it was all for. But we didn't ask enough, we didn't learn. If we had, we might not have done what we did nine years later.

Back home on leave, I was at a loose end. Mum had been worrying the whole time I was in Aden. I felt duty bound to spend some time with her and Dad. It was a strange feeling being back there; it was like the world was passing me by. Almost everyone I'd known from school had settled down. Mum was always telling me who'd just had another baby or who'd got a new flat. Dad was a union rep then. He was involved in proposals for a new wage structure, while the members were still pushing for a big pay rise for everyone, regardless of their job. All the talks of grades and who deserved what went over my head. I wasn't part of that world. I didn't want to be part of it.

In a newspaper that had found its way out to Aden, there had been an advert offering emigration packages to Australia. It said nearly everyone in Australia had a car, a washing machine, a fridge, and a telephone – and there were four TV channels on all day. For ten pounds, I could have some of that. I'd been thinking about what I had and how it all fitted in a suitcase. I could make that trip easily. Shane had laughed and said it must be some kind of con.

I'd written to Wendy a few times since she'd told me to sling my hook. I'd had no replies. I was telling myself that maybe her letters hadn't got through. But I'd got letters from home and the post system to servicemen was usually good, so I suppose I already had known it was over. Like us, the Groves weren't on the phone in those days. The only thing for it was to go round. I'm not saying I was about to go down on one knee to her, but after Aden I'd been doing some thinking and wondering whether to sign on again, and I thought I'd tell her that. I thought we could see *Bonnie and Clyde* at the pictures and go for a curry afterwards. And I was going to ask her if she'd seen the adverts about Australia.

Mr Grove opened the door. Like everyone else round there, he worked at Fords and he knew Dad. He was a quiet, good-natured sort of bloke, big built and usually smiling. His smile was a bit awkward that evening. From the doorstep, he explained about Wendy's fiancé from Rainham, who worked in insurance. He said he'd told her off for not letting me know. I thanked him. As I left their street, I decided to sign on for another six. I saw *Bonnie and Clyde* on my own.

# Fiona

I WAS TEN in the April. Mum had been dead for two weeks and Hettie had gone back to Ebwich. Even then, it was obvious that Dad didn't want her at our house in Beckenham. He was never comfortable with her around. He'd always been at sea when we'd stayed at Hettie's, but there must have been times when he could have come. He never did. There was something he feared about Hettie and something she disapproved of about him. These things circled around them in separate orbits, pushing out at each other, never colliding. I didn't understand it, but I felt it.

Cervical cancer meant nothing to me. Hettie had said it was something to do with 'women's bits' and that Mum had been very poorly but had kept on going for mine and Dad's sakes. She told me to stop calling her Auntie, that she felt old enough without that tag. She said Mum had been very brave, and now I had to be brave too. I didn't want to be brave. I didn't see how my mum could die when she wasn't as old as a lot of other people and they even had their mums still. It wasn't fair.

When Gran and Grandad had died, they were old. Mum still cried, and I cried with her, but they were old, it was different. Other than distant cousins in Scotland, Hettie was my only living relative then. I had no grandparents left on Dad's side and he'd been an only child. His father was killed at sea in 1917, not long after Dad was conceived. His mother struggled to bring him up on her own, doing cleaning jobs and taking in washing. I don't remember her and he hardly ever spoke of his childhood.

Before she went home, Hettie said she'd talk to Dad about my going to hers for the school holidays. That promise was the only reason I stopped clinging on to her at the front door. But I never got to go. I didn't go back to Ebwich for another eight years.

I preserved every memory from my time with Mum. Even now, I replay the things we did together, scared they'll fade away. Theme tunes from TV programmes are the most evocative. The soundtrack of *Robinson Crusoe*, those rolling waves of music, still transports me back – bringing the smell of her skin and her lilly of the valley soap. Then there were those children's adventure tales, made in Europe and dubbed for British TV, set in sunny foreign-looking places. Dad would often be away and Mum would watch them with me, as keen as I was to see what happened next. I had to sleep in her bed after watching *The Singing Ringing Tree*, when the face of the bear kept appearing between my curtains.

Much later, Hettie told me how Mum had played down the hospital appointments, how, when she'd suddenly deteriorated, Dad had been flown home and how they'd still kept it all from me. She'd said it might have been better if they'd told me something of what had been happening, but nobody thought I should know. Neither did I know how much passed between Mum and Hettie in all those letters they used to write. Sisters separated by eleven years and many miles, they'd been unusually close, despite being apart for much of their lives. We'd often hurry out to 'catch the post' when Mum had another reply to send.

Dad said he'd been given a special job in head office, so he didn't have to go back to sea for a while, and he'd be there with me. But who was going to look after me if Mum wasn't there and he was working up in London? The answer was a lady called June. Dad arranged for her to come in every day and help out. I cried and said I wanted it to be Hettie. She used to phone every Sunday evening to talk to me. I told her what had happened. She said she couldn't come down, but she was thinking of me and we'd meet up soon. Dad was annoyed. He said I had to get used to things, just like he had.

June was a nice-enough woman, but she wasn't Hettie. She walked me to school and back, looked after me, and cooked our main meals. I got used to it. I started adjusting to our new life, and Dad looked happier too. Then some nights he started coming back later and June had to stay later to put me to bed. After that, June's daughter, Lizzie, used to look after me on Saturdays and in the school holidays. Then, not long after that new regime had begun, another regime took its place – Margaret and Jo arrived.

It was the summer holidays when I met them. I'd been asking and asking when we could go to Hettie's, and Dad's answers were getting more and more evasive. When he got back one Friday evening, I'd tried again, thinking we could drive up there the next day. He wouldn't be at work, so why not? He said he had other plans. I said Hettie could come and get me and I could stay there on my own, I didn't mind. He looked annoyed at that. Then he told me.

'We can't go tomorrow. There's someone I want you to meet.'

'Who?'

'A lady from work and her daughter. Jo's the same age as you – someone for you to play with.'

'I play with Rachel next door.'

'Well, you can play with Jo tomorrow.'

When Margaret first walked in, she looked around the hallway, taking in the house, not looking at me. Jo was behind her, behaving much the same. As young as I was, I got the feeling they were appraising the place, checking it out. When Margaret did look at me, it was a passing glance, before directing her smile at Dad. Because we were the same age and looked alike, I thought Jo and I must be alike. But we weren't. I soon discovered we could hardly have been more different.

'You girls can go and play together,' this woman with her make-up and strong perfume said, following Dad into the lounge, looking around her again, still taking it all in.

I think I asked Jo what she wanted to do and got a sulky shrug for a reply. I asked if she wanted to see my bedroom. Margaret answered for her, telling her to 'run along'. When I showed Jo my room, my books and the paints set I'd got for my birthday, she just said her dad was getting her a new bicycle soon. I found out it was one of the many things he was always going to get her, yet somehow never did.

That day, Dad took us out to lunch at a restaurant. At some point, Margaret took her attention from Dad and looked at Jo and me, side by side, and commented that my hair needed cutting. Mum always liked my hair long, and I looked to Dad for some kind of support, but he said nothing. By then, I'd decided I didn't like Jo or her mum. When they were in the toilets, I told Dad how I felt. I couldn't understand why that annoyed him. If she only worked with him, what did it matter? They'd only come round to see us for the day, hadn't they? We didn't have to see them again. He said something about me having to learn to get on with people.

In the car on the way home, watching Margaret sitting in the front next to him, where Mum used to sit, where I'd started sitting, telling him how brilliant Jo was at maths and geography, I couldn't understand why they'd come to see us, come to lunch with us, or why Jo's dad wasn't with them.

That evening, after they'd left, after Jo had spat out the walnuts from the cake we'd given them for tea, Dad was tucking me into bed, telling me about them. He said Jo's mum and dad hadn't been getting on together. He said that happened sometimes and sometimes people who are married get unmarried, and sometimes they find a new husband or wife to be happy with. He was trying, in his clumsy way, to prepare me for what was to come. I'd only just stopped crying every night for Mum by then, but that night I started it again and he had to come in a few times before I went to sleep.

That summer, we saw more and more of Margaret and Jo. Dad encouraged me to take Jo to the park sometimes, to give him and Margaret 'some time to chat'. But they did that all the time anyway, at least Margaret seemed to. Once, when Jo got bored, and we went back early, Dad came downstairs, tucking his shirt in, ushering us out for a walk to the shop for sweets. Margaret had been up there with him. Jo sniggered about that and I couldn't understand why. Just after that, we went to Cornwall and stayed in a cottage. There were only two bedrooms. Dad said he'd share with Margaret and I could share with Jo. He said it would be more fun for us to be together. Jo sniggered about that too and Margaret told her off.

Jo and I were tolerating each other by then, but there were times when we fell out. It was usually when she started bragging about her dad and how he lived in a huge house and his family had all this land. Sharing the room with her, I'd got fed up with these stories and asked her where was he then, why wasn't he there too? She didn't have an answer, and I said it was my dad that took us all out places so she should shut up talking about her stupid dad. She went off squealing to her mum, and I got told off.

Before we'd set off to Cornwall, I'd been asking Dad why we had to go to there and why didn't we all stay with Aunty Hettie. He'd said the boarding house wasn't 'suitable'. I said it had lots of bedrooms, and he told me to stop asking because we weren't going. Hettie had phoned every week until then. Dad used to answer, say a few words and pass her on to me. I'd missed her call when we were in Cornwall. When we got back, I said I wanted to ring her. Dad said he'd do it and to wait upstairs until he'd spoken to her. He seemed to be ages. I heard his voice get louder, increasingly frustrated and annoyed. I crept onto the landing and heard him saying something had nothing to do with her, before slamming the phone down. He wouldn't let me call her back. He got angry when I had a tantrum about it, and I had to spend the rest of the evening in my room. When he came up to say goodnight, he told me was going to marry Margaret, and we'd all be a family, a new family, and I should be happy. I refused to let him kiss me goodnight and cried myself to sleep.

Dad's only concession to the phone calls was to say I could write to Hettie from then on. Maybe he thought I wouldn't, that I'd tire of it. But I did write, and I never tired of it. It was as if I were keeping up Mum's letters. Right through my schooldays, we wrote to each other. In all that time, we never went to stay with her and she never came to stay with us. She didn't come to Dad and Margaret's wedding either. Later, she told me she hadn't been invited. Yet in all the years she wrote to me, she never badmouthed Dad. When I'd written about Margaret and Jo, and how I didn't like them, her replies were sympathetic but diplomatic, urging me to put it aside, work hard at school and make Mum proud of me, because she was watching over me and her love hadn't gone away.

The wedding, that November, marked out fresh lines of combat between Margaret and I. From overheard discussions, I got the idea it had taken some manoeuvring to get the church ceremony she'd insisted on. They had to marry in the registry office and have the wedding blessed in the church. The part in the church looked pretty much like a full wedding ceremony, with Margaret in a white wedding dress and Dad in a fancy long jacket. Margaret wanted Jo and me to 'match' and decided I should have my hair cut to shoulder length when Jo had hers trimmed for the big day. Dad cajoled and persuaded me to do it for his sake. I think he thought the whole matching thing would make us closer, like 'real sisters'. But I wanted nothing less. Jo wasn't all that keen either. She came out with some spiteful remark about having my hair like hers wouldn't make her mum like me. I shouted back I didn't want her mum to like me, that she could keep her mum. I hated my new haircut and hit back by refusing to wear the frilly, puffed-out dress that matched Jo's. It marked the start of a long war with Margaret, a war than neither of us won.

At the wedding reception, a friend of Margaret's asked her where she and Dad were going for their honeymoon. That got my attention because they'd said nothing about it. I had it in my head people who got married a second time didn't have honeymoons. I had only a vague idea what it was. The word had always confused me. I saw this light brown moon in my head and couldn't connect it to getting married. I couldn't hear Margaret's reply, but she and her friend had glanced my way, and that glance worried me. I went and found Dad and asked him the same question. He was different with all the guests around him, smiling and saying things to everyone, not really like him. He brushed off the question with something like, 'we were going to wait a little while.'

I found out the reason for his answer, and Margaret's look, just a few days later, about the same time as all of Margaret and Jo's things turned up in a big van. Jo had finished school early for the Christmas holidays on account of their move, and Dad and Margaret had taken holiday from work to join up with Christmas. In the New Year, Jo would go to my school, twenty minutes' walk away – at least that's what I'd thought. I still had a week or so before the end of term, and Dad said I'd be going on my own until then. I didn't understand why that was. Leaving them all in the house, and returning each afternoon with them still in the house, upset my routine. Then Dad said that June wouldn't be coming round to help out anymore, that Margaret was giving up work and she'd look after everything. That upset me too. And all this time, Jo kept giving me her little smirk, a sign that I came to realise meant she knew something I didn't.

I missed June. She'd become part of my world. The way she bustled around the kitchen and the way she called something 'blessed' instead of using a swear word were just like Hettie. I never saw her again. That last week of school, I had to get my own breakfast – Jo watching smugly, wearing her flowery nightie and her little smirk. Just before Dad walked me to school, Margaret would breeze downstairs in her long dressing gown to say goodbye and pretend to be nice.

On the last morning of that term, on that walk to school, Dad told me I wouldn't be going back there after the holidays. He said I'd be going to another school with Jo. To begin with, he didn't tell me what sort of school. He kept saying how much fun it was going to be, how there would be all these people to make friends with, that there were big grounds, a swimming pool and all sorts of things that the local schools didn't have. It was going to be great fun, and I was going to live there during term time. I cried and he got annoyed.

When I got home that evening, I discovered Jo not only knew already, but she'd known for a while. She knew all about Frentons, the school near Folkestone that Margaret had chosen for us – or rather for Jo, having been assured they had excellent maths teachers. Jo knew this and could list all its other facilities. She sounded like an advert for the place. When I said I wasn't going and ran up to my bedroom, trying to pull the chest of drawers across the door, Margaret said I could stay there until I got hungry enough to come down. She didn't know how little appeal her cooking had, that I looked forward more to school dinners than her soggy vegetables and burnt pies. It was way past my bedtime when Dad asked me to let him in to talk to me. Even then, Margaret was hovering behind him and I could see Jo's face smirking in her doorway. I told him I'd only talk to him. Margaret tisked in the background when he finally agreed.

I poured it all out. I cried and told him how much I missed Mum and how I didn't want 'them' in the house. He listened to me; he let me say it all. But even as I was saying it, I knew he wasn't going to budge. He said things were different now, that we both loved Mum, but now she wasn't there we had to go on and do new things. He said going to this school was one of those things, that it was much better for me, that I'd 'get on' better and meet other people. But no matter how many times he said it, it made no difference. I said Jo could go there and I'd stay at home, even with Margaret. He said that wasn't possible because soon the job at head office would be over and he was going back to sea. They had given him a new ship, a huge oil tanker, and Margaret would go with him on his next trip. I said Mum never went, and he just said she hadn't wanted to, that things were different now.

Dad stayed in my room after I'd turned away from him and buried my head under the pillow and refused to listen to any more explanation of why it had to be that way. When Margaret came to the doorway and urged him to come to bed, saying 'she'll feel different in the morning when she sees how nice it will all be', he left me alone. I know now that was the moment it all started, how I ended up doing what I did. That feeling of utter betrayal was the catalyst.

I stopped talking to Margaret and Jo. I trudged behind them as we visited the shops to complete the list of purchases that the school had sent. Jo kept up a cheerful stream of chatter, overplaying how much she was looking forward to it. Margaret replied briefly, between looking at her list and checking the prices of the clothing. Jo's knowledge of where we were going was based on The Four Marys in her *Bunty* comics and annuals, and her Enid Blyton books where all the children went to boarding schools. It was a dream come true for her and she couldn't wait to get there. After listening to her enthusiasm all day, I took the sharp scissors from Mum's sewing basket, locked myself in the bathroom, and hacked off as much hair as I could manage. I don't know why I did it. I suppose it was the only way I could hit out. But it was worth it for the look on Margaret's face when I went downstairs for dinner. She stared at me, unable to believe what she was seeing. Jo's expression was equally rewarding – until it turned to a satisfied smile when she realised how much trouble I was in. Then, with her face all scrunched up, Margaret screamed at me.

'You nasty little bitch! If you think this will make any difference, you're wrong.'

Another line had been crossed; another battle front had been set up. Only then did it occur to me that the school wouldn't take me with my jaggedly short hair – that hadn't been the plan. I felt doubly triumphant and told Jo to get stuffed when she started telling me how much trouble I was in.

Dad showed a rare flash of humour when he saw me. I'd tried to brazen it out and stare back at him as he came through the front door. He just shook his head in disbelief and laughed. Then he phoned Mum's old hairdresser, Rita. She was fully booked for Christmas. But knowing Mum as long as she had, she agreed to fit me in at the end of the next day to attempt a repair job. Margaret was not amused by Dad laughing, and Jo looked distinctly disappointed.

When Rita had finished with me, she stepped back and said. Well, eat your heart out, Jean Seberg. Dad had to explain what she meant as we headed home in the car. When we got back, Margaret ignored me and I could see Jo was envious. I had a film-star haircut, and she had a little girl's one. The next time I had my hair cut that short was in Holloway in 1976, only then it was to save on precious shampoo. In 1967, my new haircut didn't stop me from going to Frentons.

# Chapter 3      1979

## Fiona

It DOESN'T TAKE her long for her to repack her stuff in the little suitcase that Hettie lent her. The reception desk is on the other side of the building to the function room. She hopes she'll get away without anyone seeing her. The woman on duty is the same one who checked her in earlier. She looks confused when Fiona says she's checking out and wants to pay for a phone call. While she's working out the charge, and confirming the room has been paid for, Jo walks purposefully along the corridor towards them. The receptionist says the phone call is two pounds thirty – a bloody joke. But Fiona doesn't have time to argue and puts the money down. Jo is behind her as she goes through the door.

'Well done, Fiona. Happy now?'

Fiona keeps on going, but Jo catches the door. She's not giving up.

'Why did you even come?'

Fiona stops and turns to her. 'I came to see Dad – *my* dad. Where was yours?' She knows that was cheap, but it just came out. Now she's started, she can't stop herself. 'And that creep, that new relation of yours, was pissed out of his head and feeling me up. But I don't suppose you're interested in hearing that, are you?'

'Oh, that makes it alright, does it?' Jo bats back.

Fiona steps right up to her and looks her in the eyes. If Jo had seen some of the women she'd spent two years locked up with, if she'd seen some of the things she'd seen... But she was at university, everything paid for by Dad. 'You should go back to your guests,' Fiona says. 'And tell your husband his cousin's an arsehole.' She turns and walks on.

'That's right, mess things up and run off. Same old Fiona,' Jo calls after her.

Fiona keeps walking. She already regrets what she's said. This is pathetic, she thinks, like we're ten-year-olds again. She hears Jo's footsteps behind her. She fights the urge to turn and say more, that she and her mother are parasites, that they're both using Dad for what they can get. Then Jo says it, shouts it after her.

'You know he was seeing Mum before your mum died, don't you?'

Fiona stops again, thinking she can't have heard that right. She stays facing away from Jo, processing the words. She knows she shouldn't, but she can't help turning. As she does, Jo's face has a shadow of that smirk that she knows so well, that satisfaction of knowing something Fiona doesn't. But this is on another level. Did she really say that? Of course she did. Her face confirms it.

'You didn't, did you? He'd been coming to our place for ages. He'd even stayed over when you thought he was still at sea. That's what your precious father is like.'

For a fraction of a second, she tells herself Jo is lying. Then the words take root. It makes sense. It explains the speed of Margaret's arrival. It explains a lot of things. She holds back. She feels the impact on her posture; it's sucked the breath out of her. If she speaks, she'll give Jo the satisfaction she's looking for. It takes every shred of her self-control to turn and walk on. If Jo follows her, it will be different. She will let go. But Fiona knows Jo. She knows she isn't that brave. Maybe even Jo knows she's gone too far. Besides, she's fired her last shot, the bullet she'd been saving for so long. Fiona keeps walking.

At the car, she curses the decision to come. She had wanted to see Dad. He'd invited her. She tries to tell herself that whatever he did, he's still her dad. But the thought that the three of them conspired against her is digging in sharp and hard. How could he think that would work? How could he imagine she wouldn't get to know or that Jo wouldn't tell her? She sits and holds the steering wheel. Now he's probably thinking she's spoilt the evening for Jo. Margaret is doubtless telling him she'd known something like this would happen, that she'd told him not to invite her.

Fiona turns the ignition key, praying the car won't do the thing it sometimes does and need coaxing to start. But it starts straight away, a tiny consolation, confirmation she should go. She doesn't put it into gear though. She thinks how it would feel to go back inside and throw what she's heard in his face, scream it at him so everyone hears, smash some of those glasses of free drinks, smack Margaret in the face, smack Jo in the face.

She's gripping the wheel tightly.

Then she breathes out. She doesn't have to be here. She can go right now. She'll be running away, but she doesn't care. This isn't where she should be. She winds the window down, lets the cool air in. She's glad she hasn't had anything to drink. She puts the car into reverse, backs out, and pulls away. She hopes she'll remember the way back. She pictures the last bit of road to Ebwich. The sun might just be appearing over the sea when she gets there. That's all she wants.

Leaving the Blackwall Tunnel, she thinks of Clive again. She does the sums in her head. If he was still alive, if he hadn't lost any remission, he'd have been out soon. He'd have had another chance at life. If she hadn't told him it was over, he'd be alive. But she's done her crying for that. She remembers what her cellmate, Angie, had told her, shaking her roughly when she'd ranted about being to blame. She'd told her he'd have done it eventually anyway, no matter what Fiona had done. If only she could be certain of that. She turns the radio on. She has to hit the station selector button a few times to get it to work. She drives on.

She notices how many people are on the roads in London late at night. At Ebwich, you're surprised if you see another car. Supertramp's The Logical Song starts playing. It's been played a lot lately. It's been playing in her head too. She turns it up to just below where the speaker distorts and absorbs the words. She wants someone to tell her who she is; the questions are too deep for her too. Did she just want to be accepted? Is she jealous of Jo getting married, of Dad getting who he must have wanted instead of Mum, of all those couples side-by-side that she's seen today? Is it logical? She doesn't want to admit to herself she needs someone. She wonders if she can just stay like she is now. Would she end up like Hettie – on her own? Who is she?

She gets a little lost before she finally sees the signs for the M11. It's a new motorway. It will make her getaway quicker. Hettie's Maxi hasn't been on many motorways. When Fiona first arrived at Ebwich, it had sat on flat tyres round the back of the café, developing a layer of moss and looking forlorn. Hettie said it had been like that for nearly two years. She'd said she felt guilty every time she saw it. She'd said it had been put out to pasture, just like she had. Fiona had been determined to prove her wrong on both counts. Not having a car had made Hettie's small world shrink. Even if she wouldn't drive it anymore, Fiona could.

She'd washed the layers of dirt off, got rid of the moss, pumped up the tyres and found a charger in the shed to put on the battery. Her knowledge of cars wasn't great, but there was a handbook in the glove box and she knew that oil and water were important. She'd checked the levels and they'd seemed okay. It took several attempts for the ignition to fire. After puffing and blowing, the engine kept on turning. The body creaked and juddered when she'd let the clutch in. The brakes reluctantly released, and the car finally moved.

After a few runs up and down the road, she'd had enough confidence to take it to the garage in the village for a service and MOT. It jumped out of gear a bit, but they got that fixed. Hettie reminded her it needed tax and insurance and said she was happy to pay. Now it brings a smile to Hettie's face every time they go out in it. The run down to London proves it isn't finished yet. All the same, she takes it easy.

Mum's Austin 1100 had smelt like the Maxi did. A bit oily, something from the seats too, the cooked vinyl when the sun heated it up. When she was little, and Dad was away, they'd make this same journey up to Aunty Hettie's in that car. From Beckenham, it was quite a trip. They'd leave early, but they'd still crawl through London. After that, came town after town before the houses and streets finally thinned out. Then the road flattened, the fields opened up all around them, and they'd drive on and on until they'd stop for lunch at Spalding or Boston. Then came the even quieter, easier run to Ebwich. She was the map reader in those days, and the names on the signs are still familiar. They bring back the anticipation of another summer break, Hettie's café and the beach, the days out with Mum.

But those memories can't keep Clive out of her mind. He's back again, raising another question she never likes to answer: whether she'd let her lawyer, Mr Youngman – who was in fact an old man, more like a grandfather – talk her into saying Clive had coerced her.

Dad had sent that white-bearded, three-piece-suited, soft-spoken man, and she'd let him take over. She'd been scared, then relieved it was out of her hands. She'd been in the middle of something she'd had no experience of. When it sunk in that she really was locked up, she'd been glad of Mr Youngman's wrinkled smile and his calm voice saying he was there to help. Within half an hour or so, he had her saying that Clive had pressured her into going along with everything, that she'd acted under that pressure, that she'd been controlled by him. It was her best defence, Mr Youngman said. Had she? Was she? As time went on, as she served her time, she knew that wasn't entirely true. It wasn't even that it made that much difference. She'd still been convicted. She'd still got a four-year sentence while Clive had got six. But she'd got out; she was here. Clive had only got out to be buried.

Hettie had never asked her about Clive when she'd gone to live with her. At the time, Fiona was glad. There'd been all that trouble at home, and Hettie had let her move up to Ebwich. The hassle about transferring the probation had been sorted out and Fiona was just glad to get away from everything. Ebwich had seemed a tranquil pool then, somewhere she'd wanted to submerge herself in and forget the past. She didn't want to talk about what had happened. Hettie seemed to understand that. Getting out of that safe pool to travel to Jo's wedding, feeling the air of the outside world on her, had been a shock. Now she's heading back, anxious to re-submerge herself, yet knowing this isn't the way to tackle her problems, knowing that hiding isn't the answer.

Oncoming headlights assault her eyes – eyes that are prickling with the lack of sleep. Yet she's not feeling drowsy. Hidden energy has come to her aid, steering the car back to where she'll feel safe again. But all the time she's asking herself how long can she go on like this. Is she using Hettie as a substitute for Mum, running back to her apron strings? What else is there?

The miles pass. The hours pass. The tarmac rolls under her. She stops for petrol on the A1. She wonders if the young woman who serves her, working the night shift, has kids at home asleep. She looks like she doesn't get much herself, apologises when Fiona brings the key to the toilet back, says it's impossible to keep it clean, the sorts of people that use it. Fiona tells her it's okay, gets back in the car and drives on.

Finally the light cracks the sky, the sun low down to her right. Soon she's heading towards it, thinking how they used to cheer out loud when they got to this bit, knowing that Hettie would have put aside scones and the best cake for them. She can almost taste the jam and cream.

The Maxi rolls to a halt behind the café. She gives the dashboard a pat. It's done alright. Since it's rebirth, it no longer skulks in a corner. She parks it in its new position near the back door, running her hand it over, like it was a reliable old horse that's got her safely home. Before she's even inside, Hettie has started down the stairs. The sound of the car will have woken her. She'll be worried, wondering why she's back so soon. Fiona waits for her to appear in the hall.

'Sorry, I didn't want to wake you.'

'You didn't,' Hettie says.

'I couldn't stay.'

Hettie looks hard at her for a second and makes for the kettle. 'You shouldn't have driven all that way at that time. You could have killed yourself.'

Fiona is thinking about what she heard about Ted, killing himself late at night in his car. She looks at Hettie, wondering if she's thinking that too. If she is, she shows no sign – she never does with Ted.

'I had to.'

'That bad was it?'

'I snapped.'

Hettie turns from filling the kettle, alarm in her eyes.

'A cousin of the groom had too much to drink. He came on to me and I kneed him between the legs.'

Hettie laughs. It takes Fiona aback for a second. Hettie can't stop. Perhaps it's relief. Fiona joins in. Being back there makes that possible. When they stop, Hettie looks at Fiona and shakes her head.

'What did her ladyship think of that?'

'Margaret? I didn't wait to find out.'

Hettie gets out cups and saucers.

Fiona wants to tell her what Jo said about her dad seeing Margaret before Mum died. She wonders how much Hettie knows, but she says nothing. She can't speak of it. They're quiet until the kettle boils.

'Did you talk to your dad?' Hettie asks.

'A little.'

Hettie looks like she wants to ask more but breezes on. 'Well, it's a start. Maybe now Jo is married he'll be thinking...' She stops and looks out of the window, changing the subject back in the sudden way she sometimes does. 'I bet he regrets leaving the sea.'

'He could have done that for Mum,' says Fiona. 'He could have been there more for her.'

Hettie fills the teapot, looks at Fiona and squeezes her lips together before letting herself speak. 'Roni wouldn't have asked him. She...' She stops herself and looks away.

Only Hettie called Fiona's mum Roni, her shortening of Veronica. Fiona liked to hear her say it. There was something so intimate in that name, more than just a nickname, a deep connection, a lasting connection. Every time she used that name, Fiona saw the love Hettie had for her dead sister.

'She never complained when he was away,' says Fiona. 'Months and months on end.'

'She had you, love,' says Hettie. 'And anyway, she was tough like that. She was the evacuee in the family, don't forget. It wasn't easy in the munitions factory, but at least I was at home still. She was up here, miles away from home.'

That was the other thing about being at Hettie's. It had hardly changed since Mum had been here during the war. She'd have been just eight years old when it started, a big chunk of her childhood away from her family. She'd been here, where they were standing now, in that kitchen. Hettie had told her how her mum had sat at that same table, doing her colouring when she'd first visited to check on her. Fiona knows Ted was here then too. It was when Hettie had first met him, her future husband. And now they're in that room, with that sink, that table, those cupboards, probably even those teacups; still the same.

'Self-sufficient, that's what she was. You're like her,' says Hettie, stirring the teapot.

'At that age though,' says Fiona.

'Like I say, she was tough. We were all tougher then,' says Hettie. 'And it wasn't like Dagenham up here. But she liked that. Even before she brought you here, she'd come up when your dad was away.'

Fiona sits down. Hettie sits opposite her, wanting her to carry on, always interested to hear about her mum.

'Ted's mum and dad doted on her,' Hettie goes on.

'Their little cockney sparrow, they called her. They loved her to bits. I was always grateful for that, knowing she was safe up here, that they cared for her. Don't get me wrong, our mum and dad loved her too, but Dad loved the pub a bit too much and Mum, well, she were so nervous to start with – and then with the bombing and that.'

Fiona has heard most of this before, except perhaps how much Hettie felt in debt to Ted's parents. She thinks maybe if it hadn't been for that, Ted might not have stood a chance. There's no visible trace of Ted in the house now, and Hettie never refers to him directly. It's as if he's never been there, despite it being first his childhood home, then his married home with Hettie. She wonders why he's so absent. She wonders why Hettie married him. She wants to ask, but she doesn't.

'We just had to manage,' says Hettie. 'And it weren't all doom and gloom, even then, you know. We had some right old times, I can tell you. Me and my pal Jean and the other girls. It were different then. When we were doing our bit. We felt different. They have all these big words for it now, but it was like we were more in charge of ourselves.' She pours the tea.

Then you were here, thinks Fiona, living and working with your in-laws. She tries to imagine how different that must have been.

'Course it all went back to how it was before,' says Hettie, finishing her train of thought. She puts milk and sugar in her tea, almost putting sugar in Fiona's, then stopping herself. 'And here I am still.' She looks over at Fiona. 'But you mustn't feel you have to stay any longer than you want to.'

'I'm glad to be here,' says Fiona. 'You know I am. I just wonder what I'm going to do next.'

'That's natural at your age,' says Hettie. 'And this place...' she gestures at the walls. 'Once I stopped taking guests...'

Fiona thinks how quiet the café is sometimes, and how Hettie won't let Iris, her helper, go. She'd said it wouldn't be fair, Iris depends on the money.

'We could start taking guests again,' Fiona says. As she says it, she realises how much they'd have to do. The three rooms that used to be let out need redecorating, fresh mattresses, new bits and pieces. The guest rooms share a rudimentary bathroom at the back of the house; she can't see many people liking that these days – not if they're going to charge enough to make it worthwhile.

But Hettie doesn't dismiss it. 'Be a lot of work...'

'The rooms just need papering and painting,' says Fiona. The idea is appealing to her now. 'That bathroom though...'

'If we just get a new loo and sink, maybe one of those electric showers over the bath.' Fiona's enthusiasm is rubbing off on Hettie. 'I've got a bit put by – we could find out how much it'd cost.'

'I wouldn't mind doing the decorating.'

Hettie smiles at her. 'Got yourself a little project, I reckon.'

'I'll strip the paper off the back room first,' says Fiona. 'It needs doing the most. I'll move into the front.'

Hettie waves towards the door. 'What are you waiting for?'

# Roy

HE WAKES LATE for him – gone nine o'clock. Geri is already up. It was one in the morning when he'd got home. He wonders if Geri heard him come in. He doubts it. He's got home late before and got in the house, in the bed, without her waking. If it were her out that late, his ears would be tuned to any sound of her coming back. They were different like that. He'd eased the lock back on the door, quietly shut and relocked it, and slipped off his jacket and shoes. He'd been very conscious of the money in the bag. He needed to hide it. He'd decided on the cupboard under the stairs, right at the back behind some boxes. He'd closed it silently and stood listening for any sound from upstairs.

Luiz's bombshell and the dilemma about Sally and Tina were still circulating in his head. It had supposed to have been the night he told Geri how he felt, that they weren't right for each other, that he was leaving her. It had supposed to have been the start of something new for him – painful but at least honest. His head had ached with the strain of it, the prospect of telling her. He'd been tempted to get back in the car and drive away, drive anywhere. But he couldn't. Instead, he'd climbed the stairs one step at a time, silently, and slipped into the bathroom. He'd undressed, peed quietly without flushing, and slipped into bed with her, not touching her. He'd put it off.

'Where the hell were you?' she says from the doorway. He sits up. She's up and dressed. He could tell her now. He could just come out and say it. Just say he has to go. He's doesn't have to tell her he's got that money, how he's got it, just that he's going to do something else, that he can't stay there any longer. He nearly does it. But he doesn't. It feels too cruel. There must be some other way.

'Sorry, it took longer than I thought it would. Then we got talking...'

As far as Geri knew, he'd taken the day off to help Luiz move out of his old flat into Sally's place. He was supposed to be clearing the place up, ready to hand it back to the landlord at the end of the month.

He shifts back down under the covers and looks at the ceiling. He still can't say it. Geri comes into the room and sits on the bed.

'What's going on, Roy?'

'Nothing,' he says.

'Is everything alright?'

He hesitates. He should say it now. But she's been good to him. So has her dad. 'Yeah, course it is.'

But it's not. He's never going to be happy here. He knows it. He should be able to talk to her, tell her everything, but he never has. They work, they come home, they make love every couple of nights or so, they go out occasionally, they go through the motions of being a couple – but there's nothing else, nothing deeper. She's as bad at this as he is. Was it like this with her ex-husband? Or had there been more between them? He wasn't jealous or even curious, but it seemed strange she'd wiped this bloke out of her life so easily. Roy thinks now he's planning to do the same to her. Being here, getting into all this, was his mistake – he knows that. She's still looking at him, waiting for him to say something. He can't. She gets up and leaves the room. He's missed his chance again.

He looks back at the ceiling. This should be normality, a normal Sunday morning. There was a time when this was all he'd wanted – craved even. When he'd got back from Angola, he'd have given anything for this – something steady and routine, boring even, a chance to forget what had happened. Now he's messed it up. He keeps making desperate, stupid decisions, and he still doesn't know what he wants. Will Geri hate him now? It would be better if she did. He wouldn't blame her.

But he has to do something. They usually go to her mum and dad's around midday for lunch. He has to get away before then. He needs to take some things with him, at least some clothes. He still doesn't own much. When he'd moved in, Geri had looked at his two bags in the boot of the car and asked him where the rest of his stuff was. He'd never got in the habit of owning much. That had perplexed her. The steady stream of carrier bags with new clothes, and the frequent additions to the house, perplexed him. One case would do this time, he thinks.

They keep the cases in the spare bedroom. He slides out of bed and goes out to the landing. Downstairs, Bob Marley is asking 'Is This Love?' Geri likes that one. He knows she'll stay down there to hear it to the end. A few minutes, that's all he needs. He grabs his soft-sided suitcase, battered and scarred. Geri had said to chuck it and get a nice new one. He'd said it was still fine. The zip isn't great, but he gets it open and puts it on the bed.

Two trips back to their bedroom does it. Two armfuls from the chest of drawers, then that fucking zip again, then he slides it back out of sight, under the spare bed. Now he's just got to get it, that bag of cash and himself out of the house.

In the kitchen, he's getting some cereal when Geri gives him the solution.

'I've got to take a dish back to Carol,' she says, making for the door.

Carol, a couple of houses down the road, is always giving them things she's cooked too much of. Roy knows they'll have a long chat. He's got his chance. He feels a coward, a heel, for doing it like this. He tells himself it's better like this, better for her too. He knows it's a pathetic excuse, but it's the best he can do. As soon as Geri closes the front door, he dashes up the stairs and grabs the case.

He hesitates. What else? He gets his toothbrush and shaving stuff. Downstairs, he pulls the holdall from the cupboard. He shoves his jacket on top of it and grabs his car keys. Then he's out of the door. He doesn't lock it. She won't have taken her keys. His car is round the corner, out of sight, pure luck. He's there in seconds, bags in the boot, and away.

Before Edmonton Cemetery, he stops at a phone box. He pictures Hettie's hallway as he dials. He can see the wallpaper, the table where the heavy Bakelite phone used to sit. Is that where the phone still is? The pips go. He pushes a ten-pence in and hears her say the number.

'Hettie, it's Roy, Jean and Alan's Roy,' he says, thinking he's not theirs, they're dead.

'I know whose Roy you are,' says Hettie.

He's relieved. He'd wondered if she'd made the offer, thinking he'd never take it up.

'How are you, sunshine?'

Again, he thinks how she hasn't changed. He feels that stability, wants it for himself. He asks if her offer still stands. She said of course it does. Then he says they'll be three of them. She doesn't even ask who.

'The more the merrier,' she says. 'So long as you don't mind taking us as you find us.'

Us? He remembers she'd said something about a niece. He's thinking that's not ideal, but she's asking him when he'll be there.

'Is today too early?' he says.

'No time like the present,' comes her reply.

When he says they'll be there that afternoon, she tells him she'll have the kettle on and what about that sponge cake he used to like? Her remembering that brings him up short. Part of him wants to run there even more; another part of him tells him it's wrong bringing his shit to her. Too late now.

He's back in the car. He should be at Sally's sister's place around ten thirty. He's not looking forward to it. Tina must be wondering what's going on. And how's Sally going to be? She's going to be a handful, that's for sure. She's bound to be worried about Luiz. He tells himself he can't be responsible for who she falls for. But he'd promised Shane to look out for her and Tina. He hasn't kept that promise; he's messed up. But since Luiz came into Sally's life, she's been happier. She deserves that too. She won't be happy now, he thinks.

There had been a time, before Luiz, when Sally had dropped a lot of hints. It had been awkward then. He'd always liked her. He'd always thought Tina was a smashing kid. But he'd never wanted anything more. He realised he'd probably been given off signals himself, nothing direct, just things he'd said about how hard it was to settle down. It had been embarrassing that time when Tina was in her bedroom and Sally had kissed him. She'd misread him, that's all. They'd both got over it. They'd stayed friends.

When Luiz had said he was moving in with Sally, Roy was worried though. By then he knew what Luiz was into, and he didn't know how much Sally knew about it. He'd realised how close Luiz's determination was to recklessness. Perhaps he should have warned her. Too late now – now Luiz is in deep shit and she's had to leave her home. He wonders if she knows just how deep that shit is. They'd never spoken of what Luiz was waiting for from Angola when Sally was around. Nothing was said about those 'friends' of his who were probably looking for him right now. No, he really hadn't kept his promise to Shane; he hadn't looked out for Sally and Tina.

Sally hadn't spoken of Shane for a long while. Roy wanted to talk about him many times, but no longer felt he could. By the time Shane and he had gone to Angola, things between Sally and Shane had long been over. When Roy had turned up with the news Shane was dead, it was Sally that had to explain it to Tina. He hadn't elaborated on what had happened and she hadn't pressed him to, not after what had been in all the papers. He told her he and Shane had been stupid and he was lucky to be alive, that Shane hadn't been so lucky. He thinks he should have been able to tell Geri something about that. That he couldn't, only goes to prove he's making the right choice now – for both of them.

As he parks the car, Sally's face appears at the window. Her dark brown hair is scraped back. She disappears from view. He knows from that glimpse she's worried. She was waiting. He'd always thought of her as a tough woman, coping with Shane's absences, ditching him when he didn't measure up, coping with bringing up his child, managing with so little money after his death. It hit him then how much of that toughness must just be a protective layer, maybe even a fragile layer. Dragging her up to Lincolnshire will bring no comfort to her. Tina might like the beach, but there won't be much else to do. Maybe it's not such a great idea. But he can't think of anything else.

When Sally opens the door, he sees the bags inside, ready. He says hello to Tina and asks her what she's been up to, pretending this is all a big adventure. Sally is having none of it. She's tense, in a hurry to get out, and doesn't even look at him.

'Let's get going,' she says.

They're out the door and making for the car before he can ask her how she is. As Tina calls goodbye to her aunty somewhere in the house, he puts the bags into the boot of the car, registering the distress on Sally's pinched features. She gets Tina into the back seat and closes the door so they can talk without her hearing.

'Luiz said you know somewhere we can go,' she says.

'I do, but it's not ideal,' he says. 'Haven't you got any other relatives or something?'

She looks at him like he's suggested going to the

moon.

'No, and I'm scared. What's he up to?'

'He's in trouble,' says Roy. 'He says he can sort it out.' Even as he says it, he's aware how much she's been messed around here, that none of this is her fault.

She opens the car door. 'Can we just go?'

# Chapter 4  1975

# Roy

I LEFT THE ARMY in July '75. Shane left the year before. Our reasons were completely different. He'd met Sally, and he'd got her pregnant; I'd met no one and decided it was time I did – and being in the army made that hard. It wasn't exactly a great time to be looking for a job though. School leavers were going straight on the dole; a lot of them joining their parents who'd lost their jobs in the last few years. The country was back into the whole pay-freeze pay-demand thing after the miners brought down the Heath government the previous year. Ted's boys were borrowing money to keep the lights on. Exports were in the red and optimism was in short supply. I soon wished I'd stayed where I was.

Going back to live with Mum and Dad made things worse. It's only temporary, I said. Of course, they said. Just until I get fixed up, I said. Stay as long as you like, they said. And there I was – right back where I'd started. Mum was fretting about what I'd do, and Dad's running commentary on the miners' pay demands, the rescue bids for British Leyland and all the other industrial woes, did nothing to lift my spirits. Every afternoon, after scanning the papers and visiting the job centre, I'd end up lying on my teenage bed. I was thirty-one years old, with even worse prospects than when I'd last occupied that room, staring at those four walls, trying to work out what to do. When Dad suggested working at Fords, saying he could put some feelers out, I'd said no. By the end of the month, I'd told him maybe he should. It would only be temporary, of course.

One evening we'd just finished dinner and Dad was reading out something from his Daily Mirror, some report on an ex-paratrooper called John Banks, who'd recruited a bunch of ex-soldiers for a campaign against Ian Smith's Rhodesian regime. It all sounded like a massive cock-up. Dad was saying it wasn't surprising these ex-army lads were going in for these sorts of half-arsed schemes – that's how bad things had got. And by the way, he'd had a word at work. He was sure something could be sorted out for me.

That same evening, I went up the West End to meet Shane. With Sally having had Tina, and him having to settle down and make a home for them, we'd not seen much of each other. I suppose I envied him a bit. He seemed to have something to aim for and a purpose in life. When he'd suggested a night out, I jumped at the chance. It wasn't just that I couldn't stand another night in front of the telly; I needed to talk to someone who might understand how adrift I was feeling.

The minute I spotted him, the way he was standing, looking down, I knew things weren't right. I'd gone out to moan about how I was feeling and ended up spending most of the evening listening to him telling me what a mistake he'd made, how much he hated the job he'd got driving a delivery van, and how all his savings had gone on the flat, and how he wished he was back in the army. Worse still, he and Sally weren't getting on. She said he was miserable to live with, and he felt the same about her. The only good thing for him was Tina. When he talked about her, some of his old bounce came back and the gloom lifted from his face. She was the only reason he was sticking it out, he said.

We had quite a bit to drink before we got the last tube. He staggered off at Mile End, saying he didn't know how long he could put up with things, and I went back to Dagenham, equally pissed and pissed off.

Taking the job Dad had found for me was all I could do. It seemed better than nothing, and maybe in a few months something better would come along. But I had no idea how hard it was going to be. It should have been the easy option, just doing what everyone else had done – stay at home and work at the factory. There'd be some kind of social life and I'd be earning money. Surely I could find something to get into, surely... But I couldn't. I just couldn't.

I did try to make it work, to make the best of it. I bought a car and new clothes. I was single. I could go out as much as I wanted. But there was no one to go out with. Everyone I'd known from before had settled down, got married, and had kids. Most of my workmates had been at Fords since leaving school. They'd done their apprenticeships, and some of them were foremen or managers. I was a nobody. When I'd left them behind, I'd felt special. I'd gone off, travelled, been places, had people around me who were like me. Now it felt like my workmates were looking at me with amusement. Here he is, back at home, starting at the bottom, lucky his old man put in a word for him.

I had the mechanical skills. I'd worked on stuff a lot more complicated than a fucking Ford Cortina, but there I was fixing the doors on, with seconds to spare before the next one on the line had to be done, then the next one, then the next. It was mind-numbing and tedious, and I'd count the minutes to a break, the hours to the end of the day. I think Dad understood. He told me to stick at it and keep an eye out for something better, that it was only temporary, something would come along.

Yes, I tried. I tried hard but I couldn't do it. When Shane rang me in the November, I hadn't heard from him for months. I wasn't keen on hearing more about his problems, but then he said he'd left Sally and Tina. He said it had been hard, that he was going round to see Tina still and he was a lot happier. I was glad for him. He said he'd found a flat in Enfield, his old stamping ground, and he'd chucked the driving job to do some casual work, stripping out places for renovation. When he asked me how things were and I said they were shit, he said there was a room for me at the flat and he needed another bloke to work with him. It was cash in hand, but he was making good money. He said it would be a laugh, no one breathing down your neck and money to be made on the side too. He said I wouldn't believe what people paid for some of the stuff they were pulling out of these old houses.

Mum looked worried and Dad just shrugged when I told them I was going. I felt bad, but I felt a lot better when I walked out of that factory for the last time a week later.

It was one extreme to another. From the mundane routine back home and that job at Fords, I went to a free-wheeling, laugh-a-minute, almost holiday life, with Shane. We pitched up in his old pickup, different places all over London. We were gutting houses that this bloke he knew, Larry, was converting into flats. There was no paperwork, no rules, and no plan. So long as everything got stripped out on time, no one was bothered how we did it or what time of day we started or finished. We had the radio on full blast and bacon sandwiches from the nearest café while we watched the girls go by.

We knocked seven kinds of shit out of the places in the mornings, sold off what we could in the afternoons and headed for the pub. We claimed our dole money on Thursdays and got paid in cash by Larry on Fridays. Evenings were spent eating out and drinking. The weekends were a blur of more of the same. It felt like we lived in pubs and clubs, not in the tatty little flat where we never even kept a loaf of bread in the cupboard. The girls we brought back there didn't stay long, but we didn't really care and neither did they. I went with it. I let it all happen. I didn't think of anything else. I was having the youth I thought I'd missed out on.

It couldn't last. Of course it couldn't. When the work slackened off, I was spending more than I was making, eating into my savings from the army and telling myself it didn't matter. One Friday, Larry said he had nothing for us the next week. He said it was just temporary, and he'd be in touch. A week after that, we heard his nephews from Dublin were over and helping him out, doing what we used to do. That was the last we heard. We got a few odd jobs on a dodgy building site, but they evaporated after a site inspection shut the place down. Shane said it didn't matter; we should think of it as a holiday and enjoy it. So we did – until the money we'd earnt so easily ran out. Our dole money would never cover our drinking and clubbing, and we were still eating most meals out too. I dipped into my savings again and again, and I subbed Shane for stuff he had to get for Tina. Then Christmas came round.

Shane was going to spend the day with Sally and Tina. I kept expecting him to say he'd move back in with them, but somehow he and Sally always seemed to fall out after being together for more than a couple of hours. I didn't have any choice. I had to go home to Dagenham and pretend everything was going great.

I'd made it home for Christmas a few times when I'd been in the army. Mum got a huge kick out of us all being together. We'd do our best to make those few days like they used to be when I was young. Even as an adult, those times were special. The Christmas after I'd moved in with Shane marked the end of all that. I wasn't coming home like I used to. I no longer felt I had anything to be proud of, any purpose in life even. I was ashamed to be going home, not having a proper place of my own, or kids to take to see their grandparents. Even Shane's Christmas arrangement had some of the ingredients that mine didn't.

A couple of other things happened that Christmas,

tiny things on the face of it, things that changed the way I saw Dad. We'd done our usual thing, gone down to the club a couple of hours before Mum was going to put the dinner on the table, pulling on our coats to the sounds of her strict warning on when we had to be back. As we walked along, I found I was having to slow my pace, noticing that Dad couldn't stride out like he used to. That seemed to have happened all of a sudden, or I'd just not noticed it. I remember feeling disappointed, almost annoyed – not about the pace we were walking at, just at the unfairness of it. He'd worked hard all his life. Now he was approaching retirement, he'd lost so much of his vigour and drive.

He still had plenty to say about the unemployment situation, rampant inflation, and the fallout of the industrial unrest in the summer; but physically he was struggling. That morning, Mum had made references to him seeing the doctor, inviting some kind of discussion or disclosure. But he'd shut the discussion down and she hadn't pushed it. Worse still, I never asked, never got her on her own and asked – and I could have, if I hadn't been so wrapped up in the mess I'd got myself into.

The second thing about that Christmas happened when we'd sat down in the club and I'd got the drinks in. We'd been talking to a few of Dad's old workmates and a few of the blokes who'd been at the factory during my short stint there – lads I'd been to school with. I'd tried to brush over what I'd been doing since leaving, describing the work I'd been doing with Shane as 'salvage stuff', making good money, doing okay, you know. Then someone came past our table, someone I vaguely remember working with Dad. Ron, his name was. Dad and Ron had many a run-in over politics and union stuff. Dad used to say Ron was to the right of Genghis Khan, while Ron regarded Dad as being to the left of Karl Marx. Usually, they just sparred with each other in the club – and even when it got heated, it was only politics. That day was different. I heard later Ron had lost his wife a few months earlier. Being a few years older than Dad, he'd just retired. He wasn't coping well on his own. His two sons had given up on him and he'd been in the club every day, drinking heavily and getting into arguments, hovering on the edge of being banned. When he stopped at our table, he'd already had plenty to drink and I could see the bitterness in his face when he saw I was there with Dad, doubtless knowing we'd be on our way home to our Christmas dinner. It started with a sarcastic comment.

'Surprised to see you here,' he said, looking at Dad. 'I would have thought they'd have got you up at BL to sort out their mess.'

He was referring to the news reports of huge losses at British Leyland, another nail in the coffin of the British car industry. Dad fixed him with a stare when he replied.

'I'd go back to the bar and have a seat if I were you, mate – before you fall down.'

I could see straight away it would have been better if Dad had ignored him. Ron leant on the table next to ours and gave us a cracked grin. Then he looked at me.

'Home for Christmas, are you?'

'That's right,' I said.

'Not got yourself hitched yet then?'

'No,' I said, wondering why he'd come out with that.

'Young, free and single, playing the field?' he couldn't stop the slurring now.

'Something like that,' I said.

'Not that being married made any difference to some,' he went on, aiming a lopsided grin at Dad.

I couldn't work that one out. It must have shown on my face because he turned the grin on me and went on.

'It never stopped him.' He indicated Dad with the long ash on the end of his fag.

'Bugger off, Ron,' said Dad.

'No, you bugger off. Have you told him about your bits on the side? You had more than your share, didn't you?'

Another one of Dad's old workmates, Harry, at the next table, called over. 'Give it a rest, Ron.'

'Keep your fucking nose out!' Ron called back.

Everyone else was looking away. Denied his audience, Ron snorted and waved his arm dismissively, shedding the ash off his fag. 'It was his missus I felt sorry for.' He seemed to lose his focus then; he scanned around the room like he was trying to remember where he was, before shuffling off towards the bar.

I waited to see if Dad would say something. He didn't. I had to speak first.

'What was that all about?'

'He always talked out of his arse,' Dad said, before taking a long drink. 'He ain't changed much.'

He wasn't going to discuss it. We talked about this and that, chatted with some of his other workmates, and made our way home.

That night, I stayed over – back in my old bedroom

again. I hadn't been looking forward to it. It was another reminder of how I'd still not moved on, still had no one of my own, just girlfriends that came and went. I wondered if they sensed something in me, a lack of ambition perhaps, no plans for the rest of my life. Lying in my old bed, I went over Ron's words and tried to decide if he was off his head and just talking rubbish or had Dad really been a womanizer in his younger years. I started thinking about the last holiday at Ebwich, the hurried departure, nothing being said about Hettie all the way home, never going back there again. Hettie had been Mum's oldest friend, yet they'd lost touch after that visit. It's not that I hadn't considered the idea before – that Dad and Hettie had something going, right under Mum's nose – but I'd brushed it aside. After all, Mum and Dad had stayed together, and I'd never heard Mum complain about him or suggest anything like Ron had been ranting about. Or maybe Mum had just tolerated Dad, and maybe Hettie, her best friend, had been the last straw.

The day after Boxing Day, I went back to the flat. We had to stretch the little money we had left and find something to do in those dead days before the New Year – two things that don't go well together. I was hoping Shane had some ideas, or he'd found us some work. But when I arrived, the first thing I saw was two police cars outside. Apart from some of the demolition stuff we'd syphoned off, I didn't think we had anything to worry about, but I was glad to see the commotion seemed to be centred on the pavement where a small crowd had gathered. Then I saw Shane being restrained by two police officers and a bloke with blood coming from his nose, shouting and pointing at Shane. Behind him, a young woman was screeching and crying. I called out to Shane and got told to move away. Shane said it was alright, but clearly it wasn't. My questions to the police were ignored as Shane was put into one car and the bloody-nosed man and the woman into another. The rest of us were told the show was over and to go home.

Shane was charged with assault and released just before midnight. He was angrier than I'd ever seen him. He'd heard shouting outside the flat and looked out to see the bloke smacking the woman around the head. What he didn't know was that someone had already called the police, and they were on their way. By now, the woman was being dragged off down the street. Shane had run out and grabbed the bloke. Their struggle escalated into a fist fight and Shane gave this bloke a bit of a pasting. The woman, instead of being grateful, had turned on Shane. By the time the police arrived, she was backing her bloke up. She'd said their argument was nothing and Shane had attacked her boyfriend for no good reason. Shane said that one of the coppers who'd attended, a sergeant, had been at school with him. He thought this copper had believed him but couldn't do much because the boyfriend was pressing charges. All Shane got out of it was a load of bruises and an appointment at Enfield Magistrates' Court. It was a crap ending to a crap Christmas.

# Fiona

By the time I left school, I'd been with Jo for eight years. During that time, we'd learnt to accommodate each other. But there were still distinct boundaries and flashpoints. When one of us broke the unwritten rules – usually Jo, out to impress someone or spouting something to cover up her insecurities – there would be trouble. The rules included not calling my dad 'Dad' and me not badmouthing her mum. If we stuck to those rules, things weren't too bad.

Our status as step-sisters of the same age made us curiosities at school and we got more than our fair share of comments and questions. We got asked how come we had so little to do with one another. We got asked if there'd been a salacious affair between our parents. I'd even been asked if my mum was really dead. I ignored the thoughtless prattle and kept my thoughts to myself. But Jo enjoyed the attention. She couldn't go for long without some boast about either her real dad – still claiming he was heir to a huge estate where she'd soon be living, just as soon as he completed his overseas business ventures – or her boasts about her stepfather being captain of a ship, which she'd transformed from an oil tanker to a prestigious command in the Royal Navy. When I debunked these myths, she'd exact revenge in any way she could, damaging my books and clothes or informing on my misdemeanors, real or made up.

Jo knew how to hit back verbally too, just where it

hurt, usually with references to Mum coming from the East End, a daughter of factory workers. To begin with, I'd lash out, and she'd smirk with satisfaction when I was punished. Frentons' punishments were designed to humiliate, usually involving cleaning the toilets or the baths which Jo and her friends would have ensured were as disgusting as possible. But I learnt that attack wasn't the way to handle Jo. I got good at letting her show how petty she could be, guiding her into revealing her own flaws with a carefully chosen word at just the right time. I learnt a lot more about people at school than she did.

When I wasn't dealing with Jo, there were some good times. During the electricity cuts in the early 1970s, the teachers seemed to lose their power along with the national grid losing its. In the blackouts, the winter evenings became ours. With candles and blankets, we made our own little enclaves where stashes of cake and chocolates were eaten, the teachers were discussed and mimicked, and favourite books were read out loud. When there was electricity, our ration of early evening TV was another escape. To begin with, it was a painful reminder of those evenings watching TV with Mum. Then I discovered by pretending she was there with me, watching *White Horses,* I could feel her presence, the warmth of the side of her body and her voice in my head, telling me everything would be alright. Julia's adventures on the stud farm in Lipica and her bond with the magnificent Boris would take me from the grey winter evenings at Frentons, back to the warm glow of life at home with Mum. The theme music still has my heart swelling and my tears flowing.

The strange thing was, despite Jo's keenness to fit in – she even changed the way she talked at school – as we got older, I managed better than she did. For one thing, there were fewer expectations on me. Margaret was convinced Jo was a genius who would soar to the highest academic heights, and pressured her to prove it. Dad had no such expectations for me. I could go along with the flow, enjoying the small pleasures, keeping under the radar and making the best of things. For all her cunning, I could always read people better than Jo could. I learnt how to defuse trouble and persuade; Jo still preferred revenge. She never grew out of hitting back in some sneaky way, usually with something she'd discovered and stored up, ready to launch. But it did nothing to improve her life at Frentons. As her circle of friends diminished, mine grew. Frentons never matched the boarding school world of her books and comics.

I also discovered I could handle a lacrosse racket while she was useless with one; I was pretty good at netball and she wasn't. I didn't want the attention these skills brought, but I enjoyed it all the same. And from Mum and Hettie, I'd learnt to cook. I could fry sausages and eggs on the little primus stove I'd sneaked in from home. I got on with most of my classmates and had two close friends, Lolly and Frieda. I was learning how to make the best of things. It must have irked Jo that she'd wanted Frentons so much and I hadn't, yet I'd made the best of it and somehow she never could. But throughout it all, she could always muster that smug smile that said she knew something I didn't.

By the time we were in the sixth form, Jo's life at school revolved around her academic success – a narrow track, more like a treadmill. Any suggestions or help I offered were scorned and often triggered a fresh wave of petty attacks. So I left her alone, she left me alone, and our remaining time at school passed with few incidents.

The holidays were always the worst for me. If Dad was away at sea, Margaret would accompany him, and various arrangements had to be made for us. Those times were worse than school. For the short breaks, we stayed at school, cared for by a couple of the domestic staff and one of the younger, keener teachers. There were girls from overseas, and from service families there too. It was like school without the lessons. A few outings were organised during these breaks, but most of our time was spent in the eerily quiet school. Summer holidays were usually spent with other families, acquaintances of Margaret or people she'd found and paid to have us.

Of all the things I hated Margaret for most, was her refusal for me to stay with Hettie in the holidays. I never understood why Dad wouldn't overrule her – no matter how much I pleaded. Neither could I stay with Lolly or Frieda, who always asked me to, who even got their parents to write to Dad. Margaret said it wouldn't be fair on Jo unless she was invited too – and she was never invited. I made sure of that. But of all Margaret's crimes against me, her veto on visits to Hettie came top.

Hettie had driven down just before we'd started at Frentons. It took a lot of tantrums and tears for Dad to agree to that. It had been a strained visit – spoilt for me by Jo and Margaret always there, lurking around in the background. Hettie tried her best with them. But her

East End cheer did not melt Margaret's icy reception, or even bring a smile to Jo's sulky face. Only once did she manage to corner Dad. Despite hearing nothing of their exchange, I could tell she'd given him a piece of her mind, because he was angry and jittery for the rest of the day. She was supposed to have stayed for a few days but left early, getting me on my own to tell me to keep on writing to her and not to forget she was always there for me.

I never did forget, and I wrote to Hettie almost every week, putting more effort and sheets of paper into those letters than any I sent to Dad, which went via the shipping company's head office and could take weeks for a reply. Hettie's replies were prompt. What she didn't have in the way of news, she made up for with stories of Mum. It had started with my letters saying how I much I missed Mum. In her replies, she'd write a little episode of her and Mum's life when they were young. I kept asking for more. I looked forward to those installments with more relish than any of my favourite TV series. I got the other side of the stories Mum had told me. I learnt where they'd both come from and how they'd coped with being apart in circumstances far worse than mine. I think it made me realise I could cope. It made me determined to cope.

It would be a long time before I found out what she and Dad had argued about that day she'd gone back home early. Margaret and Jo had oozed satisfaction after Hettie had driven away, while my loathing for them stepped up a notch. Hettie never referred to that visit in her letters, but I knew it was the last movement in a split between her and Dad, a crack that had become a chasm. The only contact I had with Hettie after that was through her letters and the occasional call I made from a phone box when I could sneak away and get her to call me back. But nothing stopped us from keeping in touch.

Keeping in touch with Dad brought little comfort though. When we'd gone to Frentons, Margaret had decided Jo and I should always write jointly to her and Dad and they would write back to us in the same way. It was one of the few grievances Jo shared with me, having to write our separate sheets to put in the same envelope. I soon worked out it was another of Margaret's ways to keep control. This was how my requests to stay at Hettie's in the holidays were quickly rebuffed with various excuses that Dad went along with. All this time, my resentment of Margaret grew and grew.

During a bad patch when I'd first gone away to school, I wrote to Hettie saying I was planning to run away to Ebwich. She wrote back and told me not to. She reminded me that Mum had coped when she was younger than me and she wouldn't have wanted me to do it. She reminded me Mum was watching over me. In time, as I coped better, it felt like she really was.

When school ended, everything changed. Even Margaret's control slipped away. Dad had changed too. I thought I detected signs of regret, of the realisation he'd missed out on a lot during those years I was at school. He called in some favours to make sure our leaving school coincided with his shore leave. When he and Margaret collected us from school, as he told us about the holiday he had planned for us, Margaret said very little. I was sure he'd overridden her on that occasion. He made a point of spending a lot of time with me during those couple of weeks in France. Jo and Margaret pretended not to notice, but I could see they hated it. They compensated with constant talk of the plans for Jo's future, the wonderful career she was going to have. Dad had asked me what I was going to do, but I didn't know. Lolly had written from Yorkshire to say she was hoping to get a job in the civil service in London, while Frieda had landed a job in an estate agency in the West End. They both had plans. I still had nothing, and I missed being with them.

With Jo set for Bath University, my lack of plans constantly irked Margaret. The more she brought it up, the less I felt inclined to cooperate. She got very imaginative with her suggestions though – usually via Dad. We went through all the women's military services, then various overseas organisations, until we got to opportunities for nannies in Canada and au pairs in Austria. It came to a halt when I announced I'd got a job in the office of a local factory. I took the job to spite her, to do anything but move out and satisfy her. It wasn't very adult of me, but it felt good at the time.

But I really didn't know what I wanted to do. Careers information was non-existent at Frentons. The staff assumed most girls would do a stint of secretarial training, then a few years in an office while they looked for a husband. Even Jo was one of the few exceptions there. Although Margaret had pushed her towards a degree, I knew Jo was more capable of it than I was. Over the years, I'd realised that Margaret wanted more for her daughter than she'd had herself. Her marriage to

Jo's father was a product of the same attitude that I'd seen at school. Her own family had money, but her brother had inherited it all and showed little inclination to help Margaret. Just a few years out of school, she'd met the man she'd thought was her ticket out of her problem – Laurence Belmont-Hart. Laurence had inherited his family estate, Warltonley, in Somerset. Death duties and taxes had taken their toll on the place over the years, but it was Laurence's lifestyle that finished it off. His get-rich-quick schemes and his incompetence finally got to Margaret. After Jo came along, she left him. She moved with Jo into in a decaying flat in the Belmont-Harts' London house while she divorced Laurence and tried to make a living with her meagre qualifications.

Margaret got just enough money out of Laurence to get Jo into a good prep school. She worked as a secretary until she met Dad. It took me a long while to realise that she'd done most of this for Jo, that she hated her dependence on her husbands and it came out in the way she exercised whatever power she had. That's how she coped, how she carved a better future for Jo. For all my dislike of Margaret, I could see she was making sure Jo would have better prospects than she ever had.

By the time we'd left school, Jo's fantasies of her father getting back the family estate had ebbed away. Realising she was smart enough to do well, and with something of her mother's determination, Jo had decided on an Economics degree and a career in finance. It peeved me she had all these brains but still couldn't wash her own clothes, and she'd still steal my clean underwear. But I had to admit she had something to aim for, which was more than I did. My office assistant's job at Grey and Garton's Engineering already felt like a big mistake.

I was due to start work two weeks after we got back from France. After that, it wouldn't be long before Jo went away to university. Then Dad would go back to sea, and Margaret would go with him. The idea of my being there alone in what Margaret now saw as her house tormented her. Rearranged, redecorated and refurnished, so that every trace of the past had been stripped away, it was her domain. I had to look very hard for a remnant of Mum's influence on the place. But I realised that despite Margaret's efforts, the best traces of Mum were in my memory and that's something she couldn't erase.

Something else Margaret couldn't do was to prevent me from seeing Hettie anymore. As soon as we were back from France, I rang her. Then I told Dad I was going up there to visit her before my new job started. He was annoyed, almost scared about it. I couldn't understand why. But he knew I was going, whatever he said. I let him tell Margaret. Jo pretended she didn't care what I did, but outside of the routine of school, and having to wait for university to start, I could see she was at a loose end. I'd stayed in touch with Lolly and Frieda and a few of the other girls since we'd left school. No one we were at school with was in touch with Jo. It wasn't long before Dad was given the job of suggesting Jo went with me to Hettie's. I just looked at him and shook my head and he didn't ask again.

Hettie couldn't pick me from Lincoln station as the café was busy, so it was late afternoon when I arrived on the slow, meandering bus at the crossroads in Ebwich. During the last few miles, I'd looked out at the villages and the countryside and remembered the last time I'd been there with Mum. When I got off the bus, it was with an odd mixture of sadness and joy. I told myself she was there in spirit. The sun was out and there was an onshore breeze. I could smell the sea. The village was exactly as I remembered it. I knew then it had been the right thing to do, exactly the right place to be. As the bus pulled away, I stood and soaked it all in. It was like coming home. It had been her home once, that's why.

The two weeks at the café went by quickly. I was helping in the mornings and going to the beach in the afternoons after we'd finished serving lunches. Only one of the rooms Hettie let out was occupied. The elderly couple from Sheffield were faithful regulars. They had often been there when Mum and I had visited. They were another reminder, another connection to her. Hettie's other regulars had drifted away. The caravan site on the edge of the village was the preferred choice now. They had built a clubhouse, a pool, and a playground for the children. Hettie's seaside boarding house was a pre-war relic by comparison. She was philosophical about it. The café still held some attraction, especially for day trippers, and, as she said, keeping the rooms up was getting too much for her. When the time came to go home, I told Hettie I wished I hadn't taken the job in Beckenham. She said I should give it a go, and give Margaret another chance too. She said things might be different now. They weren't.

# Chapter 5     1979

# Fiona

FIONA THINKS HOW odd it is that scraping off wallpaper reminds her of Holloway. It was the idea of making a place your own. Some of the women went to great lengths to do that. They cut out pictures from magazines to stick to the walls, made curtains and runners, and coveted any little extra they could get hold of – a potted plant, a photo frame, anything that made the space theirs. At the time, she'd thought it sad, sad that it was their home, that they were going to those efforts to make the place more homely. Was this old place going to be her home now? She didn't want to think that, yet there was comfort in that thought.

She finds a second layer of paper. The faded roses give way to delicate fairies and stars. She scrapes on, contemplating that idea of home, somewhere to settle down properly. A sting of anger catches her unawares. She had a home back then. She had a home with Mum. Was Dad really seeing Margaret before Mum died? She still doesn't want to believe that, but it explains so much. Yet it makes no sense. Margaret never brought Dad any joy, at least not that she'd ever seen. Why would he do that? She fights the urge to pursue that line, to keep looking back, keep dwelling on how things could have been different. She knows she needs something for herself now. She knows that living in the present and making a future is the right thing to do, the only thing to do. And there must be someone to do it with. Surely there must. But it scares her too. How do you know it's the right person? Was that what Dad had wanted, or had he fallen into a trap that Margaret had laid for him?

When Margaret and Jo first appeared in her life, she used to look at Dad and wonder why he'd done it, wonder if he was just being carried along with something, convenience maybe. She'd wondered whether he thought of Mum when he was with Margaret, or if he ever missed her at all. He'd never said he did, never even hinted he did. That's why she'd asked him. And still she didn't know. When she'd cried about Mum, asked him why she had to die, he only ever said they had to get over it. She'd stopped saying things about Mum to him then. He didn't like it when she reminded him. She'd kept it all inside herself and carried it with her off to school as hidden luggage.

Wrapping all that up inside her, learning not to reveal too much, had become Fiona's normal state. Even with Clive, she'd stifled her emotions, let them exist on the surface, like they were just on her skin, something that didn't soak in, that she could rinse off. She knows that now. She'd ignored it then. She'd gone along with Clive. And no, he didn't coerce her; she'd just rode along beside him, going his way. He'd talked and dreamed and schemed, getting almost manic with what they could do and why they didn't need to conform to anyone else's ideas. He'd impressed her, but he didn't seduce her. He'd kept his distance in that department for quite a while – she'd seduced him in the end. She wonders if she'd handled things better it might have been different. She knows it's a pointless line of thought, that it's all too easy to say what you might have done, could have done, and it doesn't help. What she did to him was cruel. She did it for herself.

As she looks at that wallpaper, scraping into the last layer, she thinks of Clive's bedroom, years out of date, not unlike this one – the brown wooden furniture, the high wooden bed with the shiny quilted eiderdown over the worn blankets and sheets. She remembers the first time she went in there. His mum was out. They'd had the house to themselves. His dad had left years ago. She was just beginning to see how hard his mum had to work to keep that house on her own. That's why nothing was new. That's why his room was twenty years out of date, wallpaper like this, layer on layer, with stains in the corners. She'd looked up at it when she lay on his bed that day, teasing him, watching as he looked down at her and hesitated, as he realised what she was doing; shocked when she produced the Durex packet, her knowing he wouldn't have any, her coming prepared. She wonders now if he ever got over that shock, if he was always a little awestruck with her, despite her being younger, despite him being the one with all the plans.

The next layer of paper is more stubborn. She wets it

and scrapes harder. She thinks how different they were. He'd been at home with his mum when she'd been at school all those years. She'd been so much more ready for sex than he was. He saw that. But their differences went beyond what she had in mind that afternoon. He was looking for someone to enact his non-sexual fantasies with. And he'd met no one else like her. But even then, she knew it wouldn't last. She'd thought it was a phase, that they'd both move on. She considers how it might have been if he'd found someone else, if he hadn't killed himself. The thought makes her wonder what kind of man is right for her. Is anyone right for her, or will she be here scraping off the paper she's going to put on these walls, then scraping the next lot off and the next?

When she gets to the plaster, pencil lines appear. At first she thinks they're just random marks. But as she scrapes, she realises they're lines of a drawing. It looks like a child's drawing. She scrapes faster to reveal more. There's a boat of some kind, an old-fashioned boat with a paddle wheel. The artist hasn't quite mastered perspective, but gradually it becomes clear that they've drawn a long line of stick figures winding back from the boat. She's sure they're children. Behind them stands a large building with a tall chimney. As Fiona steps back from it, Hettie enters the room.

'Well I never!'

Fiona looks at Hettie. 'What?'

'Roni.'

'Mum did it?'

Hettie steps up to it and points. 'That's the Ford jetty where all the kids went from. I took her down there.

There was this long line, all the way back to Valence Avenue, kids all walking along, three or four lines of them.'

Hettie has told her before how thousands of children were evacuated to the East Coast from Dagenham. She could never really picture that scene from September 1939. Now she's taken aback by how real this childish drawing makes it.

'Mums bringing their kids from all around the town,' Hettie says, indicating the stick figures carrying what looks like sacks. 'A lot of them had their stuff in pillow cases. They didn't have suitcases or bags.' She looks closer. 'It was very early. The gates were still locked when we got there.' Her voice cracks. 'They'd organised milk for them, all these crates stacked up.' She points to the rectangles with the distorted bottles that Roni had tried to draw.

Fiona turns to see Hettie's eyes are wet, locked onto the image. She can see she's back there.

'You can't imagine it now, can you? Some of the mums went with them. Roni kept asking why our mum wasn't going too. I kept telling her she couldn't, that she had her work. She were trying so hard to be brave but at the last minute she couldn't keep it up and she started to cry. I held her and held her till the last minute, when I had to let them put her on the boat. One of the volunteer women took her by the hand and she kept looking back at me. I cried all the way home. I felt I'd let her down.'

Fiona takes the scraper and uncovers the last bit of the picture, hoping there'd be more, a message she could take comfort from. But there's nothing. She's reached the edge of the picture, the last child in the long winding column.

Hettie wipes her eyes and carries on. 'They took them to Lowestoft to start with. Then by bus up the coast. I came up to see her when she'd settled in. The woman they'd put her with meant well, but Roni found it hard being with all these other kids in the family. We were all adults in our house bar her. She wasn't used to the rough and tumble. Then I got talking to this woman who knew Ted's mum and dad. It was a long way, but I had no choice. That's how she ended up here.'

Fiona's eyes are fixed on the stick figures in the snaking lines looking for her mum, the eight-year-old child, away from her family, away from everything she knew. She's twenty-three; what does she have to be so scared about? She gently runs her hand over the lines on the wall. She stops on one child. There's another stick-figure tucked under its arm. She points at it.

'Her dolly,' says Hettie. 'It went everywhere with her.'

Now she can't keep the tears back either. 'I don't want to cover it over again.'

'We could put a frame around it,' says Hettie.

'I'd like that,' says Fiona. She wipes her eyes.

'Ted's mum papered this room, you know,' says Hettie. She picks up a fragment of the stars and fairies from the floor. 'She got it special for Roni. I never knew it was still under there. Ted must have papered over it. Typical of him not to strip it first.'

Hettie's voice has changed with the mention of Ted. The softness has turned brittle. Fiona wonders why, wonders what Hettie felt for Ted, if that brusqueness when she talks of him is for real, or just some protective layer she pulls over herself when she needs it. There must have been something there. Or why did she marry him?

'Do you miss him?' she's asked it before she can stop herself.

Hettie seems to have to think of the answer. It was like when she asked her dad about her mum. She shouldn't have asked.

'Me and Ted...' she starts to say. 'It weren't—' she stops again. 'I was very fond of Ted. But I felt sorry for him. And the thing is, if you just feel sorry for your bloke...' Hettie shrugs as if what she's saying is a universal truth that Fiona will understand.

'I think I felt sorry for Clive,' says Fiona. It's the first time she's said that, thought it out loud.

'Well, you know what I mean then,' says Hettie.

'I thought I loved him. But I was just getting back at Margaret and Dad.'

'Stop blaming yourself,' says Hettie. 'You're young. You can put it all behind you. You are putting it behind you.'

'I can't forget what I did – what I did to him.'

Hettie turns away. 'I know. I do know.'

'And coming here... I mean, I'm grateful, you know that. But what am I going to do?'

Hettie picks up some more scraps of paper and looks at them. 'You're going to take your time. The trouble with being your age is, you think everything has to happen in the next week or the next month. You've got years.'

Fiona ponders that for a second, not really getting it,

unable to forget how she'd come to be there.

'I was bloody stupid.'

Hettie looks her in the eyes. 'We've all been bloody stupid.'

'And last night,' says Fiona. 'That was bloody stupid.'

'That's not how it sounded to me.'

'It wasn't very grown up though, was it?'

'Sounds to me like he wasn't very grown up. Hope it taught him a lesson.'

Fiona smiles. She's so glad of Hettie. Just then, when she'd said that, she could see Mum in her face. They were probably never very alike, but just then, the way her face narrowed slightly, the earnest look in her eyes, she could see the same expression.

'And Dad,' says Fiona, 'selling the house and giving Jo and David the deposit for their place.'

Hettie sits on the bed. 'He's just trying to do his best for her. He means well. He always—' She stops, like she's said too much.

'You know, all that time in prison, I thought about it a lot. I thought I'd got it straight. I knew why I'd done what I'd done. And I'd seen all these girls and women worse off than me. I thought I could sort everything out. Then, when I got out and saw Jo and Margaret again, it was just like it was before, resenting them, resenting him for what he did.'

'He might not be as bad as you think,' says Hettie.

Fiona looks at her, puzzled that she could say that, about to ask her why. Before she can, Hettie goes on.

'Give it some time.'

Fiona puts down the scraper. 'I thought I needed nothing from Dad. I thought I was over all that stuff with Jo and Margaret coming into the house. There she is with her new husband, her job and her new house. Miss goody two-shoes, with her degree and her big church wedding.'

'You don't really begrudge her that, do you?' asks Hettie.

'No, it's just—'

Fiona stops. The phone's ringing downstairs. Hettie gets up and makes for the door. 'Give it some time.'

Fiona wets and scrapes, working away from the picture, hoping there could still be more. She hears Hettie's voice from downstairs, a note of surprise in it, saying something about rooms. Surely not people wanting to book, not now she's started making this mess. She scrapes away, onto unmarked plaster now, a little chalky with age, revealing cracks inexpertly filled in, thinking they'll need attention before any new wallpaper goes on.

Hettie starts back up the stairs, calling up, surprise in her voice. 'We've got visitors coming.'

'Oh bloody hell!' Fiona says.

Hettie reaches the doorway. She stands uncertainly, like something's just occurred to her. 'No, it's alright, not paying guests.'

Fiona looks at her, bemused. 'Who?'

'Roy Brady. I knew his mum, way back, from the factory in the war. I asked him at her funeral. I never thought he'd come.'

'You said guests.'

'I think it's his girlfriend and a little girl. I didn't think he...' Hettie trails off, looking at the wall, realising it's going to mess up Fiona's decorating plans. 'We'll have to manage. We'll need the double room at the front though – so the child can be next door.'

'It's alright,' says Fiona. 'I can tidy up and move back in here. I don't suppose they'll stay for long, will they?'

'Just a few days,' says Hettie, uncertainly.

'When are they getting here?' asks Fiona, thinking she'll have plenty of time to sort things out.

'Today,' says Hettie. 'And I should be opening the café now.'

'I'd better get cracking then,' says Fiona, her resentment diminishing with the challenge of something urgent to do, something happening.

# Roy

'FOUR OR FIVE hours,' Roy says, turning to answer Tina in the back seat.

'You're kidding, aren't you?' says Sally. 'Tina's never been in a car for that long.'

'We'll stop, don't worry,' he says.

'Where is this place? I've never heard of it.'

Sally's tetchy tone isn't improving his mood. He's doing his best. It would be better if she just went along with it, he thinks. He tries to lighten things up.

'It's at the seaside. A bit quiet, but...' He doesn't want to tell her how quiet. He aims the next words at the rear-view mirror. 'You've been to the seaside. You went to Southend with Luiz.' He regrets the comparison. There's no pier or rows of amusement arcades where they're going.

'She was sick on the way back,' says Sally.

He breathes out. Shane used to say she'd get into these negative moods.

'Probably all the junk Luiz let her eat,' he says, just suppressing his exasperation.

'Are you driving straight back?'

He wonders why she's asking. She must have seen his bag in the boot when he put their stuff in with it.

'No.'

'Are you staying too?' asks Tina.

'Just a few days or so,' he says. He feels Sally's eyes on him, knowing she wants to ask more about that. He breezes on. 'I had some great holidays there when I was a kid.'

'Is there sand?' Tina asks, sounding more interested.

'Miles and miles of sand,' he says. 'And usually hardly anyone else there, loads of space – that's why I loved it.'

'How old were you?' asks Tina, more interested still.

'Oh, let me see now. The first time was 1952, so I was six.'

'Same as me!'

'Yes, the same as you. We went there for a few years running.'

Tina takes this in. They're stopped at some lights. The morning traffic is heavy. Sally turns the tuner knob on the radio. He stifles the urge to tell her to leave it alone.

'The last time we went was 1956. There were still horses working on the farms.'

'I wasn't even born then,' says Sally.

'Then you didn't go anymore?' asks Tina.

'No, we didn't,' he says, not noticing the green light

until a horn from the car behind blasts out, unnecessarily long.

'Why not?' Tina sounds puzzled.

'I think my mum and dad fancied a change.'

It's odd, he thinks, her asking that. What the hell was Dad thinking of? After that last holiday, Mum didn't even want to go in that direction. They went to the Kent coast, Margate, or Folkestone, instead. They went to busier beaches, busier boarding houses with strangers, not as friendly, not like with Hettie and her few regulars. It just wasn't the same.

He glances over at Sally. Her face is set. He can't work out what she's thinking. He wonders if this isn't a big mistake, but at the same time it feels right to go there now, like it was on the cards somehow, as if this reason for going was all part of a plan. But he doesn't have the rest of the plan – that's the problem. He has the money in the boot and he has these two in the car. Then what? Sally's saying something. He was tuned out, he hasn't heard.

'… when we stop.'

He looks across at her. She looks back, thrown by his blank expression.

'Find a phone box,' she says.

He looks out at the road, not knowing what to say. 'Sorry, I was miles away.'

'I want to call Tomás. Luiz might be there or someone who can take a message for him.'

'Yeah, of course.'

He doubts Luiz will be there. He could have disappeared forever. Despite the comings and goings and the shady 'business' he does with his friends, she cares about Luiz. She's upset by all this. He sees that. But she must know the stuff Luiz is into is risky and illegal. Roy hasn't talked to her about that. He's not planning to, and she's unlikely to say anything about it with Tina in the car. He doesn't want her to. He doesn't want to admit his part in it.

He glances over at her. He's never understood her. It didn't matter before. When she was with Shane, she was just his mate's girlfriend. He'd not seen that much of her back then. Later, when he'd had the task of telling her that Shane was dead, it had almost felt as bad as when it had happened. There wasn't the chaos and the noise, the explosions and the ripping of steel and flesh when he'd turned up to the flat that day to break the news, yet his guts were more liquid and his head felt more of a mess. There was no adrenalin to carry him through that.

Tina was two years old then. Sally and Shane had split up over a year before, but Tina's dad was still her dad. Except, all of a sudden, she didn't have a dad anymore. Shane used to talk about getting back with Sally, that it wasn't over between them. But that possibility had gone then. And Roy had been the only one who could bring that news. He was the only one because no one else knew – no one. No one even knew where they were when it happened.

When he'd told Sally Shane was dead, she didn't react. Her face was blank. He'd not known what to expect, but he'd prepared himself for all sorts of things – her hitting out at him, angry that he'd gone with Shane and he'd come back alive, her breaking down and crying, her throwing him out. Instead, she just took it in, expressionless. She asked where and when and he'd told her. But she didn't ask anything else. He told her he'd promised Shane to look out for them, to look out for Tina, help if he could. Again, she just took it in. But he'd done it. He'd told her. There'd been no one else to tell. Shane had no other family. A few days later, when he went round to check on her, she said she'd told Tina her daddy had got very sick and had gone to heaven – not that he'd had been ripped to pieces by machine gun fire on a dusty African roadside.

He glances over at her again, remembering how only a few months back Luiz had been in the car with him when he'd dropped Tina's birthday present off; how she'd seen Luiz in the car and insisted he came in too, and how she'd looked at him, how he'd looked at her. Roy had been intrigued by the instant attraction. She was a good-looking woman, self-contained and confident; he wasn't surprised Luiz was interested in her. And there had been no one else – as far as he knew – since Shane. Or maybe there had, but that wasn't his business. There had been that kiss, though. He'd held back. Not for Shane's memory, not for Geri even, but for himself, and for Sally too. They just weren't a match. He couldn't say why they weren't; he just knew it. He was glad that phase had passed, even relieved when Luiz had been so drawn to her. But what if he hadn't held back? Could there have been something? Where would they be now? Not in this car going into hiding. Better or worse?

'I need a wee,' says Tina.

Her voice pulls him back. 'Okay, darlin'. Next place we see, we'll stop.'

At a roadside café, Roy gets some drinks and Tina visits the toilet. Sally heads to the payphone, returning shaking her head. He doesn't say anything. At Alford, they stop to get some lunch. Roy knows Sally is itching to phone again. When Tina runs to the counter to look at the cakes, he puts his hand on Sally's arm to stop her getting up.

'This place we're going is owned by a friend of my mum and dad.'

She waits for him to carry on. She looks slightly bemused.

'I don't want her to know what's going on, why we're there. I don't want to worry her. I feel bad enough about this as it is.'

'How are you going to explain us then?' she says.

'I don't know. Just let her think...' he doesn't want to say it.

'That I'm your bit on the side?'

It's not such a bad idea, he thinks. 'Yeah. Don't worry, we'll work out something with the sleeping arrangements.'

She doesn't respond to that. Instead, she asks, 'So, are they're after you too?'

'No,' he says. 'I just need a break.'

'Have you left Geri – is that it?'

Is it that obvious? he thinks. 'Yes, I've left her.'

Sally looks at him, waiting for more.

'I don't want to get into it,' he says.

Tina has chosen her cake and comes back from the counter. Sally gets up. He watches her cross the road to a phone box.

'How much longer will it take?' Tina asks.

'Not long,' he says as he finishes his tea. 'Still loads of time for a paddle.'

He tells her the things he used to do there when he was her age. As he does, he watches the phone box, sure that Sally hasn't put the ten pence into the slot, that there's been no answer. From the set look on her face when she returns, he knows he was right. She stares at the table, mouth tight. They don't speak until they're back in the car.

'He'll be okay,' says Roy, trying to sound like he believes it.

'He can't do this to me,' she says quietly.

As they get into Ebwich, Sally looks out, finally paying attention to her surroundings. Tina is trying to see too. He can tell from the blank look in Sally's eyes she's not impressed.

'It won't be for long,' he says. Then, mindful of Tina, 'We'll find things to do.'

They're passing the caravan site. When he was there as a child, it took up less space. There are signs and roadways and buildings that weren't there before. The caravans are bigger too. At the crossroads, where the larger of the two pubs is, the street and the houses look tatty. It probably looked like that before, he thinks, but that black-and-white post-war world was all like this, hand-me-down and worn. It's just the contrast now, he decides. This has stayed the same; everything else has changed. Hettie's place, near the other side of the village, is coming into view. It looks tatty now too. He drives round the back, where Dad parked the car. He parks in exactly the same spot.

When the back door opens, it's not Hettie who stands

there. The woman is more Sally's age. She has short blond hair and brown eyes that take them in. The niece, of course, he thinks. He can't decide what that look means. He wonders what the set-up is now. It was months back when Hettie said her niece was staying there. It looks like it must be long term. It's a complication he could do without. He gets out.

'I'm Roy,' he says. 'Is Hettie around?'

'She's in the café,' she replies. 'She's expecting you. You'd better come in.'

She's talking to him, not Sally and Tina. He steps back to include them. 'Sally and Tina,' he says. 'Are you Hettie's niece? I don't know your name.'

'Fiona,' she says, going back inside, walking through the kitchen to the hall like they should follow her.

He waits for Sally and Tina. They're mute. Sally looks at him quizzically.

'It's okay,' he says. 'Go inside.'

Even the smell of the kitchen is the same. Hettie usually baked for the shop the night before and the sweet smell lingered all morning – it's there now. He's certain that the crockery on the drainer is the same too. Even with that reception, and Sally and Tina's reticence to distract him, he's back. He absorbs it. Yes, it's just the same. He looks down the hall. The carpet runner is the same too – and the stairs, the stair rods lining up in front of him. The young woman is going up. Sally and Tina are following her. When he'd last come down these stairs, he'd felt something was wrong, something he didn't understand. He follows them up, remembering that feeling.

On the landing, she's talking to Sally now. 'You've

got the two rooms at the front. We're decorating. We weren't...'

He's trying not to resent her. There's nothing wrong with her, but he'd wanted Hettie to meet them.

'You can use the bathroom there.' She points to the door. 'We're in the back so you'll be... You should be okay. The hot water's a bit erratic.' She seems distracted, trying to think of what to tell them.

'I remember,' he says.

She turns to look at him.

'My mum and dad used to have this room,' he says, following Sally into the front double bedroom.

Sally looks around, taking in the pre-war furniture, the square of worn carpet and the high bed. There's that expression again, saying she's not impressed. Her response annoys him. Tina has gone into the room next door. He follows her.

'This was my room,' he says. He doesn't say that the wallpaper and curtains are the same, or that the rug, more modern, covering the lino by the bed, might have changed.

'Where will I sleep?' asks Tina, looking confused.

He doesn't want that conversation now, not in front of this Fiona. She's taken a few steps back on the landing.

'I'll let you sort yourselves out,' she says and starts down the stairs. She stops and looks back up. 'Shout if there's anything you need.'

Her accent is odd, he thinks. There are notes of refinement, overlaid with something harder. He's puzzled that she's a relation of down-to-earth Hettie, who he'd noticed at Mum's funeral had kept her East

End cockney twang.

'Thanks,' he says to her. 'We'll sort ourselves out. I'll be down to see Hettie.'

She's looking at him. He thinks she's suspicious, that she senses something's going on here. He returns the look, trying to make it a smile, until she turns away and carries on down the stairs.

'I'll tell her you're here,' she calls back. And she's gone.

He turns back to join Sally in the double bedroom.

'You and Tina have this room. I'll have the small room. They don't have to know.' Then to Tina, who is in the doorway now, looking at them. 'You share with your mum, darlin'. I want my old room.'

Tina looks at her mum.

'So long as you don't kick like you used to,' says Sally.

Tina goes to the window. 'Where's the sea?'

'Not far,' says Roy. 'I'm going down to get our things. Then I'll show you where it is.' He heads down the stairs calling back, 'Bet you didn't bring a bucket and spade.'

Downstairs, Hettie and Fiona are behind the counter in the café. Hettie puts a slice of cake on a plate Fiona is holding and smiles over at him as he walks in and looks around.

'Don't say it all looks the same,' she says. 'Just because it does.' She gives him a hug.

'That's not such a bad thing,' he replies.

As Fiona takes the tray to a customer's table, he uses the opportunity to say it.

'The woman I'm with, and her daughter, it's

complicated. She needed to get away, and I needed to get away.'

'And you have. So stop fretting. It's okay.'

'Just so long as—' He stops. He doesn't know what to say.

'I said it's okay, didn't I?'

Fiona is back at the counter. More customers are coming in the door.

'Thanks, Hettie. It's a big help. I mean it.'

'Get down to the beach,' she says. 'Not much has changed their either.'

He catches Fiona's eye as he leaves. He's still not sure about her.

Upstairs, he gives Sally her bags and takes his holdall into the little bedroom. He closes the door and jams the bundles of cash between the chest of drawers and the wall. Back on the landing, he looks in on Sally and Tina.

'You'll like Hettie,' he says.

Sally stares at her bags, like she doesn't know what to do with them. Tina is still looking out of the window.

'And she loves kids,' he goes on.

'Who was it that showed us in?' Sally asks.

'Her niece,' he replies, sensing Sally knows this other woman's presence has thrown him, not wanting to discuss it, unable to pinpoint what bothers him about her.

'Hettie came here after the war to live with her husband's family,' he says, for something to say. He can see Sally's feeling lost. He hopes she'll be alright here. He hopes she'll find something in common with Hettie: two East Enders, years apart in age but not so unalike, having to cope with what life has thrown at them. He's not sure she'll get on with Fiona.

'When are we going to the beach?' Tina says.

'Now,' says Roy.

'I didn't bring towels or anything,' says Sally.

'You get ready and I'll sort that out,' he says.

Downstairs, the café is quiet. Fiona is in the kitchen, stacking plates at the sink. He thinks he should break the ice a bit. She turns as he walks in. What is it about this woman? He can't decide.

'Everything alright?' she asks.

'Fine, thanks. Sally didn't pack towels. I don't suppose...'

'They're in the bathroom.'

'For the beach, I mean. Maybe old ones?'

He meets her eyes. There's something more to her, more than her age suggests. She holds his gaze for a second, unflinchingly. He wants her to talk. He doesn't know why.

'Did we mess things up turning up like this? I mean, you said you were decorating.'

She shrugs. 'It's been waiting long enough. Another few days won't make much difference.'

'You've got your work cut out.'

'I know,' she replies. 'It looked like this in the sixties.'

'It looked like this in the fifties,' he laughs. 'Hettie and Mum worked in the same factory during the war. They were old friends.' He stops himself from adding more and waits for a response.

She dries her hands. 'I'll find the towels.'

He follows her up the stairs, still asking himself what it is about her. She turns at the top and, level with her rear, he looks away, like he's not been watching it.

'She doesn't talk much about friends.'

He's thrown by her remark. He follows her to the big cupboard.

'They sort of lost touch,' he lies. 'Hettie was at Mum's funeral back in February. I hadn't seen her since I was a kid.'

As she sorts through the cupboard, he gives way to his curiosity.

'Have you been here long?'

'Over a year now,' she says and hands him the towels. 'I think the tide's out. You'll have a long walk.'

# Chapter 6  1976

# Roy

THE MONEY WE'D got from some temporary delivery work over Christmas had gone. Shane had spent most of his on Tina. I'd tried to put some by, but it wasn't going to last long. The New Year period was slack for work and the rent was due. I sold my car. Shane held on to the pickup, saying we needed some wheels or we'd be out of the running for any casual work. We didn't keep out of the pubs though. We were trying to live like we had months back, when we had plenty of cash. But the zest had gone.

Shane also had the worry of another round of questions from the police and his magistrates' court hearing that had been set for early February. The woman he'd gone to help was sticking to her story and had expanded it to include Shane hitting her too. No one in the street had seen what Shane had from the window and no one witnessed what happened when he'd intervened. He was talking about doing a runner and not appearing for his hearing because he thought he didn't stand a chance. Nothing I said helped, and we were in danger of falling out over it. He was more pissed off than I'd ever seen him.

It was the last week of January that he told me about an ex-squaddie he'd been talking to on a building site where we'd got a couple of days' labouring for cash. According to this bloke, there was good money to be made with some outfit providing military training in Angola. He'd told Shane he knew an ex-para in Camberley who'd been asked to put the word out. Neither of us knew anything about Angola. There'd been stuff on the news about the place being in chaos after the Portuguese had pulled out, and I remembered something about Cuba and Russia being involved on one side and South Africa on the other, but neither of us had a clue about any of it.

I thought it sounded too good to be true, but Shane said this bloke had told him there'd been adverts in the papers, so it must be legit. I pointed out we'd never get jobs doing combat training, it wasn't our thing. I said we should hang on for some more local work to come up, that I still had some money in my savings. I could tell he was ashamed I'd paid for the petrol we'd just put in the pickup. He said he wasn't sponging off me any longer, and he wasn't hanging around to get a jail sentence for an assault he didn't do – he was going to look into this Angola thing.

It was a day or so later that he found the advert in a paper and rang the number. He was told it wasn't just combat trainers they needed, but mechanics and other trades too. He'd said there was at least six months' money to be had – at least double what most half-decent jobs paid, plus food, gear, and our fares all thrown in. I still didn't think he was serious. I pointed out he wouldn't see Tina if he was in Angola.

'Maybe Sally would see things different if I wasn't around for a while,' he said. 'I could come back and give it another try, if she'd let me.'

'Or she'll find someone else while you're out there and the police will be waiting for you when you get back,' I replied.

'They might work out what really happened. That stupid bitch might drop the charges,' he said. 'It could be a good thing not being around.'

We went round this loop a few times – me telling him he'd make things worse with the assault charge and just look guilty for not turning up, him saying he had nothing to lose.

'If you're serious about making up with Sally, you should tell her how you feel about her, and go and tell the truth at the hearing.'

He stopped talking then. When Shane chewed things over, he'd clam up. I said no more. I was hoping he'd see sense. We'd been having this debate on our way down to The Angel where we'd heard they were looking for labourers on a building job. All we got was a soaking hanging around the site, only to be told there was nothing doing. It had been a cold, miserable month, and the wasted trip made everything seem worse. We found a local café to warm up in and kill some time. We were avoiding going back to put money in the meter to run the poxy two-bar electric fire.

'Bet it's not this fucking cold in Angola,' Shane said.

I still didn't think he was serious.

'Bet the beer's crap,' I said.

'I can't fucking stand this fucking country.' He gestured at the rain on the windows.

We'd started the week on a downer and there was nothing I could say to change things. I'd never seen Shane this pissed off.

'What about it?' he said. 'Why the fuck not?'

He'd got me. The thought of going somewhere – anywhere – to do something and get paid, having some kind of purpose instead of going back to that flat, was very attractive. He knew from my hesitation I was wavering. He grinned at me. If he was determined to dodge his hearing, then he would – whatever I said or did. I had to smile.

'Yeah?' he said.

'We just check it out, okay?'

When he came back from the phone, he was looking more chipper than he had in a long while.

'They still need mechanics,' he said. 'This bloke explained it all. There's this Roberto guy, he's trying to get the country back from the commies. His outfit is called the FNLA – something liberation of Angola. He's got loads of backing, American money, weapons and kit, armoured vehicles, air cover, the whole lot.'

'So why does he need the likes of us?'

'That's just it; he's more like a politician. He's got all the money and local blokes willing to fight, but they don't know what they're doing. They need trained blokes and proper support.'

'What about all this stuff on the news about the Cubans and Russians?' I said.

'He said the FNLA are in the north of the country,

they're going to push south. They just need to get started. We don't have to stay if we don't want to.'

He was motoring – a bit too quick for my liking.

'We could be on our way on Wednesday. A couple more days of this shit and we're out of here.'

'I don't know,' I said. 'It sounds too easy.'

'Alright,' he said. 'But we can find out more at the recruitment meeting they're doing.'

'Recruitment meeting?'

'Yeah, tomorrow night. We go to Paddington station. A bloke called Frank will meet us and we'll get the full SP. We stay the night in a hotel – they're paying – and, if we want in, we're on our way the next day.'

I still didn't believe we'd do it. But there didn't seem any harm in finding out some more.

The next morning, Shane sold the pickup. He spent the rest of the day with Sally and Tina. When he got back, he was a bit subdued. I couldn't work out if he was going to change his mind or if he'd made up his mind already. As I shoved some kit in a bag, I offered him a get out.

'We've just paid the rent on the flat. How about seeing the month out before doing this? Then if they're still recruiting, we could pack up and go.'

'Nah,' he said. 'I got two hundred quid for the pickup. I gave it to Sally. She'll sort the rent out if need be. Our stuff will be alright here.'

The packing didn't take long. He'd said we only had to take wash gear and a change of clothes. I asked him if we needed documentation – passports, proof we were in the army, stuff like that. He said he hadn't renewed his passport and the bloke on the phone said he wouldn't need it – everything would be taken care of.

'That don't sound right,' I said.

'I told you, this has got backing,' he said. 'If they can handle all the travel and that, they must be well set up.'

I didn't argue. I half expected to be back at the flat that night. I took my passport anyway and we set off.

Sure enough, we were met under the clock at Paddington Station by this Frank bloke. He seemed in a hurry and didn't even ask our names. We followed him round to a nearby hotel, where he gave us reservation slips. Mine said Harold Hobson and Shane's said Reginald Guilder. I said that wasn't us. Frank said it was all part of keeping a low profile and not to worry. There was a group of other blokes checking in then too. Some were overweight, and some were young lads who looked like they couldn't train a budgie – let alone a bunch of African soldiers. I can tell if someone's been in the services just by the way they look and behave and I said to Shane that most of this lot didn't look the part.

'You're right,' he said. 'There's some right Herberts here. All the better for us, I reckon.'

'This don't smell right,' I said. 'What if it's illegal? I don't even want to give anyone my name.'

'Alright, we'll use the ones from the room reservations,' Shane said. 'Happy?'

I wasn't happy. But I still thought we'd be out of there that night, so I said nothing and we went up and put our gear in our rooms.

In the bar, we got talking to an ex-para. There was a bunch of them in the bar. They'd gravitated together, like ex-service blokes seem to. In amongst this crowd, Shane was keener than ever – like he was back in the army. A bit later, we were all shepherded into a conference room and a bloke who called himself Colonel Banks gave us all a briefing. He was a short, wiry kind of guy in one of those safari suit things. He didn't look like a colonel to me. The name rang a bell though. I was sure this was the John Banks who'd been in the papers, the one involved with the Rhodesian mercenary cock-up.

Until then, I hadn't thought of this as mercenary recruitment, but as I listened to him, I realised that's what it was. Looking around, that was hard to believe. Of the hundred or so in that room, most didn't look the type. When Banks started talking about coaches being outside the hotel the next morning to take us to Heathrow, I still couldn't work out what we were supposed to be doing. I said it to Shane, but he seemed to be on a roll now. The idea of going somewhere new, flying off somewhere, seemed to have blocked out any doubts as far as he was concerned. We were told that if we were still interested, we'd be interviewed later on. Shane was already working out what to say. He said we should play up our Aden service a bit.

'Why?' I asked. 'We're doing training, aren't we?'

'We don't want to look like some of these tossers,' he said.

Later that evening, we got to meet Banks in one of the other rooms. Shane went in first. He nearly missed his name when they called out Guilder. As he came out, he gave me a thumbs up and I took his place. A couple of other blokes were in there too – just watching, letting Banks do the talking and ask the questions. I told him what I'd done in the army and where I'd been. I did mention Aden and some stuff about FLOSY and the NLF. From the way Banks was nodding and talking about the mutilated soldiers, I knew Shane had laid it on thick. He confirmed we'd be helping the FNLA kick out the communists. He said the opposition troops, the MPLA's army, were poor soldiers, and the Cubans were the only real fighters, but they didn't want to be there and it wouldn't be long before the FNLA pushed them out. The different sides were only groups of letters to me at that point, but I gathered that the MPLA were communists. I was regretting not taking more notice of the stuff on the news. I told him more about my REME service and said I could do transport support and vehicle maintenance and that I could train the Angolan soldiers to do the basics in that area.

Banks seemed happy with what I said. He asked me if I had a passport. Knowing that Shane didn't, I said mine had expired too. I thought that would be it. We wouldn't be flying out to Angola without passports. But he just took a Polaroid photo of me and made a note against my name, my false name, on the list and said they'd make up an ID card for me and the travel formalities would be taken care of. Then he told me we'd get an advance payment of hundred and fifty US dollars, our first week's pay, when we were on the coach the next morning. He said there was a twenty-five thousand pound insurance on each man too, which, in the unlikely event of death, would be paid to his next of kin. I was still taking this in as I was shown out of the door and a young lad was being shown in. I doubted he'd been in the boy scouts let alone the army. He grinned at me and I started wondering if we weren't all just a bunch of idiots.

I went back to the bar to find Shane. As expected, he was with the group of ex-army blokes. A fair bit of booze had already gone down and a lot of loud talk and bragging was going on. After a couple more rounds, someone said this whole thing was paid for by the CIA, and the US would provide support. Apparently, Banks had told him everything would be explained when we got there, got acclimatised and kitted out. It sounded like bullshit. I wanted to get Shane on his own and say it wasn't too late to pull out. We hadn't taken their money, and they didn't know who we were – we could just walk. I didn't get the chance until the bar closed and he'd had a lot more to drink than me. He just shook his head and slurred that it beat the hell out of going back to that fucking flat and having no money. I left him struggling to get his key in his room door and went on to my room thinking at least I wasn't paying for the heating and hot water that night and Shane might see things differently in the morning.

At breakfast, Shane hadn't changed his mind. He kept saying we'd get ourselves a nice little set up over there, enjoy the sun, and watch the money building up. Looking out on the grey London street where our two coaches were already jamming up the busy traffic, I didn't have much of an argument to offer. Then Banks and one of the others doing the organising told us to finish up our breakfasts and get moving. We went upstairs and grabbed our stuff. Shane didn't hesitate getting on the coach and I followed him, wishing I'd tried harder to talk him out of it. A few of the heavy drinkers had to be woken up, but it wasn't long before we were on our way to Heathrow. We really were going to Angola.

We were flying to Brussels first, then to Kinshasa in Zaire. Banks had already said something about the operation being run out of Zaire, which bordered the north of Angola where we were headed. I thought about this as we stared out at the people on the pavements, as we did the stop-start in the morning traffic. They were on their way to work, wrapped up against one of the coldest winters in years, while we were off on an adventure, travelling to somewhere warm and sunny. That's what I told myself. But it didn't stop the cold feeling in my stomach that said this wasn't right, it was too easy.

On the coach, we were given a form to fill in. It was for our next-of-kin details. I thought about Mum and Dad then. I'd been trying not to. They knew nothing of this. I used to phone every week if I hadn't been over to see them. It had been a week since my last visit and I should have called. The last time I'd been round, Dad seemed to have aged years. His remaining hair had gone grey, and he was getting a slight stoop. He looked so tired. Mum said he'd started looking forward to his retirement. For him, that seemed odd. I'd nearly picked up the phone in my room the previous night and rang them. Then I thought how much they'd worry and how Dad would probably tell me I was being an idiot and to get out of there fast. Shane was just staring at his next-of-kin form too. He was a Barnado's boy. He had no family apart from Tina.

'We'd have to put our real names on these,' he said.

I hadn't thought of that.

'I ain't getting killed,' he said. 'This is bad fucking luck.'

We handed back the forms without filling them in. One of Bank's lot collected them without even checking. As he did, he handed out the hundred and fifty dollars advance payments. I counted the crisp brand-new notes. I'd never seen a dollar bill before. Shane just shoved his into his wallet. He was quiet for a long while. I could tell he was chewing something over.

'If anything did happen to me,' he said, 'would you look out for Tina – and Sally?'

'Yeah,' I said. 'Course I would.'

It looked like that insurance form had got him thinking.

'Really? Make sure they're okay?'

'Course I would, mate, you know I would.'

'Thanks,' he said, staring back out at the passers-by.

'Anyway, we're doing training and stuff, aren't we? We've been in riskier places, haven't we?' I said, trying to convince myself now.

'Yeah,' was all he said, and we didn't talk much more. We just watched the slow wet streets become faster, wet roads.

At the terminal building, we didn't get off the coach straightaway. Someone said the press was onto us and we had to keep a low profile. Some of the lads seemed impressed, like this was part of the 'mission', that we were involved in something important. I kept thinking back to the stuff about Banks and Rhodesia, the false names in the hotel, and just the way he handled things, selling us the idea. Maybe the press was there because there was something wrong about this whole thing.

While I was thinking this, something was going on at the front of the coach, some paperwork being done. Next thing, we're handed our boarding cards with our names hand-written on them. That seemed odd. A shout goes out for those who had passports to get off first and those without to follow behind. Shane and I joined the second group and were given 'Security Advisor Service' ID cards with our mugshots on them, cut from the Polaroids from the night before. I couldn't see how anyone would take those seriously, but we were being ushered swiftly towards the departures area with a pack of press photographers running after us. Banks was trying to avoid getting his picture taken at the same time as telling us to say nothing to anyone.

It was a messy scrum getting through to passport control, where we were handed more forms to fill in while Banks talked to the security staff. When it came to going through to Departures, our IDs just got a quick glance. Before we knew it, we were done and heading for the gate, simple as that. Months later, I heard accusations that this had been arranged in advance and the British authorities were doing the CIA a favour getting us out there. It was just another thing that made me realise how ignorant and naïve we'd been.

At Brussels, there were more photographers and more chaos. The first group of recruits had got there before us and had put in some time in the bar, waiting for us and dodging the press. Again, we were ushered through to Departures without any hassle about not having passports. It felt like everyone was in on this thing. It was about half past three by the time we boarded the flight to Zaire. Shane and I were sitting near two lads who'd served in Northern Ireland. One of them told us that the part of Angola we were going to had no international airport. The capital, Luanda, and most of the rest of the country, was in the hands of the MPLA. That didn't sound too promising – and there we were, heading right into it. No one said it, but I could see we all had a lot of questions and no way of finding the answers. Instead, we ate the tray meals they brought us, drank a few more beers, exchanged stories about our service time, and, eventually, just put our seats back and slept.

# Fiona

BY THE TIME the New Year came round, I'd been working at Grey and Garton's for over three months. Dad's secondment to the office had been extended before Christmas – I was sure Margaret had something to do with that – and with Jo being at Bath, it was just the three of us in the house. Margaret was still determined to accompany Dad on his next trip, but still couldn't stand the thought of me living in the house on my own if she did. I was sure she was biding her time and was cooking up one of her schemes. When Dad started telling me his company was recruiting female deck officer cadets and brought home some leaflets about it, I knew where the idea really came from. I played her at her own game for a while and showed just enough interest to keep her hopes up. I might not have known what I wanted, but I knew it wasn't following

Dad into his career.

Jo had been home for Christmas, full of stories of how wonderful university life was and how many nice people she'd met. The good side of that was that we didn't argue. She fired a few salvos my way about dead-end jobs and the difference having a degree was going to make for her, but they just bounced off. My new job might have been a dead-end one, but I was gradually fitting in. I'd made friends with Hilary in the sales office. She was the same age as me and had introduced me to some of her friends. Everyone in that little group was intent on having fun and I was soon carried along with it, aware of how little experience I had in their world of pubs and clubs, that whole nightlife world, dancing and drinking and sizing up the blokes who were interested in us. I hadn't met anyone special, but I was learning how to enjoy the process of looking. I was soon going out a couple of nights in the week with the girls, as well as most weekends too, and it made life bearable.

My newfound social life meant Jo's presence over Christmas had very little effect on me. She still had that air about her that said she knew more than I did, that she was party to some secret that I wasn't, but the effects were wearing thin by then. I was happy to leave her at home with her little smirks when I went to work or out in the evening to have fun.

Work wasn't as much fun though. The two women whose office I'd been crammed into the corner of were Brenda and Joan. They were middle-aged, been there for years, very aware of their places in the pecking order and very keen to make sure I knew my place was at the bottom of that order. The men in the factory called them the gruesome twosome. Brenda was the personnel manager. She was also responsible for the payroll. Joan did all the admin. I did everything they didn't want to do. I did the photocopying and the filing, and took the post and paperwork to and from the managers' offices in the factory. I ran errands, made the tea and did anything else they told me to do. If things looked a bit slack, one of them would create a task for me, usually involving clearing out or reorganising stuff they couldn't be bothered to do.

At my interview, I'd said I could do an evening class in typing. The idea was I'd gradually do more of the clerical work. I was regretting being so enthusiastic about that, as it would mean more time in the office with the Gruesomes. But compared to school, the regime was a holiday camp, and I wasn't about to give Margaret the satisfaction of seeing me quit – at least not until she was away at sea with Dad and I'd had time to work out what else to do.

Then I met Clive. He'd started at the factory in the November, but it was the first pay day of the New Year before our paths crossed. Grey and Garton's paid the office staff and the managers monthly into their bank accounts, but the shop-floor workers were paid weekly in cash, the same as they'd been for decades. It meant a lot of counting of money, filling in pay slips, and making up envelopes. Brenda and Joan made a big fuss about this procedure. Handing out the pay highlighted the divide between the shop-floor workers and the office staff; it gave the Gruesomes a real buzz.

That particular Friday, Joan had phoned in sick. She'd

been sneezing and coughing the place out for the last two days, and I was glad not to have to listen to it. Brenda looked like she was coming down with the same bug and was agitated because she'd have to make up all the pay packets. I said I'd help her. Reluctantly, after stressing the great responsibility it was, she agreed. She did the slips while I counted the money into the envelopes and put them into the ancient office safe. After lunch, she checked every envelope, sealed them and, with some ceremony, put them in department order into two wooden trays with straps on them.

Like two cinema usherettes serving ice cream, we went through the factory, getting a signature for each envelope and making sure the recipient checked the contents. Brenda loved this ritual. I found it embarrassing. It was an excuse for the blokes to pull my leg and, in a few cases, make ribald comments. I doubted they did that with Brenda or Joan.

I'd skipped over Clive's name – Clive Gerald Rathley he was down on the form as – several times, as he didn't seem to be where he should be. His became the last envelope in my tray. The consensus was he was probably skiving in the toilets. This came with a lot of innuendo as to what he was doing there, and a few suggestions I should go in and find him. Finally, one of the older blokes, shaking his head with exasperation at the others, told me to hang on and he'd go and see. The young guy that emerged to the catcalls of his workmates, didn't look like a Clive Gerald. He was a couple of years older than me, shaggy fair hair, green eyes and a smile that melted away my annoyance. When the comments had died down and he'd signed for his money, he asked me if I was always going to give out the pay. Before I could explain, the foreman was telling him to get back to his lathe and get on with his work.

The same evening, crossing the yard from the office, on my way to the gates and home, I saw him ahead of me. He spotted me when he turned to get into his battered Mini Clubman. He called over, saying he was sorry for holding me up earlier. I just waved and walked on. As he drew level with me to turn into the road, he opened his window and asked if I wanted a lift. I said he didn't know where I was going. He said it didn't matter; he'd go anywhere I was going. That made me smile, but I brushed him off and carried on walking.

Clive was there the next night and the one after, with the same offer. The factory finished before the office, so he was either doing a lot of overtime or he'd been hanging around to wait for me. I couldn't help but admire his determination. On his third try, I accepted a lift. I liked the look of him and it was raining.

'Why are you working in a dump like this then?' he asked as we joined the stream of traffic.

'Why are you?' I replied.

'That's a good question,' he said. 'Best answered over a drink.'

I said I'd meet him later.

When I did meet him, that evening, I wasn't in the best of moods. I'd had a blazing row with Margaret. I'd discovered the top I was planning to wear was missing. I was sure Jo had taken it back to Bath with her. I knew she liked it because she'd been looking at it when it had been drying. I told Margaret she could tell her daughter

I wanted it back. Margaret had called me a liar and said Jo would never have taken it. Then I listed all the other things Jo had taken over the years. She demanded an apology that I refused and said she wanted me out of her house. That did it. Dad was out at the time and I told her it wasn't her house, it never was and it never would be. I said I was there before she was, and if she didn't like it, she could get out. It was a stupid exchange, but I couldn't stop myself from hitting back. Her last words were 'we'll see about that, madam,' before she shut herself in the lounge. Her retreat was a small triumph. She knew Jo had taken that top, and she also knew she didn't have the power over me she used to – things had changed.

My anger stayed with me all the way to The Cross Keys where I was meeting Clive. He was waiting at the bar as I went in. He'd dressed up: smart trousers and shoes with a white shirt, collar folded out over his jacket. I felt underdressed in my jeans and jumper. His smile faltered when I couldn't return it.

'Who's been upsetting you then?' he asked.

'My stepmother,' I said.

I hadn't intended to tell him about Margaret and Jo. I didn't want our date to be a moaning session. But I needed to vent, and the thing about 'her house' had been eating at me the whole way there. We'd sat down at a table and I gave him a condensed version of Jo, Margaret and Dad, finishing with her threat.

'There's always some fucker who wants to control you,' he said. 'It's like at work, all these little Hitlers, power fucking mad.'

He then recounted the long list of his previous jobs

and his grievances with each of them. They'd all seemed to end with him refusing to do something and walking out. I wanted to say that wasn't what I was talking about, but he was on a roll. I got the idea that his trouble with authority figures was a thick strand in his personality, but I was glad to have someone to tell my troubles to. And I liked him. And I'd felt some empathy with him too. A lot of the people he described were like Brenda and Joan. When he related how he'd got back at one of his old bosses, it made me laugh.

'Yeah, I left his car on bricks and sold the wheels a week later.' He said. 'Oh and I did leave a little pressie in the fuel tank too.'

I didn't get that. I must have looked confused.

'You know, not taking the piss, more like giving it.'

At the time, it seemed funny. His impression of a car running on a mix of urine and petrol made me laugh even more, and I was glad I'd agreed to our date. It took me a while to realise that with Clive, these things weren't really funny.

Then he asked me if I wanted to go on to Tites, Beckenham's answer for a night club. I said I wasn't dressed for a night club but he said it was no problem; he'd drive me home and wait for me to change. This 'let's-do-it-now' attitude of his was something else I liked about Clive. I wanted to stop thinking about everything so much and be impulsive too. Also, the idea of turning up at home with a boyfriend held too much shock appeal to pass up. 'Why not,' I said.

I made sure Dad and Margaret heard me getting out of Clive's car and going upstairs. When I came back down, makeup on, wearing my latest night-club wear –

a fitted black dress, sheer tights, my newest going-out shoes and a white cotton jacket – I put my head round the door of the lounge and said I was going back out again. Dad said something about taking care. Margaret stared, affronted, then looked at Dad expectantly. I had the door shut before he could say anything. I saw the curtain go back and Margaret's face look out as I got back into Clive's car.

That's how it started with Clive. And it was fun. We went out as a couple, and in a group with Hilary and her mates. We went to the local pubs, to Margate at the weekends, to Tites of course, to the Chinese restaurant and up to the West End when we could afford it. Dad tried unsuccessfully to get information about Clive from me, while Margaret just watched every time Clive turned up to pick me up.

When Margaret tried to bring the subject of Clive up, I stonewalled her. I never gave her the satisfaction of voicing her opinion. I was soon spending more and more time with Clive, glad to get out. Nothing had got too physical at that point. The stories of being pounced on by older men that I used to hear at school hadn't been borne out. I was doing the leading in that department, but I decided that was okay too. I was in control. For the first time in ages, I felt alright.

While all this made my working life bearable, it wasn't doing the same for Clive's. I knew he was running out of excuses at Grey and Garton's. He rarely got in on time, and he'd had a few warnings about it. His work was okay – when he did it – but he often wasn't there when he should have been, and production was held up waiting for him. When I met his mum, some of this made more sense. Having brought him up on her own, inevitably her relationship with him was close. It wasn't just that though; she'd cut Clive a lot of slack. Since his schooldays, she'd made excuses for his problem with authority and his poor timekeeping. But he wasn't at school anymore and she hadn't done him any favours when it came to coping with the outside world. I got the idea she depended on him emotionally as much as he did on her. Mrs Rathley, Denise, was an intelligent woman though. I could see she was trying to break that dependence. A few months before I'd met Clive, she'd met someone called Jeffery – a name Clive liked to draw out with derision, especially after he'd once tried to have a man-to-man about Clive's numerous job changes.

Once, when she'd sent Clive out for some groceries and we were alone for a while, Denise touched on her new relationship. She'd said she was getting out more and doing new things, doing things for herself. She talked a little about her life; how she'd once wanted to be a teacher, and how she'd ended up married young instead, then on her own with Clive. I could see she might have had a very different life if she hadn't met Clive's dad. She alluded to being pregnant with Clive before she married, and how that was avoidable now, like she was sending me a message. When I look back on that time, it's as if I was taking her place in Clive's life. It happened without me realising it. I took Clive on as a welcome distraction from my own family life. I became as dependent on that distraction as he became dependent on me, as he used to be on his mum.

About this time, I lost touch with Lolly and Frieda.

Lolly's parents' phone number no longer worked, and when Frieda's parents answered her number, she was never there. They just said they'd pass on a message to her. Lolly had been talking about going to her brother's house in Yorkshire for a while, but I didn't have the address. It hurt me they'd not been in touch and I kept wondering why. There was something that no one was saying, and I spent hours thinking about what it might be.

At work, Brenda and Joan had heard on the grapevine I was seeing Clive. They didn't refer to it directly, but when the pay packets were made up and Clive was being docked for his late starts, Brenda made a point of stating it out loud so I could hear. It irritated me, but I didn't let her see it. I think that made her worse. Then, one morning, barely two months after he'd started, Clive got the sack. Brenda announced it to Joan in a satisfied, we-knew-that-was-coming tone. I kept my head down and ignored the glance from Joan. As soon as I had the chance, I slipped out to find out what had happened. One of Clive's workmates told me Clive had been even later than usual that morning. He then took a toilet break just after starting. There'd been an argument with the foreman and Clive was told to 'get his cards'.

On the strip of waste ground at the side of the factory, there was a gap where Clive's Mini Clubman usually stood. As I walked home that evening though, he pulled up beside me and I got in to hear his side of the story.

'That wanker Munroe has always had it in for me,' he said bitterly, accelerating too hard and slamming on the brakes at the first lights. 'I'll get my fucking own back. You wait and see. And if that arsehole Jeffery says anything about it...'

I let him rant on a bit before trying to make light of it, saying he could get another job.

'I'm fed up with all these dross jobs,' he said. 'And these bastards we have to work with! You know what I mean. Look at those two hags in your office. The only joy they get is from other people's grief.'

Having heard Brenda and Joan's conversations for a good while by then, he wasn't far off. Doubtless, I was being discussed along with Clive whenever I was out of the room. I told him it didn't matter. If that's what did it for them, who cares?

'But don't you ever want to do something outrageous?' he asked. 'Really shake the fuckers up?'

'Yeah,' I said. 'Of course I do. They really annoy me.'

He started letting his imagination run: kidnapping the foreman, faking photos of Brenda and Joan in an orgy and posting them up around the factory.

I went along with his ideas, thinking we were just fantasising, just letting our imaginations run wild and letting off steam. Then he came out with it.

'We could rob the payroll,' he said. 'You're in there when the security blokes deliver the cash – it'd be a cinch.'

I just laughed. He wasn't serious.

# Chapter 7    1979

## Fiona

FIONA'S NOT SURE about this Roy bloke. She wonders why, if his parents were such good friends with Hettie, she hadn't mentioned it before. And this girlfriend of his – she doesn't look at him or talk to him like there's anything between them. It's almost like she's his sister. And his light brown hair is unfashionably short. She doesn't normally like that in a man. But he carries it well. On him, it adds to the solid, capable look. There's something about him, those little crinkles in the corners of those blue eyes, like he's seen things, done things. Her interest puzzles her. Maybe it's just that he's the complete opposite to Clive, and he's older than her. But that doesn't explain it. She needs to get a grip, she tells herself, going for older men now. But still, she wants to know more. Before he'd arrived, all Hettie had said was he'd been in the army and had trouble settling down afterwards.

Hettie was funny about personal things. There were some areas she would never talk about, places she didn't like to go. She never criticised Dad, despite what he'd done, and Fiona still couldn't understand that. She'd talk about some things, like Mum being there in the war, and then she'd clam up about her own husband. When Fiona had been there as a child, she'd never even known about Ted. She doesn't remember Mum saying anything about him either. He would have been dead five or six years then, and there'd been no trace of him in that house.

It occurs to Fiona that Roy must have been there when Ted was alive. He might know something. She wonders if she could ask him. She's back to thinking about Roy. There's something going on there. He's carrying something. She can tell. Her time in Holloway honed the skill of reading someone, watching a face, watching how they move, noticing how they phrase things, evade things, try to camouflage things. Sally is very different to him, Fiona decides. She's worried about something too, that's for sure. She was using the phone earlier, not getting an answer by the look of it, then trying again later. The way she'd come away from that phone, on edge, tight, trying not to show it. She'd seen that in Holloway too. Why are they here?

Hettie has told Roy to bring Sally and Tina into the kitchen for the evening meal. Guests, when Hettie used to have them, had their evening meal in the café after it was closed. Fiona remembers Mum and Hettie preferring the privacy of the kitchen, her being a little miffed at not having the privilege of eating in the café when the sign on the door said closed. When they all sit down, she notices Tina calls him Roy, not dad. She watches how Sally talks to him, still trying to decide what their relationship is. She's Tina's mother, but that's all. From his glances, Fiona can tell that he's noticed her watching them. As she ponders this, Hettie tells Sally how she came to be there.

'I'd never heard of the place until Fiona's mum was evacuated. Back of beyond, I thought. But we struck lucky. They looked after her like she was their own. I married their son and ended up here myself when the war was over. Funny old world, eh?'

Hettie's oblique mention of Ted makes Fiona look up, glancing at Roy, checking if he noticed it too. He looks at her and looks away. Yes, he noticed. Sally is explaining to Tina what 'evacuated' means. Tina looks confused.

'On their own?' she asks.

'Most of them were,' says Hettie. 'Fiona's mum was a little trooper. She used to bite back the tears and carry on. It makes me well up to think of it – even now.' And her voice confirms it, cracking a little as she goes on. 'When I think of her, with her little bag and her little dolly under her arm.'

Fiona tells them about the drawing on the wall. Tina wants to know all about it. Fiona promises to show it to her later.

'But they came home?' asks Tina.

'Yes, they did, my darlin'. Yes, they did. I came and fetched her. I came into this room and she was sitting at this table where you are now, as good as gold. She'd put her coat on hours too soon and sat there in it waiting for me. I cried like a baby, I did. They were all comforting me in the end.' Hettie gets up to collect their empty plates. 'Right, I've got apple pie and cream here.'

The subject is closed. Fiona looks across at Roy again. Their eyes meet briefly before he looks away.

Hettie insists on doing the dishes. Iris could do them with the café stuff when she gets in to help in the morning, but Hettie won't hear of it. Roy and Sally go to watch TV. After showing Tina the drawing, Fiona goes outside. She'd meant to check the oil in the car after the drive back from the wedding. The Maxi uses a bit, and she knows she mustn't let it get too low.

The evening sun hovers above the trees in the field behind. She stands and takes it in for a second, remembering how her cell window faced north and she'd promised herself she'd never take a sunset for granted ever again. She goes to the shed for the rag and oil can and opens the car to release the bonnet catch. She hears the back door and looks over to see Roy crossing the yard to the shed, looking inside and picking up her old bucket and spade, the beach toys that have been there since she'd last used them, a long time ago. Out in the light, he examines them, puts them back, and turns to her as she raises the bonnet.

'Bet it uses a bit.' He walks over.

'Yes it does,' she says, wiping the dipstick, then pushing it in and pulling it out to check it.

'They usually do.' He watches her remove the oil cap and walks over to pick it up to look at it. 'Head gasket not going yet then.'

She finishes pouring. 'How do you know?'

'The filler cap is clean. It would have a creamy gunk around it if water was getting through. They're not great for that either.'

She's curious. It's a chance to talk. She checks the

level again, and he hands her the cap to put back.

'Hettie said you were a mechanic.'

'She said you'd adopted this and got it going.'

'I didn't do that much,' Fiona says. 'It was a shame she'd stopped using it.'

'I bet she's glad you're here,' he says.

'I'm glad I'm here,' she replies. 'I see you found my old bucket and spade.'

'Mine, you mean,' he says.

She goes to contradict him, suddenly seeing the humour in it. She drops the bonnet down. 'I won't argue over a bucket and spade.'

He laughs. 'Not so long as we agree they were mine.'

'They might have already been here,' she says. 'So perhaps they were yours.'

'When was that?'

'I must have been four or five,' she says, crossing to the shed to put back the oil. 'So it would be about 1961.'

'A while after me then,' he says. 'We came here until the mid-fifties.'

She turns, more interested now. 'Ted was alive then.'

'Yes,' he says.

She waits for him to elaborate. He doesn't.

'What was he like?'

Roy blows air out of his lips and creases his eyes at the sunset. 'I think the word is aloof.'

She can tell he could say a lot more. She wonders why he won't.

'What did he do?'

Roy turns, unease in his eyes.

'I mean, did he have a job?'

He relaxes a tad. 'I think he did driving work.'

'She hardly ever mentions him. I used to think he was killed in the war.'

'No,' says Roy. 'He didn't serve. They rejected him because of his health.' He reflects on this for a second. 'His family didn't have much luck in the health department.'

'And then he got killed in a car crash?'

'Yes,' he says. 'That's what they told me.'

'I just wonder why she never talks about him.'

He shrugs. There it is again, something that says he knows more. She thinks maybe he'll say more if she gets to know him. He's self-contained. He has no urge to talk all the time – a bit like her. She wants to know more about him now.

'She said you were in the army.'

There's that unease again. But he replies.

'Yeah. Came out five years ago.'

It feels like he's not going to elaborate on that either. But he does.

'I thought it was time for something else. I'm not so sure it was a good idea. But there you are; you can't always tell, can you? Do you like it here?'

Now he's asking the questions, she thinks. But it's nice he doesn't want to just talk about himself; so many people do.

'It's alright,' she says.

She follows his gaze as he looks around. The back of the house could do with painting, but in the evening light it doesn't look so shabby.

'Not such a bad place, is it?' he says.

She almost says she'd been in a lot worse, but she doesn't. He might expect her to say where. I've got my secrets too, she thinks. He's waiting for her reply.

'It was strange coming back here, but I like it,' she says.

'It is strange coming back here. It's like a what-do-you-call-it – time capsule. That's what I like about it. Going back to when you didn't...' He stops, seeming to regret the track he's got on.

'When you didn't have stuff to worry about,' she finishes for him.

He gives her a brief smile. 'Yeah, that's it.'

'It feels like running away. But sometimes I think that's okay too,' she says. She's embarrassed she said that. She puts the oil back and closes the shed door, intending to go back inside.

'Have you been here a lot since you were a kid?' he asks.

She turns back to him. 'We stopped coming when my mum died. Then I came back once after I left school.' She turns to look at him. 'Did you ever come back? Before now I mean.'

'No,' he says. 'I think Mum and Dad fell out with Hettie.'

She's got to ask it. 'Why now?'

He looks at her. There's regret in those eyes, she thinks; something from the past, shame even, fear too maybe.

'Just needed to get away,' he says. 'This seemed the right place.'

'I'm being nosey,' she says. 'Sorry.'

He shrugs. 'We're probably a pain in the arse to you. I know Hettie hasn't had anyone staying for ages.'

'No. I'm sorry if it looked that way. I suppose I've got

used to it just being just the two of us in the house. It's not healthy though. I don't see anyone much. There's the café customers – but it's not the same.'

She can see he's taken aback by her candor and struggles with his response.

'You're, I mean… You'll make friends. You're young, you're…'

I'm what? she asks herself later. What was he going to say? Stupid that she wants to know that, that she wants him to say something nice about her. But he's got his own problems and there's been enough trouble in her life without adding someone else's.

She leaves him there, saying she's got things to do inside. As she passes the sitting-room door, Sally looks up. She probably heard them talking outside. Fiona gets a flash of something from that look. Not quite hostility, not even possession over this man, but some kind of resentment that she can't fathom. Again, what is it with these two? She carries on to the front room, where Hettie sometimes sits after dinner, the room that the guests used to use, a place Fiona doesn't associate with her time there as a child. They always used the back room in those days.

Hettie sits in the armchair by the window. The chair, part of the long-faded Damask three-piece suite, had been supplemented by several other armchairs to accommodate the guests that no longer come. Fiona has already resisted saying they should take some of them to the tip. This chair is Hettie's favourite and there's a view of the road that she's contemplating. Or perhaps she isn't. After all, she must have looked out at it thousands of times. Fiona hesitates. Hettie is so deep in thought she hasn't noticed her. She's about to back out when Hettie looks over.

'You and Roy were just kids when you first came here,' she says. 'Like Roni was – like Tina.'

Fiona sits on the settee.

'Roy and I were just talking about it,' Fiona says.

Hettie turns away to look outside again. Fiona waits, knowing there's more, realising she'll have to ask.

'He said he came here in the fifties.'

Hettie doesn't answer for a few seconds. 'Yes, me and his mum were workmates during the war.'

'You didn't stay in touch then?'

Hettie turns back to look at her. 'No.' The memory strains her features, squeezes at her eyes for a second. She turns back to the window. 'Life's mistakes.'

'Mum said I've got to say goodnight.' Tina's voice comes from the doorway.

'Goodnight, my darlin',' Hettie says.

'I'm sleeping in the big bed with Mum,' Tina says as she slips away.

'Sleep tight,' says Fiona.

They hear her down the hallway, asking if Roy will read her a story. They hear him go upstairs with her, telling her about the stories he used to get read at her age. Fiona looks at Hettie, trying to frame what she's going to ask. Hettie beats her to it.

'They just need somewhere for a few days. He's trying to make it nice for Tina. A bit of an adventure…'

'Him and Sally,' says Fiona, 'they seem, I don't know, there not, like, *together*…'

Hettie makes a tight line with her mouth before answering. 'I think he just needs some breathing space.

We shouldn't pry.'

Fiona feels she's overstepped the mark. She asks herself why she wants to know, and why does it matter? But even as she does, she remembers him, that look in his eyes. She tells herself she's not interested, but she knows she is.

# Roy

TINA IS SETTLING after her story. The novelty of sleeping in a big bed with her mum is gradually being overtaken by the need to sleep. The walk to the beach had seemed a long way to her. Roy knows Sally and Tina don't really walk anywhere much. They get the bus or the tube when they go out. Tina had kept asking why they hadn't taken the car. He'd said it was part of the fun of being at the seaside. Sally hasn't got the right shoes for this place either. He'd wanted to walk there like he used to, look around and see how much he remembered. They'd never taken the car back then. He'd thought the beach was much closer. Maybe it was because he always used to run ahead, impatient to get on the sand.

As he watches Tina lose her battle to stay awake, he thinks this is good. She's been on the beach, she's enjoyed it, she's tired – it's uncomplicated. If only everything was like this. But there's the money in the room next door, there's Luiz and the people he's upset, there's Geri and there's Hettie. And there's this Fiona – and what is it about her he can't get out of his head? All these complications, things to work out, try to be honest about, decide what to do about. He needs to put them in some kind of priority order. First, he needs to decide what to do about Sally and Tina – and how long they can stay here.

Tina's asleep now. She's fine. It's Sally who'll be at a loose end. He noticed it all evening. Now they can be alone, he should talk to her. He goes down to the sitting room, the back room, like they used to – after eating their evening meal in the kitchen, after being on the beach, just like today. He noticed earlier that the big Bakelite radio has been consigned to a corner, no longer centre stage. There's a TV in there now. Sally sits upright on the couch. Anthony Quinn is being made mayor of an Italian town which is about to be taken over by the Germans. Roy knows Sally's not really watching the shenanigans, he knows she's worrying. She turns to him.

'She's asleep,' he says.

'I should have kissed her goodnight,' she replies, guiltily, getting up.

'She's fine.'

'I'll just check.'

He wants to talk right away, but he lets her go. When she'd used the phone earlier, she'd only been a couple of minutes. No answer again. He'd said nothing. Even if someone had picked up, he's sure it wouldn't have been Luiz. But what can he do? There are a couple of places he could look for Luiz, but that means driving back to London. He can't take her back with him. He decides he'll go back alone if she can't contact Luiz after a couple of days – if she can last that long. He hears her coming back down the stairs, then he hears the phone dial whirring. There's a long wait before the receiver is put back in the cradle.

She's back in the doorway. He waits for her to say it.

'Still no answer,' she says. 'What am I going to do?'

'Just wait,' he says. 'This time in the evening, they could all be out. Ring first thing tomorrow.'

She looks hard at him, eyes blinking a little, trying to contain her fears. Then she turns and goes back upstairs before he can reassure her any further.

He crosses over to the radio, remembering how he used to read the stations off the dial, asking Dad where Athlone was, Oslo, Vatican or Hilversum. He'd turn it on with a big, satisfying click and wait for it to warm up, humming gently before giving out that intriguing hiss between stations. He remembers being perplexed how you knew you'd found those faraway places when more than one voice came from the same strip on the dial. And there'd be so many more at night; strange languages, carried over the airwaves, music, voices in big empty rooms, voices you couldn't understand. Dad showed him the wire aerial suspended above the garden, the earth connection under the window, and tried to explain how the voices got there. He's tempted to turn it on, to see if it sounds the same, to rotate the tuning knob and move the pointer across the world.

'It still works,' says Fiona from behind him, startling him.

'I used to read the places from the dial,' he says, 'try and tune them in.'

'So did I,' she replies, crossing to stand next to him and look at it.

'The guests used to have the front room.' He looks around. 'We were allowed in here though.'

'You must have been special guests,' says Fiona. 'Like we were.'

He's curious. 'Were they family holidays?'

'Not exactly. Just Mum and me,' she says. 'Dad was usually away at sea.'

He runs a hand over the smooth case. 'This was Ted's sanctuary from the guests. He'd turn the wireless on and keep that door shut.'

'No one ever talked about him,' she says. 'I never understood that.' There's a questioning focus in her eyes, looking right into his.

He thinks for a few seconds before replying. In his mind, he sees Ted in that armchair. The way he stared around him sometimes, the moods that nowadays would be called depression and treated as an illness. Distracted Ted, friendly enough but somehow never looking comfortable in his own skin, never comfortable in his own home, the place Hettie came to live. It was like he'd never lived there.

'He wasn't much for socialising,' he says finally.

'Did he—'

'There you are.' Hettie looks in.

'Reminiscing about the wireless,' he says, catching the awkward glance from Fiona.

'I only put it on for The Archers now,' she says. 'Are the rooms okay? I know they need redoing.'

'They're fine,' he says.

'Was dinner alright?'

'Lovely, thanks. And thanks for having us like this.'

'Don't be silly. It's nice for me. It's been nice having

this one here too,' she looks at Fiona. 'I was thinking of packing it all in until she came along.'

Fiona looks embarrassed. 'You were doing alright.'

'No, I wasn't,' says Hettie as she turns to go.

He follows her out, sensing Fiona hanging back, wanting to ask him more about Ted.

In the kitchen, Hettie says, 'It's none of my business, but are you really alright?'

'A bit worried,' he says. 'It's complicated.' He's not going to tell her why. He's thinking she shouldn't have to hear his problems, that he'll be gone in a couple of days.

She waits for him to elaborate. When he doesn't, she indicates the back room with her tea towel. 'I worry about that one.'

'Why?'

'She's had her troubles. She says she doesn't know what she wants. But it's been lovely having her here. It's like having a bit of her mum, Roni, back again.'

'She asked me about Ted,' he says.

Hettie stops drying a plate and looks at him. He regrets saying it, but at the same time thinks it might be better for Hettie if she talked about Ted.

'It's all in the past now,' she says.

'I'm sorry,' he says. 'I didn't know what to tell her. I never really understood.' He's standing awkwardly at the table, wondering if he should sit down.

'It's not you that has to be sorry.' She puts down the plate and puts one hand on the sink.

He interprets her silence as an invitation, and takes a chance.

 'Dad said something to me years ago – just the once,

and he never mentioned it again. He said it was his fault.'

She sits down. He takes the chair opposite her. It's the one Ted used to always sit in, the one by the door – where he could make a quick escape, unwilling to sit and talk after the meal. When she speaks, it's almost a whisper.

'Some things are best left unsaid.'

He can't understand that. Surely it can't matter now. He waits for her to go on, but she doesn't.

'It couldn't have been easy for you,' he says, giving her the chance to cut herself some slack.

She shakes her head, drops her eyelids. 'Things were very different back then. People get divorced now without batting an eyelid. You don't even have to get married to start with, these days.'

He doesn't know what to say. He feels a sting of guilt for how he left Geri. He wonders what she's doing, if she's worried about him. Being there now seems all wrong.

'It wasn't like that for us,' Hettie goes on.

'Mum and Dad kept going,' he says, not sure if she meant them or her and Ted too.

'Kept going. That's just it, isn't it? That's what we had to do then. Keep going through the bloody war, keep going when there was nothing much afterwards, keep going in our marriages. You can do too much keeping going.'

'Did you really mean it about packing this in if Fiona hadn't been here?'

'Yes, except I don't know that I'd do with myself if I did. I never minded the holidaymakers, you see. Ted bloody hated them.'

'I remember.'

'Laughable isn't it? He hated the people who were paying our bills and keeping the roof over our heads!'

'He never seemed happy,' Roy ventures.

'It wasn't all his fault. He had his troubles too. He never fitted in – even as a kid. Then when people round here were losing their husbands and sons, and he was still at home... He got a hard time over it. It got so no one would talk to him.'

'But when you met him,' says Roy, 'I mean, you must have...'

She looks hard at him, the candor in her eyes saying here's the truth coming. 'You don't make a marriage on sympathy. It took me a long while to work that out. Then it was too late.'

He understands. He thinks of Geri. Did he feel sorry for her, or did she feel sorry for him, or perhaps it was it both – double the problem.

'When your mum got back in touch, she talked a lot about you; how you'd left the army. She was worried about you.'

A pang of guilt digs into him. 'I didn't know if I'd done the right thing. When I went back there, it was like turning the clock back – and not in a good way. I didn't want her to worry.'

'She was more of a mother than your own mother could have been,' says Hettie. 'She was bound to worry.'

'I did some stupid things,' he says.

'Join the club,' she says. 'But you've got time to put things right.'

'Sally and me,' he says. 'We're not a couple.'

Hettie laughs. 'I can see that.'

'Tina's dad was with me in the army. He was killed.' He pauses. He's not ready to say how. 'I promised him I'd look out for her.'

Hettie looks puzzled. He knows it doesn't explain why they're here.

'She got involved with this friend of mine and he's in trouble. I helped him out with something and I'm involved now too.'

Hettie shakes her head. 'You don't keep things simple, do you?'

'I know.'

'And the woman you were with at the funeral, Geri, wasn't it?'

'I've left her. That's why I came here with Sally and Tina.'

Hettie leans forward in the chair. 'You are in a bloody mess.'

'I'm sorry. I didn't want to bring all that to you,' he says. He can see she's pondering what he's said. It was the edited version, but even telling that much has brought some relief. 'Anyway, it's for me to sort out. We'll be gone soon, I hope. If I come back again, I won't bring anything like that with me, I promise.'

'Well, I hope you will come back.' She reaches across the table to squeeze his hand. 'None of it makes any difference to me. You're still welcome.'

Back in the sitting room, Fiona looks up from the armchair as he opens the door. The news is on the telly. He hesitates in the doorway. She raises the magazine from her lap.

'I'm not watching it,' she says.

He closes the door and sits on the settee. She gets up and goes to turn the TV off.

'Unless you want it on?'

'No,' he says, wondering what he's going to do instead of pretending to watch it. It's too early for bed and the room seems very quiet now. He picks up the local newspaper and flicks through it. He glances over at Fiona. She looks up.

'We can watch Tina if you and Sally want to go out,' she says. 'There's only really the pub, of course – unless you take the car.'

It feels like a test, like she's assessing his relationship with Sally. It won't take her long to realise there isn't one, not of that sort anyway. She probably already knows he's in the little room on his own. But why does that matter?

He puts the paper down. This could just be another complication, another mistake. He gets up.

'Goodnight.'

'Goodnight,' she replies.

# Chapter 8     1976

## Roy

SOMETIME AFTER MIDNIGHT, we walked across the tarmac. We'd landed at Kinshasa. There was a moist, almost spicy sort of heaviness in the air that I've never forgotten. We grouped together as we walked towards the terminal building. It was good to be moving and stretching after our confinement. We were all looking around, feeling the strangeness of a foreign place, noticing how the airport looked unfinished. I was expecting us to go through some kind of security check, customs maybe. I was wondering how it was going to work with no passports, if we'd really just get whisked through again. But after entering the terminal building, a tired security guard filtered us off into a separate corridor and out through a door to two battered coaches. For a second, I thought we were being taken to another building for security checks. But there were no checks and only our contingent was sent to the buses. This was our transport; we were on our way. From the comments and banter, some of the lads thought we were getting special treatment, passing through the airport with no formalities, like VIPs. I was still thinking it was all too easy.

There was already a tang of sweat in that old bus that the open windows didn't get rid of. After a quick head count, we were away. I overheard someone saying a few of the group had done a bunk at Brussels. I wondered if they'd known something we didn't. At that point, all we knew was we were doing a stopover to get kitted out. Some of the lads were saying it was so we could get used to the climate, and speculating on the likelihood of some drinking and local girls.

From the airport, we crossed the city through a hotchpotch of modern buildings on wide avenues with layers of tin shacks in the shadows behind them; an odd mixture to our eyes. After that, we followed the thick exhaust of the first bus, climbing to higher ground that overlooked the city. The place we pulled up at was not what I'd expected. I suppose I thought it would be a barracks or camp, but this was a huge house behind high walls surrounded by the remains of what would have been impressive gardens, now housing wrecks of vehicles. The gates were guarded, and the walls were patrolled. I thought maybe it was a military set up after all. It wasn't until later we found out it was the home of Holden Roberto, leader of the FNLA, the man we were working for.

Big house it might have been, but we were shown to some outbuildings to lie down in for a few hours' sleep. We found one functioning toilet and one outside tap. We never got to see the inside of the place. No one was impressed with our treatment. When the place came to life, one of the lads found where we could get some coffee. We'd hardly drank it before Banks appeared and started handing out kit from a pile of cardboard boxes. The state of this gear would have been amusing if we weren't already pissed off. Boxes were dragged out, and torn, shabby mismatched fatigues were dumped in a pile for us to pick through and find anything that would fit. The musty, stale sweat smell suggested none of the kit had ever been washed. Shane's quick-wittedness got us a pair of boots each that actually fitted, while the others were left foraging through some more boxes of boots that had appeared and looked worse than the first lot. Whoever supplied them didn't know men have different sized feet.

When the rifles came out, I started saying we wouldn't need them, but Shane gave me a look and I went along with him, scavenging through a stack of tatty Belgium FNs, Shane made up two complete weapons from four or five he'd grabbed, recognizing them as similar to the L1A1 SLRs we knew from the army. He'd always been into that stuff more than I'd ever been.

From the way some of the others took the first weapons they saw, and the way they handled them, we could tell they hadn't got a clue. The ex paras among us had followed Shane's cue, picking the best of the bad lot, unlocking them and removing and separating the bolt and carrier, checking the gas pistons, checking the firing pins, stripping them down in no time at all and swapping bits around. I caught the bemused but impressed looks of some of the others, probably thinking, like me, they wouldn't need a working rifle if we were there to provide non-combat training.

After putting our civi gear into cardboard boxes and putting our names on them – to collect them on the way back, we were told – we were divided into groups. As the others handed over their passports, I tucked mine away in my 'new' kit. Then Banks returned in uniform – now being called 'Major Banks'. He looked down his list and consulted with a couple of overweight guys – supposedly sergeant majors. Then another worrying farce took place as he promoted some of the group to corporals and sergeants, seemingly based on what they'd told him in London. Shane and I were passed over. We exchanged confused expressions with a few of the other ex-army lads, and I wondered how any of this could work.

They didn't seem capable of feeding us in that great big house, so we were put on the buses again and taken to a hotel in town. I was wondering what sort of place it was that would feed two busloads of men in combat fatigues, but nothing was a surprise anymore. Shane reckoned our meal was horse meat, but there weren't many complaints – we were too hungry by then. Before we sat down, we were warned to behave ourselves. I discovered later that white mercenaries were not exactly popular in this part of Africa – they'd be even less popular by the time our Angolan debacle was over.

Back at the big house, we were left to our own devices while Banks went ahead of us across the border into Angola to check things out. Some of the other characters we'd seen with Banks in London went ahead with him. We were told they were off to São Salvador, an FNLA stronghold. From what we could work out, there had been some disagreements about when and where the rest of us were going. The uncertainty did nothing to improve my opinion of the whole set up, or Banks either. It triggered a lot of discussion in our little groups about what would happen next. Some of the more experienced ex-military amongst us were asking where the air support and armoured kit was coming from, while the younger lads were either looking very worried or buoyed up with having been given weapons to play with. Shane and I tried to find out more about the vehicle maintenance side of things. No one knew anything – maybe it all happened at São Salvador, we concluded. When we heard a few more of the group had pulled out, and arguments broke out about whether we'd ever see the rest of our pay, we kept out of it and waited to see what happened next.

When Banks got back – after we'd been scratting around for meals and queuing for the one manky khazi – we heard he wasn't staying. He was hightailing it back to London. He looked at the end of his tether by then and in no mood to give explanations. We wondered what he'd seen on his trip over the border. All he said was he was going back on business for President Roberto and we'd be under the command of a Colonel Callan. It was a name that none of us knew, but would eventually be in the news all over the world. It turned out it wasn't even his real name.

The sudden change of leader did nothing to reassure anyone. Like me, most of them had been taking in what they'd seen so far and weren't impressed. The only assurances Banks offered were about our money being paid. Then he and his cronies got on their way. Soon after that, we were back on the stinking buses.

I hadn't seen a map, but I gathered we were just north of the border with Angola, and our journey out of Zaire would be south to this São Salvador place. It sounded like we'd go from there to where we'd be stationed. At that point, we all imagined that this FNLA army had some kind of command structure – bases, field headquarters, stores, workshops, barracks and so on. Once we got to São Salvador, it should make more sense. What we didn't know was that the FNLA was a rag-tag army of native Angolans – with no training and no motivation – and some competent but outnumbered Portuguese mercenaries bolstered by us lot. Neither did we know we'd been recruited to fight for a so-called president who hadn't a clue what he was doing and, in desperation, was buying in British ex-soldiers, who he'd been told were the best in the world.

Holden Roberto's plan had been to bring many more like us to Angola. He'd been funded by the CIA for a proxy war, a warm offshoot of the cold war. Fighting communism was something most of us on those buses were used to hearing about. Countering the threat from the Soviet Union was what we'd been trained for. We thought the Soviet-backed Cubans fighting for the MPLA were just another threat from the USSR. We'd been brought up on that sort of stuff. This was more of the same, only much further south. But the FNLA were never a match for the MPLA's forces, and we didn't know that yet. Besides, whatever we told ourselves, we were only there for the money.

Our bus ride, two hundred miles we worked out later, the best part of a day, was a sweaty and thirsty one. It started on tarmac – a modern highway while we were in Zaire – before we joined a dirt track which might have been at the border. It was hard to say as we'd passed through a few sentry points before joining that red dusty road. Each checkpoint was guarded by listless, bored young blacks in odd mixtures of uniforms, like the ones back at the big house in Kinshasa. We discovered this was the FNLA. These were the soldiers we'd come to help. As if to remind us, those four letters were painted on walls in the towns and villages we passed through.

Between the widely spaced pockets of habitation, thick high grasses, six-foot or more, bordered much of what passed for a road. Sometimes we had to leave the track to avoid the worst of the potholes. We bounced and lurched on, hot and thirsty. We passed over tight bridges and climbed hills with the buses' worn-out engines struggling and belching oily smoke. Now and then we saw clusters of wrecked vehicles, military and civilian, and sometimes family groups carrying their possessions, heading the opposite way to us. None of what we saw gave us the slightest confidence in what we were getting into. I could see Shane looking out at all this too. I didn't even want to ask what he was thinking.

The so-called FNLA headquarters at São Salvador was another mansion surrounded by walls, even more trashed than the one we'd left, reached by pot-holed roads where black guys in rags, apparently FNLA soldiers, drifted around carrying rifles. We heard the house was the ex-governor's mansion. Later, I realised it was a remnant of wealth from the Portuguese days, not all that long ago, stripped out and looted, local people taking back some of what had been taken from them.

The town did have an airstrip. We heard talk this was where the FNLA had their planes. Later on, we found out they were only a couple of light aircraft with no combat role whatsoever. They were no more use than the stripped-out vehicles that were scattered around on what had once been the lawns of the mansion. Things were looking worse by the minute. Then we were told São Salvador wasn't our base; we'd only be there long enough to get our heads shaved and switch transport. We did hear more about Colonel Callan though. Rumours went round that he was an out-an-out bastard. You used to get that kind of wind-up in the army. Sometimes it was right, sometimes it was bullshit. Shane and I decided to wait and see. We could hardly do much else. Besides, we were soon to be on our way again.

A few of our lot went ahead in Land Rovers and a few stayed in São Salvador. The bulk of us set off later in a convoy for a place called Maquela on the evening of that first day in Angola. Like everything else we'd seen since getting off that plane, the Dodge personnel carrier we crammed into had seen better days. The canvas roof was missing and, to add to our discomfort, the road was even more rutted than on our last journey. Then it started to rain. I always thought of Africa as a hot dry place, but at that time of the year Angola was still in the rainy season. The rain was intermittent and sometimes heavy. The idea it could be roasting hot at midday, pissing rain in the afternoon, and cold at night was just another bizarre twist to this whole fucking disaster.

The rain turned the dusty road to slime. In the open trucks, we got soaked. The wheels were soon spinning and losing grip. Just to add to the fun, there were more hills too. The trucks were quickly at their limits, sliding sideways and losing all traction. A mad run at an oncoming hill worked for a while until one ridge did for the Nissan truck in front of us. Despite the 6x6 drive on the Dodge, we were stuck behind it. Behind us, an ancient three-ton tipper that was carrying drums of fuel was also immobile in the mud. The Land Rovers at the front of our column left us behind. After a lot of arguing and debate, word went out that we just had to sit tight and we'd be rescued.

After a couple of hours wait, trying to keep out of the rain, a battered recovery truck turned up driven by an ex-British soldier, Chris Dempster. This guy seemed to know what he was doing. He said with the rain still pouring down, there was no point in tackling the stuck vehicles yet. Some of the lads started complaining to him they were there to do vehicle maintenance and not to carry a gun. I heard him tell them they'd best drop that line and keep their heads down if they knew what was good for them. Shane heard that too, and we looked at each other. If we hadn't known already, we knew then we weren't going to be handling any spanners in Angola.

We waited it out, soaked, cold, completely dispirited, and asking each other if we can't even get transported to where we needed to be, what was the rest of this outfit going to be like? It was getting light when the rain stopped and the process of dragging out the vehicles finally started. Callan had turned up by then, screaming and cursing in the way we'd soon get used to. It looked like the rumours about him were correct. After nearly losing the truck over a cliff edge, we were finally back on our way, prospects even gloomier than before.

# Fiona

CLIVE DIDN'T LET up on his idea of robbing Grey and Garton's payroll. I had plenty of time later to analyse why I went along with it, not least when I was questioned by the police, and later when I was on remand. After the trial, serving my sentence in Holloway, I had even more time to think about it. I concluded I hadn't done it to shake up Brenda and Joan, to please Clive, or even for the sheer exhilaration of it. The best explanation I could come up with, and the worst reason for doing it, was that I did it to lash out at Dad and Margaret. All the time I thought I was in control, doing my own thing, showing them I could earn a living and not be dependent like Jo, I was incubating the resentment and loss that had swamped me since Mum died.

I think Clive's resentment fuelled my resentment and separated me from everyone else I knew – even Hettie. Since meeting Clive, I'd phoned her less and less – always saying I was sorry for leaving it so long. She'd brushed off my apologies, saying she was glad I was so busy, and she was happy for me and hoped I'd come up to see her soon. I'd stopped thinking about seeing her then; I was just too wrapped up with Clive. I'd stopped thinking about everyone – Lolly and Frieda too. It was just after I met Clive that Lolly wrote to tell me about her brother had bought a farm in Yorkshire and she was going to stay there. I found the place in Dad's road atlas, a small village near Skipton. I couldn't work out why she'd do that and why she'd made no mention of Frieda either. But again, I was too wrapped up with Clive to think any more about it.

I think I'd always known Clive was not the one for me, that his manic streak, those spikes of excitement he brought, were just distractions, short-lived ways of kicking out at Dad and Margaret – Jo too. When it came to the crunch, I let my defence counsel play heavily on Clive coercing and manipulating me. I let them present me as this ex-private-schoolgirl, naïve and inexperienced, led on by an older man who'd seduced her and took advantage of her. Even my physical relationship with Clive was adjusted to fit that line. Even worse than what we'd done, at the time anyway, was hearing this twisted version laid out in court as Dad and Margaret sat listening. Dad's face was impassive, frozen in sadness, looking down at the floor, more painful to see than Margaret's upright pursed features with that gleam in her eyes. I knew I'd done it to hurt them, and how stupid that was. All I'd done was hurt Dad – and myself too. I just was glad Jo wasn't in court with them. To have seen her face would have been too much.

Clive's plan, if you could call it that, had been to strike when the payroll cash was out in the office, after it was delivered and before the pay packets went into the safe. Our office was upstairs on a little side corridor of its own, where a fire escape went down to the factory yard. All I had to do was slip down and wedge open the latch on the fire door. There was even a little block of wood that the cleaners left there for just that purpose. In the fantasy version that we'd laughed over so often, Clive would burst into the office toting a sawn-off shotgun, masked and clad in black. Brenda and Joan would wet themselves and simper as they packed the money into the bag he'd sling at them. Then he'd vanish down the stairs before anyone could raise the alarm. The sound of a powerful stolen car was the last anyone would hear, and the mystery of the Beckenham Panther would never be solved. When all the fuss died down, I'd resign, perhaps saying the robbery had left me traumatised, and we'd take a sumptuous Caribbean holiday, toasting Gray and Garton's with Champagne in some beachfront, palm-fronded bar. Yeah, right...

As the weeks passed, the fantasy version was amended and what actually happened was this. Not having access to a sawn-off shotgun, Clive could only think of one alternative. His mum's cleaning job was at the local comprehensive – his old school. Her work was in the evenings and holidays. When he was younger, Clive used to help her. He'd often been in the school with her when the place was empty. One of his jobs was to lock all the rooms when she'd finished them. He'd soon worked out the key system – one master key for each building. There was very little control over the numbers of master keys, and teachers were lazy and careless with them, leaving them in desk drawers. Clive soon had his own set. He used these to take revenge on various teachers he'd fallen out with, hiding their stuff, loosening the legs on their chairs, that sort of thing. One evening he was poking around in the PE office cupboard when he found the starting pistol they used for sports day. It was in a shoebox at the back of a high shelf, their idea of a safe place. The cartridges were next to it. He liked to go in and handle this gun that wasn't really a gun, but looked and felt so like one. This was his weapon for the robbery. He let himself into the sports block late one night and took the starting pistol from where it was still kept. He had the robbery weapon.

The mask, the black clothing, and the bag weren't easily to hand, so he'd taken one of his mum's plainer scarfs to tie round his face, supplemented by a pair of sunglasses and a wooly hat. A long mac that had hung for years in their spare room completed his disguise, and an old army rucksack found in the loft became the swag bag. As for the powerful stolen car, he said it wasn't necessary. He could park the Mini Clubman behind some derelict sheds on the other side of the road and get away down a side round before anyone would see him.

It was all a long way from the dashing Cadbury's Milk Tray man that he'd originally imagined himself as. He said it would have to do. That's when it hit home that he really was going to do it. I tried to stall him. I said I wouldn't be in the right place that next Friday morning, that I'd have some filing duties at the other end of the building. I thought if I put him off, he might drop the idea. He didn't. He said I could wedge the fire escape open first thing in the morning, no one would notice. So I did, still hoping he wouldn't appear.

He did appear – bang on cue, bursting through the door, pointing the harmless pistol, and shouting at us not to move. Joan froze in disbelief and just stared wide-eyed. But it was the utter terror on Brenda's face that made it all worthwhile – at least for those first few seconds. I felt no sympathy for her fear. Since Clive got the sack, she'd maintained a steady campaign to get me to break my silence over him. As I'd shared nothing with her and Joan about my personal life – not that there was much opportunity with Joan bleating about her daughter's marriage and Brenda detailing her family's ailments – she'd had very few ways into the subject. She'd resorted to oblique remarks about 'shiftless young people today' and 'work-shy good-for-nothings like that Rathley character'. She'd taken this up a few notches the day before the robbery when the subject of job references had come up, saying he'd never get a job if he was stupid enough to give the firm as his last employer – she'd see to that. She'd glanced my way to check for a reaction. But she hadn't been to my school. I knew when I was being baited and I'd let it wash over me. So that look on her face, when Clive pointed the gun at her, 'like someone had shoved a broom pole up her arse', as one of my fellow inmates used to say of her victims, felt like payback time.

But things had already gone wrong. I wasn't supposed to be in the room when Clive arrived. On a normal Friday, when the pay packets were made up, they sent me over to do photocopying and filing in the Sales office. That Friday, the Sales Manager had sent me back with some details of a vacancy he needed advertising. I'd hurried over, hoping to dump it on

Brenda and go, but she'd told me to wait as she had a letter for me to take back. So I'd been standing there when Clive made his dramatic entry. Even through that stupid scarf and glasses, I could see it had thrown him.

He did his best to forge on, shouting at us to put the money in the bag and waving the starting pistol around. There had been a few horrible seconds when Brenda and Joan had seemed rooted, and I really thought they wouldn't cooperate. I knew I had to wait for them to move first and pretend I was as shocked as they were. Then Clive made a pretty good job of cocking the gun and pointing it at Brenda, trying to sound like a villain off The Sweeney, telling her it was her last chance. She did as she was told, followed by Joan and me. There should have been over three thousand pounds. But in the drama, I didn't spot another bag of cash by the side of Joan's chair. Clive didn't know he was only getting three quarters of the money – things had already gone wrong. Then, when he told me to open the door for him, the accent he must have been practicing got forgotten and he'd sounded just like himself. That might not have been so bad had the production manager, Mr Garton, son of one of the founders, not been crossing the yard as Clive ran down the fire escape.

Mr Garton suffered from emphysema, not helped by his Senior Service habit. So when Brenda appeared at the bottom of the stairs shouting we'd been robbed, his attempt at chasing Clive across the yard didn't last long. Clive was over the road and sprinting for his car. He was getting away. The plan had worked. Except it hadn't. He'd been seen. One of Clive's ex-workmates had a doctor's appointment that morning and was cycling in for a late start. He had no idea what Clive was up to, but he had seen him pulling up the scarf and putting on the sunglasses before he'd even got into the factory yard.

Word rippled round the factory from department to department. It reached our office just as the police did. Uniformed officers arrived first. They were getting names and details of what had happened when the production manager hurried in and repeated what Clive's ex workmate had seen. Brenda's trauma turned to triumph, claiming she'd recognised his voice and was sure Clive was the culprit. Joan just looked stupefied at her. Then they both turned their gaze on me. They couldn't know I'd opened the fire escape door for him, but I imagined the suspicion forming in their heads. I was giving my name to a constable just then, just as Mr Garton was coming along the corridor from the main staircase with two men I guessed were detectives. Between coughs, he was telling them what he'd seen and confirming the robber was carrying a gun. I stepped out into the little lobby just outside the office to let the others in. In a few seconds, Brenda or Joan would tell someone I was Clive's girlfriend. At the very least, I'd be kept there answering questions when I needed to warn Clive they'd identified him. I had to get out.

Our office was full to bursting now and Brenda's voice, repeating Clive's name, was all I heard. This was my chance. I walked past the drawing office, smiled at the receptionist at the bottom of the main stairs, and headed through the back corridor to the main production area. This way, it wouldn't look like I was leaving the premises. At the end of that corridor was another door to the stores area and the loading bay. I'd seen the police cars outside the main entrance and I knew I had to get out through the side gate. My route was deserted; everyone must have been too busy talking about what happened. I had a horrible thought that the side gate might be locked, but I could soon see it was wide open. I was through it without being seen. The first phone box was too near for comfort, so I hurried on to the one near the small parade of shops.

The plan had been that Clive would take the money home and hide it in the loft. He'd arranged a job interview for late that morning and was going to attend it like nothing had happened. No one robs a payroll and then goes to a job interview, do they? As I dialled his number, I was trying to work out if he could have left for it already and if he'd even answer the phone. But he did. As I told him he'd been recognised, I was scanning around me, expecting a police car to pull up at any second.

Whatever he was, Clive wasn't slow-witted. He'd got another plan. Everything was going to be alright. We had money. We could escape. I should make for the train station and get the next train to Orpington, where he'd meet me. I put down the phone, considered going back, thought about what it would be like, thought about the questions, and thought about what it would be like at home. Then I headed for the station.

As the train pulled into Orpington, I looked for Clive, not believing he'd be there, thinking he'd already be caught. But there he was, on the platform with the rucksack and another bag by his side, grinning at me.

*Truth*

# Chapter 9      1979

# Roy

It's just after seven in the morning and it's bright and clear. Roy walks to the village shop. He can smell the salty seaweed on the breeze. He thinks this is how mornings should be – if only he wasn't so worried. A few early risers from the caravan park are also out. They're picking up milk for breakfast or, like him, they're buying a newspaper. He could have read the paper Hettie gets delivered, but he needed an excuse to get out. He wants to phone Luiz without Sally overhearing, without her even knowing. He doubts Luiz is still at Tomás's place, but he has to try.

In the phone box opposite the shop, he listens to the ring tone go on and on, already sure it won't be answered. Maybe Tomás has done a bunk too. Just as he's about to hang up, the phone is picked up and the pips go. He pushes a ten-pence into the slot. He doesn't recognise the voice. The English isn't as good as Tomás's. The man, half-asleep, says no, Tomás isn't there and no, Luiz isn't there. Roy gives him Hettie's number, reading it twice, slowly, telling him he must get it to Luiz. The man, irritated now, says he'll pass it on and hangs up. Roy stays in the phone box, staring at the dial as if it will tell him what he wants to know. How bad is this? Is Luiz alright?

He buys his newspaper. He gets a few hundred yards in the direction of the café and turns back. Back in the phone box, he dials another number. It's answered straight away. He pushes another ten-pence in, not knowing how to start.

'Roy?'

Geri's voice sounds strange here. He's only been away for a day, but it feels he hasn't heard that voice in ages. It's part of somewhere else now.

'I'm sorry,' he says. 'There's things I should have said.'

'What's going on, Roy?'

He still doesn't know what part of this mess to start with. He knows he can't shirk it any longer, so he goes for what he's most ashamed of first.

'I'm not coming back,' he hears himself say, like another part of him is talking, taking over out of necessity. 'It's not fair on you and it's not right for either of us.'

'What?'

'I'm sorry, Geri. I can't do this anymore – I can't. I should have told you to your face, but I couldn't.'

She doesn't respond. He thinks he can hear a sniff.

'You need to find someone who's right for you – and it's not me. I'm really sorry.'

'Have you got someone else?'

'No,' he replies. 'It isn't that.'

'Where are you?'

'I can't tell you.'

'Then you have got someone else.' Her voice has risen in tone and volume. 'You're lying!'

'I swear to you there's no one else. I've come away to try and sort out what to do.'

'Where?'

'You don't need to know.'

'If you're telling the truth, you'll tell me where you are.'

He hesitates. She's right. He should tell her something. She doesn't have to know about Luiz and he won't be there much longer anyway. 'I'm at Ebwich. Do you remember Hettie – from the funeral?'

She takes a few seconds to get this. 'Why there?'

'I just need some time and some space,' he says.

'We had something, Roy,' she wails. 'I really thought we had something.'

'It's not your fault,' he says. 'It's mine. I wasn't honest with you. I'm the one in the wrong, Geri.'

'What about the garage? What about Dad?'

'Tell him I'm sorry to let him down. He'll find someone else.'

'It's not about someone working at the garage. He thought you were—'

'I can't do this,' he cuts in. 'I can't.' He wants to stop this now. He wants to hang up before he gives in and says he'll go back. But he knows that's not the right thing to do. He forces himself to go on. 'I'm going now, Geri. Look after yourself. Find someone better than me.'

Putting down the receiver felt crueler than anything he'd just said. He keeps his hand on it, gripping it, feeling sick from the base of his stomach, closing his eyes, listening to his own breathing. He wants to get away from Ebwich now. He tells himself he'll wait until tomorrow. If Luiz hasn't been in touch, he'll drive down and find him and tell him that's it. Luiz can collect Sally and Tina and take them somewhere else; he's helped him all he can.

An hour later, after they've had breakfast, Roy is upstairs persuading Sally to come to the beach with him and Tina.

'What for?' she asks.

'Tina wants to go. It'll do you good.'

She looks at him, lips compressed.

'You can't just sit here waiting for the phone to ring.'

'What if he calls while we're out?'

Tina's excited feet pound up the stairs.

'Hettie or Fiona will take a message. You can call him back.'

'Are we going now?' Tina asks.

Sally sighs. 'Alright, I'm coming.'

Roy goes downstairs ahead of them. The café is quiet. Hettie told them at breakfast that Mondays often start like this. Fiona finishes cleaning the windows at the front. He'd like to talk to her, but doesn't know why or what he'd say. It bothers him. He tries to forget it and goes outside to get the bucket and spade. As he closes the shed door, he sees Fiona in the kitchen. She's watching him from the window. He looks back, certain there's something in her face, something he wants to believe is for him. She breaks the gaze first and moves away. He stands looking at the empty window, unsure, wanting to go inside and say something, anything, but he still doesn't know what.

Tina runs the last few hundred yards to the sea, Sally calling for her to hold on, Roy telling her it's okay, let her run, that's what kids do on the beach, remembering that's what he did. But it was different then, he thinks. Everything was taken care of. Nothing was complicated. That's what he wants now. He wants simple. He knows it's an illusion, but he clings to it, avoiding the reality surrounding it. Somewhere like this would do just fine, he thinks. He makes a picture in his head of a house, one of those houses where nothing much happens, where there's someone to come home to, weekend afternoons with nothing much to do, late sunlight coming in the window of a quiet bedroom, safe nothingness. Sally's voice breaks the silence that has hung between them from the road to the beach.

'You were fostered, weren't you?'

'Yes,' he says.

'Do you know why?'

'I was a war baby.' He says. 'Left in an air raid shelter, 1944. The little blitz, they called it, Hitler's last attempt to bomb us out.'

They're following Tina's footprints along the shoreline. She's taken off her shoes and socks, squealing as the water washes over her feet and foams at the tide's edge. They stop to watch. He thinks how Dad had told him that detail of his birth and how his mum ruffled his hair and said, 'And there you were – something good out of all that bad.'

'Do you ever wonder?' Sally asks, not needing to say what.

'No,' he replies. 'Mum and Dad *were* my mum and

dad as far as I'm concerned.' He tries to decide where she's going with this. She must know Shane didn't know who his parents were. He's thinking she's going to say something about that. She doesn't.

'I worry about when she'll start asking more about her dad,' Sally says. 'She's going to want to know what happened to him, why it happened to him. And I don't even know myself. You know more about him than I do.'

Tina is kicking up the water, walking way ahead of them now.

'We were idiots,' he says. 'I regret it every day. And I was lucky. Shane wasn't. That's all there is to it.'

'I can't tell her that.'

'I don't know what you should tell her. The whole bloody thing was a mess, a stupid mess caused by people making money out of someone else's war. We should have kept our noses out. It's better she knows nothing about it.'

'I won't lie to her,' says Sally.

'You can't tell kids everything,' he says. 'Better she doesn't know.'

Tina runs back and takes the bucket and spade from him. She starts making a sand castle. They spread out the towels and sit on the sand to watch. He doesn't want to think about Sally telling Tina about what happened to Shane. She'll have questions for him if that happens, things he's not even told Sally, not told Geri, not told anyone. Perhaps he won't be around when Sally tells her. He wonders where he will be.

They sit a couple of feet apart, saying nothing, listening to the wash of the waves, looking out to the horizon. He wonders if he's sat in this exact spot before. Being back there has released more memories, drifting up to the surface, floating around, reconnecting him. Over the years, he'd asked himself if he'd imagined what happened the last time he was here. Now he's here, he knows he didn't imagine it. There was something in the fabric of that house that's confirmed it, something locked in the air of the place, echoes of that argument on the day they'd left.

Sally looks at her watch. She's been doing it a lot. He knows why.

'He'll leave a message,' he says.

She doesn't reply.

When Tina's construction is finished and he's helped create the moat and a channel to let the tide fill it, they admire their work and head for the little shop on the road back into the village. He tells Tina how he'd get an ice cream from there every day, how they'd known his name and would pile the cone higher than anyone else's. As the shop comes into view, he notices how it's expanded. A flat roof section projects out now, hiding the cottage behind it. Inflatable beach toys blow in the breeze; bright, alien plastic colours. The woman who serves him wouldn't have been born when he bought his last ice cream there, like Sally, like Fiona.

Roy doesn't want to go back to the beach. Sally's anxiety has got to him. Now *he's* worried whether Luiz has rung and left a message. Tina wants to hurry back to the beach though. She has plans for a bigger sandcastle, and Sally has bought her a windmill to go on the top of it. He says just for half an hour. He helps with the larger-scale version while Sally watches. When they've admired it for long enough for Tina to agree to leave it, debating whether to leave the windmill, Sally looks at her watch again and catches Roy's eye.

'Time for lunch,' he says, holding out his hand to Tina. 'Bring the windmill. We'll need it tomorrow.'

She soon lets his hand go and skips ahead, holding her windmill up to turn as she goes. They walk faster to keep up.

'It's so different here,' Sally says.

He's puzzled. It's like she's suddenly aware of the contrast between the Lincolnshire coast and Poplar.

'I couldn't live somewhere like this,' she goes on. 'But somewhere with some more space would be nice.'

'Do you really think Luiz—' he hesitates, toning down his question. 'I mean, what are you expecting?'

'You know Luiz,' she replies. 'I'm not sure what to expect.'

'You're right there,' says Roy.

'Are you doing this for him or for you?'

'It's complicated,' he says.

They walk on. He knows she's waiting for him to elaborate.

'I'm doing it for Shane.'

'You've already kept that promise,' she says.

'That's not how it feels.' He can't tell her how it feels. 'Geri and me... I needed to get away.'

'How bad is it with Luiz?' she asks. 'Who's he upset?'

'I don't know. He says he can sort it out.'

'Do you believe him?'

The café comes into view. Tina disappears around the back.

'I don't know,' he says.

He follows Sally through the back door. She calls to Tina, telling her to wash her hands before lunch. He goes through the kitchen to the back of the café. Fiona stands at the counter. She smiles at him before serving a customer. He's aware he's staring at her and turns back to the kitchen.

Sally is in the hallway, phone to her ear, waiting. He goes to sit in the back room. He hears her putting the phone down. Whoever was there before has gone. She calls up to Tina and returns to stand in the doorway.

'I can't stand this,' she says.

Roy doesn't answer straightaway. They look at each other. She's determined, but so is he.

'Give him a couple of days. If we've not heard, I'll go down and find him.'

'We're coming too.'

He doesn't answer her. He's not having that argument, not now. Tina's rapid feet pound down the stairs and past them to the kitchen. Sally follows her through to the café and he trails behind, hoping she's not going to say any more about Luiz. Fiona looks up from clearing plates away as they sit down at Tina's favourite table in the window – his favourite table. He sees the afternoon stretching out, waiting to hear, hanging around; going over and over the things in his mind, having to watch Sally trying the phone again and again. He can't face it. He tries talking Sally into a trip to Mablethorpe, using Tina as an excuse, saying she'll enjoy it there. Reluctantly, Sally agrees.

Later that afternoon, they're back in the café having tea when Sally returns from the phone after only a minute. He doesn't need to ask. He avoids her glance and looks outside as a car draws up. It's Geri's car.

# Fiona

THE WOMAN WHO'S just walked in is looking right at him. He gets up, crosses to the door and says something to her. Fiona can't hear what he says. The woman points to where Sally and Tina are. He moves between her and their table, opening the door, motioning her outside.

Fiona looks at Hettie. She's seen the woman too. They both watch them talking outside the window.

'Who's Roy talking to?' Fiona asks.

Hettie hesitates before answering. 'That's Geri. His girlfriend, or ex-girlfriend.' Hettie's words are brisk, trying to play it down.

Fiona regrets asking. Her interest was too obvious. She takes a glass of squash over to Tina, unable to stop herself looking outside to where Roy is walking with the woman towards a car. They stand there talking. They stand for a long time.

Fiona is by herself behind the counter when Roy comes back inside. She sees the woman driving past. Roy looks like he's going straight to the kitchen.

'Everything alright?' she asks, this time not caring that she's giving away her interest. She wants him to talk. She wants to know.

He pauses at the kitchen door. 'Not really. Complications...'

'Well, I hope it turns out alright,' she says.

'Yeah, so do I.' He looks out to the road, on edge, like he's making sure his visitor really has gone.

'Is Sally okay? This doesn't seem her kind of place,' she says. She wants him to stay and talk.

He breaks his focus outside to turn to her. 'No, it's not her kind of place.'

'Tina likes it,' she says. 'It's different for kids, isn't it?'

His features relax. 'Yeah. I never had a care in the world when I used to come here – except that my pocket money would run out before the end of the holiday. And even then, Mum and Dad would sub me. Funny what you remember, isn't it? I wonder what Tina will remember of this.'

'Does she see her dad?'

The question throws him. He stares at her, and she wonders if she's offended him.

'Sorry, none of my business.'

'Shane's dead,' he says.

'How old was he?'

'Thirty-two.'

By the way he looks outside again and then back at her, she thinks he's going to say something else. Then Hettie is back with Tina's sandwich and he carries on to the kitchen.

After their evening meal, Fiona takes out the rubbish. Roy is in the yard, unscrewing the hinges from the shed door. She remembers he'd promised Hettie he'd fix it.

'Tina enjoyed Mablethorpe then,' she says, referring to Tina's detailed account over dinner. But her opening is more a comment on Sally's silence than Tina's chatter. It had been obvious Sally was upset, and Roy had been trying to camouflage it. She's offering him the chance to talk. She senses he wants to.

'Sally just wants to go home,' he says. 'Hold that just there. Lift it up a bit if you can.'

She lifts the door while he gets screw into the top hinge.

'Is everything okay?' she asks, conscious of being so close to him.

'It's a long story. No doubt you saw my visitor today.'

'Yes,' she says. There's no point pretending she didn't.

He's facing her now, looking straight at her. They're very close, closer than they've ever been. She looks straight back. She doesn't want to stop. She likes his eyes.

'Just let me get another one in and you can let go.'

As he puts the rest of the screws back in and tries the door, she doesn't want him to finish this so quickly.

'It's the best I can do with the frame being rotten,' he says.

She steps inside the shed. He stays in the doorway. She reaches out and takes his left hand. He looks at her. He knows. She pulls him inside and closes the door behind him. It's warm. The smell of old creosote, timber and years of dust will be forever associated with that moment. It's dark too. The one window has long been covered by ivy. She pulls him closer until she can feel his breath. She misses his lips and then finds them. His arms go round her. This is what she wanted. She puts hers around him, satisfied to feel his flesh through the thin shirt, conscious of her breasts squashing up against him, aware of the contours of his back. It's a lingering kiss, like it's been waiting a lot longer than a couple of days. She wonders if it's the same for him, if he's wants this as much as she does.

They stay together for several minutes like that. At one point, he takes her face in his hands and holds it before kissing her again. She likes that. It's not been like this before, that feeling of inevitability, that this is right. The only doubt in her mind is whether he thinks that too, that by pulling him in there she's acted too soon, that he might get the wrong idea, that this is all there is. She wonders if he's going to do more, wanting him to slide his hands down her, undress her, even in there, even in that dusty space, get down on the floor. The day's heat is trapped in that space too. She can feel the moisture breaking out on her forehead and in the small of her back. It would be good to get her clothes off, good to get his off. But she doesn't, he doesn't make a move to, and neither of them has said a single word. The longer the silence goes on, the more intense it gets. She's worried something is wrong. Finally, finally, he speaks.

'You're a lovely woman, Fiona.'

She doesn't know how to reply.

'But I'm in a mess and I won't be here much longer.'

'I don't care,' she says.

'You will,' he says. 'And so will I.'

He slides his hands down her arms, slowly until he breaks the contact.

'Did I make a mistake?' she says.

'The nicest mistake to happen to me in a long while,' he says.

'What then?'

'Come inside. I put some beer in the fridge.'

It's not the let-down it could have been. He wants to talk. It's something. She's not going to refuse. She wants to know more and follows him inside. He opens the fridge and hands her a can. She gets two glasses. They sit at the table. He smiles across at her. Then he looks down.

'This afternoon... She came up to ask me to go home.'

'Are you're going to?'

He looks up and shakes his head. 'No.'

'And Sally and Tina?'

'I promised Shane I'd look out for them,' he says, rotating his glass on the table top.

It wasn't what she wanted to hear, but he seems to need to say it. She should let him, help him. 'What did he die from?' she asks, expecting it to be an illness or maybe an accident.

'Stupidity,' he says. 'His and mine.'

She looks bemused, raises her eyebrows for more.

'Do you remember all that stuff in the news about mercenaries in Angola 1976?'

'Yes,' she says. 'I was on remand in Holloway. I read a lot of newspapers then.'

There, she's said it. His eyes contract, the corners wrinkling more. He gives a tiny nod, like he understands. But how can he? She knows Hettie won't have told him how she'd ended up there. But she wants him to finish before any of that.

'Go on,' she says.

'Shane was ex-army, like me. We were both out of work. We went out there to make some money. It seemed like a good idea at the time.'

'There was a trial,' she says, trying to recall. 'That maniac. What was his name, Callan? They executed him, didn't they?'

'Him and three others,' says Roy. 'After he'd killed at least a dozen of us and God knows how many others.'

She's remembering the stuff in the papers, the raw reporting, how incongruous it had sounded, how shocking it was. 'Wasn't he a psychopath?'

Roy nods. 'Not half.'

'Did he kill your friend?'

'Not directly.'

She looks at him, wondering what he'd done there. 'You weren't… I mean, what did you do there?'

He looks her in the eyes. 'We were supposed to be training mechanics or doing maintenance. We were shanghaied. We ended up having to fight. We either went along with it or risked being another of Callan's victims.'

'What happened to you?'

'I got out. The person who helped me is Sally's boyfriend, Luiz. That's why I'm here – that and promising Shane I'd look after Sally and Tina.'

She can't help herself. 'You owe too many people favours.'

His face cracks into a reluctant grin. 'You're right there.'

'And Sally's bloke is in trouble?'

'Big time,' says Roy. 'So what's your excuse? How did you end up in Holloway?'

She hesitates. Does she want to tell him? Was it like in Holloway, where eventually, with those you trusted, you told your story? But this isn't just passing time.

There's no need to tell him. She could brush it off. She could just get up and go. She does neither. She pours the rest of the can into her glass. She tells him about meeting Clive. Then she backtracks and tells him about Mum, Dad, Margaret and Jo – even about school. She manages to smile when she tells him about the robbery. He doesn't look shocked. He just listens.

'You might have read about us in the papers,' she says. 'Donney and Clive?'

He looks quizzically at her.

'Donney, my surname. They thought it was amusing.'

'I wouldn't have seen the papers then,' he says. 'And when I got home, I didn't want to read anything or hear anything about it.' He empties his glass. 'Donney and Clive! At least you didn't end up like they did.'

# Chapter 10    1976

## Fiona

ON THE FIRST night, tucked away off a quiet lane, I asked Clive about the money. He'd been lamenting over leaving his car behind, speculating on when it had been towed away from the station at Orpington, where he'd left it in the no-parking area. He'd not said how much the camper van had cost. He'd gone in on his own to the second-hand car place where he'd spotted it. The dealer was probably still smiling at the fastest sale he'd ever made, about as long as it took to count the cash.

Then we'd bought clothes for me, cooking things, a gas bottle, bedding and food. Neither of us had thought how cold it would be, so our next purchases would have to be more blankets and warmer coats. I don't know what I was expecting, but I thought there'd still be plenty of cash left. There wasn't.

'Sixty-three pounds! Is that all?' I said when I finally got it out of him.

'I thought you said there'd be three and a half thousand – and we needed this van.'

'Joan had another bag under her desk,' I said.

'The fucking bitch!' He got out his wallet and looked in it. 'I've got thirty quid,' he said.

He knew I'd left my purse and my bag when I'd dashed from the office.

'I've got money in my post office savings,' I said. 'We could go back and get my book.'

'It's too risky,' he said.

I was trying to work out how long we'd survive on ninety-odd pounds. Not very long.

'Anyway,' he said, 'I've still got this.' He took the starting pistol from the glove compartment, weighed it in his hand, and grinned.

A few weeks ago, I'd have thought he was joking, that having just got away, he'd even think of taking another risk like that.

'This is our savings book,' he said.

He was still on a high. This wasn't about getting back at the people at work now; it was a thrill he wanted more of. I was worrying about getting caught; he was thinking of the next time.

'They'll know the gun's not real now,' I said.

'How? It's only taken out for sports days. It won't be missed for months.'

'We'll give ourselves away. They might already have worked out where we are,' I said.

'We'll go somewhere much further away,' he said, like he'd just had the best idea ever. 'Tomorrow, we'll really put some miles between us and them.'

So we did. The next day, we started a long loop west and then north: Brighton, Worthing, Portsmouth, Southampton, Bournemouth, then up to Bristol. It was sleety, grey and cold. Passing Bath, I thought of Jo at the university and wondered if her last driving test had been as much of a disaster as the others. I'd passed my test the previous autumn, but Margaret had made sure I didn't get to practice. That Jo had failed her test twice already had a lot to do with it. Somehow, the car was never available for me to practice in. She'd always have an excuse for needing the car when I asked to use it. Dad never stepped in, so I hadn't driven since I'd got my licence. To deprive her of the satisfaction of saying no, I'd stopped asking. So my driving experience was limited. When Clive said I should take a turn, the camper felt very different to my driving instructor's little Datsun Cherry. It was a strange feeling, driving along, departing from the norms and rules. It was so easy inside the bubble we'd created for ourselves to pretend nothing else mattered.

Clive got pleasure from me regaining my driving confidence. I soon got over the feeling I was steering a boat. I stopped floundering to find the handbrake, and waggling the stick to find the gears. We drove on. The tax disk had expired months ago, and we had no insurance either. But they seemed trivial details at the time. We were above those things. We'd become a team, aligned against the rest of the world, taking turns at the wheel, increasing the distance between us and where anyone might look for us. We headed north – Gloucester, Hereford, Shrewsbury, Oswestry, then Chester. It got colder and colder. We drove and we talked.

It wasn't that we hadn't talked before. Clive already knew a fair amount about me. He knew all about Dad and Margaret and he knew about Jo. But somehow, in the cosy partnership of that journey, in the cocoon of that van – despite the heater not being that great – it was different. We revealed more. We talked about who we were and what we wanted and what we didn't want. For the first time, Clive talked about being brought up by just his mum. I'd wondered about it, but I'd never been able to ask. Then, looking out of the windscreen, as that grey January became a grey February, he wanted to tell me.

He told me how his dad had suddenly left them and how he hadn't seen him since he was five. He didn't blame his dad for anything, but I could see why that was the landmark he started from. It had separated him from the other kids at school; it was the root of many things that happened to him.

Left with his mum, Clive was still loved and protected – that wasn't the problem. It sounded like he was too loved and protected. He didn't have many playmates, and if any of them hurt him in any rough and tumble, he wasn't allowed to play with them again. His mum walked him to and from school, back home for lunch and back again. She'd be there waiting at the end of every day.

Outside of school, his world was tightly knitted to his mum's. They did everything together, and she arranged her day around him. Her three part-time jobs, mornings in the greengrocers, afternoons cleaning in a nursing home and evenings cleaning at the local comprehensive school, were timed to fit around his schedule. In the school holidays he either went with her to work, having to sit tucked away reading or amusing himself, or she took holiday to look after him. When he was older, they'd spend a week or two at his cousins' house in Dorset – the farthest he'd even gone from home in his whole life until our journey together.

His dad never showed up again and his mum never mentioned him. If he ever asked about him, she'd brush the question aside, reminding him they didn't need anyone else; they had each other. At school, his sheltered life was all too obvious to the other kids. And kids being kids, they needled away at it. His mum always made a special effort with his appearance, which, in the nature of these things, just made things worse. His clean, pressed uniform came in for comments and teasing, and his briefcase, seen alongside the battered sports bags of the other kids, made things worse. But what he dwelt on most – his biggest shame – was his mum being a cleaner at the school.

He'd tried to keep it a secret. He'd never mentioned his mum had a job. He'd implied she didn't need one – not when his dad worked in Saudi Arabia, earning huge amounts of money, due back anytime soon. But his stories didn't hold out for long. He'd been seen in town with his mum at the shop and, because after-school events often overlapped with the cleaners being there, it wasn't long before someone was mocking him about his mum's work. Then the lies about his dad came out and everyone joined in with the teasing.

My school life might have been very different to his, but there was one thing in common – your standing in the pecking order, your status, if you like, counted for everything. I had a different way of coping than Clive did. I got through it relatively unscathed. But Clive took the taunts to heart. He was ashamed of his mum. He kicked back at her and at everyone. Flying off the handle at his tormentors at school got him into a lot of trouble. The more cunning kids used to set him up for it too, and he usually reacted and lashed out at someone, anyone. He only just got through his school years without being expelled.

When I asked him if he had any friends at all back then, he didn't answer straight away. He carried on looking out at the road.

'Not really. I bet you did.'

'I managed,' I said. 'I made some good friends. We helped each other.'

'I'd have bloody hated it. I'd have run off.'

'You accepted it. You survived it. You hear people say it toughens you up, not having your mum and dad to run to, having to deal with it yourself. Sink or swim.' I said. 'I couldn't even phone home. They'd usually be away, Dad on a trip and Margaret clinging along, making sure she was where I couldn't be.'

'You can make phone calls to ships,' he said.

'You can,' I said. 'But it wasn't that easy. It depended where they were and what time of day it was. And we were only allowed calls on Sunday evenings, and there'd be a queue for the phone. On the rare occasions we got to speak, Margaret would hog the call, talking to Jo. When it was my turn, Jo would be next to me, listening. I could never say what I wanted to say to Dad.'

'Bitch,' he said.

'If the holidays coincided with Dad's leave, Margaret begrudged every day I had with him. If they didn't, I wouldn't see him at all.'

'You're better off without them,' he said. 'All of them. We're okay together, aren't we?'

'Yes,' I said, touched by the change in his tone, the vulnerability when he'd said that.

'Whatever happens, we'll stick together – promise?'

'I promise,' I said.

But even as I said it, I wondered what it would mean and if I could do it. I looked across at him, wondering how much of this was bravado; whether he was even more scared than me, if *he* wanted to phone home. I thought I should make it easy for him in case he did.

'Have you thought about phoning your mum? She's probably worried.'

'We shouldn't risk calling anyone,' he said. 'Besides, she'll be too busy running around after fucking Jeffery.'

I doubted that. I'd seen how torn she was between her life and needs and those of Clive. My arrival had brought some hope for her. I felt bad about that then. When I'd first gone round there with Clive, it had been obvious that despite being older than me, he'd never brought a girl home before. Sitting in their lounge, as his mum brought the tea tray in, it had been awkward for us all. She'd asked me polite questions about work and my family and I'd given polite, bland answers. At the time, I couldn't decide if she wanted me to take him off her hands – or the opposite, she wanted me to leave him alone. Did she still want to keep him close to her, just like when he was at school? I realised then it was neither. She wanted him to be happy, and she wanted her life too – hardly unreasonable. That tight connection between them felt uncomfortable though, too intense. It was there in the way he kept looking at her, not me, when she was in the room. Doing that robbery, taking off like we had, he'd broken that bond. But what had it done to him? I couldn't decide.

Yet despite these worries, despite our situation and the fear of being caught, that first few days was a good time. The steady thrum of the VW engine, our long chats, the road ahead of us, meals in quiet spots along the way, cooking on a two-ring burner, were the best parts of our time together. Even coping with the cold and the lack of a toilet and proper washing facilities felt part of the adventure. We drove on, in a private rhythm, in our own world.

We became adept at finding public swimming pools with hot showers, splitting up so no one saw us together. The cold weather helped us there. We kept our hoods up and wore our scarves round our chins. We didn't look that different to anyone else. One of us always stayed in the back of the van when we were in a petrol station or car park, so we weren't seen together. We continued north – Liverpool, Blackpool, Kendal, Carlisle – but the money was running out.

We stayed off that subject for almost a week. But after our last visit to a supermarket, and with less than half a tank of petrol left, it couldn't be ignored any longer. We were north of Carlisle then, passing through Brampton, heading east. We needed to buy food. Clive took us off the main road to a quiet side street. We felt safer now we were a long way from Beckenham, but we still split up when we left the van. I was going to buy some sausages, bread and eggs with the last of the money. Clive said he wanted to take a look around. He was nervy and distracted when he handed me the van keys and said he'd meet me back there in half an hour, stressing not to be any later. I knew what he was going to do – and I said nothing.

As I stood waiting to pay for the groceries, I couldn't stop the dread building up in my stomach. It wasn't like before; when I hadn't thought it could really happen. I hurried back to the van, hoping he was okay. I sat in the driving seat, checking my watch, trying to work out how long he could be, knowing we had to get out of there as soon as he got back. When the side door suddenly slid open, I hadn't even seen him approach. He must have come a different way back.

'Drive!' he said, pulling the door shut and lying on the floor. 'But take it easy.'

And I drove. Out of town, getting stuck in some traffic on the main street where a police car was trying to make its way through. I took it slowly, fighting the urge to push down on the accelerator, holding off until we were on the main road and Clive got up and slid through to the front passenger seat. He took the cash out of his jacket pocket and counted it. We were criminals already, but just then it felt worse, much worse, than before. And there was that look in his eyes as he turned to me, that smile that he had when he was on a high, as he told me what he'd done. He hadn't even covered his face when he'd threatened the shopkeeper with the starting pistol.

'That was bloody stupid,' I said.

'I had to move fast. How else were we going to get any money?' he replied.

But the money he'd got was only seventy-five

pounds. I wanted to say we couldn't keep this up for much longer, but it wasn't the right time.

We put a good few miles between us and that newsagents, driving on into the evening, up to the Borders when we were on the last dregs of petrol and had to risk filling up. Going further north meant it was wetter and colder, and the places we stopped were more exposed. Cooking inside the van without letting too much of the elements in became a condensation nightmare, and although it was cosy under our pile of blankets, listening to the wind outside, we'd wake up to streaming windows and penetrating damp.

We headed towards the Northumberland coast to Berwick-upon-Tweed. I said we had to risk using a launderette and we should use the showers at the local swimming pool too. The previous night had been particularly cold. We'd lain awake until the early hours debating where to go next – me hoping he'd suggest giving up, and him giving no clue he'd consider it. After Berwick, it looked like we'd be carrying on.

I'd gone to the pool first. To avoid attracting attention, I swam for ten minutes before poaching myself in the shower, letting the heat soak in. It was in this grand old building with a tower. When I was swimming, I'd had the whole place to myself, looking up at these columns and enormous windows, letting myself imagine I wasn't going back to that van, that I was going back to a nice warm house instead. When I was getting dried, I found a copy of the Sun newspaper in my changing cubicle and all the warmth left me in an instant.

On the front page, my own face stared back at me – a

grainy enlargement cut from a school hockey team photo. Next to it was one of Clive that must have been even older, his hair shorter and neater than I'd ever seen it. The headline said, *DONNEY AND CLIVE* and underneath, *Dangerous Duo Go North!* I abandoned my trip to the launderette and hurried back to the van.

Clive stared at the paper. The column under the photos connected the robbery at Grey and Garton's with the one at the newsagents in Brampton. Clive's abandoned car was mentioned too. Whoever wrote the piece had been talking to someone at the factory. I wondered if it was Brenda. 'Posh girl Fiona Donney and unemployed boyfriend Clive Rathley…' The parallel to Bonnie and Clyde was pathetic even for that newspaper, but they milked it all the same. We'd carried out a 'Heist' we'd 'sped off and disappeared into hiding', and the police were in 'on the trail'.

Clive loved it. He was grinning all over his face, reading about himself. I was angry and scared.

'It's not funny,' I said. 'We'll be spotted now for sure. We might have already been.'

'What, from those photos?' he said. 'Donney and Clive!'

He was still savouring the words and still smiling. I was thinking all we had in common with them was our naivety. I was thinking about how they ended up.

# Roy

I THINK IT was the Saturday, the last day of January when we finally arrived in Maquela. It was an FNLA stronghold, an unknown place that would hit the world news not long after we got there. We'd been told it was close to the front, where all the action was, and where Callan recently had some success against the MPLA forces, despite being heavily outnumbered. None of this did anything for morale though, especially after our journey there. The whole thing about acclimatization and training had been forgotten. The whole thing about support and the need for mechanics, back-up, medics, whatever, had gone too. We were going to be fighting, like it or not.

Maquela might have been a nice place once. It was a small town, with lots of single-story buildings, some with verandas on columns, surrounded by walled gardens. A lot of the buildings were derelict though, with rubbish and wrecked vehicles littering the streets. Again, the surroundings did nothing for our spirits. Everyone was hungry, tired, and pissed off. No one cut us any slack. Instead, we were lined up for Callan's inspection.

Unlike us, Callan was smartly turned out. His kit fitted his muscular frame, making up for the fact he wasn't that tall. He carried himself with arrogance and a taut aggression that didn't bode well. He wore an undisguised sneer on his dark features as he took us in and snapped questions at us about our experience, regiments, and trades. Equally well turned out was a 'Captain' Wainhouse, Callan's second in command. While they were taking in our answers and assessing us, one of the ex-paras who'd served in Northern Ireland said he was sure these were the pair who'd held up a post office over there. He said they'd got jail sentences for robbing some piddling amount of cash. Later, I heard another ex-para saying something about Bloody Sunday and Callan being a psychopath.

It was obvious from that inspection that Callan had been expecting something else, something more like a keen, lively bunch of professionals. Instead, as he ran his dark, angry eyes over us, he saw a shambles. At least Shane and me looked like we'd been soldiers, and the ex paras and some of the other army lads were doing their best too. But he wasn't much impressed when we said we were ex-REME. The lads who had less experience came in for some real stick though. Callan couldn't contain his scorn and disdain for them, spewing a stream of abuse in their direction. But it was two royal navy blokes who'd been in submarines that put the tin lid on it for him. He took their presence as a personal insult. As for the civilians, he looked at them like they were something he'd picked up on his shoes, or polished boots in his case.

When he'd finished ranting, he put us into groups and gave us a quick rundown on what we were there for. That's when it our suspicions were confirmed. This wasn't an army about to rescue the country from communists; this was more like a suicide mission. The Cuban-backed MPLA had T-34 tanks, other Soviet hardware and plenty of men. Their army was known as

FAPLA and they were bolstered by Cuban soldiers. We were going to attack them using 'killer groups', more like guerrilla tactics I suppose, hit and run. I looked around and wondered what we were going to attack them with.

I wasn't the only one thinking this. Some of the lads were asking the same questions, others piped up that this wasn't the deal, that they'd come here to train the local soldiers. One of them even said he thought he'd be flying a plane. A much-older guy said he was there to translate Russian. As this all came out, derision crept up Callan's face until it poured out of his eyes. He let rip at the dissenters, shouting that if they didn't want to fight, they could step aside and get out of their combat gear.

While this was going on, I was watching the faces of Callan's henchmen. As well as Wainhouse, there was a so-called Sergeant Major Copeland, and another nutter called Shotgun Charlie. We worked out later that Callan and these buddies of his had got there a couple of weeks earlier. These sidekicks might not have been the full shilling themselves, but they were shit-scared of their commanding officer and were going to do whatever he told them.

As about twenty of our group started taking their gear off, I exchanged a few quiet words with Shane. He was keener to stay put than I was, but we were sticking together, so I stayed put too. I couldn't help noticing that some of those who'd opted out were experienced soldiers. That shook me. After that, we grabbed some of the combat rations that had come in the trucks with us and were told to get ready for a weapons inspection.

As we looked for cleaning gear and checked the place

out, we tapped up anyone we could for more information on what was really going on there. On the one hand, Callan seemed to have had some major successes, taking out hundreds of FAPLA soldiers with this 'killer group' tactic of ambushing, doing the damage and disappearing back into the bush; on the other, there were reckoned to be thousands of MPLA soldiers moving steadily north, already controlling much of the country. I heard later that they had grossly overestimated the FNLA mercenary force. Had they seen what we'd seen, they'd have been pushing towards us a lot faster than they were, especially as the South African forces were withdrawing from the south of the country.

But Callan's successes had gone down well with Holden Roberto. He had carte blanche for how he did things. The worst of this was his treatment of the black FNLA soldiers. According to the lads who'd been talking to some of them, Callan had had dozens of them killed – usually where they stood quaking after upsetting him. They had lost others because of malaria or dysentery – made worse by lack of medical facilities. Deserters, or potential deserters, had been slaughtered too, chucked off a bridge, apparently. Local civilians had fared just as badly, especially if suspected of being spies. We worked out that another group at Maquela were Portuguese mercenaries and gathered that Callan regarded these as a notch or two above the Angolans; in turn, they seemed to be more loyal to Callan. We were told these 'porks' would do whatever he told them to, including getting rid of anyone who upset him. The more we found out, the worse it got.

On top of all this, there was still no sign of the sort of heavy weapons needed to fight a ground war. There was also a complete lack of comms gear. No one had any decent maps, and no one had even seen a compass. There were a few Land Rovers, a couple of light armoured vehicles, plenty of machine guns and ammunition, but the only serious hardware we could see were LAWs, 66mm light anti-armour weapons – our only defence against all those Soviet tanks. We weren't even given basic stuff like knives and forks, blankets or even something to drink out of.

It became clear that the group who'd got here before us were more tightly knit than our lot. I suppose they'd had more time to adapt too. Also, a lot of them already knew each other and had no need to mix with or help us. But enough was said for us to conclude this Callan was the para with a Greek name who'd robbed the post office in Northern Ireland, and he'd only had his current name and rank since he'd been in Angola. The word psychopath kept coming up again too. Away from the others, stripping and cleaning our FNs, we decided the best plan was to act keen, keep our heads down, and look for a way out.

The twenty-odd lads who'd opted out were now on jankers. But it would need a lot more than cleaning to make that place bearable. There was also talk of them being sent back to São Salvador. It looked like they were the smart ones. Before I could draw any more conclusions, we were rounded up, ready to move south towards a place called Quibocolo. We were told this was a base camp. Five or ten kilometres beyond this was enemy territory, with no FNLA presence at all.

Callan had plans for us.

As this was sinking in and we prepared to leave, there was a sudden change of orders. A lot of confusion and shouting eventually revealed that FAPLA columns were on the move, advancing on two fronts. One thrust was towards somewhere called San Antonio do Zaire, to the west of us, where another group of FNLA mercenaries were; the other column was to the south of us. If these advances were successful, we'd be surrounded and cut off. Callan was on fire, balling orders for his own group to get into Land Rovers to head west, where he planned to intercept that advance. Watching the dust of his departure, it seemed like a suicidal response, given what we'd heard FAPLA had to throw at us. Our group was now under the command of Copeland, not much of an improvement from what I could see.

Copeland called us together and told us we'd be dealing with the attack from the south. It was raining heavily by then, following the usual pattern we were learning to expect. Copeland's plan was that we'd drive to Quibocolo that evening, then continue on foot in two groups and use the anti-tank rockets to ambush the approaching column. As he said this, a couple of the Portuguese mercenaries translated it to the rest of their lot and they all exchanged worried glances. Looking around at our group, I could see no one else relished his plan either. Clearly, no one had any confidence in Copeland. The younger lads, especially the ones who'd never served in any army, looked terrified. Copeland found this amusing, then annoying. His only concession to these virgin soldiers was a demonstration of how to use the LAW rockets, followed by some basic weapons training before we set off. At least the rain had stopped by then, but watching some of those kids handle their weapons, did nothing to raise Shane's or my spirits. This was going to be a bloody mess.

Copeland's mission started badly and came to nothing. He intended to lead off with a hand-picked group of his favourites, but that meant there wasn't enough space in the remaining Land Rovers for the rest of us – especially with M40 guns mounted on their truck beds. After a lot of messing around to organise another vehicle, we finally got going on the rutted road, heading south.

All I remember of Quibocolo was a little chapel and the villa that was the FNLA base. Like the other outposts I'd seen, it must once have been a substantial house and was now a ruin. As we waited for the orders to set off again, two mercenaries turned up on foot. I recognised one of them from our flight out there, a guy called Max. I remembered Max because I'd heard him say he'd been in the Foreign Legion. I'd been meaning to ask him more about it because it was one of those things you didn't really think anyone did anymore. After Copeland had questioned Max, all hell broke loose and our great leader and some others piled into Land Rovers and took off without us. It sounded like we might have lost Maquela. No one knew what would happen next. We were left in limbo, finally bedding down in some old canvas and sacking, hoping we weren't going to be surrounded and wiped out too.

The next morning, Callan arrived. Even for him, he was in a foul mood. He hadn't engaged any FAPLA forces, and he'd heard the news of the attack at Maquela. He ordered us back into the Land Rovers and armoured cars and we headed back there with him. Word was going round there'd been a mutiny, not a FAPLA attack, and Callan had already caught the offenders who had been making for the border with Zaire. We were trying to fathom this out all the way back. It made little sense.

When we arrived, we heard Copeland and his crew had been mistaken for FAPLA. Their Land Rover was shot up by the lads who hadn't wanted to fight. The place had been looted and Copeland's attackers had taken off with a load of supplies. We didn't know what to believe, but then Max told us it was right, he'd been in the Land Rover when they were attacked. It was a wreck. How none of them weren't killed or hurt was a mystery. It seemed unlikely that the lads left at Maquela had done all this, but all the evidence was there and it had been confirmed by at least one of the Angolans who'd witnessed it. Besides, if it had been FAPLA that had attacked, we wouldn't be standing there gawping at the bullet holes and mangled metal.

As this all came out, two trucks and an armoured personnel carrier arrived. We were surprised to see the runaways were on board. Callan really had caught them. They stared out at us, doubtless wondering what was going to happen to them. Right then – despite everything I'd heard, and seen, of Callan – I just thought they were in for the shittiest jobs, the worst food and maybe a good hiding, and I had little sympathy for them.

As Callan and Copeland shouted at them to get out of

the trucks, I noticed a few of them still had their weapons, so I decided things couldn't be that bad for them. I was wrong again though. A head count was taken, and it sounded like a couple of them had got away. While this was going on, I realised that the Portuguese mercenaries had circled round the outside of us all and the machine guns on their vehicles were manned and ready. Callan was going to scare the shit out of everyone, that's all, I thought. Wrong again.

As we were lined up to watch, I couldn't help thinking this sorry lot should have made a better job of their escape. I still didn't have much sympathy for them. From what we gathered later, Callan had come across them almost by accident, heard that they'd been attacked by FAPLA at Maquela and was told they'd put up a fight and had to retreat. He'd positioned them along the road as a precaution against another attack before Copeland had turned up. That's when he'd heard there'd been no FAPLA attack and that his own men had been attacked in the Land Rover by a rocket and machine gun fire from the non-combatants.

Something in the way he walked towards them hinted this was worse than I'd thought. Even from where I was, a good ten yards away, I saw the anger and hatred oozing from his face before he bawled at them to drop any weapons they still had. He called forward Copeland and the others who had been ambushed and, indicating them to the line of fugitives, let rip, shouting that these men were worth ten of them. Then he told them the penalty for desertion was death. And even then I didn't think he meant it – he just couldn't, could he? I wasn't the only one thinking that either. Quite a lot of the lads being bawled out weren't looking that bothered. No one had been killed in the 'accident', so they probably thought they were just in for a bollocking. Then it all changed.

Callan had pulled out his pistol and asked who fired the rocket, and a young bloke stepped forward and piped up that he'd done it. I didn't even know his name. Maybe he thought that if he owned up, had the guts to say it was him, he'd get respect from Callan and, whatever else happened, the situation would be defused. It must have been what he thought, because he didn't even look scared. But what happened then still brings a chill to my guts. Callan stepped forward, said something about this being the only law, raised the pistol and shot the poor bastard in the head, following it with two more shots. Everything froze. As this young kid's blood oozed into the ground, I looked at Shane and he looked back at me with the same thought – that didn't happen, did it? But it had happened. We'd just watched a murder, and no one had said a thing.

While this was sinking in, Callan ordered the rest of the escapees to strip and the young lad's body to be got rid of. It really looked like he meant to kill them all. Everyone could see that. Everyone's faces said it. Eyes were staring, heads trying to understand where this had gone. And we knew, we knew from things we'd heard, that the stripping off thing was Callan's prelude to execution. But not right away. First, he called for volunteers to fight. Why everyone didn't jump at the chance, I don't know. They'd seen this lad killed in cold blood – wasn't that enough for them? Four stepped forward. Then Callan asked for a driver and another guy volunteered. Someone else got a reprieve too. That left about a dozen of them. The Russian translator guy, a Scot I think, starts saying something about no one meant any harm. A burst of gun fire at the ground from Copeland silenced him. This was looking worse and worse. Then Callan told Copeland to take them away – that he knew what to do with them. It was horrible to watch as they looked over at us, as if we could do something to help them. What could we do? We looked at the guns pointing at us from all around as they were herded onto the truck to the sound of Copeland's goading, telling them they were going to die.

I still clung to the idea that this was some elaborate charade, designed to get them to fight. But then we'd just watched someone killed, put down like an unwanted animal. We were still reeling from that and didn't know what to believe. Shane's face, creased in confusion and disbelief, reflected this. At the same time, I was thinking why didn't they escape? Was it possible for us to escape? And still, as the trucks pulled away, followed by two Land Rovers, one with a heavy machine gun on it, I hoped they'd be back, shamefaced and toeing the line.

But the trucks came back empty. And with those empty trucks came a horrible atmosphere that settled over the whole place, a depressing mist of despair and fear. You could feel it all around. That and the regret that we'd got ourselves into this unbelievable mess. Callan and his henchmen were objects of silent loathing from most of us now. I'm sure it wasn't just Shane and I that were talking quietly about how to get out of there and how far we were prepared to go to do it, but we kept it to ourselves. I'm ashamed to say we were only thinking of ourselves. It wasn't a mass mutiny we wanted; it was a quick exit with no passengers. We didn't have long to dwell on any of this though. That same day, we were called together and told by Callan we were going to intercept the advancing FAPLA to the south of us. We were soon on our way, passing a grassy sloping valley on our left where we saw clumps here and there, then realised they were bodies lying discarded, crumpled and shattered – the lads who'd gone off in that truck. We could so easily have been amongst them.

# Chapter 11     1979

# Roy

THEY'VE TALKED FOR over half an hour. He'd listened to the Donney and Clive stuff with interest; she'd grimaced at his account of the killings at Maquela. There's more to tell, but Roy knows it's enough for now. He realises it's the first time he's ever told anyone what he'd witnessed. There was so much in the papers about it at the time. And when the trials came up later that year, when it was all regurgitated, there'd been enough people talking about it, enough piecing together of what happened, for him to think his account would add nothing. So he'd kept quiet. It wasn't that he'd planned not to talk of it. After all, Luiz knew he'd been there, and Sally knew he'd been there with Shane. She knew Shane had died there – but that's all she knew. He'd always thought it would get easier to talk of it. It never had – until now.

He wonders what Fiona thinks of him now, and why that matters so much to him. Was it because of what had happened in the shed? No, he decides, it's more than that.

'Being here has helped me decide what to do,' he says as he pours the last of the beer into their glasses. He pauses as the froth settles. 'I'm going to do something for me for a change.'

They listen to the murmur of the TV in the other room until Fiona speaks.

'This place... It's strange, isn't it?'

He looks at her. He knows what she's getting at. Something about coming back here when he did – why?

'Yes,' he says. 'Everything seems connected to here. It isn't, but it feels that way.'

'Even when we've not been here,' she says. She's looking right at him. 'What happened to Ted?'

He's thrown by the question. He understands why she's asked it. It's been hovering around the place for the last two days. He doesn't reply straight away. But she's still looking at him. She's not about to let him off. 'Hettie would tell you if she wanted you to know,' he says finally.

'I'm not sure she can,' says Fiona. 'I'd like to understand.'

It's something else he's never talked about. He looks down at his glass. He's going to refuse to tell her. Then he changes his mind. He trusts her. And who else can he talk to?

'The last time we were here,' he says, 'I was twelve.' He considers this before he goes on. 'When you're that age, you don't understand everything the adults are doing, but you notice things.'

She nods.

'I was adopted,' he continues. 'I'm not saying that

made it any different, but I think in some ways I watched Mum and Dad more than other kids watch their parents. To start with, I used to doubt it could be permanent. I thought I might get taken back to the children's home. Then when I didn't, watching had become a habit.' He stops, not sure if this matters.

'Go on,' she says.

'What I'm trying to say is that the last time we were here, there was something else here with us. I didn't know what it was, just something. None of the adults seemed to be relaxed. And Hettie was different when Dad was around – sort of watchful. Mum was different too, on edge, less fun than she usually was. They were all skirting around each other.'

'And Ted,' she says. 'What about him?'

He looks around the room like he's seeking some inspiration. 'Ted was a strange one. He hardly spoke at the best of times. He was mostly out of the house, doing haulage work for the local farms. He was a loner. He'd sit in the back room in the evening smoking his pipe, listening to the wireless or staring at nothing. He spent time in the local pub too, but I can't imagine him having friends there. He would have been a few years older than I am now, but when I think of him, it was like he was an old man. Him and Hettie just never looked right together.'

She waits for him to go on. He knows she knows he's going to tell her now.

'We used to go to the beach every day,' he says. 'They'd sit and read or Dad would mooch around with me, digging in the sand or paddling. Dad was teaching me to swim too. Usually, Mum and me would set off first. Dad liked to stay behind and read the paper, maybe tinker with the car, before bringing the sandwiches down and joining us. The last day we were here, I'd forgotten to put my trunks on under my shorts. I was just getting my confidence in the water and desperate to swim. I wanted to go back and get them. Mum wasn't keen. She kept saying I could swim in my shorts. I got a bee in my bonnet about that and kept badgering her until she let me run back to get my trunks. I could see she wasn't happy about it, but I didn't care.'

She's watching him closely. He feels her eyes, even when he looks away.

'Anyway, I came back here and heard voices from upstairs – Dad and Hettie. I couldn't hear what they were saying, but I could tell they were arguing. They were in Mum and Dad's room. I don't know why, but I knew something wasn't right, something was happening, something secret. I crept upstairs, intending to get my trunks on and slip out again. The stairs creaked – just like they do now – and they went quiet in the room. Dad came out. He looked angry. Hettie's voice came from behind him, asking who was there. I just wanted to get away. It felt wrong to be there. At the same time, I wanted to know what was going on. He asked me what I was doing creeping about, eavesdropping. His face was strange, like he was scared of me. I knew this was something different, something I couldn't understand, and I knew it was between him and Hettie, but I had no idea what it was.'

'What did he do?'

'Nothing. He asked me where Mum was. I told him

I'd come back for my trunks. He followed me into my room and made sure I got them.'

'It was definitely Hettie in there?' she asks.

'I heard her voice and it couldn't have been anyone else.'

'They were having an affair?'

He doesn't answer. He goes on. 'I went back to the beach. He watched me go. I said nothing to Mum about it. It felt strange. Wrong, I suppose. But she knew something had happened.'

'How?'

'She just did. She could always read me. I was very timid as a young kid. She'd worked really hard with me when I first came to live with them. You have all these child psychiatrists these days – she knew nothing about that stuff – but she made sure she knew how I felt. She knew when something wasn't right with me.'

'But she couldn't have known what you'd seen.'

'I think she did.'

Her forehead creases in confusion.

'She probably already knew about them. I don't see how she can't have. Anyway, when Dad turned up, he hadn't got the packed lunch. I was building a sand castle. He usually helped, but instead kept talking to Mum – quietly, so I couldn't hear. She kept talking too, getting upset. I could see this was no ordinary conversation. Then Mum came over and said we were going back – home, I mean. She said she'd explain later. The way she said it, I knew not to ask why. We walked back here, and I had to sit in the car with Mum while Dad got our things. She was trying to pretend nothing was happening.'

'Had she given him an ultimatum?'

'I think so,' Roy says.

'And that was it?'

'No, it wasn't. As we sat there, Ted turned up for his lunch. He saw us in the car. It was strange. Mum said nothing, but I could see she was worried. He'd been in the house a few minutes when we heard Dad shouting. He wasn't the sort of bloke that shouted much, so that was unusual too. Ted and Hettie were shouting too. Mum went to get out of the car, but Dad was already coming out to us with our cases. He put them in the boot and we were off. That was it. We never came back.'

'But what happened with Ted?' Fiona asks.

'I didn't hear about that for a long while,' says Roy. 'They found him dead the next morning. They said his car came off the road into a drainage channel and he drowned.'

'They said?'

'I don't know for sure. But he knew all the roads round here. He drove them often enough. It probably wasn't an accident. More likely, he killed himself.'

'Did they talk about it, your parents?'

'No,' Roy says. 'Not a word. I think Mum made him agree to that. And I think he regretted what he'd done. He seemed to work hard to get things back to normal. You've never seen a house and garden better looked after than ours did after that holiday.'

The sounds of The Waltons saying goodnight to each other reach them from the TV.

'I wonder why Hettie stayed here after that,' she says. 'Ted and his family were all dead then.'

He considers this. 'She probably had nowhere to go.

And we do these things, don't we? We get ourselves into places where it's just easier to stay.'

The sound of a woman singing drifts down the hallway. A country music programme has started on the TV.

'I know I have,' he adds.

She gives him a tiny smile. He'd like a repeat of what happened earlier. As he's thinking this, the singing stops and they hear Hettie's feet in the hall. They won't be on their own for much longer. Just as well, he thinks. That kind of involvement is no better an idea now than it was earlier. Hettie stops in the doorway, surprised to see them. Roy feels guilty, conscious of what they've been discussing. He wonders if Fiona feels the same.

'There you are,' Hettie says, like she's trying not to show she's registered something.

Fiona drains her glass and gets up. 'I'm going to have a bath,' she says and slips out.

Hettie turns to rinse a cup in the sink. 'She's a good girl,' she says.

'She told me a bit about what she did and about her stepmother,' says Roy.

'None of it would have happened if her dad hadn't taken up with that bloody Margaret woman. I wish she'd come here earlier. If I'd have known...' She turns and starts wiping down the sink.

He senses an opportunity, a chance to get it all out now, tidy it away. 'I told her how it was the last time I was here.'

He wants to know what's on her face, but she keeps her back to him. He needs to finish it.

'She asked me what happened to Ted.'

'He went out drinking. He knew how sharp that corner at Butcher's Dike was. He'd have known what would happen.' She turns, pain straining her face. 'He couldn't even swim. Not that it would have been any good boozed up and trapped in that thing.'

'I'm sorry,' says Roy pointlessly.

'So was I,' says Hettie.

He realises this is as far as she'll go. It doesn't tell him much more, but she's said it.

'Why did you stay after that?' he echoes Fiona's question.

'Out of habit, I suppose. I didn't know where else to go. You probably think that's strange, don't you, staying here in Ted's family's place?'

He shrugs.

'The thing is,' she pauses to frame the words. 'Me and Ted, we were, I don't know, more like a brother and sister who tolerated each other – there wasn't anything else.'

He looks surprised.

'Ted couldn't, or didn't want to,' she says. 'I never found out which.' She sits down at the table where Fiona had sat. 'I promised his mum and dad I'd look after him.' She laughs. 'I'd always thought it would be the other way round when I'd found a man.'

Roy doesn't know what to say. He hadn't considered that until now. He thinks about his mum and dad, what they seemed to have, and how his dad had betrayed her. It seems like Hettie paid the price for that, not him.

'You need to forgive yourself,' he says.

'And you need to take some of your own advice,' she bats straight back at him. She lets him take that in before asking, 'Did Geri get the wrong end of the stick?'

'Yes. She saw Sally and Tina and she thought...' He shakes his head.

'She was bound to.'

She starts putting crockery away. Enough has been said. The room suddenly feels too small. He stands up.

'I'm going out for a walk.'

# Fiona

FIONA DRIES HER hair, pulls on her jeans and tee-shirt, and taps gently on Sally and Tina's bedroom door. She waits, about to give up, when she hears movement in the room and the door opens a fraction. Sally looks out, surprised. Fiona thinks Sally probably thought it was Roy. She feels awkward now.

'Are you alright?' she asks through the gap in the door.

'Yeah, I'm alright. Tina's asleep,' Sally whispers.

'Are you coming back down?'

Sally opens the door a little wider and looks out. Fiona senses she wants to talk, that she's really more shy than standoffish, that she's not as hard as she likes to pretend. She's seen that look many a time – girls starting their first sentence, trying to fit in, trying not to show weakness, trying to look like they're coping when really they're in turmoil.

'Bit early to stay up here,' she says.

Sally hesitates, glances back to the bed, then follows Fiona downstairs. Hettie is humming to herself in the kitchen. Fiona wonders where Roy is. She wonders if he told Hettie what they'd been talking about. It's going to be awkward if he did. She closes the sitting-room door behind them.

Sally sits on the settee. 'Have you ever had to give someone up who wasn't good for you?' she asks.

Fiona sits in the chair by the fire. 'Yes,' she says. 'I have. We'd been apart for a while, but it still wasn't easy.'

'That's men for you: never there when you want them; always around when you don't.'

Fiona smiles at this simple creed. It wasn't quite that simple in her case, but she isn't going to explain, at least not yet. She wants to ask Sally about her man, this Luiz person, but she thinks that would betray Roy. Sally would know he's confided in her. She should tread carefully. But she doesn't need to. Sally wants to talk.

'I think I've been kidding myself,' she says.

Fiona smiles. 'We're good at that, us girls.'

'I don't need all the trouble he's brought me,' Sally goes on. 'I've got to think about Tina.'

'Stay here for a while,' says Fiona. 'It's a good place to think things over.'

Sally looks around the room. 'No offence, but I don't know how you can stand it. There's nothing here. And I want to be in my own place.'

'This place has healed me,' says Fiona.

Sally looks quizzically at her.

'I'll explain sometime.'

Sally looks down at the floor. 'Did you think me and Roy were..?'

'Not really,' says Fiona.

'Don't get me wrong, Roy's alright – I even had a thing for him once. But he never... He had Geri. Then Luiz came along.'

'Did you know she was here this afternoon?'

Sally looks up. 'No.'

'Looks like Roy has some problems.'

Sally gives a hard laugh. 'Yeah, don't we all?'

She's right there, thinks Fiona.

'I know what Luiz does isn't on the level, and I know I've been kidding myself he'll change, but I can't stand that worry any longer – not after this, not after having to leave my own home. It was different when we first met. I had no idea then.'

Neither speaks for a minute or so. Fiona remembers how it was the same with Clive to start with and how relieved she was when it ended, and the pain that followed.

'Roy likes you,' Sally says suddenly.

Fiona looks at her, wondering why she said that.

'You could do worse,' Sally adds.

Fiona ignores the suggestion and risks saying what's on her mind. 'He told me a bit about Tina's dad, about what happened to them in Angola.'

'Then you probably know more than me,' says Sally. 'I never wanted to know. I know Roy's not had it easy, and he's done enough for us. He should do some things for himself now, have something he wants – someone.'

The suggestion is clear. 'Bit old for me,' Fiona says, still thinking about what happened in the shed, about how he was afterwards, then thinking about how her dad was older than her mum.

'He's about the same age as Luiz – and you and me

must be about the same age.'

'It's probably not a good idea,' Fiona says, and picks up the newspaper. She finds the TV page. 'It's the horse show thing on BBC, a documentary on BBC2 and that army series on ITV.'

'I don't fancy any of those. I think I'll go to bed,' says Sally, getting up.

'If you're sure,' Fiona says. She wants Sally to stay. It's still early. She doesn't want to sit there alone.

But Sally is in the doorway. 'Night,' she says, and she's gone.

Fiona switches on the TV. The documentary about parents battling with their social services department isn't what she needs just then. She switches channels. There's some kind of border incident between East and West Germany in *Spearhead*. She watches it for a few minutes, thinking about what Roy had told her earlier, not really seeing him as a soldier, let alone a mercenary. The door opens and Hettie stands for a second looking at the TV.

'Never watched that,' she says crossing the room to her chair. She shivers. 'I'm not all that warm and it's supposed to be July. Roy's gone out for a walk.'

They stare at the screen for a few minutes.

'He told you what happened to Ted,' Hettie says.

Fiona looks over and back at the TV. 'I asked him. I'm sorry if I was being nosy. I just wanted to understand.'

'Did he tell you what happened the last time he was here?'

'Yes,' Fiona says. She waits, expecting Hettie to go on, but instead she focuses on the screen. Fiona knows she's not really watching the programme. She wants to say something about not judging her, but she can't find the words. Besides, it was a long time ago. No one should be bothered, surely.

They often watch TV together in the evenings. It feels different this evening though. Neither of them is taking any of it in. She glances at Hettie's face. Her blank look doesn't quite hide the pain. Her eyes flick to Fiona before she speaks.

'Water under the bridge.'

Fiona doesn't know how to respond. Again, she waits for more. When the silence goes on, and Hettie picks up the newspaper and starts flicking through it, Fiona gets up and turns off the TV. The room is so quiet. The whole house is quiet. She's thinking about Clive – remembering how it had between them, and thinking how it hadn't been as inevitable as she'd once thought. On her side, it was a protest; on his, she couldn't say, even now. Except perhaps he needed someone to perform in front of, someone who'd agree how bad his lot was and how nothing he did was his fault. The thought is broken by Hettie, looking over and suddenly revealing that her thoughts were on the past too.

'Ted never liked them coming here, but they were my friends.'

Another thought occurs to Fiona. She can't keep it in. 'Was Ted ever violent?'

'No,' Hettie says emphatically. 'Never. He hardly ever raised his voice, let alone his fists.'

Fiona thinks there's something missing. She wants Hettie to explain.

'It wasn't just him not serving in the war – though he heard enough about that at the time from people round here – he had no confidence. I could never understand how his mum and dad could be like they were with your mum – and yet with him...' she closes her eyes. 'He was their own, but they were never that kind to him. Later on, I think they regretted how things had been. They knew they should have done more. But he was a grown man then, and it was too late to change him. It was as if your mum was a second chance for them.'

She smiles at her next thought. 'You should have seen their faces when she came back to visit. They couldn't do enough for her.' Her smile drops. 'That must have hurt him. I didn't think it at the time, but it must have.'

'I think she thought of this place as her real home,' says Fiona.

'But she knew other places, you see. He saw nothing, living here,' Hettie goes on. 'If you think it's a backwater now, you should have seen it in the forties – you were something special if you had an indoor lavatory. He even thought because I came from London, I wouldn't marry him.' She shakes her head. 'The hints I had to drop.'

'Why did you?'

Hettie's reply is instant, like it's something she's dwelt on for a long time. 'I was grateful to his mum and dad and I felt sorry for him. And if I'm being honest, I had nothing else. The thought of staying in Dagenham... It wasn't going to be like during the war, working at the factory. I could see that.' Her voice is wavering, going higher with the frustration. 'It would be back to women staying at home, having kids and doing the bloody washing.'

She stops to collect herself. Fiona watches her face

and realises how much pain this is bringing. But she wants her to go on. She wants to know.

'Ted's dad wasn't well then,' Hettie says. 'And his mum said to me I could run this place, that it would pick up again after the war. Ted wouldn't interfere. It'd be like my own business – one day it would be. And it did pick up, and in the end it did become mine because he was dead. They were all dead.'

In the silence that follows Hettie's words, Fiona thinks how this doesn't explain everything.

'It was lovely when your mum came here – and later when she brought you.'

'Mum and Dad came here together too, didn't they?'

'A couple of times,' says Hettie. 'Just after they were married. He wasn't much impressed with this place. He had ambitions. He wanted to forget where he was from, wanted your mum to forget it too.'

'Maybe that's why he likes Margaret,' says Fiona.

Hettie looks over, almost says something, but stops herself. She gets up. 'I'm going to bed.' She turns in the doorway. 'No one needs to be ashamed of how they came to be born.'

Fiona sits puzzling over what Hettie has just said, knowing there's more, noticing, again, how Hettie avoids criticising Dad. She knows from the little he'd said about his childhood, he just wanted to forget it. She recalls how he didn't like to hear her mum reminisce about where they came from. But they'd never have met if they hadn't come from the same place and he hadn't been back there visiting his mother, second mate on a ship that had tied up in the Royal Docks after a run from South America. Did he regret that too? She thinks of the old photos of him, usually in tropical whites, smiling and leaning on the rail, the sea behind. That was him doing what he loved. She compares those images with him now – going to work on the train every day, playing golf at the weekends, entertaining with Margaret, never really looking happy, something eating away at him.

She sits in the silence, thinking it's too early to go to bed, and not wanting to lie alone with her thoughts. Since the wedding, she's avoided sitting alone just thinking. It tends to bring back Jo's words. She'd like to doubt those words, but she can't. And just thinking about them is giving in to Jo, letting Jo get to her. But she can't help it. She's doing it now. Does Jo know that? Did she know that long after they'd parted, her sting would still hurt, would leave her with all these doubts? She considers how long Jo has kept that barb hidden, how many times she must have been tempted to use it and didn't. She puzzles over why she did it when she did – on the day she was getting married – and whether it really was what happened with that wanker on the dance floor that brought it out, or was it just her last chance to do it and she simply couldn't resist it? She'd have said it eventually. Fiona is sure of it.

She has to put Jo out of her mind. She thinks of Lolly instead, how her name had never come up as the informant who'd phoned the police to report her and Clive, giving details of the camper and the route they were taking, the information that got them caught. She knew it was Lolly. Officially, it was a 'member of the public' who'd made that call. Well, Lolly was a member of the public, but she was also her friend. Fiona knows

Lolly did what she did because she thought it would help her. And it did. Once she'd got over being taken into custody, the relief had been so welcome. Even the bed in the cell had felt welcome. Lolly must have felt guilty about what she'd done, unable to face her. Worse than that, she'd been unable to tell her about Frieda and her. Strangely, that felt worse and Fiona realises she felt more pain from that reluctance than the phone call to the police. Why did Lolly not know Fiona would understand? Why did she cut herself off like that? She misses that friendship. That gap is still unfilled, that wound is still open and hurting.

She can't move from the chair. She goes over everything again and again, but the conclusion is the same: she has to talk to her dad and she has to talk to Lolly. These are the things that will let her move on. She's pondering this when the phone rings. She gets it to it as Sally's bedroom door opens upstairs. It's a man's voice, with a slight accent. There's no preamble.

'Is Sally there?'

# Chapter 12     1976

## Fiona

THE TEMPORARY FEELING of wellbeing from my swim and the long, hot shower vanished as I drove us out of Berwick–upon-Tweed. We'd needed petrol and Clive had got in the back out of sight while I'd filled up and went inside to pay. I was already wary of places where I was the only customer, where the person serving might take more notice. I'd got my hood up and my scarf as far up my chin as I could without it looking too suspicious. But having seen that newspaper, and then noticing a stack of copies as I approached the counter, I felt like I had a sign on my head with my name on it. Everything I did felt like a risk. When the grizzly old man behind the till looked at me, I couldn't meet his eyes. There was no one else on the forecourt, so I didn't need to say which pump it was and just held out the right money.

'Not the best weather for camping,' he said, with a nod outside towards the van.

I was going to say I wasn't camping, make up some

story about visiting a friend, but I just forced a smile instead. 'No, it's not,' I said and turned and tried not to hurry for the door.

It felt like he was watching my every step towards the van. I wondered if from my few words he'd noticed my accent and known I wasn't local. Even if he hadn't, he'd remember the camper van. I took my time getting in. I didn't start the engine straight away. Clive asked me what I was doing. I pulled gently away before answering.

'Trying not to look like I'm in a hurry. He noticed the van. It's only a matter of time now before someone recognises us.'

He shuffled forward and into the passenger seat.

'They don't know we're in this,' he said.

He was trying to sound convincing. He wasn't fooling me.

'It's not enough,' I said. 'We're visible. We're driving around all the time and we don't have any money left. They know we've gone north. Everywhere we stop, we're strangers; and in small places, people notice strangers.'

Before I'd seen that paper, we'd decided to get off the A1 and go towards the coast. We hadn't even decided where. It seemed too random now. We needed to be out of sight. Then I thought of Lolly. She'd still be at her brother's house. From her last letter, it sounded like it was out of the way. The address was easy to remember – Highridge, Burnsall. What would she think? There was a good chance she'd either seen the stuff in the papers or someone had told her, maybe someone from school, maybe Frieda. As I looked out at the road, I considered it. I thought of the scrapes we'd got into at school, how she regarded the authority of the teachers as no more than a game that you played any way you could. She knew how it had been at home for me. She'd understand what had happened, I was sure of it. I just had to convince Clive. I tried sowing some seeds.

'What we need,' I said, 'is somewhere to hold up for a while, get off the road out of the way. Newspaper stuff blows over. They'll be some other thing next week they'll be focussing on. We just need to be out of sight until they do.'

He looked over at me. 'Yeah, but where?'

I told him about Lolly. I didn't say we should go or even could go. I let him take it in. I knew with Clive that was the best way. By the time we'd turned off for Eyemouth, he'd got the map out and found Burnsall. He'd seen the sense in the idea.

'Let's do it,' he said. 'Turn around and go back down the A1. We could be there by late afternoon.'

We had enough petrol to reach Lolly's place. We found a quiet place to stop before we got to Newcastle and ate a cold lunch. Then we drove without stopping. Having made good time, we then spent half an hour trying to find the house. It had been a grey day, and the light was already fading. I didn't want to stop and ask anyone. I was trying to hide my fear that we'd never find it. Then, just when I was about to suggest abandoning the idea, thinking that the van going backwards and forwards on the roads around the village would surely attract attention, I saw it. The sign 'Highridge' had almost fallen over, but we'd found it. In a dip off the road, surrounded by farm buildings, mostly falling down, the stone farmhouse had a light burning and smoke coming from the chimney. I suddenly realised how much I'd missed contact with other people. It struck me then how I'd probably spent more time with Lolly than anyone else I knew except Mum. Why hadn't I made the effort to see her more since we left school? Maybe if I had, I wouldn't be in this mess.

Pulling up in the yard set a dog barking and I remembered Lolly had said Richard hadn't told her she'd be looking after his brown labrador, Beans, as well as the house. The back door opened and Lolly, holding Beans by the collar, peered out. Then she saw me and I knew from the worried look on her face that she knew what had happened. When we'd let go of each other and I'd patted Beans and introduced Clive, she confirmed it.

'Is it true? The stuff in the papers...'

'Mostly,' I said. 'I'm sorry to turn up like this.'

She hesitated. 'It's okay.'

She'd glanced at Clive, a touch uncertain. That bothered me.

'Could we stay a few days? Until things quieten down,' I asked.

Again, she glanced at Clive. Neither of them looked comfortable. It irritated me. They'd never met, never spoke, yet they didn't like each other.

'Would that be okay?' I was trying not to sound as desperate as I felt then.

'You're welcome. You know you are.' She looked towards the van. 'Maybe park that in the barn, out of sight.'

Clive was looking sulky as he went back to do what she'd suggested. I followed Lolly inside. She'd told me in her letters that her brother had bought the place with grand plans to renovate it and make the most of the views. Then he'd taken a job that involved long periods in New England and the renovation work had stopped. The result was a mixture of new, needing finishing, and old, needing an awful lot of work. She apologised for the mess as we avoided the building materials on the way to the kitchen, where the big stone fireplace had a good fire in it. Judging by the sofa, the chairs and the TV in there, this was where she was living. For the first time in ages, I felt warm and safe.

Even then, as Lolly asked me what had happened, and I tried to explain, I was trying to remember if I'd mentioned where she was living to anyone, anyone who the police might have talked to. I decided I hadn't. We were reasonably safe for a while. She didn't pass judgement, but I could see she was shocked by what we'd done, and I found I couldn't explain it away anymore. I was about to blurt out what a big, stupid mistake I'd made when Clive joined us. If I'd started saying it, I wouldn't have been able to stop. I told myself I had to get a grip and think this out.

Lolly made us all drinks, pulled a couple of worn chairs close to the fire for us, and started telling me how she'd ended up there, how her brother had plans to raise rare breeds of sheep and how then, like with the house, he'd lost interest again. She seemed to have taken over his plans with the sheep. I knew she loved animals, but this was a surprise. As she explained about the breeds, I could see Clive glazing over with boredom.

I asked her which Frentons' girls she'd heard from and we swapped some news about them. I noticed she didn't mention Frieda. I was puzzled. I concluded they must have fallen out and didn't ask. Clive looked distinctly out of it by then. I tried to explain who we were talking about and the background to various escapades, but it made no difference. He hardly spoke. He no longer had me all to himself, and he resented it.

Lolly picked up on the signals and asked us about the van and where we'd been. It almost worked. We almost had a three-way conversation for a few minutes. She said there was a spare room we could have, the only other decent room apart from where she slept, warning us we might find it cold. She said she'd take up an electric heater and try to air the bed. I said it would be fine and no matter how cold it was, it couldn't be worse than it had been the last few nights. I was wondering if I could face another night in the van ever again.

'It's not the van, it's the crap weather up here,' said Clive, sounding offended.

Lolly's reply didn't help. 'You get used to it,' she said. 'It's lovely in the summer.'

'I don't want to get used to it,' he said.

I knew then it was a mistake going there. It felt nice to be somewhere solid and safe. But it couldn't work. How long could we stay, and what then?

We brought our things in from the van, along with all the food we had left to pool with Lolly's fairly slim supplies. There was enough for a somewhat mixed meal of fried eggs, sausages, boiled potatoes and carrots – not unlike some of the concoctions we made secretly at school. I could tell Lolly was thinking the same thing. I said nothing though. Clive's set features put me off launching into any more stories of Frentons. Despite this inhibition, being indoors, eating in that warm room and then helping Lolly wash up, felt so homely and normal. I was still glad to be there.

Going to bed was strange. As Lolly was explaining about the immersion heater, and saying if we wanted separate baths we'd have to wait a while for the water to reheat, I realised it was the first time the intimacy of my relationship with Clive was being seen, or perhaps acknowledged, by anyone else. That we might share a bath highlighted it. For the first time, I was embarrassed in front of Lolly, the person who had shared my most intimate thoughts. It was odd. It was a kind of break point, a transition from being schoolgirls to being women maybe. I didn't refuse the bath. My shower in the swimming baths at Berwick seemed like an age ago, when it had only been that morning. And it was a chance to think, to absorb my doubts.

After that, and after saying goodnight to Lolly, Clive and I were back together on our own – and it felt strange, not as inevitable as it seemed in the last few days. We were together in that square, solid, stone-walled bedroom with its bowed ceiling and stubby door, in the big iron-framed bed that must have been left there when Lolly's brother bought the house. It was one of those beds where children were conceived, then born; where they would have eventually died many years later – the entire circle of life in those few square feet. Yet, while we were in that bed, in that house, nothing physical happened between us. Clive made no response when I cuddled up to him. He lay still, flat on his back, and eventually we fell asleep.

We lasted just two nights at the farmhouse. In that time, the friction between Clive and Lolly steadily grew. My frustration grew too. Having got somewhere safe and comfortable, he wasn't even prepared to give it a try. We weren't burning money in petrol, we weren't skulking around avoiding people – all he had to do was stay put, relax and let some time pass. I was sure we'd make better plans when we weren't just driving from place to place. But Clive couldn't see that. And he couldn't share me with anyone, especially someone who'd known me much longer than he had, that understood me better than he did. And I knew Lolly; I knew how she was when she didn't like someone. I could tell she found him shallow and abrasive. It annoyed me – annoyed me because she was right. I tried hard not to let my conversations with Lolly dominate things. But with Clive saying nothing when she was around, it was hard not to talk just to her.

On the first morning we were there, Lolly had to go to Skipton for groceries. Her brother had left her his old Volvo to get around in. She asked me if I wanted to go with her and I said yes before thinking. When I told Clive, he got angry and sulky.

'I thought you wanted to stay out of sight. Now you're going to prance around the shops where everyone can see you.'

'If I'm with Lolly, no one will pay attention,' I said. 'They're looking for a couple. Anyway, it would just be nice to do something normal for a change.'

'So I'm not normal, is that it?'

'I didn't say you're not normal. I just thought...'

'Yeah, you thought you'd just leave me here.'

His petulance and his childish tone were getting to me. We were alone in our bedroom at the time and I couldn't stop myself. 'Don't be so fucking childish! You won't stop breathing if I'm not here. We'll only be a couple of hours,' I said.

'I'm fucking childish! You're the one talking about your stupid schooldays.'

I'd tried to keep my voice down, but he was shouting, then, accusing me of wanting to chuck in the towel, of being weak, of wanting everything to be easy. I walked out and closed the door on him. Lolly must have heard. When I got to the kitchen, she tried to defuse things.

'Maybe I should go on my own. I don't want to cause problems.'

'No,' I said. 'I'm coming with you. I need a break from him.'

I knew from the way Lolly hesitated and bit her bottom lip that she wanted to say something.

'What?'

'Are you sure you're doing the right thing?'

She didn't mean about going with her to Skipton.

'I don't know what else to do,' I said. 'It's like I got on a roller coaster and I can't get off.'

'You can get off,' she said.

I knew what she meant. She could drop me at a police station and the whole thing would be over. Until then, I hadn't even thought about that. From then on, I thought about it a lot. But I didn't say so. I didn't admit it, not even to her.

'Let's just get that shopping,' I said. 'I'll talk to him later.'

Walking around a few shops with Lolly was like being camouflaged. The dread that I was going to be recognised at any second had vanished. Suddenly, I was legitimate again. We could talk freely now. I told her what had happened at home. I told her about my job and more about Clive. As I explained, I realised more and more what a stupid situation I'd got myself into. When I told her that the gun wasn't real and how he'd got it, she seemed relieved.

'If the police know that,' she said. 'It might not be so bad.'

We were putting the shopping in the car. It was the first time I thought seriously about giving in. I'd just had a taste of something like freedom and I didn't want to go back to those feelings of persecution.

'I doubt it will be that simple,' I said.

'Where does he keep it?'

'In the glove compartment,' I said.

When we got back, Clive wasn't in the house. For a few welcome minutes, I thought he'd just upped and gone. And that was another turning point. After a pang of fear for him, I suddenly felt relief. I didn't know what I'd do, but I felt an immense weight had lifted. It hit me I could spend a few days, a week or two even, with Lolly and then give myself up. It had suddenly become easier to do that. It was like the sun coming out after a rainstorm. After looking around the house for him, I went out to the barn. The van was still there. Clive was sitting in the driver's seat, staring ahead at some imaginary road. He glanced at me and looked ahead again. I got in the passenger seat. Him just sitting there like that tore at me. His almost helpless state, him being who he was, just being him, bit at me inside. I waited for him to speak. I noticed how cold the van felt and, again, thought how I didn't want to spend another night in it.

'I can't stay here,' he said, finally.

I didn't want it to turn into an argument. I made myself wait a couple of seconds.

'I just want us to be safe,' I said. 'I'm sorry you don't like Lolly.'

'It's nothing to do with that,' he snapped back.

It was everything to do with that, but I let it go.

'I feel safe here,' I said. 'Can't you just wait a while, just to let things die down?'

He turned to look at me.

'Please,' I said. 'Just give me a bit more time.'

I got out of the van and he followed me back into the house where Lolly pretended nothing was happening.

When we sat down to eat, Clive was more talkative than usual. He had a plan.

'Ireland,' he'd said. 'Southern Ireland.'

Lolly kept her eyes on her plate. I didn't reply. I was wondering where his idea came from.

'You don't need a passport,' he said, 'and we can take the van over. We'll be safe there. If we could get some cash before we go – one last time, a decent haul, we could get a ferry, head somewhere quiet – maybe find a place to rent for a while.'

Lolly glanced quickly at me. Clive caught the glance and looked at me for my response.

'Let me think about it,' I said.

I'd have said anything to stall him then. I didn't want that discussion in front of Lolly. He gave me a hurt look. He must have thought I didn't need to think about it, shouldn't need to think about it. But I just wanted to buy some time. I hadn't thought of it before, but I was thinking more and more about how it would look for Lolly if we were found there, as unlikely as that seemed. It would be kinder to her if we did go. Maybe then I should give myself up – before anything else could happen.

'We can talk about it later,' I said.

# Roy

WE CONTINUED SOUTH, passing through Quibocolo where two of our group were dropped off and two more Land Rovers joined us. Every mile on that dusty, rutted road was a mile closer to the MPLA forces. We were heading towards them and they were heading towards us. It couldn't be long before we met. There must have been fifty or sixty of us in that group, crammed into maybe eight Land Rovers – a piddling little force compared to what we were going to meet. But it wasn't just an overwhelming enemy we had to fear. There were landmines on the road – our own bloody landmines. And Callan's solution to this? An armoured car in front, followed by his Land Rover, then the rest of us, keeping in the same tracks – about as half-arsed as you could get. This was his style: macho, headstrong and fearless to the point of stupidity.

Three men paid the price for that stupidity, even before we saw any FAPLA. I don't know what happened exactly. Maybe a vehicle up ahead disturbed a mine and moved it into the path of the Land Rover in front of ours. Maybe the driver in front was an inch or two out of line; either way, a mine ripped into the vehicle in front of us and tossed it into the air. Some of the lads in our Land Rover didn't escape when lumps of metal blew back at us. Shane and I were lucky; the others shielded us from the shrapnel. The engine had taken a hit too and was spouting hot coolant. By the time we'd scrambled out and worked out there was no one firing at us, there were three dead and eight or nine with serious injuries. We'd not even seen the enemy, and we'd lost blokes already. A great start to Callan's offensive, I thought, as we piled the bodies and the wounded into one Land Rover to be taken back to Maquela. Did Callan think again? Did he change his plans? Did he hell. We squeezed into the remaining vehicles and carried on just as before.

We stopped frequently. When we did, I could see Callan standing up in his vehicle using binoculars to scan ahead. At one stop, taking the chance for a quick piss, Shane turned to me and said he was worried about what would happen to Tina if he didn't get back. I tried to laugh it off, saying we'd be okay. Then, making sure no one could overhear, I said we needed to look for a chance to take a vehicle and get out of there. He nodded in agreement and said he'd be ready.

The road we were on went to a place called Damba. Aerial surveillance suggested FAPLA had been sighted along that road. And what were we going to do? Drive straight for them and make a frontal attack, Callen-style, that's what. These tactics had worked for him in the past, and he had no doubt they'd work again. So that was his plan. Then, the next time we stopped, the atmosphere changed. Tension rippled down the convoy as word was passed along that the MPLA's army was just ahead. I thought we'd pull off the road. Instead, we drove like maniacs right at them.

Callan and Copeland were out of the vehicles in front of us firing rockets at the approaching tanks, while the rest of us tried to get some cover to use our machine guns. We were lucky – at least to start with. The audacity of the attack really had taken them by surprise. The poorly organised return fire and the headless chicken display – evident even through the smoke and dust – worked in our favour. FAPLA soldiers were being killed wholesale. However much hardware they had, they couldn't have had much training or experience with it. It seemed they were firing as much at themselves as they were in our direction.

But they did have tanks. Even if their foot soldiers were incompetent, a lumbering monster of a Soviet T34 can take a lot of stick. Our M40 guns with their anti-tank rounds weren't having much effect, so the 66mm rockets had to be used. To give them credit, Callan and Copeland took two tanks out fairly quickly. A third, an even tougher T54, I think, took longer. It eventually succumbed to a close-range rocket, but not before one of its shells hit the Land Rover carrying most of our ammunition. That shot reaped a massive explosion – injuring three blokes, including the one who'd had the guts to run forward to make the killer rocket shot.

Chaos doesn't describe it. Then, just when I thought this was the end, that we couldn't be that lucky for much longer, that they'd surely regroup, work out the size of our force and take us out, Callan shouted to everyone to get back in the vehicles and get out of there. Shane and I did good impressions of keenness, keeping up our firing until the last second, not even trying to hit anything or anyone. Then you couldn't see our arses for dust. They even didn't come after us – lucky, again.

It was back to Maquela, where the newly injured were joining the first lot at the rudimentary hospital. Apparently, it was easy to find. You just had to follow the sound of the screaming – there was no morphine or anaesthetics. On the journey back, exhaustion replacing the adrenaline, we did what we could for the poor sods that had been hit.

As soon as we were on our own, we started planning our escape. We'd already noticed some of the Land Rovers had more jerry cans than the others, and we'd earmarked these as the best escape vehicles, intending to be in one or near one of them next time we went out. And there was going to be a next time. Despite the losses, Callan wasn't put off. We were told we'd be doing the same again the next day.

We got the rest of the night to recover. But the following morning, as we contemplated our next outing, wondering if we'd survive it, there was another example of Callan's psycho behaviour. We heard him shouting at someone, then a gunshot. From what we could make out, he'd lost it again and another poor sod had died. In this case, a local baker who Callan thought was cheating him on prices. Then we heard sobbing as the baker's two sons discovered what had happened. Another mindless, unnecessary death that made getting that vehicle and getting away the only thing Shane and I could talk about and think about.

Callan's thoughts, though, were on adding more tanks to his score. He also had a bulldozer in his sights. Apparently, this was being used as a makeshift mine sweeper at the head of the main FAPLA column. He knew taking that out would seriously slow down their advance. This time, the plan was to dig in on the road ahead of the column and ambush from cover. It sounded a fraction less suicidal than the last effort. The fact we got comfort from that shows how desperate things were. Then we heard this was to be a smaller group, twenty-odd blokes. Knowing how unimpressed Callan had been with our non-para, non-SAS credentials, we assumed we'd be left out. But we weren't. Maybe because we'd kept our heads down and toed the line, or maybe he thought we were disposable – I don't know which – but we were included in the group, and that evening we set off towards Damba again.

Our destination was an old banana plantation, a landmark on the road. Just before we reached it, we hid the vehicles in the scrub and continued on foot. We stopped and got set up on some high ground overlooking the road. I was glad of the rest. I was sweating into yesterday's stale sweat. I realised I wasn't as fit as I should have been. The sound of a couple of jeeps had us all at the ready, but they were on their own and we were told to hold fire. We were waiting for the full convoy. And we waited all night. Someone said they'd heard the MPLA's army didn't move at night. They were probably right because the first activity came the next morning. Two truckloads of soldiers passed along the road. Again, we were told to wait. Again, the convoy didn't follow. Callan had seemed certain it was on its way, but then he decided he wouldn't wait any longer. We packed up and moved on to meet it.

It was nearly evening when we saw the bulldozer. There were trucks and tanks behind it and I thought this was it; we'd attack it head on. But Callan took us on past it, through the bush, and back towards the following vehicles. He'd decided on a different tactic: attack from behind. From the cover of the undergrowth, we let loose with everything we had – automatic fire at the trucks and rockets at the tanks. I don't know what I hit or who I hit, but there were flames and smoke everywhere. I could hardly see anything. Callan was jubilant, taking pleasure in picking off the last few poor bastards trying to get out of the tanks or the trucks. Suddenly, it was all over. The crackle and stench of burning was all that remained. The transition was disturbing and unreal. I was at the end of my rope, praying that was it and we'd head back.

But we didn't. This long FAPLA column that Callan had been told about was very spread out. What we had hit was one section of a forward party. There was a lot more to come and Callan wasn't satisfied. We cut into the bush, parallel to the road and back in again where another tank and two trucks were trundling north, seemingly unaware of what had happened up ahead of them. We attacked. It was an action replay and the tank and trucks were destroyed. Again, we melted back into the bush. But this time, vehicles behind had been alerted and were advancing at speed. There was just enough light to see a couple of trucks and three Soviet-built armoured scout cars, known as BRDMs, heading our way.

Again, we were lucky. Again Callan and Copeland took delight in finishing off the survivors. By now, I was punch drunk; incredulous I could still be alive, and also strangely united with the others that we'd survived this with. I didn't think I could have any adrenalin left. I could see Shane felt the same, shaking his head in disbelief and saying 'fucking hell' over and over again to himself. That unity was the only thing I had to cling to, to keep me going. That so many others were dead, and we weren't, seemed to cut through the exhaustion, and I was torn between a weird exhilaration and overwhelming regret. I didn't have long to contemplate this though. We were heading back into the bush again, this time back the way we'd come. Callan still wanted the bulldozer.

His obsession with that machine drove us on, and at any cost. At a jog, the noise we made, and our kit made, felt disproportionately loud. I was sure we'd be heard and wiped out. When we got close enough to stop and peer through the gloom, the bulldozer was more or less where we'd last seen it. There were at least two other vehicles, one of which had the unmistakable outline of a tank. Callan was soon firing off 66mm rockets at it. They had little effect. However, the crew were soon out and on their toes, and one of our Portuguese blokes gave chase, firing at them as he ran. All of a sudden, a menacing shape roared into view – another tank. A shell from its turret blew the Portuguese mercenary's head clean off. It was a horrible sight. I watched it in what felt like slow motion, my mind gradually processing it through the numb fear that I was getting used to.

Before any of us could do anything else, a mortar landed between us. I was sure it fell close enough to Callan and Copeland to have killed them, but no, like some indestructible ghouls from a horror film, they were okay. I think Callan had been about to fire another rocket towards the FAPLA trucks, and what I think happened next was he managed to get it away. The only explanation for the huge explosion that came next was he'd hit their munitions supplies. There was a roar, a massive expansion of air, flying debris, and a sudden wave of heat that slammed into us. I'd already got flat down, but Shane had been crouching in front of me. He flew past me in the tide of the blast.

Despite not feeling any pain, I was certain I was injured. But I wasn't – not that I could tell straight away. I turned to look for Shane, sure he must be badly hurt, ignoring the shreds of clothing and the strange, spongy wet stuff that I didn't recognise as anything human. There were fragments of metal everywhere. They'd blitzed towards us, missing me but cutting through Shane. But he wasn't there. On my hands and knees, I went around this mess on the ground, straining to see in the smoke that was still coming from the FAPLA vehicles, until I found his gun with something attached. It took me a few seconds to realise was his arm. Even then, I thought I'd find the rest of him alive.

The rest of him – when what I was seeing got through to my brain – was a scattered mass of bones and bloody tissue. By then, muffled noises, screams and shouts were filtering through the fog that had filled my head, and I was becoming aware I couldn't hear again. I could just make out some movement from our side, behind the wall of fumes and dust. It looked like some of the others were regrouping. I was the furthest away. I couldn't make out who the others were or where they were going.

Before I could decide what to do, the sound of approaching vehicles came from the direction of the main column. There was no way the rest of their force didn't know what had happened. They were on us. As the firing restarted, I knew this was my last chance. My thoughts weren't with Shane at that moment, I'm ashamed to say. I either went then or I stayed and died – and I went, as fast as I could, further into the bush, as far from the road as I could get, stumbling in the dark, blundering but moving, moving anyhow, anyway, until the gunfire and explosions receded and I just lay on my face, smelling the earth, clutching onto the ground, glad to be alive.

And that's where I stayed for the rest of that night. My rifle was far behind me. I had about a quarter of a canteen of water and the few things I kept in my pockets, including the passport I'd hung on to. That creased wedge of pages gave me hope, the possibility that if I could get far enough from that carnage, there was a chance of getting away. Pictures came to me as I lay on that earth: the single bed I'd despised in my old bedroom, Sunday lunch on the table, watching TV on a cold winter's evening. Even routine life in the army held a warm, reliable glow, a warmth I craved just then. But those visions couldn't block out the image of Shane's scattered body parts, and the realisation I was going to leave him there, his remains, the bits that were once him, in that place so far from anywhere we knew. As the cold of the night seeped into me, those thoughts and that guilt persecuted me – I was alive and he wasn't.

But when the sun came up, and I felt myself thaw, moving cautiously to look in every direction, trying to orientate myself with the road somewhere behind me, I told myself I wasn't to blame. If I wanted to stay alive, I had to move. I had to move north. I had to keep out of sight and just move and survive. I had no food, but the frequent rain of the wet season meant I should at least be able to get water. I had some money and I had my passport. And although I was finding cuts and bruises I wasn't aware of before, I was intact. I couldn't change what had happened, but I could stay alive.

What would the FAPLA soldiers do if they found me? Would I count as a prisoner of war? I doubted it. They'd soon know I was part of the group that had ambushed and killed their comrades. I knew nothing of these people, this mixture of Cubans, maybe even Russians, and the Angolans they were supporting. Those Angolans would see me as an invader, someone who'd come to do them harm, only there for money. How would I feel in their shoes? And there was the FNLA too. Callan could be alive. I was a deserter now. I knew what he'd do if he found me.

# Chapter 13        1979

# Roy

ROY WALKS BACK towards the café. It's dark. A few groups of holidaymakers are walking back to the caravan park, laughing and joking with each other. He envies their high spirits. He's done a slow circuit of the village. He knows he needs a plan. The only plan he'd had when he'd set out involved that money. He'd thought it would solve everything. But this is nothing to do with money. He knows that now. It's about not knowing what he wants, being stuck in the past, and going along with what someone else wants. He knows that has to change.

He stops when he reaches the back yard, lingering a few minutes, not wanting to go to bed yet. He knows he won't sleep. There's too much in his head. He takes the last few steps to the back door. Hettie's given him a key, but he doesn't need it. Someone's still up and there are voices in the kitchen.

Fiona stands at the stove stirring a saucepan. Sally sits at the table. There's something about the way Sally looks at him. She's got something to say. He knows it. But it's Fiona that speaks.

'Do you want some hot chocolate?'

He hesitates, like it's a difficult question, mind still tuned to Sally, wondering what she's going to say.

'Yeah, okay. Thanks.'

She adds more milk and cocoa powder to the pan.

'Luiz phoned,' says Sally. 'He got your message.'

Her voice is tight. She's angry that he didn't tell her he'd got through when she hadn't.

'Is he okay?'

'He's got a flight tomorrow evening,' she says. 'He's going to Angola.'

'Where is he now?'

'In a hotel – somewhere near St Pancras.'

Roy knows there's more though. He knows from the way she's got her hands flat on the table.

'He's got to get his passport first,' she says. 'It's at your flat.'

She must realise how risky that will be. The people he's upset know where he lives. He can see in her eyes she's asking him to do it. She waits for him to speak, but he doesn't. He needs to think about it.

'He needs your help,' she says.

She gets up, keeping eye contact with him. 'Please, Roy.'

He can't refuse. 'Alright,' he says.

'We're coming with you. We're going home.'

'Not until it's safe.'

Sally glares at him. He doesn't respond. He expects her to step things up. He doesn't want this in front of Fiona.

'It's nearly ready,' says Fiona.

'It's okay, you have it,' Sally says as she walks out.

He sits down. He's annoyed. He's trying not to show it.

'I thought it might help her sleep,' says Fiona. 'She's really worried.'

'So am I,' he says.

'She's torn between helping Luiz and doing the right thing for Tina.'

'And I introduced her to him. She'd have been better off if I hadn't,' says Roy, more to himself than her. But he's thinking maybe this is good, or it will be good if Luiz leaves her behind.

'What's he like?' she asks.

'Luiz does his own thing,' says Roy. 'She should know that by now.'

'You said he got you out of Angola. Did he come back with you? Is that what happened?'

'No,' says Roy. 'He had stuff to do. Luiz always has stuff to do – some scheme or other.'

'But he left in the end,' she says.

'Yes,' says Roy. 'He went back to Portugal. I don't know if you know about it, but a lot of the Portuguese left after Angolan independence – before even. They'd had it all their own way until then. They had the businesses and the money, but when their government started pulling out and the native Angolans started fighting amongst themselves, most of the Portuguese wanted out too. The whole place fell apart.'

She finishes making the chocolate. She pours two mugs, puts them on the table, and sits opposite him.

'No,' she says. 'I don't know anything about that.'

'It was chaos. Portugal had just gone through a lot of

political changes. They'd granted Angola independence without thinking about what would come next – same old story. In the 1950s they'd encouraged their people to go out to Angola to build up the colony, get the minerals and diamonds and grow coffee and stuff. The country made a lot of money for Portugal; they grew a lot of food there before the civil war. Then, when they pulled out, they didn't want their own people back. There were hundreds of thousands of them. They even limited what money they could take out with them – I mean, what they could exchange, something like a hundred quid. So you had all these people high and dry.'

'And Luiz was one of them?' She asks.

'His whole family,' says Roy. 'They were smart though. Before the worst of it, his old man started converting what they had into cash and buying rough diamonds. He knew they were more portable, and he'd have a better chance of getting them out. But he hung on too long. Mainly because Luiz and his sister didn't want to go – it was their home, it was all they'd known.'

He pauses, like saying this is helping him understand it. He looks to see if she's interested. Her eyes say she is.

'It had been a good life for the Portuguese who'd made it in Angola. Even they knew that. His dad had gone from a clerk in an export office in Portugal to a coffee grower in Angola – then an exporter with his own transport business. Luiz and his sister went to the best schools. They had everything. Anyway, his parents and his sister got on one of the last flights before air travel became impossible. Luiz stayed to finish the deals, get the rest of their diamonds, and make his own way out. But he had bigger plans. With the chaos of the war, he knew he could get a lot more diamonds on the cheap. The locals wanted other things just then – like to stay alive. He'd seen a way of getting rich quick.'

Roy contemplates this for a few seconds. Fiona waits.

'I'd given him my mum and dad's phone number, never expecting to hear a thing. Over two years later, Mum told me there'd been a call from him.'

'And had he made loads of money from diamonds?'

Roy snorts. 'Oh yeah, and then blew it all on some stupid schemes and was wanted by the police. That's not how he told it at the time though – that's what I got out of him later. Anyway, he was in London. He said he wanted to meet up. Later on, he said he needed my help.'

Roy blows on the hot chocolate. 'I don't think I've had hot chocolate in August,' he says.

She smiles, waiting again.

'It turns out he'd legged it here with a few hundred quid and a few bits of clothes. He'd paid someone to get him over on a cargo boat and he was on the run. But he had a plan – Luiz always has a plan. He said he still had his contacts in Angola. He was going to get a big haul of uncut diamonds from them. He knew someone who would fund it. He said if I helped him, we'd both soon be rich.'

'So what happened?' Fiona asks.

'I felt I owed him. He was on his own in a strange place and needed help – like me when I first met him.'

She's looking at him, waiting for him to go on. He wouldn't normally want to talk like this, tell someone how things had been for him. But with her he does. He wants to say it all.

'To start with, he just wanted somewhere to stay. I was moving out of my flat. I said he could have it until the rent ran out. I thought, hoped, he's be off again by then. Then he got in with some other Portuguese guys. They got him some work, cash-in-hand stuff, and his big plans kept getting delayed. I was glad. I was hoping it was all bullshit, and he'd forget it.'

Roy gets up and stands with his mug, looking out of the kitchen window at the shadows in the yard.

'Of course, he didn't forget it. He was working on it the whole time – working out how to get the diamonds to London. Meantime, I'd introduced him to Sally. I could see he liked her, and she seemed to like him.' He turns to Fiona. 'Stupid thing is, I thought that would settle him down. He'd chased around after a couple of girls since he'd been over here, but they weren't what he wanted and then he was constantly asking me stuff about Sally.'

'And his diamonds really turned up?' Fiona asks.

'Yeah, they did. And he needed someone to take them to Antwerp. He said he couldn't do it himself. That was bullshit. He was hiding from someone he'd upset. He didn't say I owed him, but he didn't have to – besides, I'd get twenty grand for doing it. I'd moved in with Geri and was working for her dad – and it wasn't what I wanted. That money was a chance to do something different.'

'What went wrong?'

He turns away from the window. 'Luiz fell out with his backers over their cut. They wanted half. He said that wasn't the deal. He said it was twenty-five percent.

I went to Antwerp, not knowing that. By the time I'd got back, he was being chased all over London. They'd even been to Sally's place to find him. They knew a lot more about him than he realised. That's when I brought her and Tina here.'

She's looking at him. He thinks he knows what she's thinking.

'Yes, I was bloody stupid,' he says. 'I knew enough about Luiz not to get involved and enough to have warned Sally. But I did neither.'

'Do you know what you're going to do?'

She's still looking right at him. She's not just asking out of curiosity. She seems to care.

'Yes,' he says. 'I'm going to go back tomorrow and find him. Give him back his money and tell him to pay off whoever's after him and bugger off back to Portugal.'

'What about Sally?'

He sits back down. 'She'll have to wait until things calm down.'

'What will you do then?'

'I don't know,' he replies. 'Back to my old flat and look for another job, I suppose.'

They sit in silence for a while. He's thinking it's all been about him. He wants to know about her. The prospect of not seeing her again hits him, disturbs him.

'What about you?' he asks. 'Do you have plans?'

It's her turn to get up and look out of the window.

'You mean what am I doing in a place like this?'

'There's nothing wrong with here. I just thought...'

He regrets asking her outright. Maybe she doesn't want to say.

She rinses the saucepan before turning back to him. 'I haven't made any plans. That's my problem. I haven't made any decisions. When I was inside, I used to think of all the things I'd do. When I got out, I stopped thinking about them. All I thought of was not ever going back.'

'That's a pretty good start,' he says.

She shrugs. 'Maybe.'

She looks back outside. It seems like she doesn't want to say any more. He doesn't want to push her.

He gets up. 'I think I'll turn in.'

There's a part of him that wants to say more though, tell her she's got some good qualities, that being here with Hettie has brought some good too. And the way she'd looked into his eyes – did she want to say more? He can't tell. He waits for a few seconds, embarrassed by his hesitation. He's suddenly aware again of the difference in age between them. It was stupid to think she might feel anything for him, he thinks. She doesn't need his problems; she's got plenty of her own. He should go. He turns to the door.

'Good night.'

'Good night,' she says.

When he reaches the top of the stairs, he regrets not saying something else. What? How much he likes her? How he wishes things were different? He listens as he passes Sally and Tina's door, certain that Sally is lying awake worrying. He should go in and say something to her. But he can't. He knows too much to allay her fears about Luiz.

He visits the bathroom. As he cleans his teeth, he thinks he can't blame Geri for jumping to conclusions.

He owes it to her to explain, even if it means telling her more, telling her more about Luiz, explaining about Sally and Tina too, about Shane even. When he gets into bed, he can't get any of it out of his head. When he next looks at his watch, it's half past two. He knows what he's going to do. He retrieves the bag of cash and stuffs it into his holdall. He packs his clothes on top of it and, passing the bathroom, shoves the rest of his stuff in. Going down the stairs in the dark, he remembers to avoid the squeaking tread. In the kitchen, he writes a note for Hettie. He takes forty pounds from his wallet and puts it with the note on the table. Then he's out of the back door, locking it and taking the key round the front to drop through the letter box. As he starts the car, he wonders if Hettie or Fiona will hear it. He wonders if Fiona will wish he hadn't gone.

# Fiona

SHE HEARS HIS car. She's been awake for the last hour. The thought of him going has made her feel empty, like she's missing something already. She's been thinking of their conversation. Not just what he'd told her, but what he'd asked her – how it highlighted her lack of direction. His question has exposed that void, that chasm that she's tried to ignore. It was easier to start with. Being there had been like some kind of extended working holiday, somewhere she'd gone to leave her troubles behind. Now it wasn't. Her troubles were still with her. Now she must pull things out into the open, things that have festered in corners, corners she didn't want to visit.

Earlier, when she'd got into bed, she'd counted the walls between her and Roy. Four, she'd decided – a short walk down the first landing, up some steps and along to his door. She'd wondered if he was asleep. Was he thinking about her or just his own troubles? What if she got out of her bed and took that short walk to his door? But she'd known she wouldn't. Now he's gone, she can't stop thinking of the things trapped in those corners of hers. He'd asked her what she was going to do. As the sound of his car dies away, she knows the answer, knows what she has to do. It's just a question of how.

A few hours later, when she gets up, she doesn't know how much sleep she's had. Not much. She can feel it in her forehead and behind her eyes. It's too early to go downstairs yet, but she knows she won't get back off. She needs to do something. But having other people in the house inhibits her. She resents them being there now, but at the same time is glad of it – someone else in the same space as her, someone with their own cares and worries. And hearing Hettie talk about Mum being in this house all those years ago, and now with another little girl being there, like she was there at her age, brings a whirl of thoughts and memories. But they're overlaid with the questions of what she's doing there now and what she's going to do next. It's no different to when she left Holloway, paying attention to Angie's advice not turn and look back at the place. She didn't, but she didn't know where her life was going then and she still doesn't.

She listens to the birdsong getting louder as the light breaks in around the curtains. She's thinking of how Dad had been waiting outside Holloway prison for her, and how it felt to be out on that grimy street, the air feeling so different. It was a raw day, but she didn't notice the cold, she just felt that different air. He'd wrapped his arms around her and held her. For the first time since she'd heard about Clive, she'd cried. He'd steered her to where he'd parked the car and they'd driven the hour or so across London, hardly speaking. After they'd crossed Blackfriars Bridge, he'd asked her what her plans were, and she'd had to admit she hadn't made any, just that the Probation Officer might help her get a job, that she wanted to get one as soon as she could. She didn't say she wanted to get her own place as soon as she could, that she was dreading living with Margaret and Jo again, that Hettie had persuaded her to go home and give it a try. He wouldn't have known that. He'd said they should 'take things easy' and that 'things would work out.' She'd wanted to believe him.

She remembers when they'd rounded the corner and she'd seen the house had new windows and the rendering was painted a snowy white. The front garden was different too. The grass and the flower beds her mum used to weed were gone. Instead, ornamental gravel and miniature conifers had been planted in a geometric pattern. The resurfaced drive had a newish VW Golf on it – Jo's, she'd guessed. She'd been hoping Jo and Margaret would be out. Margaret usually was at that time of day, shopping, getting her hair done or something, and Jo should be at work.

As Dad opened the new front door, she'd realised her old key was no use to her. She'd looked at that key earlier that morning when she'd got her things back. Mum had given her that key. Its purpose had just gone. That silly little detail worried her just then. Getting that key had been a landmark, a sign of trust.

Dad had taken his shoes off. Down the hallway, Margaret came to the kitchen door. Behind her was Jo. They were both wearing coats, on their way out, it seemed. Had they waited for her arrival or had they hoped to miss it? Standing there together, they'd presented a united front, sending her a message. But she met their gaze with ease. They didn't know they were kittens compared to the women she'd spent the last two years with. Jo looked away. Margaret didn't.

'We're on our way out,' she'd said.

Dad had stood awkwardly. Fiona knew this was embarrassing him. The way he'd moved aside to let them get to the door said he was also annoyed. She'd noticed the thick new carpet under her shoes, and realised that's what she could smell, an alien smell after the disinfectant on the hard floors of Holloway. Margaret and Jo were slipping on their shoes at the door. Fiona knows Margaret was irritated that she hadn't taken hers off, that she'd stood on her carpet at all.

When the door had closed, he'd had breathed out. 'I'm sorry. They've got to get used to it.'

'Get used to me?' she'd said. 'This was my home before they ever came here.'

'I know, I know,' he'd replied. 'Just give it a chance.'

'I don't have much choice, do I?' she'd said.

'I'll make us some tea,' he said.

She'd wondered if she'd find her room had been cleared. But it hadn't. The bed was bare but the rest of her things seemed to be there, just as she'd left them the morning of the robbery, never thinking she'd not be back that evening. Someone must have been dusted it at least. Probably Dad, she'd decided. Her suitcase – bought for the holiday in France, the year she left school – was still there too. For a second, she'd wanted to fill it with whatever she could take and walk right out. But she didn't. She put down the two carrier bags she'd brought from Holloway and curled up on the bare mattress.

Fiona swings her legs out of bed, admonishing herself for letting that memory creep up on her, knowing if she lies there any longer she'll just be thinking about Dad and Margaret. Since talking to Hettie about it, she's been blocking out the thought of them being together before Mum died. She knows that ignoring it isn't the answer. She thinks he could have phoned her after what happened at the wedding. She could have phoned him. She'd rather speak to him face to face now. He can't know what Jo told her. That nasty little revelation of hers has built the wall between her and Dad even higher. It feels insurmountable. When they do speak, she knows she'll ask him if what Jo said is true, although she's already sure it is. But she has to ask him anyway. The urge is growing stronger. And no matter what he says, whatever excuses he gives, she can't imagine ever forgiving him.

She looks at the clock. It's seven now. She dresses quickly and goes down to the kitchen. Hettie looks up expectantly, like she's alerted by her being there a little earlier than usual, sensing something from the way Fiona's moving.

'Roy's gone. He left a note and some money,' she says, taking down a cup for her.

'I heard him go,' says Fiona. 'He was talking about leaving last night.'

'What are those two going to do?' Hettie gestures up towards the front of the house.

'He'll be back for them, I'm sure,' says Fiona, wondering if he really will.

Hettie pours Fiona's tea. 'How about you? Everything alright?'

She knows, thinks Fiona. She knows I didn't want him to go. But instead of saying it, the other thing comes out.

'I want to see Dad.'

Hettie meets her eyes. 'Then you should.'

'I need to sort things out, say things. I need to hear him say things. I think he was seeing Margaret before Mum died – Jo said something before I left the wedding.'

Hettie is still looking at her, like she's taking a measurement. She nods slowly. 'Don't be too harsh, will you?'

Later, Fiona wonders why Hettie said that. She asks, 'Will you be alright if I go?'

Hettie starts setting the table. 'You don't need to worry about me. I'll be fine. And whatever you decide to do, it's okay.'

Again Fiona wonders what she means. 'Can I take the car?' says Fiona.

'Of course you can.'

They hear small feet on the stairs and Tina appears in the doorway. She'd done the same the previous morning, got up before Sally and sat in the café for breakfast, taking it all in. Iris isn't in until midday, so Hettie will soon be cutting and buttering and putting bacon on the grill. Her bacon rolls are popular with passing drivers. Tina has decided it's her favourite breakfast ever. The regulars will talk to her and she'll enjoy the attention.

'I know what you want,' says Hettie, following her through to the café.

Fiona sits staring at her cereal bowl, aware that when Sally comes down she'll probably ask where Roy is, notice that his car has gone. Fiona wants to go now too, now that she's decided. But she can't leave Hettie to explain to Sally. She has to persuade her to stay put until Roy gets back or calls. She gets up. She should tell her now.

Upstairs, she taps on the bedroom door. Sally calls out for her to come in. Fiona closes the door behind her. Sally sits up in bed and looks at her. She's expecting something. Fiona feels it. She gets straight to it.

'Roy's gone back to London.'

Alarm on Sally's face turns to determination. 'I'm not waiting for days for him to take us home.'

'I'm sure he'll be back soon,' says Fiona.

Sally doesn't reply. There's a focussed look on her face, not aimed at Fiona.

'I've decided to go down myself,' says Fiona, hurrying on. 'I want to see my dad. I'll probably be gone overnight. Will you be okay here?'

Sally does not reply immediately. She seems to be processing things still. 'I don't want to seem ungrateful, but if he's not back by tomorrow, we're leaving.'

Fiona knows better than to argue. She senses Sally has more determination than she lets on. She'll go back if she wants to.

'Where's the nearest station?' Sally asks.

'Not all that near,' says Fiona. 'I can give you a lift there when I get back. Come down and have some breakfast. Tina's having hers in the café.'

Sally smiles for a fraction of a second. 'Bacon roll,' she says. 'Then she'll want to go to the beach. I don't know if I can do it today. I don't know if I can do anything. Luiz has messed me up.'

Fiona goes to the door and hesitates. She'd never intended to tell Sally, but maybe she should. Maybe Roy already has.

'Has Roy said anything to you about me?'

Sally looks confused. 'In what way?'

'That I was in prison before I came here?'

'What? No.'

'Well, I was. The only reason I'm telling you is because I was mixed up with this bloke. I thought, or maybe I convinced myself, he was what I wanted. I ignored everything else. I ignored what he was really like, the way he looked at things. I pretended it would all be okay.'

Sally waits for more.

'We did a couple of robberies – stupid, unnecessary, pointless things that I went along with. We got caught. I know things aren't exactly the same for you, but what I'm trying to say is that it's easy to delude yourself. It's really easy to go along with something that's not right.' She stops. She doesn't know this woman. She might be presuming too much.

'I've been thinking about it a lot,' Sally says. 'I know he's not what I really want. But he brought something into my life. I wanted someone. Looking after Tina on my own... I just wanted someone.'

'I can see that,' says Fiona.

'But I don't want this.' Sally gestures at her bags on the floor. 'I'm not living like this, hiding away.'

Fiona opens the door again. 'Roy will be back for you. He said he would.'

# Chapter 14    1976

# Fiona

AS SOON AS we were alone in the bedroom, Clive was back on the subject of Ireland. This time, he would not be put off.

'It's our best chance,' he kept saying.

'I don't know anything about the place,' I said, thinking he didn't either, not wanting to say it.

He gave me that look of his, the downcast eyes, the petulance that I'd noticed in the last couple of days. He was brewing his response. I waited. I hated those silences when he turned my words sour and threw them back at me.

'You'd rather stay here with her,' he said, finally.

'No,' I said. 'I'd rather not take any more risks.'

'So just stay here? How long can we do that for? Then what?'

'I don't know,' I said.

'But you want to stay here,' he persisted.

This time I didn't answer him. I got undressed and into the cold bed. He used to warm our bed in the van before I got in. Now I was doing it. He stayed by the door, keeping his back to me, like he wanted to go right then. For a few seconds, I thought he might, and I knew I wouldn't try to stop him.

'You know she fancies you, don't you?' he said, turning to look down at me.

He had this twisted little smile on his mouth. The stupidity of it goaded me.

'That's rubbish,' I said. 'I'm her friend. That's all it's ever been. We're good friends.' I nearly say he wouldn't know what that was, but I stopped myself.

'You sure? Nothing else at school, all those girls together in the dorm?'

It was all I could do not to snap back and tell him how pathetic that jibe was. 'In your imagination,' I said instead.

Still, he didn't undress. He started putting things in his bag. 'Tomorrow morning, I'm going,' he said. 'You can please yourself.'

When he got into bed, he made sure he didn't get close enough to touch me. But I knew I'd go with him. Not for him and not for me – but for Lolly. Besides, Clive was right about one thing – we couldn't stay there forever. I was worried what could happen if we were caught there. I couldn't keep that thought to myself.

'Lolly could get into trouble over us,' I said into the dark.

'We're not getting caught,' he said.

'But if we do, promise me you'll not say we stayed here.'

'What do think I am?' he said.

I didn't answer him.

The next morning, I went downstairs to find Lolly. She'd just taken Beans for a walk and was pulling off her coat in the hall. I said we were going. She ushered me into the chilly living room, with its polythene-covered furniture and rolled-up carpet, and closed the door.

'*You* don't have to go,' she said. 'It's stupid, what he's planning. You're going to get caught. Let him go.'

She couldn't have heard Clive say he'd go on his own, but she seemed to know it – and she knew me.

'Stay,' she said.

I wanted so much to stay and I nearly said yes.

'No,' I said instead. 'We'll be okay.' I opened the door and went back out to the hall. 'Thanks though, thanks for everything.'

Clive watched me pack. He said nothing. But I could see he was pleased. He even made an effort to talk to Lolly over breakfast. He had the map book from the van and outlined the route to us. He'd decided on Holyhead for the crossing. We'd head down to Preston, then Warrington, then West into Wales.

As soon as he'd finished eating, he brought our things downstairs, saying he'd bring the van round the front and we could get going before there was any traffic around. I felt sick inside. The brief respite, the comparative comfort, and seeing Lolly again, had all fed my doubts. As I said goodbye, Clive sitting with the engine running, staring straight ahead, all I wanted was to go back inside and sit in the saggy armchair by the fire and drink tea and talk – and Lolly knew it.

'You don't have to go,' she said again.

'I do,' I replied and gave her a big hug.

She held on to me, whispering quickly in my ear. 'I've taken it.'

She let me go. Clive was pulling away before I'd even closed the door.

We stopped for petrol somewhere near Clitheroe. I'd lain down in the back until we were on our way again – our old routine. Except it was different. I wanted someone to see us. I wanted it to end. We'd just spent the last of our money and we wouldn't be getting on any ferry until we had some more to buy tickets. Then, when Clive went to get the gun, it wouldn't be there. I wanted to tell him that, but we'd hardly spoken since we'd started off. Before, we'd talk all the time or sing along to the radio. Today I wasn't hearing the music; I was hearing regrets inside my head and wishes that I'd stayed with Lolly, and I was worried what Clive would do next. After we'd been on the M6 for half an hour or so, he broke into my thoughts.

'This'll do,' he said, taking the exit for Wigan.

Like me, he could only have known the name. He couldn't have known the town itself or where to go. He just headed for the centre. We drove through, looking around us. Every face that looked our way when we stood in traffic seemed to dwell on us, like they knew who we were. I'd started to hope one of them would recognise us and call the police. Off the main road, we meandered around the side streets. Clive was looking for somewhere to park, somewhere he could get back to quickly and get away onto a clear road out of town. Still, I couldn't tell him the gun was gone. Then I noticed he was looking into the mirrors a lot. I turned to see what he was looking at. There was a car behind us, a large saloon, a Ford Granada, I think. At the next junction, Clive made as if to take us left, then swung right and looked again in the mirror. I turned again. The same car was behind us.

'Fuck!' he said.

He didn't have to explain. The front seat passenger was talking into what looked like a radio. We were back on the main road at that point. It would take us out of town. I remembered the big railway bridge when we'd come that way earlier. As we went under it, Clive was accelerating as fast as the van would let him. It was pointless. The car behind was still there, easily keeping up with us. When the siren started up, it was no surprise.

'Bastards!' Clive swerved out as the car nosed out behind to overtake.

'This is stupid, Clive. Pull over!' I said, more scared by the look on his face than by the car behind us.

'No fucking way,' he said.

The van was shaking with the effort.

'They'll catch us anyway. Please Clive!'

The road narrowed, leaving no space for the car behind to get past us. Ahead was a line of stationary traffic and we weren't going to fly over it. Clive scanned around for a way out. There wasn't one. I could hear another siren ahead. This time it was a marked police car. It was cutting a path through the traffic, getting ever closer to us. Clive slammed on the brakes, reached over and opened the glove compartment in front of me. He pulled out a bag of sweets, his woolly hat, and a rag.

'Where the fuck is it?'

'I don't know,' I said.

He looked around, like it was going to materialise from nowhere. The approaching police car was so close I could see the determined expressions on the officers' faces looking out at us. It was over.

'Come on!' Clive shouted, opening his door and turning to me.

I didn't move. 'No,' I said.

He hesitated and looked around him. Behind us, the Granada's doors were open and voices were calling for us not to move. Another siren was growing louder as a third police car came from behind. Clive took a last glance at me and broke away. I sat tight and waited. He got a few hundred yards before he was rugby-tackled by an enthusiastic young constable. He struggled for a token few seconds and was handcuffed and taken to the second police car. A voice shouted at me to get out and show my hands. I complied and the plain-clothes officer who approached regarded me for a few seconds, maybe sensing my relief, knowing I wasn't going to make a fuss.

I told myself I wasn't going to call home, that I'd got myself into this and I should take the consequences. But when I was offered my phone call, the chance to talk to Dad broke that resolve. The tears came as soon as I heard his voice. He told me not to worry and not to say anything until he'd arranged a solicitor. I was expecting a full-on interrogation, like in the police dramas on TV – the good-cop, bad-cop routine, trying to trick me into talking. But it wasn't like that. The Wigan police were waiting for the Met officers to take over and weren't all that interested.

Late that afternoon, after they'd given me two lots of

sandwiches and tea, two CID officers arrived from London. I heard Clive shouting in the corridor outside the cell I was in. He was swearing at someone, and it sounded like they were restraining him. I'd just been told that the questioning was going to happen back in Beckenham – it seemed like Clive was refusing to go. When he'd been dragged off, I was put back in handcuffs. A local female officer had been conscripted to accompany me to Beckenham, and I was taken to a car. I'd been expecting a grim van with a cage inside, but they must have kept that for Clive.

The CID officer and the female officer ignored me for the entire journey, over five hours, apart from when we stopped at a services for a toilet break when she confirmed Clive was following in a police van. The rest of the time, the CID guy chatted to her, taking the micky out of her Lancashire accent and trying hard to impress her with his tales of what he'd done in the Met.

At Beckenham police station – a place I'd only ever passed on the High Street – we drove round the back and I was led through the door from the car park. Dad was already there with a solicitor, and I was on my way down a well-trodden path of interview, magistrates' court, bail application (denied), and remand until trial. Later, I heard Clive had remained uncooperative, refused to answer any questions, and had given constant trouble to the police and the prison staff. I, on the other hand, admitted everything, and told them everything – except how Lolly had given us shelter.

I was relieved when Lolly's name didn't come up. It wasn't until I got my first remand visit from Dad – when he told me she'd phoned him after anonymously calling the police – that I realised how we'd been caught so easily. From Lolly's description of our route, they'd picked us up on the M6 and had been behind us for miles before we'd turned off. They even knew the gun was only a starting pistol, and it wasn't in the van. At the time, I was angry with her. I knew she was trying to help me, but I'd have preferred to have given myself up. I liked to think I would have done when Clive had gone off to do another robbery. But I didn't get the chance. She'd messed things up for me.

When I discovered my remand time would be taken off whatever sentence I would get, I said I didn't want to appeal the bail refusal – the sooner I got this over with, the better. I had to accept I was going to be a prisoner for a good while. My whole existence, my every thought and every daily action, had suddenly changed, and I was numb from that change. To begin with, I just sank into that new life. I wallowed in it and forgot how life had been before. It was a crude form of self-protection, but it was all I had. They say that an English public school is a great preparation for life in prison. I came to understand that a girls' boarding school like Frentons was a pretty good preparation for a women's prison.

When I first arrived at Holloway, discovering that news of mine and Clive's exploits had preceded me, I found a mix of respect, derision, sympathy and outright hostility. There were friendly smiles from some and hostile stares from others; offers of help with knowing the ropes and scowling faces thrust into mine, telling me to 'get out of my way posh bitch'. Although I'd noticed how Jo had adopted a different way of speaking at school and Clive had teased me about my accent, I'd never thought about it until then. The idea of keeping below the radar proved more difficult than I expected. Yet I found I was shedding my accent day by day and, paradoxically, calling on my skills from school to get through each of those days – trying not to count them.

# Roy

I WORKED OUT I was something like forty or fifty miles from the border, a fucking long way to walk. If I was lucky, very lucky, I could do it in two or three days. Water would be essential, and something to eat would have been nice too. But just staying out of sight was most important of all. Anyone left from our group would be heading north too, and that long column of FAPLA definitely was. I had no idea how far they'd moved since I'd seen them, or how many more were still to come, but I knew they were coming.

The road I was following was my only chance of escape. I couldn't risk being seen on it, but I couldn't stray far from it either. I already knew what the bush on either side was like – I wouldn't be moving very quickly. Keeping that road in sight was my only hope – and my biggest worry. It wasn't easy. That road wound around, crossed rocky ravines and dips in the landscape. It passed lots of places where someone could hide, and lots of places to get caught.

I told myself that thinking about that long journey

wasn't the way to do it. I had to break it into sections, an hour or so at a time. I'd have to stop and rest when it was hottest, and move on when it was cooler. I also knew I'd have to pass through Quibocolo and then Maquela. My guts felt hollow at the thought, but I had to do it. That was the plan as I walked on, keeping that road in sight. In places, the elephant grass and the tough terrain made it slow going. Two days? No, probably more. I made myself keep walking. At times, the sights and sounds of the previous night hovered around me. Flashes of that explosion – Shane's limbs and organs on the ground, lifeless, yet once alive, once parts of him – obscured my view and made me reckless, stumbling faster to put it all behind me.

Whenever I could force those memories away, I felt extra edgy, listening, worried that my own footsteps might mask any other sounds, any chance to hear someone else's movements. At one point, I thought I heard a helicopter. Whoever it belonged to wasn't going to help me. I dived under some bushes and tried to decide where it was. It faded, and I was wondering if I'd imagined it. Lying there, having stopped moving, the images and the sounds came back, and I just wanted to curl up and stay there. I let the fatigue take me. I dozed until I heard Mum's voice telling me to wake up; it was time to get up. I was in my bed at home. Then I wasn't. The fear was back. I got up and walked on.

My canteen was empty since I'd started walking. I'd been looking for a stream to fill it from. Focussing on that, pushed the other thoughts away. I made that my first goal, and it worked – I had a target. But as the day went on, the heat increased and my thirst increased with it. I was sure I'd seen water courses on our trip down there. Now I was wondering if I had. Just when I thought I'd die of thirst before anyone killed me, I saw a line in the landscape off to my right. I headed towards it and found a fast-moving stream and stuck my head in it. I drank – probably too much too quickly – and filled my canteen. Then I got my clothes off and sat in that stream and my willpower came back. I could do this. The images hadn't gone, but I was further away from them. I just had to hold on, ignore the hunger and keep increasing that distance.

I found a shaded spot near that stream and rested. Then I pushed on. If I was going to make any headway, I couldn't afford to be too choosey about my route. But the landscape had opened up, and I was more exposed, constantly listening, and searching ahead for anywhere I could hide at the first sound from the road. I was soon just focussing on the next few hundred yards, then the next, then the next. I thought I remembered passing through a small village after we'd left Quibocolo on the journey south. If I was right, I knew I should see it soon. Before I did, on a track intersecting with the road, I saw something else and my guts clenched up. – a Land Rover ahead of me, stopped in the middle of nowhere.

It was on the first track I'd seen that ran east to west, which crossed the road. There wasn't much cover anywhere around it. I had the road to my left, the open scrubland to my right and the Land Rover in front. I crouched down, wishing I had binoculars to get a better view. At first I thought it had to be FNLA – FAPLA had Soviet vehicles, and this was definitely a Series II Land Rover. It was blue, but that didn't help as the FNLA had a mix of blue and green vehicles, with only a few in daubed-on camo colours. But it had a proper cab and most of ours were open. I could only see one person near the vehicle. He was standing at the front, lifting the bonnet. If he was FNLA, then he was on his own. Did I know him? I couldn't tell. While he had his head under the bonnet, I moved as close as I dared and lay flat on the ground. Now I could see he wasn't wearing anything like a uniform – even the hotchpotch kit we'd been given. He wasn't dark-skinned enough to be a native Angolan either. I couldn't see anyone else in the vehicle and, adding everything up, I decided to chance it and get nearer still.

He didn't seem to have any weapons on him. The only thing I had was a trench knife I'd picked up at Maquela. I don't know to this day if I could have used it on him. Maybe if it had been my life or his? I can't say. I got it ready though. When he pulled his head back from under the bonnet, I was still a good few yards away. I'd wanted to be closer. I'd decided my best chance was to walk right up to him before he could reach into that cab and get a gun. But he either sensed I was there or he heard me. He turned quickly.

'Hello,' I shouted. 'I don't want any trouble.'

He hesitated. His dark eyes looked suspiciously at me. He must have wondered what this scarecrow was doing approaching him in the middle of nowhere. I lifted up my hands. It didn't seem to reassure him. He watched nervously as I approached. With his dark wavy hair and beard, he looked like one of the Portuguese FNLA mercenaries. I said one of the few Portuguese words I knew.

'Amigo.'

His expression relaxed a tad, but his eyes stayed locked on me. I wanted to say something else to reassure him, but I was assuming he wouldn't understand me. Then he surprised me. The English came out with almost no accent.

'What do you want?'

'Nothing.' I gestured to the open bonnet. 'Engine trouble?'

He ignored that. 'Are you FNLA?'

Good question, I thought. My hesitation was all too obvious. We looked at each other for a couple of seconds and I took a chance. He was on his own; his vehicle was out of action; he didn't seem to have a weapon. What could he do to me?

'Not any more,' I said.

He just nodded. Some of the tension left his eyes.

'It cuts out,' he said, gesturing to the engine. 'First just a little and now I can't get it to run at all.'

'I can look at it,' I said.

'Can you?'

'Yes,' I said and closed the last few yards between us.

He smiled and held out his hand. 'I'm Luiz.'

'Roy,' I said, and we shook.

He found a roll of tools in the back. While I checked the engine, getting him to turn it over with the starter, he told me he was heading north east 'to collect some things'. He was evasive about what and where. But when he said there had been no fighting in that area, I knew this was the best chance I was going to get.

The Zenith carburetor was my ticket out. There was a lot of crap in the petrol out there. I already suspected it was just a blockage. I got a good spark on the plugs and petrol was getting to the carb, so I removed the air inlet, stuck a rag over it, and got Luiz to turn the engine over a few times. After a bit of spluttering, the crap got pulled through and she started to run. Luiz was smiling all over his face when I put the inlet back and the engine was ticking over steadily. Now it was payback time.

'This place you're going,' I said. 'How near is it to the border?'

'There's no proper border crossing up there,' he said cagily.

'But you're going near to Zaire?' I said.

'Yes,' he said.

He produced some almost stale bread, a kind of dried meat thing and some warm beer. I hadn't tasted anything so good in a long while. He watched me wolf it down.

'I could do with a lift,' I said. 'And you could do with someone to keep this thing going.'

'Alright.' He chucked the tools in the back. 'Jump in.'

Despite the heat and the dust of that track, sitting on that battered old Land Rover seat, no longer trudging along on foot, was bliss. What's more, we were heading in the right direction – away from everything I wanted to forget. A bouncing dirt track never felt so good.

I soon noticed he had a compass and a detailed map. It was the only map I'd seen of the place so far, and a good one at that. I drank it in. This was what I needed. He'd marked out a route. It went east to a pencil cross, then north east to a second cross, then north into Zaire. I'd struck gold. He noticed the attention was giving it.

'Yes, I'm going to Zaire,' he said.

He still didn't elaborate on the purpose of his journey but, over the next couple of hours, I found out a little more about him and a lot more about Angola. If I'd have met him a couple of weeks ago, somewhere far from here, I'd never have done that trip with Shane. Luiz gave me a summary of the politics of Portugal, the history of how Portuguese families like his came to be there, and how independence had ruptured their lives and the lives of the native Angolans too. More than that, he confirmed what I'd already concluded – the FNLA would soon lose their finger-nail grip on that part of the country and anyone left behind had better be on the winning side. The way he explained this had me wondering about him even more, and I had to ask him where he'd learnt his English.

'My father had a shipping business here,' he replied. 'He wanted me to take it over one day, and English is the best language for shipping. He paid for me and my sister to learn.'

We'd just made a back-jarring detour where the trail had fallen away. He concentrated on getting back on course, working that heavy clutch and the tricky change into second gear. I tried to fathom how far we'd gone on that pencil line. The petrol tank on those things held less than ten gallons, and I doubted we'd get twenty miles to the gallon. Even with the half a dozen jerry cans in the back, I was wondering if it was enough. I was hoping those cans were full.

We stopped to confirm we were where the first cross was marked on the map. He'd written some notes on the back and he looked at them, scanning around, checking the compass until he was satisfied. It looked like he knew what he was doing, and I was bloody glad of it. I was also glad when the collection of mud huts with thatched roofs came into sight at the intersection of two trails – his second cross on the map – and he said we weren't going to drive on in the dark.

A native Angolan woman came out of one of the huts as we pulled up. A man appeared behind her and gestured for her to go back inside. He waited for Luiz to get out and they had a conversation in Portuguese. Luiz returned to the Land Rover and took a bundle from under his seat. The man took it inside the hut and returned a few minutes later with a small package. There was a lengthy, animated conversation as Luiz insisted on something and the man shrugged and kept turning back to his hut and then returning to argue. I'd got out to stretch my legs. Luiz gestured towards me and the man looked scared. After more discussion, half-a-dozen jerry cans were produced and exchanged for our empties. While this was going on, the woman reappeared with three or four kids in tow. They all stood and stared at us before the man shouted something and she pointed to one of the other huts. Luiz got some kit from the Land Rover and we went inside.

The man hadn't wanted to give up the petrol that Luiz said was part of the deal. Luiz had told him I was FNLA and he'd better not argue. At that stage, I knew nothing about diamond smuggling or that I was in the area where it was a daily business. After the woman had brought us a spicy stew that sent me looking for more water, I asked him what this deal was. All he said was that it was about survival, his family's survival. He had a package of diamonds he needed to get out of the country. Then he asked me what was my story.

I told him about the lies that had brought me there, and how my naivety let me believe them. I gave him a summary of what I'd seen at Maquela, but I missed out what happened to Shane. It was too early to speak to anyone of that. I finished by saying I just wanted to get home and asked him where I could find the British embassy in Zaire. He made a doubtful expression with his mouth.

'Do you think that's a good idea – that they won't have questions for you?'

'I don't care,' I said.

'I've heard what the FNLA has done. Did you not see how scared that man was? You think no one will be interested in what you were here for?'

I still didn't care, but I said nothing. I was going to turn myself in to the embassy and take my chances.

'You said they didn't have your real name,' he said. 'There's an easier way for you to get home – without all that trouble – and with some money too.'

'How?'

'I have a passage arranged from Pointe-Noire. You could take the diamonds to Antwerp for me.'

'I thought you were doing that,' I said.

'I was, but the old man said he can get me much more. And I know where I can get the money from. This could be something really big.'

'Why would you trust me?' It was only curiosity that made me ask. I had no intention of doing it.

'I don't know,' he said. 'Maybe I shouldn't.'

'I just want to get home,' I said.

'Maybe that's why I trust you,' he said. 'Deliver these and you go home with a thousand dollars in your pocket.'

He must have known from my face I was tempted.

# Chapter 15     1979

## Roy

HE STOPS ONCE on the entire journey, just long enough for a pee and a cup of coffee. He's hungry and he knows there won't be anything to eat in the flat. But he wants to get this over with, get that passport, get it to Luiz and get back on the road. And he knows he should go carefully. There could be someone watching the place. Given the flimsy lock on the door, there could even be someone waiting inside. The thought brings back the memory of a night out with Shane, stumbling up the stairs, realising both their keys were locked inside the place. Shane had knocked at their downstairs neighbour's door and borrowed a kitchen knife. That's all it had taken to spring the badly fitted latch. The memory hurts, the thoughts of those crazy nights out, the laughs, Shane's impetuous behaviour filling the place. And now, how empty it is without him, how nothing of him is there anymore.

He parks a couple of streets away. He plans to approach from the other side of the road. If there's anyone sitting in a car, he's going to keep on walking. He considers what to do with the holdall. He'd never imagined money could feel such a burden. He leaves it in the car, deciding it's as safe there as taking it with him. As he turns the corner into the street, blue lights are flashing outside the flat. It feels like a cruel trick, a pernicious replay. His feet stop without his control. An ambulance is up on the pavement and a police car is in front of it. A few of the neighbours are getting a good eyeful. He recognises Tony and Ruth from downstairs and they spot him. Tony is talking to a police officer. Behind them, two medics manoeuvre a stretcher through the door. He can't see the face, but he knows who's on that stretcher.

He forces his feet across the road. All he can see of Luiz's head is his dark hair matted with blood. But there's an oxygen mask on his face. He must be alive.

'Is he alright?'

'Let us pass, mate,' says the older of the two medics as they load the stretcher into the back of the ambulance.

Roy looks around, still wanting an answer. The police officer leaves Tony and heads for him. Roy looks over at Tony and Ruth, trying to read their faces, wondering what they know. They've only lived downstairs for the last year. All he knows of them is that Tony drives a lorry delivering drinks and Ruth works in a telephone exchange. They just stare back until the police officer blocks his view of them.

'Mr Brady?'

'Yes.'

'You live at 4B?'

'I rent it. I'm not living here at the moment.'

'Do you know that man?'

'Yes. What happened to him?'

The officer ignores his question. 'I need to talk to you.'

Roy looks around in despair. Luiz is in the ambulance now. They're doing something to him, hooking up some kind of monitor gadget.

'Where will they take him?' Roy asks.

'The North Middlesex, I should think,' says the copper. 'He's in good hands. Come and sit in the car.'

Roy answers the questions. He explains where he was that morning and how he'd just arrived back. He gives Luiz's name and explains he'd leant him the flat, but that's all. He says he hardly knows Luiz, and it was a casual arrangement to recoup some rent before he hands the place back. He says he doesn't know who would want to do that to Luiz. He's kept waiting until the officer has talked on his radio, returned, asked to see some ID, and kept him waiting some more. Another police officer turns up. Roy asks if he can go into the flat. He's told Luiz's injuries could constitute grievous bodily harm, and the flat could be a crime scene. Besides, they're not finished with him yet.

On the way to the police station, all he can deduce is that Tony or Ruth had called the police almost an hour ago after hearing shouting and banging. Two men had come down the stairs in a hurry, got into a car and almost hit another car when they took off. Tony had gone up to see if Luiz was okay, found the door open and Luiz sprawled on the floor bleeding from his head. After repeating everything he's already said, and that he knows nothing about Luiz's work or social life, Roy is reminded he can't go into the flat and asked where he'll go. As he gives Geri's address, he knows he's not going there. He doesn't know where he's going – apart from the hospital to find out how Luiz is. They offer to take him back to get his car, but he says he could do with the walk to clear his head.

Roy is told Luiz was sitting up and talking soon after arrival. He's had some stitches and he'll need some dental work. No matter how much he pleads, Roy can't see Luiz until he's had a further examination and some x-rays. If he comes back in an hour, they might let him visit for a few minutes before Luiz goes to the ward.

Roy stands in the main entrance near the payphones. If he calls, will Fiona get to the phone first? He gets a sensation of the distance between them, the miles of wire between here and Ebwich. He was there only seven or eight hours ago and yet it seems like years. Will she want to talk to him? Will she have anything to say other than she'll fetch Sally to the phone? Could he say he'd been thinking about her the whole journey down here? Or would he just be making a fool of himself? He walks towards the exit. He shouldn't phone until he's talked to Luiz and knows whether this is over and Sally can come home. Then he can go back, then he'll see Fiona again.

There's something else he must do now. He should go to the garage and face Kirk and take whatever flak Kirk wants to fire at him. It will be hard, but he knows he has to do it. He feels guilty for sitting at the family table with Kirk and Geri's mum on those Sundays over the last few months, giving the impression he was there because he wanted to be, when he was there because he'd just drifted into their lives and told them so little of his.

They'd been there with sympathy and comfort when his mum had died. They'd taken an interest in him. When they'd asked him about his past, he'd told them nothing about Shane and nothing about Angola, nothing about Sally and Tina, and nothing about Luiz. He'd skipped all that. He knew Geri noticed that gap, the avoidance of those last few years. She'd gently probed a few times. She probably thought there was another woman he was trying to forget. They'd all trusted him – Kirk especially. And now Roy had to look him in the eyes and tell him he didn't have the feelings for his daughter that he'd pretended to have.

He knows Geri will be at the garage too. She'll be in the tatty little office that looks out on the bins and the scrap metal pile, chasing spares' orders and phoning customers with quotes. Standing by the car, he hesitates. It would be so much easier to leave this all behind, drive back to Ebwich, tell Sally Luiz wasn't giving up on his schemes and she should give up on him, tell Fiona he hasn't been able to stop thinking about her – and stay at Hettie's, stay there, look for a job and never come back here. But he can't. He gets into the car and heads for the garage. This time when he leaves the money in the boot, he thinks maybe it won't be so bad if someone nicks it.

He can see Geri through the glass panel in the door, just where he'd pictured her. She glances up, then stares at him. He looks away and heads for Kirk. He has his head under the bonnet of a Transit van and is unaware of Roy until he's right next to him.

'Kirk.'

Kirk pulls back and straightens up to look at him. Now Roy doesn't know what to say. They're just looking at each other. Kirk's features harden. Roy braces himself, half expecting a fist. It doesn't come.

'You've got a fucking cheek showing up here,' Kirk says, wiping his hands on a rag.

Still, Roy can't say what he wants to.

'She's done your money for you.'

'I didn't come for that,' says Roy. 'I came to say I'm sorry. I didn't do right by her. I know what you must think of me.'

Kirk turns back to the Transit. 'It don't matter what I think. It's her you've let down.'

Roy's heard Kirk's take on how Geri's ex-husband treated her. He doesn't want it to end there. He doesn't want to be thought of like that, but he doesn't know what else to say.

'Is it alright if I go in the office to see her?'

'Suit yourself. But if you upset her, you'll have me to deal with.'

Roy turns and looks over. Geri is still watching. He walks across to the office. He tries to read her look. He should know what it means, but he's not sure. There's reticence in her eyes; disappointment and fear too perhaps. It hurts him to see it. He closes the flimsy door.

She looks back at the sheet in the typewriter. He thinks for a second she's going to carry on typing, but she doesn't. He sits down and starts to talk. He starts with Shane and him in the army. He can see she's wondering where this is going, but he ploughs on. Now he's started, he can't stop, and he doesn't want to. She's paying increased attention as he gets to Shane with Sally, Tina being born, Shane and him leaving the army. Once or twice, she glances behind him. He can't see, but he's sure Kirk is watching. The phone goes twice and each time she quickly takes the number and says she'll call back. He can't say she wasn't listening. By the time he's described what happened in Angola, her eyes are fixed on him. She hasn't interrupted him until now.

'Why didn't you tell me?'

'Because I couldn't,' he says.

He rounds off with how he met Luiz and what's happened in the last few weeks. She only knew Luiz as this Portuguese bloke who'd taken his flat on, just someone he'd met in a pub. He'd never told her where he'd really met him or what Luiz was into. It's hard admitting what he's got himself involved in, how stupid he's been. But the next bit is harder still. He's got to be straight with her. He owes it to her.

'I wasn't honest with you. I was glad of the job and I should have left it at that.'

'I knew I didn't know you, Roy. I knew there was something else there, but...' She shakes her head. 'And I did think...' She stops and looks down at the typewriter keys.

He's never seen Geri like this. He hates himself for doing it. He wants to get out of there right now, but he knows he'll feel even worse if he does.

She looks back up at him. 'So is that it then?'

'I sorry,' says Roy. 'I don't know what I want, but it isn't this.'

She takes an envelope from a tray on her desk and

hands it to him. 'I've done your wages up until last week. I've added the holidays to what you're owed. I'll sort out your tax form and send it to the flat. You can pick your stuff up today. Put your key through the letter box.'

He gets up and takes the envelope. There's no point in saying any more; it's better he goes. As he opens the door, he's aware of Kirk watching him. He can't meet that look. As he hurries out of the workshop to his car, he wonders how much Geri will tell her dad.

He can have five minutes with Luiz, the nurse tells him. She adds that a police officer has just left and Luiz is claiming it was a fight that got out of hand, saying it was as much his fault as his attacker's. He can see she knows it's a load of bollocks. When he reaches Luiz's bed, he looks at the patchwork of dressings. Luiz opens his right eye. The left one is too swollen to follow suit. He groans at Roy.

'Fucking bastards!' His voice lisps through broken teeth.

'The police won't believe your story,' says Roy, pulling up a chair to the bed.

'Those shits got my money. They smashed up my car yesterday too.'

It annoys Roy that money and Luiz's decrepit Vauxhall Viva are the only things Luiz is worried about. He wants to say things could be worse, but he doesn't. He doesn't ask him what happened either. He doesn't want to know.

'I've got nothing,' Luiz goes on.

'You can have my share,' Roy says. Even with the bruising, he can see the surprise on Luiz's face. Roy nearly adds it will give him a fresh start somewhere else. Then he thinks of Sally. What does Luiz think will happen there?

'You'd do that?'

'I don't want it,' says Roy.

Luiz tries to shift to face him but winces at the pain and settles for turning his head a fraction. 'I'll pay you back. I can make that money work – I don't need those bastards now. I can do it without them.'

The temptation to tell Luiz he's an idiot goes up a gear. Roy just keeps his temper and tries another tack.

'You've been lucky. What about Sally? Isn't it time to quit?'

'Everyone needs money, Roy. We can live somewhere better – Sally and Tina and me. There's better places than this for them.'

'She might not see it that way,' says Roy. 'Not now.'

'She'll be fine. She'll understand.' The anger is back in his voice.

Roy stops holding back. 'She's not fine now. She's worried sick and she doesn't want this.' He gestures at Luiz's bandages. 'She doesn't want to have to leave her home and hide.'

'She's safe now,' says Luiz. 'They've got what they want and they've done this to me. They won't touch her.'

'You'd better phone her then. She'll be pleased to hear it,' says Roy.

'It won't be like this next time,' says Luiz. 'If I can get back to Angola, I can do everything myself.' Again, he tries to turn to face Roy. Again, he winces and twists back. 'You could help me. We'd both be rich.'

Or dead, thinks Roy. 'Count me out, Luiz.'

Luiz lets his head fall back. Roy wonders what he's thinking; how he can be so bloody stupid when he's not stupid.

Roy gets up. 'Listen, this is it now. I'm done with all this. Do you understand?'

Luiz looks up at him. 'Alright, I understand.'

'And don't think the police are through with you either. They might start looking into what you're doing here.'

'I'll deal with it,' says Luiz.

Roy's not convinced, but he's had enough. 'I'd better go,' he says. 'What shall I do with the money?'

'Give it to Sally to look after,' Luiz says. 'I trust her.'

'Do you want me to call her?'

'Yes,' says Luiz. 'Tell her I'll call her soon. Tell her everything is fine.'

'Yeah,' says Roy. 'Everything's bloody wonderful.'

# Fiona

MOST OF THE morning-customers have left the café. The lunchtime rush hasn't started. Tina is at her favourite table, reading an Enid Blyton book left by a child many years ago. Fiona watches Hettie go to the kitchen for clean cutlery. She knows Hettie has something on her mind. She's been like this all morning, moving in quick bursts, glancing at her, then looking away. Fiona can't stand it any longer. She slips through to the kitchen and closes the door to the café. Hettie turns from the sink, anticipating her question.

'What Jo said about your dad, I didn't want to tell you.' Hettie's voice is tight. Her eyes brim with worry. Maddeningly, she won't go on.

'What?' says Fiona.

Hettie leans on the draining board. 'Your mum suspected he had someone else. She wasn't bitter about it. You need to know that. She knew she was dying. She told me she wanted him to find someone else, that she wanted there to be someone there for you too. She said she trusted him that it would be the right person for you both.'

Fiona can't keep the derision from her voice. 'Well, she got that wrong.'

'Yes, she did,' says Hettie. 'But she couldn't know, could she?'

'She was ill, and he was seeing Margaret at the same time!'

Hettie nods. She breathes out slowly, pain in her eyes. 'I promised I'd look out for you. And I didn't keep that promise as well as I should have.'

'Yes, you did,' Fiona says. 'It was him that didn't deserve her trust.'

'Finding the right person,' says Hettie, 'is a gamble.'

'I know,' says Fiona. 'I've worked that out.'

'You understand better than I did at your age,' says Hettie.

'I keep thinking about Roy,' Fiona blurts out. 'If he'll ever come back.'

She needed to say it out loud, to make it real or just make it vanish – she doesn't know which, she doesn't know which she wants. She watches Hettie's face as she takes this in; looking for reassurance that she knows Hettie can't give.

'I don't see why not,' Hettie says finally.

'I'm probably being stupid,' says Fiona. 'He won't want to now.'

'Give it time. See what happens.'

Fiona wants to say she can't give it time; she needs to know. Instead, she just goes back to the door to the café.

'When are you setting off?' asks Hettie.

Fiona doesn't get the chance to reply. The phone is ringing. As she crosses the kitchen to the hall to answer it, Sally comes down the stairs. Fiona gets there first. As she hears the pips sounding, even before the money goes in at the other end, she knows it's Roy.

'Hello?'

'Is Sally there?'

He sounds strained. Something's wrong. She wants to ask him if he's okay, but Sally is next to her.

'She's right here.'

'Put her on, please.'

As Sally takes the receiver, Fiona reluctantly goes back to the kitchen, where Hettie's face says she's picked up the signals. From the hallway, Sally's voice, high with panic, confirms Fiona's fear that it's bad news.

'Is he alright?'

Fiona and Hettie are blatantly eavesdropping now, standing fixed in the kitchen doorway, waiting.

'Where?' Sally's tone has moderated a fraction. 'I'm coming back. I can't stand this any longer.'

Fiona and Hettie exchange glances. How bad is this?

'No, I don't' care. I'm coming back,' Sally says,

replacing the receiver and turning to them.

'Luiz is in hospital. He's been beaten up.'

Fiona knows there's no point in trying to persuade Sally to stay now.

'You can come with me,' she says.

Sally hurries up the stairs. 'I'll get our stuff.'

'I should check the café. I heard the door,' says Hettie. Fiona goes upstairs to get some of her own things. Back in the kitchen, she waits for Hettie, glad she has an excuse to leave straight away now. Hettie comes to the doorway. Fiona hugs her.

'Get going,' Hettie says. 'I can manage until Iris gets here. Just take care.'

While Hettie goes back to serve a customer, Fiona waits upstairs for Sally, thinking in the year she's been there she's gone nowhere, and now, in the space of a few days, she'll have been away twice. She looks in her bag, wondering if she's got everything and where she'll stay, a detail she hadn't considered until now. She hears Sally get Tina up to the bathroom. She goes downstairs to wait for them. After they've said goodbye to Hettie, Sally trying to pay for the sandwiches and cakes waiting on the counter for them, Hettie refusing the money, Fiona puts their bags in the back of the car.

'I'm not telling Tina anything about Luiz yet,' says Sally. 'I need to think.'

'Do you want to see him?' Fiona asks.

'I don't know,' says Sally. 'I don't know if —'

She stops as Tina appears with Hettie. Hettie is wiping her eyes. The departure seems too quick now. Fiona feels like she's being sucked away. She's on edge. She's very conscious of driving: every gear change, every touch of the brakes, feels deliberate. She's getting too used to being there, she thinks. Leaving the place is making her anxious. She doesn't know why. The sun streams in now. She tries to absorb it and relax.

Tina may not know what's happened, but she knows something is wrong and hasn't said a word from the back seat. Fiona feels sorry for her. She wants to say something to comfort her but doesn't know what. She thinks about how this little girl is caught up in all this and she shouldn't be. Sally is mute too. It's half an hour before she breaks the silence.

'Are you going to Beckenham?'

'Near there – Shortlands,' says Fiona. 'They moved there earlier this year.'

'You can just drop us at a tube station.'

'We can go through Poplar. It's no trouble,' says Fiona. She's wondering if Sally would rather go straight to the hospital, but doesn't want to say it in front of Tina. Sally stares out and says nothing more.

At Godmanchester they stop to eat the sandwiches. While Tina is in the toilets, Sally opens up.

'I've decided I'm going to tell him face to face I'm not seeing him again,' she says.

'Do you want to go straight to the hospital?' says Fiona.

'I'm not taking Tina. I don't want her to see him. And there'll be visiting hours. I can take her to her friend's house and go later.'

Fiona wonders if her subconscious had been at work, if she'd suggested it because there was a chance Roy might be there. She feels a stab of frustration that she should need an excuse, that an opportunity to see Roy will be missed, that she can't just ask Sally for his address. Then Tina is back from the toilet, asking how long it will be before she's home, and Sally is insisting on paying for the petrol. They're back in the car before Fiona can say anything about Roy, unsure again, the impetus gone. They drive on, saying nothing more.

At Sally's flat, Tina runs inside and Sally stands awkwardly at the car, thanking Fiona for the lift. Fiona experiences a wave of sadness. Now they're saying goodbye, despite only knowing her a few days, she feels the loss. It's as if they're both alone now.

'If you need anywhere to stay tonight,' says Sally, as she turns to her door, 'you can come back here. It'd only be the couch, but you're welcome.'

'And if you ever want to come back to Ebwich,' Fiona says. 'I know it's not your kind of place but...'

'Thanks,' says Sally. 'You never know.'

They look at each other, both hesitating before Fiona gets in the car and Sally goes inside and closes her door. Fiona pulls away, glad of the need to concentrate on where she's going, glad to push down the feeling of loss. As she heads towards the Blackwall Tunnel, she realises if she goes straight to the house, Dad won't be home from work yet. She thinks about intercepting him before he gets his train. Ocean Shipping is in Moorgate, but she doesn't know exactly where, or where to park. She drives on, deciding to wait at Shortlands railway station for him, hoping it's a normal day and he'll be there around six o'clock. The traffic is heavy on both sides of the tunnel, but she's still going to get there with over an hour to spare.

She finds a parking place near the station, then kills

the time walking towards the golf club and then back along Station Road. At a quarter to six, as she walks under the railway bridge towards the station entrance, a train is pulling in to the platform above her. She hurries round as a stream of commuters fill the station exit, most still hurrying like they haven't left their work routine, or perhaps hurrying to get away from it. She scans every face. She's almost given up hope when she sees him ambling towards her, almost in protest at the rush of everyone else. He stops when he sees her. His smile fades to concern. He's trying not to show it, but she knows her appearance has worried him.

'Fiona.'

'Hello Dad.'

He hugs her tentatively, holding back. She wonders why.

'Is everything okay?' he asks.

'Yes. But I want to talk to you.'

The worry is still on his face. He looks around him. 'You could come back with me…'

'No,' she says. 'There's a pub on Station Road.'

As they walk, she can't say it – not yet. She asks him about work, if he's heard from the old neighbours, even how Jo is getting on. His answers become shorter and shorter until she stops asking.

They've reached the Shortlands Tavern now. They get a table and he goes to the bar for drinks.

When he sits down, he's still looking worried. 'Look, I'm sorry how things turned out. Not a day passes that I don't ask myself what I should have done different.'

She almost says not marry Margaret, but she stops herself. Instead, she looks him in the eyes and says what she's come to say. 'Jo told me you were seeing Margaret before Mum died.'

He doesn't flinch. His face is immobile. But there's fear in his eyes. He gives the tiniest of nods, like a welcome acceptance. 'Yes,' he says. 'Yes, I was.'

She'd known it anyway. This isn't the important bit. It's what he's going to say next that counts. She waits for more. Behind those eyes there's something else. Now he's blinking rapidly, like he's trying to stop that something coming out, that it's going to be carried on tears. She waits. He draws in a deep breath.

'When I married your mum, she was pregnant.'

Fiona had already done the sums. She knew that. It had never been talked about, and it hadn't mattered. Now it seems significant. She wonders why.

He breathes out and forces himself on. 'There'd been someone else,' is all he says before he tilts his head down.

Now it's clear, but it's not clear. He hasn't said it and he doesn't want to and she doesn't want to believe it. But she asks the needless question.

'Are you saying you're not my father?'

He only nods, like he can't say it.

'Who then?'

He pulls in some more air, like this is suffocating him. He looks up at her, but this time his eyes are softer, pained by what he's going to say.

'Someone she knew from work. I didn't want to know who.'

'But you still married her.'

'Yes,' he says. 'I loved her and I thought it didn't matter.'

Fiona tries to process it.

'I still don't understand about Margaret, when Mum was still alive – why?'

He's clenching his hands together now, looking over them at her. 'Because things changed.'

'She was sick. She was so ill!'

'Yes,' he says. 'But I wasn't ever the one she really wanted. And she knew about Margaret.'

That seems almost obscene. She can't keep the disgust from her face.

'Your mum wanted you to be happy. She wanted there to be someone…' He can't say it.

'In her place?' Fiona almost spits the words at him. It hits her that Mum and her were taken on, not unlike Margaret and Jo. Something she could never imagine having in common with Jo dawns on her – all those years and he's not her father. Something else slides in too, something else she has to know.

'Do Margaret and Jo know?'

He shakes his head. 'The only other person who knows is Hettie.'

Of course she does, thinks Fiona. She wants to hate her for it, but she knows she can't. Hettie knew because Mum told her, told her more than she'd revealed that morning.

'I thought that's why you were here,' he says. 'I thought she'd told you.'

'No,' says Fiona.

'She promised your mum she wouldn't. Hettie was just trying to protect her, help her.'

'Hettie didn't break her promise,' says Fiona. 'I came because of what Jo said at the wedding.' She feels she's opened this box that she could have kept shut. Now it's too late. Now everything's changed. The person sitting opposite isn't who she thought he was. She can't work out what it means for her.

'I'm sorry,' he says.

'Were you ever going to tell me? If I hadn't come here like this, would you ever have?'

'I don't know,' he says. 'I don't think I would. I didn't want you to think differently about me. I'm still hoping you won't.'

She takes that in. How does it change things? Does it change anything at all? While she was absorbing the shock, other emotions had been on hold. Now that shock is receding, she feels them moving up her body from somewhere in her stomach up through her rib cage, pushing up to her throat. His mouth collapses with the force and a sob emerges. He reaches across the table.

'It doesn't change what I feel for you.'

His words don't help.

'So why did you do it? Why did you bring Margaret and Jo into my life, let her send me away to school – why?'

'Because I love her,' he says. 'I know you two clashed, but that's the truth. I still love her. I'd loved her for a long time. It doesn't mean I don't love you. You'll always be —'

'Always be what – another one of your adoptions?'

She's on her feet turning for the door. He hesitates, gets up and follows, but she's in the street before he can reach the door. Outside, he calls after her.

'Fiona!'

She hears him, but she's running, running too fast for him.

'Fiona, please!' He's running now, trying to catch up with her.

She's at the car before he can cross the road. She sees him in her rear-view mirror as she pulls away, swerving out, careless of how she's driving and where she's heading. After ten minutes of driving, breathing deeply to overcome the wrenching feeling inside that wants her to turn around and go back, she recognises where she is and heads north again, knowing she can't drive all the way to Ebwich like this, and thinking of Sally's offer to stay the night – somewhere neutral.

Back on the other side of the river, she's calmer. She can't remember where Sally's flat is. She's taken a couple of wrong turnings and had to back track. On the way there, she'd blindly followed Sally's instructions. Now it takes a couple of circuits before she sees the pub where Sally told her to turn.

When no one answers the door, she guesses Sally is at the hospital. She gets back in the car. She could just keep going, drive back to Ebwich to Hettie and tell her she knows now, that there doesn't need to be any more secrets. Instead, she waits and thinks, knowing that what she'd heard has to sink in. It's on the surface still, it's raw, too recent a wound to touch. She can't help thinking what she used to tell herself – that whatever happened, Dad would never be Jo's real dad, that he'd only ever be hers. It had been her only comfort – and it had never been true. She dries her eyes. She hadn't even noticed that she was crying.

# Chapter 16   1976-78

# Fiona

WHEN I ARRIVED at Holloway, the place was being rebuilt. It seemed odd that a prison could be a building site and still be a prison, but I suppose there was nowhere else to put the inmates. That was just one of many surprises during those two years. From the first moments of stepping out of the van, when I went in on remand, to the day I finally walked out of that place, I lived in a small, detached world that was normal to both inmates and staff but alien to me. It was a world I was determined would never be mine. I told myself it was like school – it wasn't permanent, I just had to survive it.

I was admitted along with two other girls and three older women. A hatchet-faced woman, twice my size, told me to remove all my clothes and handed me a towelling gown that smelt of the previous wearers' bodies. It wasn't as bad as the smell of some of my companions, who'd been in police cells for days without being able to wash properly. The shallow bath that I spent a few minutes in made me feel no cleaner though, and the rough body search that followed left me feeling dirtier than before. I'd imagined I'd be given some kind of coarse uniform like in the old films I'd seen, but instead I got my clothes back – one of the few concessions to your individuality in Holloway – and one that most of us clung to, something of our own in a place where everything else was shared.

After being made to wait for an hour or so, a sour-faced officer, in a hurry, led me up to my cell. This was in the separate wing for remand prisoners. When I returned to Holloway after my trial, I realised how different the remand cells had been, strangely worse than the long-term cells, a place where no one cared about their temporary surroundings and nothing was done to make them more bearable. To make things worse, as the rebuilding had started, they had left these older cells to decay even more than they might have. The combination of piss, shit, cabbage and disinfectant was a smell you never forget. This was to be the smell of my home for over seven months, before my sentence even began.

Another assumption I'd got wrong was that I'd be on my own – a good and a bad thing, I'd thought. But I was wrong there too. Someone was already in the cell. As the door was closed behind me, with a wry remark about 'letting you two get to know each other', the occupant, a few years older than me, gave me a hard stare that felt like a warning. This was Angie. Still stunned by everything that had happened so far, I stared back and said nothing. By luck I'd done the right thing. I found out later Angie got to know you on her terms, not yours. When I'd just stood there taking it in, she sighed and made the first move.

'For fuck's sake, sit down.' She pointed to what I took was my bed, and I did as I was told.

I survived Holloway because of Angie. It's that simple. It was the third time she'd been there and there wasn't much she didn't know. By the time our trials came round, she'd passed on everything I needed to know – and a lot of things I'd rather have not known. Compared to the shoplifters, addicts, and prostitutes, I was already a few notches up the pecking order as far as Angie was concerned. Later, when I was sentenced, and ended up back in Holloway, and discovered not only was she back there too, but she was already working on getting me as her cellmate, it made the prospect of my sentence a lot more tolerable. My apprenticeship was complete by then. I'd learnt who to avoid, who to trust (not many), and when I was being wound up or set up for someone else's benefit – or just for plain spite. I learnt to survive.

My sentence of four years – reduced to just under three and a half after remand – was less than Clive's. His performance in court – shouting and refusing to sit down when he was told to, going into long tirades when he was being examined by the prosecution – didn't help him. From his confused stares in my direction, my more lenient sentence visibly shocked him. When the judge said he accepted I had been coerced, Clive stared at me. I couldn't look at him. He'd been given six years and was taken away, struggling and calling out obscenities. The last of my sympathy for him vanished at that moment. I couldn't see what he thought he was going to achieve. As ever, he couldn't accept anything that happened to him. He still thought it wasn't his fault.

Shortly after returning to Holloway, they transferred most of us to the new buildings, and I was back sharing with Angie. The rest of the prison was being pulled down around us then. By the summer of 1977, even the big gate house everyone associates with the place had gone too. You might think this fresh new start would make life better after the depressing squalor of the Victorian prison. It didn't. The new layout bred more trouble, allowed less observation, and for many, brought a good deal more pain and anxiety. Fights, cell fires, and prisoners barricading themselves in, became common events; leaving us locked up for long periods while the trouble was dealt with. All ideas of a fresh start with the new buildings, rehabilitation instead of containment, vanished. That was bad enough for Angie and me, but the largest proportion of women in Holloway weren't criminals, they were the mentally ill, addicts or just very sad women who needed practical help to live outside that place.

There were a few who would never live outside though. Myra Hindley was one of them. While in Holloway, she was so badly beaten up she needed plastic surgery to repair her face. We heard the alarm bells when it happened. Later that night, the catcalls out of the windows said she'd deserved it. It wasn't long since she'd won a prize for singing Joan Baez's, 'Prison Trilogy' and 'Love Song To A Stranger'. Contradictions like that highlighted what a terrifyingly fickle world prison was – a world of contrasts where conflict could quickly expand and ignite. A small, hard core of bullies and downright evil woman thrived in this chaos though – and some of those weren't prisoners either. Ex-army women, who made up the majority of prison staff, often butch lesbians, provoked trouble if they didn't get enough sport to satisfy them. Even Angie's toolkit was tested to the limits at times. I'd had to restrain her on a few occasions – despite her being the one who'd cautioned me about letting those bitches get to us.

My other lifeline throughout this time was Hettie's letters and occasional visits. For her to get to Holloway involved a long round trip that must have been hard to organise with the café. Every few months she managed it though. But it was her letters I treasured the most. We took up our correspondence where we left off when I was at school, despite what had happened in between, almost as if it had never happened. She wrote her letters every Sunday. I sent my replies on the following Wednesday so she'd have them for the weekend, ready for her next reply Each of her letters included another memory of Mum, another piece to add to the jigsaw, and a continuation of my getting to know them both better, even though Mum was gone. Hettie had a wonderful memory. Despite all the things she'd already told me about Mum, she still came up with another incident or another aspect of Mum's life to tell me about. She never mentioned Dad, and she never included any memories of Ted – omissions I wondered about at the time.

Dad wrote too. When he was on leave, he visited regularly. He was still at sea, talking about coming ashore for good. Like when I'd been at school, Margaret was still going with him, doubtless still enjoying being waited on and never having to cook or clean – not that I ever asked about her. He did say Jo was doing well at university – I hadn't asked about her either.

I settled into the routine of existing on a tiny budget, keeping my head down, and doing whatever I could to make things bearable. Angie said I even spoke differently to when she'd first met me. I'd almost reversed the change in my accent that Frentons had induced. Changes like that frightened me. They suggested the place was absorbing me too. Yet despite the worst aspects of Holloway, I found the comradery, the attempts at celebrations of birthdays, the wing magazines that some of the women put so much effort into, and all the other social facets of prison, a strange comfort. I came to understand that in a place where you're told so very little, information was a valuable currency that we all traded in.

I thought I'd convinced myself I wasn't going to do any of that and I didn't need those things. But I drew heavily on all those distractions when, after Clive's letters – and his detailed plans for us when we were both free – got too much, and I couldn't bear to deceive him any longer. I'd been trying to work up to it during the first few months of my sentence, trying to make my letters more like a friend's than a girlfriend's, trying to steer his thoughts to what he was going to do and not what *we* were going to do. But it's hard to do that in a letter. Finally, I wrote to him and said it was my last letter and it was best for us both if we put what we'd done behind us and made separate plans for the future.

Clive's letters continued for a few more months. Their

content alternated between desperate pleading and blind repetition of what we would do when we were back together. Then they stopped. One morning, I was called to the governor's office and told Clive had hanged himself in a store room where he'd recently started working. No one ever said it was because of my last letter. They didn't have to. I knew.

That was the darkest time for me. I never wanted to be back with Clive, but I never wanted him to take his life either. It was a long time before enough of that cloud lifted for me to think about myself. Again, it was Angie and Hettie that helped me do it. Angie used to laugh at my plans to get a job and do ordinary things. Her plans were to do what she'd done before – fraud – only this time not to get caught. Crime was her career. She lived it up when she had the money and took it in her stride when she didn't. That made me sad. We both knew that one day she'd be back in Holloway or some other prison. But we never said it.

In one of Clive's early letters, he'd alluded to how we'd been caught. He'd chosen his words carefully. He wrote something about 'the person you trusted letting you down'. In a later letter, he went further, saying that *someone* must have been on the phone the minute we left them. He was talking about Lolly, of course. I often thought about writing to Lolly. I even thought of asking her to visit. But I did neither. It wasn't that I still bore her a grudge; it was more that I felt we were on very separate paths, and from inside those walls I couldn't ever see those paths crossing again.

Assuming I got an early release under licence, I had about two years to serve. I decided not to count the days that passed. Instead, I focussed on each day as it came, making the best of that day. I already knew how easy my life had been compared to most of the women in there. I was going to accept that and learn whatever I could from being there. Then I was going to put that place behind me. I had Hettie's letters and visits, and the friendship of Angie and a few other women to help me. I can even say there were some times, someone's birthday, some little celebration or other, that I came to look back on with affection and joy.

Eventually, the time neared when I had to think about what I was going to do when I got out – or more importantly, where I was going to live. I'd told Dad I wasn't coming home. He'd recently been offered a permanent post in head office. It felt like he was taking it for me, that he was trying to put things right. On his last visit, he'd persuaded me I should return to the house when I got out; that despite what I thought of Margaret and Jo, we could make it work and it would be for the best – at least to start with.

I talked it over with Hettie on her last visit a month or so before I was released. I think I wanted her to say not to do it. I wanted her to ask me to go to Ebwich with her even then. But Hettie was never one to meddle. She just said Dad was trying his best and the least I could do was to give it a chance. I remember asking him what Margaret and Jo thought about my coming home. He was diplomatic. He just said it was my home too and everyone had to accept it. So I said yes, I'd come home and promised to do my best to make it work.

I tried very hard to make it work, and it was every bit as hard as I thought it would be. When Dad brought me home, Margaret and Jo were on their way out to visit possible venues for Jo's forthcoming engagement party. Dad had told me about this event a few weeks earlier, saying how lucky she was to have found David – then changing the subject when he must have realised it could seem like a comparison to my relationship with Clive. I was glad when Margaret and Jo quickly departed on their mission. It meant I had some time with Dad, and some time to settle in and get used to all the changes to the house that now felt very different. Only my room was untouched, not given the fully fitted makeover that I noticed Jo's had. It was a subtle snub that even Dad must have been aware of when he came upstairs to ask me if everything was okay and found me curled up on my mattress. I told him I was fine. I said if all went well, I wouldn't be there that long.

But I knew it wasn't going to be easy. The girls in Holloway had told me that a probation officer's idea of a job might not be the same as mine – assuming they could even find me one. But then the only job I'd ever had was at Grey and Garton's, so what did I know? Besides, who wanted to employ someone who'd robbed their last employer?

# Roy

IF I HADN'T been with Luiz, I don't know how I'd have got into or out of Zaire. I'd noticed the cartons of cigarettes in the Land Rover and thought he must either be a heavy smoker or that diamonds weren't the only thing he was smuggling. But they weren't contraband; they were essential currency. They didn't just pay our way at the border, but also at the random checkpoints where makeshift barriers blocked the road and rag tag groups of soldiers fired questions at us in French. Luiz replied with gentle, persuasive answers, accompanied by his cigarettes. I discovered he had many skills. Once, when the cigarettes didn't work, he went for a short walk with a soldier I took to be an NCO of some kind and I thought we were going no further. But Luiz came back smiling. It had taken some dollar bills that time, he explained, and we were on our way again.

We took turns at driving. At times it was slow going, bouncing on the ruts and breathing in the dust and fumes of the occasional truck in front, usually so heavily laden it just made the hills. As we drove, Luiz told me his father had contacts in Pointe-Noire in The Congo where ships regularly left for ports in Europe. He explained Zaire was once the Belgium Congo and where we were heading was once the French Congo. He said we were going to loop north then go west because in between the two Congos was Cabinda, another part of Angola, cut off from the rest of that country. The detour wasn't just safer, he said, but the roads were better too. It was good enough for me. I was just glad to be moving in the right direction, away from Angola. More cigarettes were needed to find some petrol, then, on better roads, we drove faster. Luiz wanted to cross the Congo River before we stopped overnight. The Land Rover held up well. The carburetor blocked up again just once. This time, I showed Luiz how to unblock it. I knew it was a waste of time to tell him it needed stripping and doing properly; he was a man in a hurry – but then so was I.

The next leg of the journey got us to Brazzaville, where one of his father's contacts let us stay the night in what I took to be some kind of cheap hotel or guest house – except there was no bill for Luiz to pay when we left. But there was a working shower, clean towels and a real bed. It was the first time I'd slept properly in days and I resented it when Luiz shook me out of that wonderful, blank state. We were due to reach Pointe-Noire that day, where Luiz would make the arrangements for my trip home. As we left town, I focussed on that prospect – Africa disappearing over the horizon. I had to keep telling myself it really was going to happen.

But first, Luiz left me with a family he knew – Charel, Nada and their two boys. Their house must have been in one of the better areas of town, but it would have shocked most people I knew at home. They had a tap and a toilet that flushed somewhere – from the smell, I'm not sure it went very far away – and they had electricity most of the time too. The prized possession in the house was the radio, which Charel, who worked for the shipping agents, locked away when he went to work. Nada did her best to make me welcome. I was ashamed when I realised she'd turfed their oldest boy, Dante, out of his bed so I could share a room with the youngest, Fabrice.

The delay worried me. I'd thought I'd be straight on a ship and away. When Luiz dropped me at Charel's house and I asked him what was going on, I'd already waited hours in the Land Rover while he'd been sorting things out. I was starting to worry. He said the ship wouldn't sail for a few days and I just had to wait. He wasn't going to be there though. He was heading back to Angola to finish his business before the MPLA got control of the entire country. Only the hundred dollars advance and the cloth roll of stones, along with an envelope he gave me, kept me from telling him the deal was off.

On the way to my lodgings, we'd stopped at a clothes shop where he'd paid for a couple of shirts, trousers, shoes and some underwear for me. It was the fastest shopping trip I'd ever done. He'd been in a hurry to drop me off, and that hadn't helped my state of mind either. We'd been on a precarious journey together and I felt a connection with him. The way he'd handled things made me feel vulnerable without him. Watching his departure left me feeling jittery and exposed again. On that journey, I'd gone for hours without thinking about how I'd got there, what I'd seen, and what I'd left behind. Alone again, those thoughts were creeping back.

It's hard to kill time when you're in a strange place, can't understand what anyone is saying, and, other than eating and sleeping, have no structure for your days. Those four days in that backstreet felt more like four weeks. As well as the money Luiz had given me, I still had the money they'd handed out on the coach to Heathrow. I could have done something with my time. But Luiz had left me with a strong warning about keeping the diamonds and my money safe and not wandering around. I took his advice for the first day. After that, I couldn't stand being stuck inside any longer and walked around, cautiously, in the neighbourhood for an hour or so each morning and afternoon. Whenever Dante and Fabrice were kicking a ball in their back yard, the international language of football helped pass another hour or so – and at least I could understand when they said Everton or Manchester United. Charel had little time to play with his kids, so I was in demand for those games.

I think it was the second evening, when Charel got out his radio, that I heard the news. He had a little English and proudly tuned in to the BBC World Service. Forty-odd British mercenaries were reported as arriving back in the UK. They'd been met by the police for questioning about the killings at Maquela. Callan was named as the man that gave the orders, but wasn't in the returning group. He was missing. I listened in amazement. A lot must have happened in the last few days. Out there, I hadn't imagined it would get out that soon. But it had. It was making news all over the world. Charel shrugged when the bulletin finished.

'Always fighting, always trouble,' he said.

I just nodded, hoping he hadn't seen how interested I'd been. As far as he knew, I was a merchant seaman who'd jumped ship, got into trouble and paid Luiz to get me home without any fuss. I had mixed feelings after hearing that news bulletin. Some of the others were already home. If I hadn't taken off, I might have been amongst them – or I might not. I tried not to think about it. That same night, Charel said my ship had just docked. It would be a couple of days loading and then he'd take me to it and I'd be on my way. I should be in Antwerp by the end of the first week in March. I clung on to that and played some more football with his boys.

Charel hurried me through the docks late on the Sunday evening, explaining we only had a brief window of time when the security would look the other way. I knew Charel was being paid for this but it couldn't have been without risk for him. Saying a quick goodbye to Nada and the boys had been more painful than I thought it would be. This resting place, this little family home with so few comforts, had brought me so much comfort. Also, I think that not going back home yet had lulled me into thinking I didn't have to face what had happened. I didn't have to tell Sally that Tina didn't have a father anymore. Now I was on my way, I had to face up to delivering that message.

The MV Tychon was a general cargo ship registered in Piraeus. The crew and most of the officers were Greek. It wasn't until I was aboard her that I realised my cover story wouldn't hold out for long. I knew nothing about ships. But I needn't have worried. Captain Thanos had done this before. That I wasn't his original passenger didn't seem to faze him. He said I would eat with the officers, but it would be best if I kept to myself the rest of the time. He stressed I was not to show myself when we arrived at Antwerp and not to leave the ship when we got there – I'd be told what to do when the time was right. I said goodbye to Charel, and one of the crew took me off to my cabin, my little home for the next twenty days.

During that uneventful passage, I ate very well, slept a great deal, sat out in the sun, and enjoyed long showers, the best I'd had in weeks. My only other occupation was reading a stash of Wilbur Smith novels that I found in a bookcase in the saloon. I stuck to Captain Thanos's advice and had little to do with anyone else on board. From time to time, he sought me out and practiced his already good English on me. At no point did he ask me why I was there.

The day after our arrival in Antwerp, Thanos came to my cabin to tell it was time to go. We shook hands and out on deck he handed me over to a Belgium who would take me into town. On the quayside, I got into the back of a laundry van and we passed through the docks, pausing once at the gates before we pulled away unhindered and unchecked. It was broad daylight. I'd been expecting to be taken off in the middle of the night. But there I was, in Antwerp, dropped off near a bustling European street, closer to home than I'd been in what felt like an age, only minutes from the address Luiz had given me. After all that had happened, it felt too easy. But this time it was easy.

The jeweler's shop was tiny. On entering, I thought I'd be putting the diamonds on the counter in full view. But the envelope did the trick. I was taken into the back double quick by an elderly man with a sullen, expressionless face. He checked the contents of the cloth roll. With a series of grunts, he counted out the thousand dollars Luiz had promised me and quickly showed me out. Again, I wondered what was going to go wrong. I didn't wait to find out. I changed some cash and headed for the railway station, where I took the train to Ostend. On the evening ferry, watching the rows of grey concrete buildings disappear on the shoreline, I finally knew I was going home. By late that night, I was back at the flat. My journey had been easy.

It was after that, things got difficult.

There'd been a few times in Angola when I'd held that door key in my hand and wondered if I'd ever get to use it again. Opening that door, easily finding that lock in the dark, like I'd never been away, brought a hollow feeling to my stomach. The absence of Shane, the thought that he'd been with me when we'd walked out that door, that he was gone now, torn to pieces, seemed impossibly cruel and impossibly stupid. Once inside, I stood and contemplated it all, replayed in my head the things he'd said to persuade me to go, and tried out every argument I didn't have back then to stop him. His work jacket was hanging a few feet from my face. His shoes were on the floor. The little he owned was in that flat and I didn't know what to do with any of it. I pulled his bedroom door shut without looking in. The flat was stone cold. I turned on the electric fire. With a click from the meter, the power went off. It said it all. I searched my change for a ten pence and couldn't find one. I felt my way into my bedroom and regretted undressing when I felt the cold sheets on my skin.

I put off the visit to Sally until the following Tuesday afternoon. I'd been moping around, checking the papers and the TV news since getting back. There'd been nothing on Angola. Jeremy Thorpe and the falling pound were the headlines. The gloomy financial forecasts had prompted me to exchange the rest of my dollars and pay the rent. There'd been a second note through the door that morning to say it was overdue, so I went round to the landlord to apologise and pay up. Then I got the train to Liverpool Street and the bus to Sally's place. I was missing having a car already, but my money might have to last, and some of it was for Sally. But it wasn't money that was on my mind when I knocked on her door.

At first, she just looked surprised. When I looked her in the eyes, I couldn't decide what she was thinking. She must have heard some of the stuff in the news. Did she already know? I followed her into the lounge. Tina was playing on the floor. She smiled at me and brought me some big plastic bricks to put together. It choked me to see that. It should be Shane doing this, I thought. Sally was standing in the doorway, waiting for me to say something. I just looked at Tina and tried to control myself.

'What's happened?' she said.

'Shane is dead.' I said it too quickly. The simple fact came out like it didn't matter, when it mattered so much. 'I'm sorry,' I said.

'He's not on the list of the ones who were killed,' she said. 'One of the papers had their names.'

She was saying it like it couldn't have happened.

'We didn't give our real names,' I said. 'I was there, Sally. I saw it happen.'

She sat down. Tina started taking the bricks from me and handing them to Sally. She took them one by one, robotically, silently, and put them next to her. Neither of us spoke for several minutes. Tina looked at us, puzzled. She got up on the sofa next to her mum and Sally put her arms round her and put her face into the little girl's hair.

'I still cared about him,' she said.

'I know,' I said. 'I promised him…'

She looked up at me. The anger on her face shocked

me. I wanted to say it wasn't my fault, but I knew how pathetic that would sound.

'What did you promise him?' she snapped.

'I just said I'd look out for you and Tina.'

'We don't need looking out for. We've managed alright.'

'It's what he wanted,' I said.

It seemed to make her angrier.

'He came round when it suited him. The rest of the time, he was out on the tiles with you.'

She was right. I stood up. I wasn't going to argue.

'I have some money for you,' I said. It was bad timing. I knew as soon as I'd said it.

'We don't want your money – or his,' she fired back.

'I'll come back in a day or two,' I said.

'Do what you like. You and him always did.'

She didn't come to the door with me. I left her sitting on the sofa with Tina. I walked up to Mile End tube and set off for my second visit – to Dagenham, to Mum and Dad.

I told them a pack of lies. I said Shane and I had gone to Aberdeen. I said we'd heard of some jobs in a firm servicing generators for the rigs. We had heard that, but it had been last year and we'd done nothing about it. I said we got a month's work out of it and he'd stayed on. Mum wasn't impressed. She'd said she was sure they had phones in Aberdeen and she'd been round to the flat looking for me. Dad had just got in from work and didn't say much, but I could tell from his face he'd be having words with me when she was out of earshot. And he did. When I said I'd stay for dinner, he suggested a walk to the club first and I could hardly say no. Truth was, their normal routine was more than welcome than I'd ever imagined it could be.

I took my telling off before we got to the club and we'd dropped the subject by the time we'd sat down with our pints. Dad was counting the months to retirement then, and told me he was looking at camper vans. When we'd chewed over which had the most reliable engines, he looked me in the eye.

'So where were you really?'

I had an idea he hadn't been fooled. 'You don't want to know,' I said.

He nearly said something, but changed his mind. He picked up our glasses and went to the bar. I watched him getting served and thought about coming clean. I changed my mind again several times before he sat back down. I never did tell him.

Back at the flat, someone was waiting for me – a police sergeant looking for Shane, asking if he'd got the letter about his hearing. I was getting ready with my Aberdeen story when he saved me the trouble.

'The woman was admitted to hospital a week after that trouble outside here,' he said. 'She was badly beaten up. The boyfriend's being charged, and she's changed her story about Shane that night. She's confirmed what he told us.'

I don't know what he made of my reaction. I couldn't speak. His news had just twisted the knife in my guts. I was trying to decide if that assault charge really did trigger everything or if we'd have gone anyway.

'I've been round twice,' he went on. 'He should have got a letter.'

'I've been away too,' I said. 'There's a few envelopes

and things...'

'Well, anyway, when you see him, you can tell him he's in the clear.'

'Right,' I said.

He turned back to the stairs. 'I was at school with Shane. Tell him Andy Neams says hello.'

He couldn't have known how much I'd have loved to have told Shane that.

Closing the door that night started another phase in my life. It wasn't like when Shane was there. It wasn't boozing and staying out until all hours, doing casual work when it came along. It was the start of over two years of bland routine. My first job was in security. I did night shifts in an office in the City – on the front desk until the cleaners left, then doing the round of checks every hour. In between, I'd sit reading a book or walk around trying to convince myself something better would come along. My relief would appear in the morning just as the earliest of the office workers arrived. I'd go home, sleep a bit, kill some time and go back and do it all again. I stuck that for over a year. The pay was poor and any social life was almost impossible. After that, I did some driving for a firm of couriers, mainly around London with a few runs down to the coast. The pay wasn't much better, but at least most of the work was in the daytime. About then, I finally cleared the rest of Shane's stuff out of the flat. I threw most of it away, and I only managed that by getting drunk first.

I had two relationships during that time. Pattie, a local girl I met in the launderette, who had lived most of her childhood in care and who had more emotional baggage than even I had. That lasted just over five months. She found Jesus, and I found there was no room in the flat for me, her, and the man himself. Linda came along a few months later. She was older than me, had no intention of moving into that tatty place of mine and finally met a divorcee from Swiss Cottage who had a lot more to offer than I had. I'd been visiting Sally and Tina for the whole of this time too. Usually I went round once a month, sometimes more often. Every time I did go round, Tina looked more like Shane and less like Sally. At times, I found it hard to look at her without seeing him and then seeing what had been left of him that night in Angola.

During this time, Dad retired. The meanest trick of all was played when, after a few months, his health deteriorated and he was diagnosed with coronary heart disease. I went back to Dagenham as much as I could then. Mum was pretending she was coping, but not pretending that well, and Dad was pretending it wasn't happening. He died in February 1978, the same month I got a new job in a garage near the flat.

I'd been taking cars round to Kirk's place regularly. He'd just lost his longest-serving mechanic and tapped me up about taking the job. Whenever I went round, I'd chat with his daughter, Geri, a woman with an intense look and a sad smile that I'd wondered about. I accepted the job on the spot. The hours would have made it easier to see more of Dad, but I was too late on that count.

# Chapter 17     1979

## Roy

ROY PARKS UP at the police station. He wants to know if he's allowed into the flat. He's come from the hospital. He'd guessed Sally would make the evening visiting slot, and she had. He'd tried to give her the money. She'd refused to take it. She said she was only there to tell Luiz it was over and she didn't want to see him again. They'd only spent a few minutes together. She'd told him how Fiona had driven them back and had gone on to see her dad. He could see she was in a hurry to visit Luiz and get it over with. He regretted letting her go, not asking about Fiona. All the way to the police station, he'd wished he'd found out about Fiona's plans.

Roy recognises the desk sergeant. It's the officer who came round looking for Shane after Angola, the one who knew Shane from school. He's wearing glasses, but Roy knows it's him. Now he's worried he'll get asked about Shane. When Roy gives his name and says he's here to ask about access to the flat, he can see Andy recognises him. Thankfully, he just says he'll have to check about the flat and goes off through a door at the back of the reception desk.

He returns with a plain-clothes officer who says he's Detective Sergeant Mullins. With his cropped fair hair and that clipped way of moving, the way he stands, chest out, he could be ex-army, thinks Roy. He confirms Luiz isn't pressing charges. He says Roy can go back to the flat. He's looking hard at Roy when he tells him this. Roy decides this bloke is biding his time – he knows there's something else going on. He's glad when Mullins turns and leaves.

Before he can get out, Andy leaves the counter and follows him to the door.

'You're Shane's flatmate,' he says.

'Yeah,' says Roy. 'I thought I recognised you – it was just the glasses.'

'Yeah, that's why I'm on the desk now. Had my eyesight adjusted with an iron bar.'

'Sorry to hear that,' says Roy.

'Your flatmates get into some pickles, don't they? How is Shane these days?'

He likes this bloke who knew Shane, who hadn't forgotten him. He hesitates. Just say he's still in Scotland, is what flashes into his head. But he wants to tell him the truth. It feels reckless, but he wants to say it to someone else, connect Shane back to the world he came from.

'Shane's dead,' he says. 'He was dead the last time you came round.'

Andy's enquiring look freezes on his face and morphs to shock. Now he's said it, Roy can't stop himself from going on.

'Shane and me went out to Angola that year. He got killed and I got home. I should have said, but back then it was still a bit... All that stuff in the news and that.'

Andy steps closer. 'With that maniac, what's-his-name, Callan?'

'Yeah, we were bloody idiots. They took us for a ride.'

Andy takes this in. 'I remember it being on the news.' He blows his lips out. 'Well, I'm sorry.'

'Thanks,' says Roy. 'You won't say anything, will you? I mean, I don't think we broke any laws here.'

Andy looks him in the eyes. 'I wouldn't know,' he says. 'Look after yourself.'

Getting out of the car, Roy turns away from the flat towards the phone box. Hettie will want to know what's happened, and he needs to talk to her too. He dials and only has to wait a few rings before she answers. He's glad to hear her voice. After telling her about Luiz and meeting Sally, he's aware there's something else, something not being said. It must be about Fiona. He looks at the two ten pence pieces he's got left.

'Sally said Fiona has come down to see her dad.'

The line is quiet. He knows he was right.

'Hettie?'

'He's just phoned me. When the phone went again, I was hoping it was her.'

There's something about how she says this. Something has happened and he can't think what it could be.

'He's just told her something that came as a shock,' she says.

He's struggling to put this together. 'What?'

'It's going to be a shock to you too. I didn't want to tell you on the phone.'

She's lost him. 'I don't understand.'

'He's not her dad,' says Hettie.

He's thinking that's a shock for Fiona, but why would that be a shock for him?

'Your dad was.'

For a second he thinks Hettie has lost her marbles. He's not sure whether to humour her or ask her more.

'That's what the argument was about on that last visit,' she goes on.

Roy doesn't reply. He's piecing it together. He's thinking about that last day of the holiday and that argument in the social club.

'Did you hear me?' Hettie asks.

'Yes,' says Roy. 'That can't be right. He didn't know her mother.'

'Yes, he did,' says Hettie. 'She worked at the factory. He was seeing her. He got her pregnant and Oliver married her. When you asked to stay, I should have said no, but then I thought maybe he'd said something. I'm sorry, Roy.'

'It's hardly your fault, is it?' says Roy. 'She's going to be... I mean, with her mum and that Margaret woman and all that...'

'I know,' says Hettie. 'I'm worried about her.'

'Where is she now?'

'That's just it,' says Hettie. 'I don't know. Her dad said she took off, upset.'

'She'll be coming back to you,' says Roy.

'I hope so. I hope she'll be alright. It's a long drive.'

'If there's anything I can do,' he says.

'There's nothing at the minute. Call me tomorrow.'

He leaves the phone box. He remembers about getting his stuff from Geri's. He should have gone earlier. She'll be back from work now. He should get it over with. After what's happened today, who knows what could happen tomorrow? He drives the five-minute journey, going over what Hettie said on the phone, thinking how little he knew his dad, wondering how much Mum knew back then. As he parks up, he reflects on how Geri knew so little of him, and what a shaky foundation that was for what she wanted, what he thought he wanted. It had been too late telling her everything at the garage that morning; he should have done it a long time ago.

Geri's car is parked in its usual place. He sits for a minute. He could come back tomorrow. What if she gets upset? What if she asks him to stay? But he knows he can't duck this. He gets out and hurries to the door to get it over with. When she answers the bell, he can see two black bin bags in the hall behind her. Her features are fixed and controlled. He's relieved, then unsettled by that. Before he can speak, she's handing his things to him. He hadn't decided what he was going to say. He doesn't know now either – sorry again, maybe. He puts the bags down and goes to say it.

'Geri, I just want to—'

'Your key please,' she cuts in.

She's already closing the door as he hands it to her. As the latch clicks shut, he feels worse than if she'd cried. He feels like he's been found out. He knows he's the one at fault and it hurts to know it, that it's so clear she knows it. As he drives away, he looks over at the windows. The curtains are drawn.

He's nearly back at the flat when he realises he's not eaten since getting a sandwich at lunchtime. The nearest place is the takeaway a few streets from the flat. He hesitates. It's the one he used to go to with Shane. He hasn't been back there in the last few years. He's avoided all the places where Shane was known, avoided the awkward questions. He stops outside. They'll have forgotten him by now, he thinks. And they have. He realises that the teenage boy who serves him was the lad who used to sit at the back doing his homework at a little table in the corner while his parents served. Things have moved on, Roy thinks. If only he had too.

He takes his chop suey back to the flat. He's sure it used to taste better when he and Shane got it on the way home. He wonders if it had anything to do with the quantities of beer that had preceded it back then. He eats every bit though. He wishes he'd ordered something else to go with it and goes through the fridge and the cupboards, hoping Luiz might have left something edible. All he finds is sour milk, butter, and a bag of rice. He gives up, goes into the lounge, and tidies up the mess. The blood stains will have to wait until tomorrow now, he decides.

He stretches out on the couch, trying to piece things together again, thinking of that day when Mum and Dad had cut the holiday short and they'd left Hettie's in a hurry. He's trying to remember the days and weeks that followed, sure he'll think of something that will tell him more. But he can't. He thinks he was probably too busy with his bike or playing football or what was on the telly that night. Then he thinks of Ted. If Dad hadn't been having a thing with Hettie, why did Ted do what he did? Then there's Fiona. Hettie is the only person she has left to connect her to her mum. He knows enough of Fiona to realise what that means to her. She'll be going back to Ebwich. She must. He's calculating the journey time in his head when the doorbell goes.

Detective Sergeant Mullins stands outside. Roy's guts start churning. Is this about what he said to Andy Neams about Shane or is this about Luiz?

'Sorry to disturb you, I've just got a few more questions,' says Mullins.

'Okay,' says Roy.

But Mullins waits. He wants to be asked in. Roy steps back and. Mullins comes inside. Roy shuts the door and Mullins follows him into the lounge.

'Have a seat,' says Roy, deciding that's all he's going to offer him, hoping he won't be there long.

Mullins sits in the one armchair and Roy sits opposite on the couch.

'Mr Freitas was given a right going over, wasn't he?' says Mullins, scanning around the room.

'I haven't cleaned up properly yet,' says Roy.

'He said it was his friends. With friends like that...'

Mullins waits for Roy to contribute. Roy shrugs.

'I don't know his friends. I was subletting the flat to him for a few weeks. I hardly know him.'

'I've just come from the hospital,' says Mullins. 'I wanted to see if he'd changed his mind.'

Roy still doesn't respond. He knows this bloke hasn't bought Luiz's story.

'I gather you'd been there to see him,' says Mullins.

Roy tries to sound off-hand, unconcerned. 'Yeah, I just wanted to know he was alright. I found him, you know. I just...' Roy shrugs again, conscious he's not doing a good job of lying and wishing Mullins was on the other side of that door and on his way, conscious of the money under the floorboards a few feet from where Mullins is sitting. 'I just want to move back here.'

Mullins looks around the room. 'Yes, so you said.'

Roy knows Mullins is leaving a gap for him to fill. They both wait. He's surprised when Mullins gives in first.

'You don't know his friends in Dalston, then?'

He has been doing his homework, thinks Roy. 'No. Like I say, I hardly know him.'

Mullins nods. He's not agreeing though.

'How did you say you met him?'

'I didn't,' says Roy. 'I think it was at a pub or a club, out drinking a couple of months back. '

Mullins absorbs this. 'But he's lived her for almost six months.'

He really has been checking up, thinks Roy. I walked into that one.

'Yeah, alright. I didn't want the landlord to know I was subletting. I thought I could just say he was a mate staying here for a while.'

'So, how *did* you meet him?'

That's all he's getting, thinks Roy. I'm not saying Angola. Then, for a second, he wonders if Andy has told him about Shane and him. He can't know that much, he thinks. He goes back to the lie.

'Like I said, in a club or a pub.'

'But you know him a lot better than you're letting on.'

'No,' says Roy. 'I've been living at my girlfriend's place. He's been here on his own. I only came round to get the rent off him.'

Again, Mullins looks around the room. Roy's had enough of this game. He can't know all that much – at least not yet, he decides. Mullins stands up. Roy stands too, relieved but cautious, waiting for another question. There isn't one.

'Thanks again, Mr Brady. I'll leave you in peace.'

When Roy shuts the door, he loses all inclination to go out again. He looks around the flat. He hates what he sees. But this is it. He's back here again, like before – and there's no alternative.

# Fiona

FIONA WAKES ON Sally's couch. Her temporary bed reminds her of her uncertain status. She doesn't know if she can go back to Ebwich. She's been wondering how much Hettie knew, thinking about what Roy had told her, and concluding that Hettie knew everything. She hasn't phoned her yet, she's not even sure why. She needs to talk about this. But not to Hettie, not to Dad – someone with some distance from it all. Not Sally either. She has her own problems. Fiona knows who she wants to talk to – Lolly. She hears Sally telling Tina to go back to bed and not to go into the lounge yet. She sits up. She's going to see Lolly.

She dresses and goes through to the kitchen. Sally is making coffee. Her blotchy face suggests she hasn't slept much. Last night, several times, she'd told Fiona it was over between her and Luiz. Fiona knows that must have been hard and she's worried how she's coping with it.

'Are you okay?' she asks.

Sally shrugs and turns away. Fiona feels the urge to get back in the car and go. But she feels guilty at the thought of leaving Sally after what's happened with Luiz. And she wants to ask Sally about Roy too – she'd wanted to last night. When Sally turns back, she seems to have read her thoughts.

'Roy asked about you.'

Fiona tries not to react too quickly. 'Did he?'

'He was glad you could bring us back.'

What did that mean? Fiona asks herself. Did he not want to go back to Ebwich?

'Is he alright?'

Sally hands her a mug of tea. 'I think so. He doesn't know what he's going to do though.'

'That makes two of us,' says Fiona.

Sally doesn't reply. She doesn't suggest going to see him, or that he wants to see her. Fiona wonders if Sally knows something else – if she knows Roy is going back to Geri, and doesn't want to say it. Fiona decides not to ask. She's going to do what she resolved to do when she woke up.

'If it's okay with you,' she says, 'I'll get going.'

'Yeah, of course.'

It looks like Sally's going to say more, but Tina is in the kitchen now, clattering in the cupboard for a cereal bowl. A day ago, they were in Hettie's kitchen and Tina and Sally were the guests; now it's the other way around. The sudden change in circumstances is unsettling. This boxy little kitchen is getting to her. She needs to go. This is Sally's world – her and Tina's, this flat that's so different to Hettie's place, with its square corners and big flat windows. It's their home, she knows that. It must hold something for them, but she can't feel its soul, can't imagine living there. Fiona admonishes herself for those thoughts. She thinks of Sally there on her own when Tina is at school and wonders how she manages, how she'll manage now. Tina is chattering about seeing her friends when a neighbour rings the doorbell. As Sally talks on the doorstep, Fiona hugs Tina, grabs her bag and says a hasty goodbye and squeezes past Sally. She looks hurt. Fiona stops herself going back, gets in the car and goes.

Not far from Sally's flat, she stops for petrol, impatiently watching the digits flip round, anxious to get away. Then she drives and drives; numb now, just wanting to arrive.

She passes the turn-off for Lincoln – a reminder of Ebwich, of Hettie and the café. A little later, she stops and buys a sandwich. She should phone Hettie. She doesn't. As she eats, she looks at a dog-eared, out-of-date AA map that's kept in the car. It'll take at least two and a half more hours. She fills up with petrol again. She drives on, wondering if Lolly is even there, what she'll do if she isn't.

'Satisfy My Soul' comes on the radio. Angie was into Bob Marley in a big way. Fiona remembers her singing – head tipped back, eyes closed – whenever 'Waiting In Vain' came on the radio. She thinks of how they parted, another friend she's left behind – albeit in such different circumstances. She thinks how Angie wasn't offended when she turned down her offer to be part of the next fraud scheme she'd been planning since the day she'd been caught. Angie had just nodded her head and said it was a shame, a posh-tart accent would have been useful for selling investments – adding it was probably for the best they'd never meet again. Fiona smiles at the memory and drives on.

This time, as she drives the last mile or so, she's sure she knows where she's going. But her memory plays a couple of tricks on her and she finds she's gone past the farm before she realises it, lost in a recollection of how cold it was the last time she'd driven this road. The farm looks very different now, softened by the foliage and the afternoon sun on the stone. The old Volvo is parked out front, just like before, and she can hear a dog barking as she opens the car door – it must be Beans. Then she sees Lolly's face at the window.

For a few seconds, Lolly doesn't move. Fiona stays put too, not wanting to approach the door now, wishing she hadn't just turned up like this. Then Lolly disappears from sight and Fiona contemplates turning back to the car. Before she can, the door opens and Lolly rushes towards her. Her face is creased with joy. Fiona opens her arms to her and they squeeze each other tightly. Lolly's voice, next to Fiona's ear, confirms everything's okay.

'I'm so glad to see you.'

Over Lolly's shoulder, Fiona sees Frieda in the doorway holding Beans who's struggling to greet her too. Lolly hangs on tight.

'For goodness' sake, Lolly, let her come inside before

this dog pulls my arm off!'

Lolly releases her grip and Frieda takes her place, Beans squirming between their legs.

When they're sitting inside – this time in the front room which is no longer a building site, the furniture being relocated from the kitchen – and Lolly has already said she's sorry several times, Fiona cuts her off.

'Stop apologising. It's over. It was over a long time ago.'

They still haven't mentioned Clive. Fiona doesn't shirk it. She tells them what happened. They listen. They let her tell it all. Then she tells them about the last week and how she's come to be there. When she's finished, she feels like she's let the air out of a hard ball inside her, an insidious sphere that's been occupying space somewhere behind her ribs and is now gone.

Lolly and Frieda look at each other uncertainly. Lolly breaks the impasse.

'I can't imagine how you must feel.'

'I didn't really come to say all that,' says Fiona. 'But it's so much better now I have. I'm okay, really.'

Frieda glances at Lolly, an unseen message passing between them. 'Stay here. I mean, if you want to.'

'Yes,' says Lolly. 'Stay.'

'No,' says Fiona. 'I'm grateful for the offer, but I can't.'

'Just for tonight then,' Lolly persists.

Fiona hesitates. 'I should phone Hettie.'

'Phone her and go back tomorrow,' says Frieda.

Fiona is glad to hear Hettie's voice on the phone. It's the right time to talk to her, she thinks. When she asks Hettie if she's okay, Hettie says she is and waits for her to open the subject. Fiona is ready. She wants to say it.

'Dad told me Mum was pregnant when he married her, that he isn't my real father.' Fiona thinks she can hear a quiet sob. She goes on. 'He said you knew.'

She waits. All she hears is the faint hiss of the line. It feels more telling than any words. It's the sound of sad regret.

'I promised not to tell you,' Hettie says finally, her voice catching on the words.

'He told me that too,' says Fiona.

'It wasn't my place to tell you.'

'I suppose not,' says Fiona. 'Did you know him?'

'Yes.'

'Who was he?'

'Can we talk about it when you come back?'

'Do you want me to come back?'

'Of course I do,' says Hettie.

'I'll be back tomorrow.'

She stands by the phone, replaying their words. There was something in Hettie's tone. It bothers her that she can't pinpoint it.

Frieda cooks dinner and they share a bottle of wine. In the gaps in conversation, the gaps between reminiscences and old shared jokes, Fiona feels a warmth that she hasn't felt for a long time – a time even before she met these two. She doesn't belong here. But they do. They belong together. It makes her think she could belong somewhere too. She just has to know where and who with.

When the wine has gone and they've talked about the plans for the farm and the sheep, Frieda reminds Lolly they have to be up early as they have to move some electric fencing around. Lolly discretely rearranges one of the other bedrooms so Fiona doesn't have to sleep in the room she'd shared with Clive, and they say goodnight.

The room Fiona is in faces the barn where the van had stood. She stands at the window and looks out at the shape of the building in the dark, remembering Clive there, thinking how impatient he'd been to leave. There's a rush of pain at the memory, at the thought he didn't have to do what he did, that he might have found some happiness somewhere else, with someone else. She struggles to stop looking into that blackness, wishing it could have been different and knowing it was pointless to do so. She has to close her eyes before she can pull the curtains and turn to the bed, suddenly not wanting to be there now, wanting to go down and get in the car and drive away, but stopping herself thinking it, and promising herself she won't flee like she did from Sally's that morning.

When she wakes, and she hears Lolly and Frieda moving about, the need to go is still there. Downstairs, they are already eating their breakfast, telling her she didn't need to get up so early. She can tell this is their routine, and it makes things easier. She can go without feeling guilty. When Frieda is upstairs, Lolly puts her hand on Fiona's arm.

'You will come back, won't you?'

'Of course I will,' Fiona says.

'About Frieda and me, I wanted to—' Lolly starts to say.

'You don't have to explain,' Fiona says.

'Frieda finds it harder,' says Lolly. 'Her parents are

still upset. I'm sorry we had to be so selfish about it, not getting in touch.'

'It's okay. I'm happy for you both,' says Fiona, wanting to tell her about Roy, not sure if she should, if there's anything to tell her.

Lolly goes back to clearing the table. Frieda comes back downstairs and Fiona goes up to the bathroom. She's ready in a few minutes, pausing outside the room she shared with Clive, tempted to open the door but leaving it closed. She goes down to say goodbye, repeating her promise that she'll be back.

She calculates she could be back for lunch. As she drives, she thinks about how in the last week she's been in so many places and how everything has suddenly changed. It reminds her of those journeys with Clive. Except then they were travelling nowhere. It won't be like that now, she tells herself.

Hettie is serving lunches when Fiona parks up behind the café. Her estimate was right. Once again, the old car had got her home. She stands and thinks about that word. This is her home. She wants it to be, and she doesn't want it to be, and she can't think of any alternative. She leaves her bag in the kitchen and goes through to see Hettie. She's busy with customers. She looks over with a worried smile. Fiona looks around for tables to clear. It's going to be a while before they'll have time to talk.

When the lunchtime customers have gone and they can leave Iris on her own, they go through to the kitchen.

'You mustn't blame your dad,' Hettie says, as soon as she's closed the door.

'I'm trying not to,' says Fiona, and then wonders who she means by 'dad'.

'He accepted what had happened,' Hettie goes on. 'He accepted you. He wanted you. He meant well.'

'It makes us seem like charity cases,' says Fiona. 'Like he did Mum a favour and took us on, someone else's castoffs.'

'That's not how it was,' says Hettie.

'You said you knew him – my real dad.'

'I did. He—' Hettie hesitates, wipes her hands and pulls out a chair at the table.

Fiona knows this is the crux, the something that's lingering.

'Sit down a minute,' says Hettie.

# Chapter 18     1978

## Fiona

I DON'T KNOW what deal Dad had done. But when Margaret and Jo returned that first evening, they were almost aloof. That was okay. I couldn't have stood anything else. Margaret said she was doing lamb chops and disappeared into the kitchen. Jo started a conversation with Dad about the traffic congestion her and Margaret had experienced on their search for the engagement party venue, then steered it into a moan about the overcrowding on the trains, highlighting not only that the two of them were commuter comrades, but that she had a job in London, and that she and Dad had such things in common.

I couldn't listen to any more of it. I went upstairs. I could only have been in my room a few minutes when Jo was in the doorway and I'd regretted not closing the door. She looked around, keeping her eyes off me but managing to convey how outdated my room looked compared to hers. I waited for the comment, but she had something better ready.

'We'll probably move house soon,' she said.

She'd done it again; she'd just told me she knew something I didn't. I said nothing. But even that was letting her score her point. And she wasn't giving up.

'Didn't Dad tell you?'

*Dad*, I thought, drawing on everything I had not to react to her calling him that. She knew he hadn't told me. That's why she was there.

'No, I didn't,' I said. It was pointless trying to pretend otherwise. That would have given even more pleasure.

'David and I will be looking for a house soon too.'

I didn't respond. But she still wasn't finished. I knew she had more.

'I met Pamela Tomkins the other day,' she said. 'She works in the same building as me.'

I picked up a magazine and sat back on the bed. Pamela was at school with us, someone neither of us had much to do with. Why is Jo bringing her up? I asked myself. I didn't have to wait long to find out.

'She was talking about Lolly Graham and Frieda Wilson-Smith.'

Try as I might, I couldn't ignore that. I had to look over. Despite the smirk hovering on her face, I wanted her to go on.

'Did you know they're a couple?'

She'd just landed a second, successful blow. I wanted so badly to smack that smirk off her face. I pretended to look down at the magazine. Still, I knew she had more.

'Running a sheep farm, apparently. Who would have thought it?'

I got up. The smirk vanished. Jo knew that was as far as she could go. One more remark, and I don't know if

I'd have resisted letting go. But Margaret's voice saved her.

'Is everything alright, Jo?'

Her tone managed to imply that Jo might not have been safe up there with me. I breathed in hard, made myself count to ten, and told myself to let them play their games. All the same, the thing about moving, and the thing about Lolly and Frieda, had both stung me. Jo had known and I hadn't. She'd enjoyed that little conversation very much. She hadn't changed one little bit. At least I knew what I was up against.

Margaret's cooking hadn't changed either. But at least chewing on the overcooked, dry meal discouraged table conversation about what we'd all been doing that day. Getting out of jail might have trumped their little trip out, but I wasn't about to discuss it with those two witches. All I could think of was what I'd just heard from Jo. Every time she glanced my way, her face said knew that too. As soon as we'd finished, I said I was going out for a walk and asked Dad for a door key. Margaret turned from the sink and answered for him.

'There are no spares.'

'She can have mine,' said Dad. 'I'll get one cut tomorrow.'

Margaret stayed put, pan in hand, like she was about to argue. Dad ignored her look and went out to the hall and started taking a key off his key ring. She turned away and made do with some excessive clattering in the sink.

'She'll get used to it,' Dad said in a low voice when I got to the door.

'I'm not sure I will,' I replied, taking the key. 'Why

didn't you tell me you were planning to move house?'

'Look, Fiona, I didn't want to—'

'It's alright,' I said. 'With any luck I'll be gone by then anyway.'

Margaret reappeared in the kitchen doorway, hovering, pretending not to be there. I could see Dad wanted to say more. But I grabbed my coat and got out.

It wasn't until I walked out of the front door that evening that being outside the walls of Holloway became reality. Walking to Dad's car that morning hadn't felt like I'd thought it would – the huge sense of freedom I'd imagined. Walking away from the front door, I couldn't help thinking how that house already felt like another form of incarceration, and how wrong that was. I just couldn't breathe inside those four walls. But I could get out. So I walked.

I didn't know where I was going. I headed into town and walked along the High Street, avoiding the end where the police station was. I did a couple of circuits. When I'd put Margaret and Jo out of my mind, the space was filled with thoughts of Lolly and Frieda and how Jo's tittle-tattle explained the lack of communication. It hurt that they might have thought it would be a barrier to us still being friends. But they'd made a choice and perhaps I should just respect it, or maybe time might change things. I couldn't decide.

While this was going round in my head, I was getting colder and colder. I had no gloves or scarf and realised I should have put on something warmer under my coat. The cold forced me back in the direction of home, except it didn't feel like I was going home at all.

The television was on in the lounge when I closed the

front door and went straight up to my bedroom. The prospect of sitting on the couch next to Jo, like I used to, was too much. I began a pattern that night; retreating to my room, my time capsule, the one place in that house that still felt like home. What started as a welcome refuge became an alternative prison cell. I did something then I'd never done in Holloway – I counted out the number of days I'd have to spend there before I could expect to get out.

The next morning I registered at the Jobcentre. I was through those doors as soon as they opened. My approach was to try for something local first – it didn't matter what. If I could earn some money, I reasoned, I could then look for something further afield, something where the pay meant I had a chance of a flat share, a bedsit, anything but staying in that house.

The woman at the desk went through the forms with me. She was very upbeat when I told her what A-levels and O-levels I had. She breezed on to my employment history, noting my four months at Grey and Garton's, smiled and waited to hear where I'd moved to next. Even before I replied, her smile faded as she looked down at the form again. She'd worked out where she'd heard my name and she knew there were no further jobs to put on my record. She looked up and briefly met my eyes as I told her what she already knew. But she pressed on and asked what the sort of position I was looking for. Anything, I replied. Surely, I thought, that made it easy for her. Surely they must have something. It didn't. They didn't.

While I looked at the job boards, she made several phone calls. She did her best. She gave me a UB40 form, told me to check back in a few days, and in the meantime take another form to the unemployment benefit office. At the benefit office, I was handed another form. This one would go to the DSS. I was told I'd get an appointment for an interview before I'd get any money. Next, I bought the local paper, sat in the Wimpy, and went through the meagre half page of job adverts. I scanned through the building trades' vacancies and down to commission-only sales (own transport required). I'd never built anything in my life, had no sales experience, and doubted my old bike counted as transport – assuming Margaret hadn't got rid of it. Then I worked my way round every shop in town, asking if they wanted anyone. Surely, I thought, there'd be a shop job going. And there was – just one, at H H Johnson the bakers.

I never found out what the second H stood for, but Mr Johnson, Harry to the older customers, was a nice old gent. He remembered Mum. He remembered me coming in with her, he said. He didn't say he remembered what had happened at Grey and Garton's, but I was pretty sure he did. To get things straight, though, I told him where I'd spent the last couple of years. He took it in his stride and said he needed someone in the shop, as his sister-in-law, Alice, was retiring in a couple of weeks. He even said we could work around my probation meetings. He said I could start the next day if I wanted and learn the ropes while Alice was still there. So I did.

Everyone in the shop was nice enough. No one asked any nosey questions, but there would never be a social life attached to this job. As soon as they were done, the two other women were off to cook and clean at home. There would be no trips to the pub or girls' nights out, or any of the things I'd been doing when I'd first met Clive. But I could hold my head up at home and my probation officer was happy. It was a job, and I was getting paid. When I asked Dad how much Jo was contributing towards the household expenses – so I could do the same, just like I used to – his hesitation surprised me. In the kitchen, Margaret's radar had turned on and she'd appeared in the doorway. My question had annoyed her.

'Jo's saving for a house. We don't expect her to pay anything.'

Dad gave me a look that said 'Don't push it.'

But she'd already fired me up. 'What do you expect from me then?' I said.

That threw her. It was one of the rare occasions she was lost for words. She looked at Dad.

'We'll talk about it later,' said Dad. This time his face said '*Please*, don't push it.'

So I didn't. It was more money to save towards getting out of there. A new, just-about-tolerable phase began. I went to work. I came home. I read more library books than I even did in Holloway, and I looked for things to do. I discovered I could do cookery evening classes in Bromley. Helping Hettie a couple of years before had got me interested – and we talked a lot about food in Holloway. But I think the real reason was to annoy Margaret by practicing recipes when she was out and offering to cook as my 'contribution'. I wasn't Margaret's kitchen skivvy though. I disappeared whenever she reclaimed her domain. But what peeved her (and Jo) most was how much they liked my cooking. They tried so hard not to, but the way every dish got finished up told another story. At work, Mr Johnson had picked up on my interest and had got me doing some of the baking. I came up with some ideas for different cakes. Soon the customers were asking for slices of my carrot cake and special Victoria sponge, and he rearranged the early-morning bake to fit my stuff in. I was doing more baking and less serving and I loved it. I'd finally found something to focus on, and life became more bearable.

I welcomed not being at the counter so much for another reason too. The bakery was popular at lunchtimes, especially with workers in the town. Usually someone from Grey and Garton's called in to do the sandwich run. I'd always known I'd have to serve people who knew me, and knew what I'd done. It was only a matter of time before one of them stood in my queue. So it was no surprise when, one lunchtime, I had to serve Hilary. She was more on edge than I was, fluffing the order and avoiding looking at me. I'd have liked to ask her if she still had those raucous nights out like we used to, maybe get an invite to join them again, but she didn't give me the chance. She just grabbed her order and almost forgot the change.

After seeing Hilary, it wasn't meeting my old workmates that bothered me. It was just Clive's mum I was dreading seeing. I had this premonition that one day she'd be standing on the other side of that counter too. But the dread gradually receded. The weeks passed and I was doing okay.

About then, Margaret did a U-turn on the cookery

front and even asked me to cook a couple of times a week. It usually coincided with David's visits. He was often at the house in those days. His presence had the benefit of Margaret being on her best behaviour. She avoided any conflict with him around, and I think it pleased her to have me in the kitchen while she entertained.

Jo had two states whenever David was in the house: glued to him like they shared the same blood supply, or watching me closely as if I was about to steal him from her. Neither state was pleasant. I avoided being with them whenever I could. Being the family cook on those occasions suited me as much as it did Margaret. Besides, I was making plans. I was going to visit Hettie as soon as I could. We'd had lots of phone calls about it. I'd already cleared things with my probation officer, and I was ready to tackle Mr Johnson about some holiday. Then Clive's mum turned up.

The other bakery on the High Street had suffered a fire. While the place was being stripped out and refitted, we were getting a lot of their customers. We were extra busy and we were all on the counter. One morning, I looked at the queue stretching to the door and saw Denise's eyes focussed on me, hard and loaded with pain. We needed more white rolls. That gave me the opportunity to get away from that stare. I found a few other things to do in the back too. I waited until she'd been served before I went back to the counter.

When I'd first got out, I'd thought of going to see Clive's mum, but I never had the courage – or the words to say to her. I hoped that encounter was it. She'd seen me, she knew I was back, and it was done with.

But it wasn't. That evening, after we'd closed up, she was waiting for me. I was about to cross the road at the Bricklayers Arms when I was aware of footsteps speeding up behind me, then her voice, a strangled, angry shout.

'You've got a bloody cheek!'

I turned, but I already knew who it was. I crossed over and walked on, faster. She kept up. There were plenty of people around. I didn't feel threatened, but I didn't want this to happen on the High Street.

'Coming back here!'

She kept this up until I got to Village Way. I stopped. Maybe if I said something, tried to explain.

'I'm sorry about what happened to Clive,' I said. 'But that was his choice.'

'His choice? You conniving bitch!'

I started walking again. She was soon behind me again, calling me a murderer and saying she hoped I rotted in hell. I'd got as far as the catholic church when a voice called out. 'Denise!'

I glanced back and could see a man waiting for a car to pass before he crossed. I guessed it was Jeffery. She'd stopped, torn between pursuing me and waiting for him.

'Denise, love.'

She turned back to shout at me. 'Saying those things about Clive. He'd never have done any of that if it hadn't been for you!'

I didn't look back, but Jeffery must have caught up with her. He was pleading. 'Denise, love. Leave it.'

I got going as fast as I could, thinking she'd said her piece, that was it. It wasn't.

Jeffery probably tried to persuade her to keep away from the shop. He must have managed it for a few days and I really did think that was it. Then she came back one lunchtime and made another scene, shouting the same things, like she'd prepared a script and couldn't depart from it. Mr Johnson got her out of the door and told her he'd phone the police if she came back. She was back that evening though. This time, Jeffery didn't rescue me. This time, she screamed at me and clawed at me until I only got away from her by running, and I could run faster than she could. The next few evenings would have been the same had I not gone out through the back and avoided her. She soon worked that out. Whenever I left, I had to play a ridiculous game of checking back and front, then dodging her to get away.

Mr Johnson said I should talk to the police. I didn't want to. Apart from being out on licence and not wanting to jeopardise anything, I felt sorry for her. Some of what she said was true. The pain of those months after hearing what Clive did came right back. My bearable time seemed over; another punishment seemed to have begun. I dashed home every night and retreated to my room. I avoided going out anywhere. Then a week or so passed when she didn't appear. Surely that was it. It wasn't.

Mrs Rathley had worked out where I lived. She must have had an idea from when I was going out with Clive. She'd have known the street at least. But, one night, around ten o'clock, the doorbell rang and Dad went to the door. I heard her voice. I knew she'd found me. At full volume, she started on her script – this time telling him what his daughter was, what I'd done, this time adding that I was a little slut who'd messed her son up and had his death on her conscience. Dad handled it well. His voice was calm as he tried to persuade her to leave. But she wasn't giving up. Her shouting grew to a screech. He didn't know what to say or do then – he just stood there and took it. Jo and Margaret had come into the hall to see who it was. I was behind them. I didn't know what to do. If she saw me, it would surely provoke her; if I stayed inside, she might do something to Dad. I didn't think about it for long. I told Jo to phone the police and pushed past her and Margaret.

'We're calling the police,' I said. 'So you'd better go now.'

'You're calling the police! You murdered my boy and you're calling the police!' And she was off on the same trail about everything being my fault, hoping I'd 'rot in hell.' Then she bent down and took a rock from the ornamental edging. I could hear Jo on the phone, but even if the police came straight away, someone was going to get hurt. Dad must have decided the same. He grabbed me and pulled me back inside, just closing the door before the rock made contact. As we all stood inside, wondering if she would beat the door down, we heard a more metallic bang from outside. I went to the window in the front room in time to see her pounding Dad's car with the rock and making a good job of it too.

She didn't wait for the police to arrive though. I saw her stagger away, drained, disappearing out of sight and leaving more than the damage to a car behind her. Margaret's urgent tones had already struck up in the kitchen, telling Dad she wasn't standing for this in *her* house and asking who would pay for the damage to the car. This time I didn't hold back. I pulled open the kitchen door and told her it wasn't her house, that she'd wormed her way into it and into our lives because she'd been looking for a meal ticket and someone to take her and her sly little bitch of a daughter on. The colour drained from her face and her eyes bulged. I knew there was no going back, and yet saying those things brought an enormous relief. I'd wanted to say them so many times – and it felt good. Her face crumbled, and she looked towards Dad, expectantly, waiting for his support. I looked at him too. He was torn. I'd put him in an impossible situation, but I wasn't about to have the last remains of control taken away from me. I wasn't going to ask him to choose. I was going to make it easy for him.

'I'll talk to my probation officer tomorrow,' I said. 'And I'll find somewhere else to live.'

'Fiona, you don't have to do that. We can —' Dad had finally found some words, but I didn't let him finish.

'I do have to,' I said.

Dad went back to the kitchen for more words with Margaret. When the two police officers turned up, I told them what had been happening at the shop, who Denise was, and why she'd been there. Dad said he didn't want her charged with the damage to the car, overriding Margaret's protests.

As the police officers left, bemused, Jo stood by the stairs. She'd been listening with a growing gleam of satisfaction on her face. I stopped a foot from her and looked into her eyes. She tried hard to return my stare.

'If I see a smirk on your face,' I said. 'I'll wipe it off for you.'

Even she knew this was something different. Her stare wavered, her eyes got watery. From the kitchen doorway, Margaret's voice, thin and wailing, attempted a rescue, appealing to Dad.

'Are you going to let her talk to Jo like that?'

But he didn't reply and Jo was withering. She slid to one side, giving the space to me.

'Good idea,' I said. 'Stay out of my way.'

The satisfaction only lasted until I'd reached my room. After years of self-control, in far more dangerous situations than that had been, I'd lost it. Yes, it felt good at the time, but my original plan had been much better – to have stayed long enough to have somewhere to go had been the smarter move. Now I had to go. But I was determined to go, no matter what the cost. And there was only one place to go. That's when I phoned Hettie.

# Roy

I CAME TO realise that Geri's sad smile was her attempt to conceal how life with her husband, Vic, was. One of the other mechanics, Ronnie, had already told me Vic was an arsehole that didn't know when he was well off. Despite being nearly forty, Vic was living the life of a teenager. His weekends seemed to start on a Thursday and last until the following Monday. He'd either be found in the bookies or the pub next door, except for Saturday when he'd be wherever Millwall was playing and wherever the fans were drinking. He often didn't make it home on the Saturday night and it could be the Sunday afternoon before he'd turn up with his hangover and his bruises from whatever fracas he'd got involved in. His solution was to keep on drinking. How he kept his job at the builders' merchants was a mystery to everyone, although, apparently, his boss wasn't much better. I used to see Kirk in the little office every Monday, in earnest conversation with Geri, her gesticulating in frustration and looking tearful for the rest of the day. The word amongst the other lads was that Vic was on borrowed time and Kirk was just restraining himself from giving him a taste of his largest adjustable spanner.

Despite the background drama, or maybe because of its distractions, I was settling in at the garage. Kirk was a good boss. I was earning a bit more and liked working there. It was still a tough time when I was on my own in the flat, between my abortive attempts at relationships. Everyone I knew in the area, I knew through Shane, and I avoided them, knowing what their first question would be.

It didn't help that everyone at work knew each other, knew their friends, went to school with them or their siblings. It wasn't deliberate, but I was an outsider. I'd never be part of their world. I don't think I wanted to be. When we did talk over our tea breaks, I never felt the inclination to say much about what I'd done. Life in the army and the stuff I'd done afterwards, especially Angola, wouldn't have meant much to them anyway. Even if they were interested, I couldn't imagine talking about it. I still thought about it though; I still thought about Shane, and I still visited Sally and Tina, but I never spoke of my past with anyone.

On one tea break, Vic appeared. He went straight through the workshop to the office to see Geri. It must have been a Tuesday because he was sober, and he must have known Kirk was out because I doubt he'd have turned up otherwise. We could hear their raised voices from the other side of the garage. The other lads reckoned Geri had told Vic to sling his hook, had the locks changed and dropped his gear off at his mate's place. It sounded like Vic wasn't happy with the arrangement and was demanding to be let back in. Our conversation dwindled as the volume from the office increased. I could see the door from where I was sitting up on the workbench. It looked like Vic was leaning over the desk at Geri. When I saw her pull back, I was off that bench double quick.

Vic's reaction to me pulling open the door – a cursory 'And you can fuck off!' before he turned back to Geri – was his first mistake. I got hold of him by the neck of his jacket and pulled him back, switched my grip to his throat and rammed him into the back of the door. I'm no street fighter, but Vic was only a hard man when he was with his football mates and someone was on the ground they could kick. I doubted he could do much face-to-face stuff. He gave it his best shot though. He got one in on my left ear before I put his head through the flimsy glass panel in the door. He was lucky with that glass, but his nose was spouting blood and he'd had enough already. The other mechanics left their tea. We all watched Vic stagger to his feet, look around at everyone, call Geri a fucking cow, and head for the street.

I couldn't do much wrong in the garage after that. My

mistake was to think that it had been fate, that Geri's split with Vic had happened because me and Geri were meant to be. To start with, that's how it seemed. It's not that we fell into bed that same night either; it was more than a month before I even asked her out. Both being on our own, and neither liking it, was the main reason. At the time, it seemed a good enough reason.

Geri split up with Vic in May. By that September, I was spending a few nights a week at her place and everyone at the garage knew. Kirk seemed happy about it and happy that Geri seemed to take things slowly, making no plans other than getting a divorce from Vic. By December that year, Geri was saying it was daft, me living in my flat when I was spending so much time at her house, and why didn't I just move in? I made excuses and held off for a few weeks. Mum had been getting dizzy spells, and I'd been going over to Dagenham a lot more then.

Mum wouldn't admit much. She just kept saying she had tablets from the doctor and didn't want a fuss made over it. But I knew it was serious. She'd been talking about Dad a lot then, about their life together and how it had been when they adopted me. That wasn't like her. It was as if she was summing up her life for me, drawing it to a close. She hadn't managed well since Dad died. I noticed how the house wasn't clean like it used to be. She wouldn't let anyone help her with it either. She seemed to have given up. Later, I realised I'd been downplaying it all, pretending even to myself, ignoring the signs.

On my last visit, I'd been trying to get her to talk about Christmas, saying I'd stay over and we'd do a

Christmas lunch like we used to. It would have been the first Christmas we'd done that without Dad, and I could see the prospect was too much for her. I told her we had to do something and as Christmas day was on a Monday, I could come over on the Saturday and we'd do the shopping together. I didn't tell her Kirk had asked me to go to their house for Christmas lunch and I'd said I couldn't with Mum being on her own. Geri was disappointed and had been scheming to get me to bring Mum over too. But the way Mum was, I knew that wasn't going to happen – she hadn't even met Geri's mum and dad.

In desperation, I put the idea to Mum and she got annoyed with me for suggesting it, finally agreeing that I'd go over to her and we'd have Christmas together. I was about to go, mission accomplished, when she said someone had phoned for me, a few days before, someone called Lewis? Luiz, I said, after I'd finally worked out who it could be. She recounted a confused conversation with him and how he'd given her a number and wanted me to phone. She couldn't understand why he said he'd met me in Angola. Had I been to Angola? She decided it must be something to do with my army days and she'd written the number down.

As I drove home that evening, it hit me how little I'd thought about Shane, Angola or Luiz since being with Geri. I took that as a good sign. I'd still been seeing Sally and Tina though. I'd go over when Geri had her 'girls' night out' on Saturdays. She'd started that routine when Vic had been doing his weekend disappearing acts and I'd encouraged her to keep it up, saying I didn't mind a night in on my own. Having told that little lie, it had got harder and harder to tell the truth about where I'd been going; how I'd pick up a takeaway every Saturday evening and that it was Tina's treat to stay up and eat it with us in front of the telly. Or how, when the weather was nice, we'd go to Victoria Park. Or even how Sally had suggested I spent Christmas day with them.

A part of me wanted to ignore Luiz's message. But I did phone him. I was curious to know what happened after he left me in Pointe-Noire, no more than that. Then, when I heard his voice, and we talked of our journey out of Angola, I felt a connection to him. And it was a distraction from the worry about Mum's health, the confusion over Geri, and the fear of being nowhere and going nowhere. When I'd last seen Luiz, I'd been going somewhere, going home.

Luiz was upbeat on the phone, telling me he'd come to London to make some money, barely mentioning going back to Portugal, and answering my questions about his family with short answers that veered back into his optimistic plans. He said he was living in Dalston and we should meet up the following night. He suggested The Cat and Mutton on Broadway Market. It sounded like he was finding his way around. I agreed straightaway.

But I didn't see Luiz until the New Year because the next day I got a phone call at the garage to tell me Mum had been admitted to hospital. I spent most of that Christmas worrying about her or driving back and forth to see her. With Dad gone, I was suddenly aware she was the only person I had left that really knew me. And even then, I'd lied to her about so much.

Christmas lunch reverted to Geri's original plan – me going to her mum and dad's place. By now, the flat was even less bearable than it had been before. I'd given up chasing the landlord's promises to fix up the bathroom and kitchen and spent as little time there as I could. Kirk and Judy's Christmas decorations and generous welcome were just what I needed. When I caught Geri's eyes over the table, I told myself this was what I wanted, something a bit more permanent and somewhere that felt like home, like home used to feel.

Mum only lasted until the end of December. She never came out of hospital. The night I dashed over to see her before she died, I was surprised by how much she had to say. She seemed to want to spend her last drops of life in words, words to me. She wanted to tell me, all over again, about the day she and Dad brought me home and what it had meant to her. Then she said some things about Dad, things I never expected to hear. She said she knew what he was like when she married him, that he had 'a roving eye' and that her friends, including Hettie, had warned her about him, but she didn't listen. She said she didn't regret what she'd done, that he couldn't help how he was, and she always knew he loved her and that was what mattered. She said I needed to find the right person too, and she hoped I would. After that, she lay quietly. Twenty minutes after that, she was dead. Geri had come with me. She was waiting outside. She said I shouldn't go back to my flat, I should move in with her. So I did.

# Chapter 19      1980

# Roy

AFTER RETURNING FROM Ebwich, Roy took the first job that came along – in a tyre fitters in Waltham Cross, where he knew no one. He lasted five months there before he made his decision. Christmas on his own had been the worst time, the trigger point that decided what he was about to do. His memories of the previous Christmas when Mum had gone into hospital, along with hearing his workmates' plans for the holiday period, made the decision easier. Pride had kept him from doing it before. Throughout that autumn, he'd wondered what Fiona was doing, and often thought about phoning her. Putting it off meant he couldn't get a refusal. If he did nothing, the possibility, miles away, was still there – so long as he didn't call her and hear what he didn't want to hear. It might have stayed like this if it Sally hadn't told him Fiona had written and asked for his address. But there'd been no letter from Fiona – why not?

Then the Christmas card arrived from Hettie. She'd

written in it 'Give us a call. We'd love to hear from you.' There was something significant about the 'us' and 'we'. He looked at those words and read them over and over again until, on New Year's Day, he stuffed some clothes in a bag, locked the door of the flat and hurried to his car.

Now he's on his way. He's not going to let anything hold him up – and snow is forecast for tomorrow. The flat and the job can wait, he thinks. This is the most important thing now. He makes good progress. In less than half an hour he's on the A1. He turns on the radio. There's no traffic news. The roads are quiet. He's not in the mood for Dave Lee Travis. He pushes another pre-set. Terry Wogan is working through the most-played tracks from the year just gone. Gloria Gaynor tells him 'I Will Survive', and it makes him think how lucky he's been, how much worse things might have turned out. He has survived. The watery sunshine and the snap of the cool air outside, seems to endorse it.

After he'd found Luiz in the flat, things had gone quiet. He'd been expecting the police to come back again. They never did. When he'd collected Luiz from the hospital and told him he'd take him anywhere but the flat, he'd meant it. Things with Luiz were not going back to how they had been, no matter how dismal the alternatives looked. He'd expected Luiz to protest, he'd even expected him to ask for a lift to Sally's place. He'd already promised Sally he wouldn't do that. But Luiz gave him an address in Shoreditch, saying Tomás had sorted out somewhere for him.

Roy knew Tomás had been to the hospital. He knew that because Luiz had asked him to give Tomás a thousand pounds from the money under the floorboards. And Luiz already had plans for the rest of the money – he'd said so when he'd taken it from him. Roy had cleared his debt. He didn't need to tell Luiz not to contact him. He could tell from the way he'd looked at him, eyes a little sad, mouth tight; and from the way he'd half-heartedly offered him in on the next deal and how he'd said no more when Roy hadn't responded. They had shaken hands. That was it.

As the tarmac of the A1 rolls underneath him, he thinks how so many of his journeys with Luiz were landmarks, markers of things that would stay in the past now. They were done. As he crosses the Brampton Hut roundabout, the news on the radio breaks into his thoughts. Soviet troops have been moving to seal off the border in Afghanistan. President Carter is promising tough action. Two soldiers in Northern Ireland have been killed in some kind of shooting accident. He thinks about how their families will be feeling at the start of the New Year.

It's a relief that Christmas is over, that New Year's Eve is over. For the first time in a long while, the coming new year seems significant, worth considering. Sally and Tina spent their Christmas with Steve, her new bloke. Roy has met him a couple of times. They get on okay, but Roy knows Steve is still weighing him up, probably wondering about his relationship with Sally. He's not sure how much she's told Steve about Shane and him. She must have told him something, but Roy senses Steve has some concerns, some questions maybe. When the moment's right, he'll tell him some things.

Since Steve came along, Roy's seen less of Sally and

Tina, something that saddens him, something else behind his decision to set off on this journey. Seeing Sally with Steve was another nudge too. He has to give her credit there; she's moving on. He recalls it was her that gave Shane the heave-ho. He wonders where they'd all be if she hadn't, then tells himself how stupid it is to even consider that.

He's past Spalding. He's done a hundred miles now. He's thinking about the last time he'd driven north on this road, that warm summer's day, worrying about Luiz, trying not to resent having Sally and Tina in the car, worrying about them and about what he'd just done to Geri. He thinks about how he'd never even met Fiona then. This time it's different; it's Fiona he's thinking about now, already planning how to save face if he's wrong, if she's not interested. Art Garfunkel is singing 'Since I Don't Have You' and he drops his speed a little. There's nothing to overtake; the miles are slipping by all on their own. He can think now.

He's had plenty of time to think since last summer. He's come to the conclusion that blame or bearing a grudge won't solve anything. It was hardly an earth-shattering conclusion, but it helped, it focussed him. Alone in the car, going somewhere at last, he feels that focus. It feels good. Wogan is playing Herb Alpert's 'Rise'. The trumpet notes blend with the passing trees and fields. He drives on.

Wogan's show finishes. He turns the radio off. He stops at a petrol station. He fills the tank to the brim. He buys crisps, a Mars bar, and a tin of Coke. There won't be that many places open today and he'd been in too much of a hurry for breakfast. He used to like those roadside stops when he was a kid. Usually he'd wangle a fizzy drink or an ice cream, Dad kidding him he wasn't getting anything, then letting him out of the car to choose, and Mum telling him to mind the seats. As he rejoins the road, he's thinking of her. She knew what Dad had been up to. She knew everything, he decides. She always did. But he still can't understand her acceptance and tolerance of Dad

And Fiona never met him. She never met her real father. He wonders about that too. There are things he can tell her. At least that's something he has to offer. Of course, Hettie could tell her about him too. Or does she not want to hear? And how was Hettie now? His assumption, that she was the one his dad was involved with, had been Ted's assumption too. What happened between them that afternoon after Dad had driven him and Mum away? Whatever it was, she's had to live with it for almost twenty-five years.

He pulls into a lay-by for a pee. He's passed the turn off for Skegness. He knows it can't be much more than half an hour now. How's he going to play this? He thinks he should have phoned. He could find a phone box before he gets there. He sits in the car wondering why the hell he's done this, doubting himself now. Then he thinks of what it will be like if he goes back, if he'll ever do this again. He starts the car. He drives on.

Ebwich is on the road sign. There hasn't been another car on the road for miles. He's recognising farms and bends in the road. He can smell the sea. He wants to hurry now, but the curves of the road don't let him. He passes the turn where Ted's car was found. Then it's the last mile. It's come up quickly. On a straight section of the road, another car approaches. He knows the shape. It's an Austin Maxi. It could be anyone. But he knows it isn't. He knows who it is. Yet even as they close on each other, he can't react. As they pass, he looks at her and she looks at him. Like a camera shutter, he registers an image of her face and then she's gone. He doesn't know what to do.

It's a few miles before he feels his foot come off the accelerator. There's a gateway coming up. He brakes hard and reverses into it, swings round and heads after her.

# Fiona

HE'S GONE. IT was definitely him. She can't react. She keeps going, confused. Then she knows he's coming there to see her. She knows it with certainty. Since July she's thought of him every day, hoped every day he'd phone. They don't get that many phone calls. Every time that phone has rung she'd hoped it was him. Hettie knew it. She was almost apologetic when it was just a call about a delivery or from the plumber doing the new bathroom, or someone about the other refurbishments they'd had done. Now that the work is nearly finished, and it's too early for spring bookings, there's less to do. It's so cold there today. She can't imagine anyone booking a holiday. Weeks ago, she'd written to Sally, asking for Roy's address. Sally had finally replied with a short note telling her the news that she'd met a lovely bloke called Steve. She'd looked at that address every day since then. Today she'd decided that's where she was going.

Hettie has been talking about taking more of a backseat, hinting that Fiona could run the place, that it's going to be hers one day. Fiona's touched by that trust, the generosity that she doesn't feel she deserves, and yet it only makes things worse. If she was here and he was there, what chance can there ever be? She's lain awake so many nights thinking that if Roy hadn't been adopted, he'd be her half-brother. The things about him she'd liked so much, that seemed such a deep part of him – where had they come from? It's a strange thought that her real father was the man who'd brought him up.

That morning, she'd hesitated so many times before telling Hettie what she was going to do. It was a ludicrous idea, setting off on New Year's Day to find him, but she knew it had to be then or she'd never do it. When she'd said it, Hettie hadn't looked surprised at all. She'd said she should take some sandwiches, as there'd be nowhere open on the journey. That had made her smile.

Then Hettie said she was worried about the car, that the weather was going to get worse. Fiona had said it was all the more reason to get going, get ahead of it. As she pulled away, glimpsing Hettie's face in the rearview mirror, it dawned on her Hettie might be scared she'd be on her own again. She'd wanted to jam the brakes on, run back and reassure her. But she couldn't. She might not set off again if she did.

She's braking hard now though. He's here. He's heading for Ebwich and she's heading the wrong way. She turns. She pushes the car harder than she ever does.

She's just thinking she'll be behind him before he reaches the café when she sees his car approaching from the opposite direction. He's turned around too. What's he doing? Is he running away? But from his face behind the windscreen, the smile, he's not. They both slow down until they're side by side. They open their windows.

'Where were you going?' he asks.

'To find you,' she says.

'But I was coming to find you,' he says.

'Then we're both idiots,' she says.

He follows her. It's strange looking in the mirror and seeing him there. There's so much she wanted to say. She doesn't have to now, not yet anyway. It's enough that he's here.

For the first few weeks after she'd got back, she was convinced he'd be with Sally. After this Luiz person had thrown their lives into chaos, it would only be natural they'd turn to each other. And maybe his father's behaviour, his adoptive father's behaviour, had left him ashamed or embarrassed. He may not have wanted to come back there ever again. Yet something else told her differently – that he wanted her like she wanted him. Then she'd go round that loop once more, and once more decide she'd never see him again. When she wasn't thinking all this, she was thinking about the man she still thought of as her dad, despite knowing he wasn't.

It was a bitter thought when she realised that she and Jo had that much in common, that he was the father of neither of them. All that time she'd resented sharing him with Jo. All that time growing up, Jo was the one who still had her real parents – while she had no one. And she'd resented Jo calling him dad. And the person who knew her father best of all was Roy. And Hettie had known it all along. For all the things that Jo had known, that was the one thing she didn't. Fiona knew that for sure. It was a poor, grim consolation.

When she'd got back to Ebwich from Lolly and Frieda's, her dad had rung. Hettie had told her he'd already called a number of times. She'd listened to his voice – quiet, doubtless in the bedroom, not wanting Margaret to hear. He'd apologised over and over. She'd told him to stop. She still didn't know what to think, but she didn't blame him. Then he asked if he could come up and see her. She said yes, she'd like that. And he had. They'd spent a weekend together in August. They'd sat on the beach, they'd eaten in the café, they'd talked like they'd never talked before. He'd told Fiona that his mistake was to marry her mum out of sympathy, and her mistake was to let him. He also told her he still thought of her as his daughter. He always would.

# *Home*

# Epilogue

## 1990

# Lil

I'M REALLY EXCITED because Sally, Steve and Tina are coming to stay. They come here every summer. Tina is much older than me. She is seventeen and I am only six. We will go to the beach and all have our meals together in the kitchen, or in the café when it's closed. I really like that because people go past and they can't come in then. It's just ours. This year my grandad will be here too. He'll come to the beach with us. He'll tell us about when he was the captain of a big ship and all the things that happened to him. One time, pirates attacked his ship but the crew of the ship got them off. He told us how angry they were and how they went round and round them in their boat, threatening to kill them. But they couldn't because Grandad sailed his ship away. I love hearing his stories. I love living near the sea too, especially when the weather is so hot like it is now.

Actually, he's not really my grandad. Mum told me he got married to her mum before my mum was born, but he wasn't Mum's real dad. I'm not sure about that because she calls him Dad. She told me that her real dad is my dad's dad. Brothers can't marry their sisters. But I think it's okay because Dad was adopted and his mum and dad weren't his real mum and dad. It's so confusing! I talked to Tina about it. She said her dad, Steve, isn't her real dad, but she doesn't mind because she loves him and he's just like a dad to her. She said her real dad was killed when she was very small. He was in a war in Africa. My dad was there too. When I asked him about it, he said it was all a long time ago. He said it was a big mistake that Tina's dad got killed. He looked sad and his voice got all croaky. I think he wanted to cry.

Tina says my dad looked after her and her mum when her dad died. She says that's when they first came here to Ebwich. But it wasn't as nice then, and she remembers her mum being upset. My mum says that when people are upset and they come here, everything gets better. She says that Auntie Hettie makes things better. She's made things better for me lots of times, like when I got stung twice by a wasp on the same day and when I fell off the swing and hurt my leg. Mum is right. This is a nice place to live. The other children at school don't live in a café and they don't have their aunties living in their houses like I do.

Auntie Hettie is really my great auntie, my mum's auntie. Mum never calls her auntie. I don't know why. The café was Auntie Hettie's café and now it's Mum and Dad's. My grandma lived here once too. She really was my grandma. It was during the Second World War. We learnt all about it at school. The towns were being bombed and lots of children had to leave their homes to come to places like Ebwich, where they would be safe. That's why my grandma came here. She had my bedroom then. She died when my mum was a little girl, just a bit older than me. After that, my mum had my bedroom. Now Mum shares the big bedroom at the back with Dad. In my bedroom, there's a part of the wall where Grandma drew a picture of all the children waiting to get on a boat. They were leaving London because Hitler's aeroplanes were going to drop bombs on them.

My dad comes from London. He's my real dad. He's good at mending cars. He owns the garage in the village. He came here to live with my mum and Auntie Hettie before I was born. I haven't been to London yet, but Tina says I can stay there with her when I'm older and we can go to Buckingham Palace and Big Ben. I'm going to save up my money from clearing the tables in the café.

Mum's friends, Lolly and Frieda, are coming to stay for a few days too. The house is going to be full. Lolly and Frieda come here every summer. I always laugh at Lolly's name. I ask her why her mum and dad had called her after an ice cream and she laughs too. Lolly has a big smiley face. Everyone smiles when she is here. Lolly and Frieda have a farm. We have been to the farm lots of times. I love it there. My mum had to live at her school with Lolly and Frieda. She didn't come back home every afternoon like I do. I don't think she liked that much, but she says she had a lot of fun with Lolly and Frieda and it made them friends forever. I have to stop writing because I can hear a car in the back yard. Tina will want to go to the beach as soon as she gets out.

# Tina

WE'D DONE THE familiar journey in good time. After the usual stop for a drink, we'd pressed on so we'd be there for lunch. I always love going to Ebwich. I love seeing Fiona, Roy and Lil, and I was looking forward to when we all got around the table, told stories and laughed. I could go there every year forever. I'd badgered Mum for us to go back there after that first summer when Luiz disappeared. To start with, she hadn't wanted to go. I don't remember much about Luiz. But I know when we first went there, something had happened to him and things were hard for Mum. And I know Luiz went to prison for smuggling not long after that. So Mum's memories of the place wouldn't have been all that good. Even at six-years-old, I'd picked up on how scared she'd been. After she met Steve, things got better though, and she gave in to my pestering. Steve loves Ebwich too, and our visits have become something we all look forward to.

Last summer, when I finished my GCSEs, Mum told me about what had happened to my dad. I didn't even ask her to. I think she just thought it was time I knew. We didn't do anything about Angola at school. Since then, I've read all about it. I got Roy on his own on that visit and he told me what happened when he and my dad went out there. It upset him – and me – but I'm glad we talked about it. It explained a lot of things, including why he helped Luiz. I think I understand things better now. We can talk about everything more freely now. I feel even closer to him and Fiona – and Mum too. They've had quite a few things to deal with. Seeing Fiona with Oliver, her dad but not her dad, made me realise how good it was that Mum found Steve and that we all get along so well. We're lucky.

It's our tradition to go straight to the beach when we arrive. Roy says he used to do that when he was a kid. Lil was always ready to join us and, sure enough, she was out the back door as soon as we'd got out of the car. Fiona and Hettie were not far behind and everyone was hugging everyone. Roy was expected back from the garage for lunch, and Fiona had already put the reserved sign on the table – the one in the window. The café was busy – busier than when we first went there. They were run off their feet. I'd already planned to ask if I could spend a few weeks next summer helping out. Fiona was telling Hettie off for doing too much, saying she should be retired. Hettie was giving as good as she got – as usual. We left them to it and set off for the beach.

When we sat down for lunch, we all had our news to tell. Steve told everyone about he'd soon be taking on someone to help him with his skip-hire business. They already knew how he'd been swindled out of his share of his dad's firm and how he'd spent years building things back up. Then Steve and me coaxed Mum into telling everyone how her pottery hobby was turning into a full-time job and how she'd be giving up her job at the supermarket if it kept going that way. I'd persuaded her to bring one of her dishes for Fiona. We made her go and get it and everyone was admiring it. Fiona said she didn't have much news until Roy told her to tell everyone about Angie. We all looked puzzled and Fiona had to explain who Angie was and where she'd met her. There'd been reports in the newspapers of a huge property scam on the Costa del Sol and it turns out Angie was the ringleader and was wanted by the police. Fiona told us a bit about her and it reminded me how she'd ended up here with Hettie. Then Lil launched into how her grandad would arrive tomorrow and how he'd promised to bring her something for her summer holiday project for school. They were studying the Second World War, and he was going to bring his merchant navy cap for her to take into school next term. That got Hettie started on how Fiona's mum had been evacuated there and how she'd ended up there. I never get tired of hearing about what happened back then.

Listening to everyone's stories made me think how incredible it all was, how these people around the table had gone through all those things and how they'd coped. I knew from what Mum had told me that there was more behind those stories than Lil understood yet, that everyone there had regrets and had blamed themselves for things they maybe shouldn't have, and felt obligations that kept them where maybe they wouldn't have chosen to stay. But they'd got through it all. They were okay. It made me think that things that look so frightening can turn out alright. Mum got through bad times and found Steve. You wouldn't look at them and think they were a perfect match – yet in a way they are. They get on with things. They always have time for each other.

While I was thinking this, Roy joked that he was pleased to say he didn't have any news, and that's the way he hoped it would stay. He said Fiona had forgotten to mention that when she'd rang her dad, her stepmother has answered, and for the first time asked her how things were. He was saying it in a jokey sort of way, but I could see it wasn't a joke – like Fiona had forgiven her for something. Then Fiona told us that her stepsister Jo – she's a high-flier in the Treasury Department – had left her husband, David, and he'd moved to Cornwall to open a gift shop. I know Fiona has good cause not to like Jo, but she wasn't gloating. She said Jo and her husband hadn't been getting on, that they both just needed to find the right person.

I was watching Roy's face as Fiona said that. He has a way of looking at her. His eyes shine. She looked back at him and something passed between them. She gave him a big smile, and he gave her one back. I hope one day I have what they have.

# Afterword

Whilst the main characters in this novel are works of fiction, the background events are not. My research of these events often shocked me, left me saddened, and sometimes angry. However, in using them as a backdrop, and including the names of real people associated with them, there is no intention to condemn or condone any person or any ideology involved.

The post-independence conflicts that Roy experiences involve suffering, destruction, and bloodshed. They are the background canvas to his story, not a historical record. I have had no experience of such conflicts. In using them, I hope I have in no way trivialised their consequences or the experience of those, on all sides, who became caught up in them. I can only acknowledge the suffering caused and hope that the reader will too.

Similarly, Fiona's experience of prison is not intended to trivialise the often inhuman conditions of the inmates of a broken system – again, of which I have no experience. I acknowledge their suffering too.

Finally, there are many online articles and newspaper reports from the period for anyone who wants to find out more about the historical events used in this novel. I am, however, adding a list of printed sources that I found interesting and useful.

# Further Reading

Pat Carlen, Jenny Hicks, Josie O'Dwyer, Diana Christina and Chris Tchaikovsky, *Criminal Women*, Cambridge, Polity Press, 1985

Caitlin Davies, *Bad Girls A History of Rebels and Renegades*, London, John Murray, 2018

Joanna Kozubska, *Cries for Help*, Hook, Waterside Press, 2014

Stephen Rookes, *The CIA and British Mercenaries in Angola, 1975-1976*, (Africa War Series), Warwick, Helion & Company, 2021

Peter Tickler, *The Modern Mercenary, Dog of War or Soldier of Honour?* Wellingborough, Patrick Stephens Limited, 1987

Kevin Marchant, *Facing the Firing Squad, The True Life Story Mercenaries of Angola*, Kevin Marchant, 2019

Chris Dempster and Dave Tomkins, *Fire Power*, London, Corgi Books, 1978

David Tomkins, *Dirty Combat, Secret Wars and Serious Misadventures,* Edinburgh, Mainstream Publishing Company Limited, 2008

Peter McAleese (with Mark Bles), *No Mean Soldier,* London, Orion Books Ltd, 1994

Wilfred Burchett and Derek Roebuck, *The Whores of War Mercenaries Today,* Harmondsworth, Pelican Books Ltd, 1977

# Also by I D Hamilton

https://www.amazon.com/dp/B093TCWK18

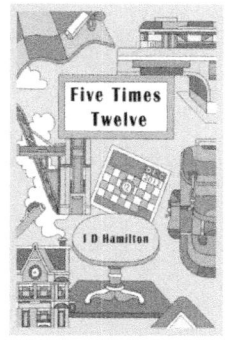

https://www.amazon.com/dp/B09CNX95FG

https://www.amazon.com/dp/B09VL8CLVQ

Printed in Great Britain
by Amazon